OATH OF RUIN

THE WARLORD CHRONICLES

BOOK ONE

KALEY KAE

OATH OF RUIN
Published by KALEY KAE
www.kaleykae.com

Copyright © 2025 Kaley Kae

Editing: Dana Alsamsam
Cover Art: Annisa Dwi Rahayu
Header and Pagebreak Art: Sydney Shopoff

For those who chase dreams that others deem unrealistic.

CONTENT & TRIGGER WARNINGS

Oath of Ruin contains dark subject matter and adult romance. Content warnings for this book include: violent fight scenes, blood and gore, kidnapping, attempted sexual assault (NO on-page SA and NOT between the love interests), anxiety and panic attacks, abuse, parental loss, explicit language, and graphic sex scenes that are entirely consensual. Please remember that depiction is not authorial endorsement.

CHAPTER ONE

What if I never get to leave?

One afternoon beyond the castle walls would ease all my woes, my dread. I don't mind the duties of being Princess of Cathros, but I always longed for more. My father never allowed me to leave the grounds, not while war raged across the seven kingdoms.

What if I jump?

It would be easy to climb over the balcony's stone railing and plummet into the ocean below. Waves crash into the rocks at the base of the cliffside, sending large plumes of water soaring skyward. I could dodge them—maybe, and swim toward the sandy shore in the distance.

My fingers tremble around the worn leather-bound book I clutch to my chest. I silently recite the lines to myself to calm my nerves. I've read it more times than I can count, scribbled notes in every margin, and pored over every page as if the words would somehow change. It was wishful thinking that I, too, could ever wield power like the warlord in this book.

What if I—?

"Good afternoon, Raelys." A voice behind me interrupts my thought.

Turning, I see my handmaiden, Eleanor. She smiles as our gazes meet, her dark brown eyes crinkling at the corners. Her braid cascades over her shoulder in a long strand of gray, loose pieces dancing around her face in the breeze.

"Hello, Eleanor," I reply softly.

"We must get you ready," she requests, smoothing her hands over the front of her dress.

"Just a bit longer…" I try not to let my pensive mood show as I glance back at the sea.

It is dry in the south, the sun's unforgiving rays beating down like heat from a forge. I wonder what the sand beneath my feet would feel like, or the waves against my skin. All I need is one dip in the ocean to cool down, to clear my head. Not that I know how to swim, but it can't be that hard… *right?*

"Are you not excited about your brother's return?" she asks.

"Oh, I'm thrilled. It's been far too long," I call out, fiddling with the frayed edges of the book cover.

A few weeks ago, my brother sent a letter announcing his plans to travel home. He is the commander of Cathros' royal army, fighting on the front lines to defend and protect our kingdom. Every year, he departs in the middle of spring and returns just before snowfall. This schedule allows the soldiers to come home and rest their weary bones in the warmth and safety of the south, rather than the snowy, barren cold of the north.

Valentin is traveling home far earlier than usual this year, which makes me suspicious. I only receive updates on war plans through my brother's letters or gossip in the castle halls, as my father never shares such information with me. Every time I ask what is happening, my father says, *'You can leave when the war is over.'*

I've been asking for fourteen years straight.

"Excellent. Let us prepare you for tonight, then," Eleanor replies.

Turning, I walk back inside my bedchambers, setting down my book on a side table as I pass. I plop down unceremoniously in front of my vanity, waiting for Eleanor to pin my long, pale blonde strands into a half-updo. After she finishes my hair, I apply small amounts of color to my lips and cheeks, blending it in with my fingertips. I pat a dark color onto the outer corners of my eyelids to complement the sapphire blue striations in my irises.

I stand and allow Eleanor to help me dress. She pulls the corset strings tight in the back, and I huff out a strained breath as the fabric settles around me. The romantic, long-sleeve burgundy gown flares at the waist, the gold details shifting in the light as I move. Eleanor places a diadem atop my head, ensuring it doesn't catch in my hair before stepping away.

"I will call someone to escort you," Eleanor says sweetly.

"Okay," I relent, a grim feeling filling me.

Eleanor disappears into the hall, returning me to my solitude. I cannot walk alone; my father forbids me to do so. The silent shadow of a guard always accompanies me. I'm never alone, but always so lonely.

My father, King Ulrik Valantis, has called for a celebration at the castle upon my brother's arrival home. We rarely have social gatherings at the castle; my father always claims they are too costly in these difficult times. I suppose it will be enjoyable to spend the evening outside of my bedchamber for once, a rarity for me.

The door opens again, and I see one of my favorite soldiers, Timothy, in the hallway with Eleanor. His armor is dented and speckled with dirt. A longsword hangs off his belt. His wavy brown hair looks somewhat messy. Timothy's eyes have dark bags beneath them, like he hasn't slept in days. I watch his lips turn up in a lazy smile at the sight of me.

"Highness," he greets me.

My somber mood eases at the sight of him. "You're back," I point out as we walk together. "I'm surprised you survived the battle at Crossgate," I tease.

"You wound me, Princess." Timothy smiles, placing a gloved hand over his chest in mock pain. "You should hope I am a good fighter, as I am your guard for this evening."

I laugh. "How did it go?" I ask curiously. "Did you see my brother?"

"It was a remarkable victory. Your brother restored all the land the Elvarrans had captured and took control of the passage." Timothy radiates with pride. "Halfway through the battle, the duke protecting those lands turned and abandoned his men to save his pregnant mistress. Horatio Horne, I think the duke's name was? Without his leadership, they were easy to conquer."

"That's good news, indeed. Cutting off that mountain pass means the Elvarrans can't travel as freely to the south," I remark, taking in the information.

"Indeed. It forces the Elvarrans to make the twenty-day journey east to Grimhold Crossing if they need to travel to the south." Timothy keeps pace perfectly with my line of thought.

"Anything else?"

"The kingdom of Erynthe is holding up better than I expected," Timothy says. "King Francis Van Buren recently sent boats with rations to Liora."

"How interesting," I muse. "Erynthe is known for being so... recluse."

The kingdom of Erynthe is on the largest island of the Southern Isles, secluding itself from the rest of Dratheria.

They are excellent mariners, spending most of their time crafting boats and fishing in the nearby reefs.

"That's putting it mildly," Timothy replies, his tone unimpressed.

I leave it at that.

As we turn the corner, the guards posted in front of the great hall allow us entry. Guests waltz in the center of the room, their bodies flowing across the polished marble floors. A string quartet plays lively music, creating a moment of respite against the weight of war.

My gaze immediately catches on my brother, Valentin, who is standing beside my father's throne. He wears a finely tailored formal coat, black trousers, and tall boots. The extravagant gold buttons stand out against the dark burgundy fabric, matching perfectly with my dress. Valentin runs a hand through his neatly styled curls, and I notice a fresh scar that runs across his left brow.

His blue eyes light up at the sight of me as I approach. "My dear sister." Valentin pulls me close for a hug. "How I have missed you."

I wrap my arms around my brother and hug him close. "Thank the gods you're home," I say in relief.

"You're late, Raelys." My father's voice is gruff.

Ulrik wears an embellished coat, the right chest embroidered with our family crest—a golden stag. Beneath the extravagant coat are brown trousers and well-polished boots. It's as if the clothes are wearing him, a bit saggy and ill-fitting. I've watched my father wither away from his illness over the years, his gray hair thinning, wrinkles deepening, and age spots darkening. No healer has been able to figure out what is causing him to decline.

Ever since I was a child, my father has had burn scars on

the left side of his jaw, down to his neck. It almost appears like a handprint, one jagged scar cutting diagonally across his chin, with four longer peaks across the side of his neck. If I even so much as mention the burn, let alone ask what happened, he would send me to my bedchamber without supper. Sometimes I would purposefully ask to get out of mind-numbing social events.

"My apologies," I say meekly, stepping away from my brother. I straighten out my gown and square my shoulders, standing with the perfect poise that he expects of me.

My father huffs an annoyed breath in response, turning his attention to my brother. "My beloved son." His tone lightens as he addresses Valentin. "You have done House Valantis a great honor by recapturing Crossgate."

"Thank you, Father," Valentin replies, bowing his head.

Ulrik has ruled over the kingdom of Cathros for over thirty years. During his rule, he has allowed our kingdom to flourish, expand, and endure through the hardships of war. Soon, the title of king will pass to Valentin, who has been preparing to rule his entire life.

Turning my attention to the room, I see King Olav Friedrich of Avelisar. I did not know that he would be in attendance tonight. It is rare for visitors from other kingdoms to come to court, as traveling can lead to a potential ambush by the Elvarrans.

As I study Olav, it becomes clear that the years have not been kind to him. His hair has thinned, showing several bald spots. The king's teeth have yellowed, and his skin is saggy and hollow-looking. He appears to be holding on by mere threads, on the edge of necrosis.

"Thank you all for joining me in welcoming my son, Prince Valentin Valantis of Cathros, home," my father announces. "As well as welcoming our guest, King Olav Friedrich of Avelisar!" He raises his glass, allowing the rest of the court to do the same. "Please enjoy yourselves!"

"Hear, hear!" Many people begin cheering, and several move around to start their conversations.

I spot my best friend and lady-in-waiting, Lady Lydia Leonora, in the crowd. She's standing with her father, Duke Raoul Leonora, who is chatting with a highborn from Avelisar. Lydia's expression is unamused as she silently nods along to the conversation. I will have to tear her away later to find some relief from the placations of socializing.

"Come, we shall get some wine," Valentin says, taking my arm in his as we walk down the platform and through the crowd.

"You must tell me of your travels," I implore him.

Listening to his tales of battle is my favorite. They are just like the tales I read in my favorite book, The Warlord Chronicles. Each page is brimming with daring exploits and strategies, as well as advice on crafting the perfect plans.

Not that I ever have the chance to plot anything. My father wouldn't allow me to set foot in the war room while they work. If he did, I would share my plentiful ideas, such as cutting off resources for the Elvarrans, leaking fake plans to throw them off, and even sending a spy to the north.

"We spent many weeks defending the border at Liora. Those Elvarran bastards travel through the Northern Alps frequently; drawing them out is much easier than crossing into the mountains," Valentin begins, guiding me through the crowd.

I nod, my eyes widening at his story. I had never met an Elvarran before, but people at the castle told me they had sharp fangs and claws to rip off human flesh. Others claim they have tall, pointed ears. Some tales include magic that could manipulate the elements, bending air or earth to their will with ease.

"We also had to travel to Nythara," Valentin continues.

"I thought the king of Nythara was dead?" I ask curiously, knowing that the kingdom crumbled long ago.

"Yes, however, we found some Elvarrans hiding out in the castle, using it as a viewpoint to spy on our movements," he explains. "We killed those dastardly rats, every last one of them."

"I see…" I glance sidelong at my brother, wondering how he survived countless battles. Many years at war made him a tenacious commander. "And what of Wrath's Blade?"

"The Elvarran king?" Valentin laughs. "I'm starting to think he is a myth. Perhaps he fears Cathros' royal army because he has yet to face me."

No one knows the king of Khalessor's namesake. People whisper in the halls the tale of Wrath's Blade, the destroyer of peace. He is the one who attacked Nythara, starting the war between the seven kingdoms. They say if you meet his blade, you will not return home, as he is no stranger to bloodshed.

"Enough of that." He gives me a playful nudge with his shoulder. "Tell me what you have been up to."

I hesitate, glancing around for my governess. When I don't spot her, I return my attention to him. "I spend most of my days in my lessons…" I tell him, a somber heaviness settling in.

Valentin scoffs. "Nonsense! What happened to my little sister who would wreak havoc in these halls? No horse racing? No sneaking into the kitchens to steal wine? What about that one time we started a fire in the main hall?"

My chest aches a little. I used to do all of those things with Valentin. Even if someone caught us, my father's soft spot for my brother meant few consequences. I would never attempt something like that on my own now. The wildest thing I have done in recent months is lie with a lord's son pressed up against a bookshelf in the royal library.

I will spare him that story, though.

"I suppose things are different now..." My voice trails off, and memories of our childhood fill me. Every year, I grow more isolated within these walls without him, a prisoner in my own home.

"I'll have a word with Father," Valentin reassures me, handing me a glass of wine. "For now, we drink."

"I'm going to need a few to get through tonight." I take the glass and drink, savoring the full-bodied taste of sweet berries and oak.

"As do I."

My brother and I were always competitive in the game of outdrinking the other, refilling glass after glass of wine. About four glasses in, Valentin shifts in his boots, wavering slightly.

"The wine we drink on the road is like piss." He burps. "This is delicious."

"Your tolerance seems to have lowered, brother," I tease, knowing exactly how to get under his skin.

He scoffs. "Don't be absurd, Rae. I am just getting started." Valentin's attention catches on someone across the room. "Stay here. I have to greet Lady Elizabeth."

"Looking for an evening of tumbling in the sheets, brother?" I raise a curious brow.

"Shh..." he shushes me, leaning in close. "Yes," he whispers before walking off.

I watch as Valentin attempts to flirt with Lady Elizabeth, who pointedly ignores his beguiling. Laughing, I turn to refill my glass of wine, staying in place until he returns so I can taunt him about the inevitable rejection. The world grows a little hazy, allowing me to relax slightly and enjoy the merriment.

I feel a sharp gaze pierce me from across the room. I look over to see Governess Margaret Pennington glowering at me. Her structured, dark-brown dress is devoid of any frills, just like her. Not a single auburn hair is out of place from her tightly wound updo. Margaret lifts one finger in the air, pointing it at an imaginary glass of wine she's holding before waggling her finger side to side to scold me silently.

I sigh.

Glancing down at the back of my hand, I see the dark purple and yellow splotches that mottle my skin. The bruises have not healed from Margaret's last lesson. I debate whether the future punishment is worth continuing to drink, numbing the misery of my abuse. As always, Margaret gets her way, and I set down the glass.

If I failed to remember even a single lesson, she would strike me on my hands and wrists, each fresh wound adding to the scars that mar my skin. I spent days memorizing geography, architecture, and history. When Margaret didn't drown me with reading assignments, it was pianoforte, etiquette, cross-stitch, dancing, and riding lessons.

The only time I am free from Margaret's iron fist is when I sleep, but even then, she sometimes haunts my dreams. Some nights, I wake up with clenched fists and a thick layer of sweat. Her voice plagues my mind, dragging me back into her grasp until I do not know what is real and what is illusion.

"I am glad to see you are all enjoying yourselves tonight." Ulrik's voice carries throughout the space, drawing all the attention to him as he stands. "I have an announcement that will strengthen Cathros's future and our fight against the Elvarrans!"

The room falls silent in anticipation.

"My daughter, Princess Raelys Bella Valantis, will wed the King of Avelisar in a showing of good faith towards our alliance!" Ulrik raises his goblet, and everyone erupts into cheer.

The cheers fade to a dull roar in my ears as my world cracks open beneath me.

CHAPTER TWO

THIS CAN'T BE HAPPENING—SHOULDN'T be happening. I didn't spend my whole life in this castle to trade it for another cage. I take a hesitant step back. Nearly every pair of eyes in the room turns to me. The weight of their expectations hovers at my throat, sharp and suffocating.

I can bear it no longer.

Turning on my heel, I storm out of the great hall. I gather the fabric of my skirt in my fists as I flee, unsure of where to go. My stomach twists into knots at the thought of marrying that old man—one who is three times my age and has a *wife*. My father has truly lost his mind this time. There is no chance that I will agree with such a slight.

Someone calls out my name. "Raelys!"

I ignore them, weaving through servants carrying large trays of food and wine toward the great hall. I duck and twist, doing my best not to collide with any of them as I race for the back of the castle.

"P-Princess—" one stammers. "Are you lost?"

"No," I bite out, angrier than I would have liked.

I push open the tall iron door to the garden with all my

strength, and it slams against the opposite wall with a loud bang. My slippered foot touches the cold ground of the garden path as I dash away from the castle. Fury and indignation pulse in my veins like wildfire, burning away every logical thought and equanimity I had left.

"Raelys!" Timothy comes rushing after me. "Come back, please!"

"I will not!" I reply vehemently, surging ahead as the world blurs past me.

"Please reconsider. It's not safe for you to go out alone at night," Timothy calls out as he tries to catch up to me.

"When do I get to be alone, Timothy?" I twist around, shouting at him. "When do I ever get a choice?" My long dress swishes around my ankles with every step, the fabric flowing smoothly behind me. "When does anyone ever ask me what I want for *my* life?"

I continue to run through the gardens, desperate to get away. The sweet fragrance of the flowers overwhelms my frayed nerves. Leaves crunch beneath my slippers as I run past the tall maple trees, heading to the back of the castle.

"I know you're upset." Timothy tries to calm me down. "But King Olav can take good care of you."

King Olav. The mention of his name makes my blood boil. I would sooner hurl myself over the back wall than let my father reduce me to a prized breeding mare. My father has continued my lessons with that wretched governess for years, learning useless knowledge and skills while keeping me in the dark about anything that matters. He only tells me things when it's convenient, or to persuade me a certain way— his way.

My brother's duty is to marry for a title and create an heir. He is the eldest, destined to be king. And my duty? Apparently, to become a pawn in a game. I refuse to believe this is my fate.

Trapped again in another castle. Safe but always hollow, aimless with no purpose.

I grind my jaw together. "King Olav can shove it up his ass."

I twist my body to the side, weaving through the tight space between the tall hedges. My skirt snags on the branches, slowing me down. I reach down and gather even more of my dress into my hands, pulling it closer to my body as I pass through the shrubbery.

The cool night air blows the stray hairs away from my face as I reach the clearing on the other side of the hedges, my breath heaving from my sprint. The full moon shines brightly in the sky, a soft illumination over the dark space. Vines crawl up the tall stone wall in front of me, signaling that I am at the barrier of my confines.

"Raelys!" Timothy's shouts.

A palm pushes my shoulder, knocking me aside. The sound of an arrow whizzes past my head and hits something with a loud thunk behind me. Turning quickly, I see an arrow sticking directly out of Timothy's neck. Before I could even think of what to do next, a second arrow lodges itself into his side, and I scream.

Timothy collapses onto the stone below, eyes glazed over in a blank stare.

"No!" I choke out, falling to my knees. "Timothy!" I cry, but there is no response.

Blood pools out of his wounds, staining the earth with the last remnants of his fading life. I grab the sword from his belt and whirl around. Three shadowy figures perch on top of the wall like hawks waiting to descend on their prey. Their forms silhouette against the moonlight, partially obscuring my view.

Elvarrans.

I take a few steps back to get a better look. I always imagined them as monsters, but the ones before me look human. They have long, pointed ears as tall as mountain peaks and faces so sharply angled that they look almost statue-like. Each time they move, they effortlessly glide across the castle wall.

"W-what do you want?" I ask, my voice trembling.

"The Princess," the petite Elvarran hisses as she crouches on the wall. She tilts her head to one side, her brunette hair brushing the tops of her shoulders. "Aren't we lucky?"

Her dark eyes narrow on me like prey as her stance shifts. It's as if she is ready to strike at a moment's notice. Two twin daggers glint in each of her hands. She wears fitted leather armor, with intricately layered shoulders and bracers that cover her forearms, signaling that she is a fierce and striking warrior.

"Should we call the king?" the Elvarran beside her sneers, knocking another arrow into his bow. The archer is tall and lean, with short, pale blonde hair a similar shade to mine. His sapphire eyes glint with menacing disgust as he aims his bow at the target—unmistakably me.

Adrenaline runs like wildfire through my veins. This could be my end. I take a hesitant step back, but it only makes the archer pull the string back further as a warning. I freeze. My grip tightens around the hilt of the sword I don't know how to wield.

"We should kill her," the third Elvarran interjects.

He is the only one who is unarmed, his posture relaxed as he crouches on the wall. He is broad-shouldered and muscular. Short braids weave through his midnight-black hair, allowing me to see his face clearly. A thick beard frames his strong jaw, accentuated by a long, jagged scar that cuts across his cheek. His deep umber skin contrasts with his striking amber eyes like swirling honey.

I have to act quickly and find a way to spare myself. If I can convince them to throw me into a dungeon, I'd have a chance to escape later. Perhaps if there is a distraction, I can dash for the castle. One thing is certain. I will not meet my end at the hands of the Elvarrans. They are clever, but I can outsmart them.

"Call your king!" I make a split-second decision.

"What?" The female Elvarran raises a brow. "Do you have a death wish?"

"Wrath's Blade, the destroyer of peace, I wish to speak to him," I tell them, forcing my voice to sound confident.

If they see fear, they will kill me.

There's a slight pause before the three of them start laughing incredulously. I falter, confusion washing over me as they exchange glances. They laugh for several breaths, wiping tears from the corners of their eyes as if I've told them the funniest joke they've ever heard.

Bloody gods.

"If you say so." The muscled Elvarran hops down from the wall. His boots thump against the stone as he lands gracefully.

He smacks the sword out of my grip with ease, and it clatters to the floor. Hands close roughly around my hips as he hoists me into the air. I shriek as he tosses me to the archer. A fist closes around the back of my dress, and I scramble to steady myself while in mid-air. The archer flips me over the wall. I fall to the ground, hitting the cool dirt with a heavy thud, the air whooshing from my lungs.

Before I can orient myself, I fall helplessly down the steep hill. Sharp rocks and tangled roots scrape my skin and catch on my dress. My diadem rips from my hair as I roll to a stop at the bottom. The wine in my belly threatens to spill, but I force the nausea away as I press my palms into the dirt and push myself up. Once standing, I see the three Elvarrans snickering at me as they move effortlessly through the gauntlet of rocks and trees.

"Sorry, *Princess*." The archer mocks, shoving my shoulder from behind to get me to walk. "Hand must've slipped."

As I walk away from the castle, something stirs in my gut. There is a world outside the walls, stretching into the unknown. I keep my expression stoic, masking both curiosity and a thin veil of fear as I press onward, eyes sweeping the shadows around me. I cannot run. This damned dress will slow me down. Even if I try, an arrow will pierce my back within seconds. In my quest to think of a way out of marrying Olav, I've tangled myself into an even tighter knot.

Wrath's Blade is the most ruthless, cunning, and wicked king in Dratheria. I will need to provide or exchange something of great value for him to keep me alive.

And then it comes to me.

CHAPTER THREE

THE ELVARRAN DRAGS me by my bicep as we trek through the forest. The rips in my dress have grown larger and more plentiful, my skirts degrading into rags. The uneven, rocky terrain makes me stumble around like a newborn doe. I thank the gods for every second I am alive, but I don't know how long my scheme will hold after I meet Wrath's Blade.

There is only one light source in the sprawling darkness—a faint outline of a camp in the distance. They are armed, well-stocked with supplies, and have enough horses to coordinate an entire cavalry if needed. As we approach, the Elvarrans slowly take notice of me, and their conversations gradually fade as the weight of unspoken tension settles in.

I am the enemy.

If the Elvarrans are this close to Cathros's castle, it could only mean one thing—they are preparing for a siege. My mind begins to work through each angle of their approaching attack, trying to figure out their plans.

Each step toward the center of the camp is a procession to my potential end. I try not to let my terror show, but I still tremble in his hold. The Elvarran yanks on my arm, stopping my advancements. I forcibly drag my gaze from the floor upward, my pulse pounding wildly in my veins.

A tall and broad-shouldered man stands before me with gray eyes and dark onyx hair. A single scar mars his olive skin, running up the side of his neck to his jaw. Each detail of his face is almost too perfect: the sharp contours of his cheek-bones, the elegant line of his throat, the arch of his brows. The sight of him makes my pulse stutter, something in me recoiling before I can name why. Looking at King Wrath is like staring at the sun for too long, distorting my vision until I inevitably go blind.

Wrath studies me with a slow, churning gaze that rakes across my skin like hot coals. I feel a strange prickling sensation down the back of my neck. Hundreds of invisible thorns touch my skin, invading nearly every part of my senses. Rage simmers in his eyes like endless pits of fire while the rest of his presence remains unnervingly calm. Every inch of him exudes power, commanding the space around him with effortless dominance.

If you meet Wrath's Blade, you will not return home.

"Gilead, what have you brought me?" Wrath speaks, his voice deep and stern.

"Found her while scouting the castle," Gilead replies, pushing me forward and releasing his hold on me. "Said she wanted to talk to you."

I stumble a few steps but manage to remain upright. Straightening my spine, I stand with a level of poise that I spent my entire life crafting. My hands shake with fear, but I clasp them together into stillness and keep my head high.

"All right. Speak," Wrath orders.

"A trade offer—" Before I can say anything else, a cacophony of laughter echoes through the camp.

"And if I don't like your offer?"

"Then I'll meet Wrath's Blade." I hold firm, unyielding among the crowd.

Several Elvarrans invade my space, inching closer with a feral prowl. Some jump at me, trying to get me to flinch, while others pull at the lace of my dress, ripping off small pieces of it to take for themselves. I try not to let fear show on my face as I hold Wrath's gaze, clenching my jaw tightly.

"I don't have all day, human," he continues, unfazed by the antics surrounding us.

"A kingdom conquered—"

He cuts me off. "And how would you accomplish that?"

"I'm to wed King Olav Friedrich. Upon entering Avelisar, you can disguise your forces as my guard to enter the castle," I say confidently. "And expunge them."

It's us or them. If I must trade Avelisar for Cathros, so be it. It is despicable to trade an entire human's kingdom life for my own freedom, but it is precisely the kind of bait Wrath can't resist. He's conquered one human kingdom before, and I believe he'll want to make it two.

Wrath's brows draw together. "Who are you?"

"Princess Raelys Valantis of Cathros."

The camp goes deadly silent.

Wrath takes a few slow steps toward me. The Elvarrans around me scatter like flies on a carcass. A black leather-gloved hand shoots out. He pulls the necklace from the inside of my dress, and the chain yanks my head forward. Bewilderment crosses Wrath's gaze as he traces his thumb over the crest embedded in the metal—a sword with two wings on either side. It's all I have left of my mother, and I pray he won't take it from me.

He releases the pendant and steps away. "A few questions, Raelys."

My name is a hymn on his lips, one that's his to claim. It

sends a chill down my spine. His inquiry feels suspicious, a misdirection to gain something from me. Perhaps he doesn't believe my identity and wants to test me.

I play along, stunned that I made it this far. "All right."

"Why did King Olav Friedrich and his court travel to Cathros?"

"To ease tensions." I keep my answer vague. Wrath did not say I have to give detailed answers. He will likely use what I say against the humans, which will lead to more conflict between the North and South.

"The motive?"

"Olav skipped sending winter rations to the villages on our shared borders last snowfall," I explain. "He used the guise of coming here to make amends, but I believe it is to hide the fact that he has no winter rations once more."

"Why are you in a marriage arrangement with a king who has a wife?" he asks.

"He has no heir," I tell him truthfully. "I think they are weaker than they appear on the surface."

For this to work, I need him to believe Avelisar is an easy target. I want him to give up on his conquest of Cathros and set his sights on a different kingdom. It's the only path that lets me slip past Olav and safeguard my home in one maneuver.

"Your people will view you as a traitor," Wrath counters.

"I see it as joining the winning side." I boost his ego, wondering if flattery will sway him.

He remains irritatingly placid. "You're aware of the tales surrounding my name, and yet you're brainless enough to seek me out…"

The Warlord always said that the enemy of my enemy is my ally.

"I'd rather make a deal with you than go near Olav's wrinkly dick." My words are blunt, but they strike something within him.

A flicker of bemusement ripples across his stoic features. He chuckles softly under his breath. It catches me off guard. The laugh is harsh and has a slight bite to it, like striking steel against stone. Some nearby Elvarrans snicker at my words, making offhand, vulgar comments in the distance.

"Crass, Princess," Wrath replies. "Your father wants to wed you for a failing alliance?"

"He's punishing me for not marrying the inbred Prince of Oderris." I continue with my candid rant, dropping the royal formalities for a more authentic tone.

I can see the wheels turning in his mind with a malevolent fascination as I feed him information. Every exchange is a game. He is an unassailable fortress of conviction. Wrath saunters around my side, and I remain facing forward. Even after he steps away, his presence lingers on my skin like heat that won't fade.

"The army stationed in Liora. How strong is it?" He turns the conversation away from me, a calculated move.

I must be cautious; the wrong answer can lead to many lives lost. Valentin frequently uses the town of Liora as a staging point for attacks due to its closeness to the northern border. I try to think of a good diversion, but something tickles the back of my throat. My windpipe suddenly closes up. It burns like wildfire, forcing me to speak.

"They use it to draw out your kind—" I choke out against my will, a hand flying to my chest. "You're using magic on me!" I whirl to face him, a flurry of shock and anger filling me.

"Please answer quickly, Princess," Wrath says calmly.

"And what if I don't?" I scowl back.

"When you agreed to answer my questions, you agreed to answer them truthfully." Wrath continues to pace around me, like a predator stalking its prey. "The magic can tell when you're skating around the truth."

Yielding is inevitable. I am experiencing firsthand what it is like to face the blade, and I may not escape with my life. Wrath demands compliance, leaving little room for resistance. His magic is a power that rank cannot bestow.

"Who else is Cathros in an alliance with?" Wrath continues his line of questioning.

"Oderris."

"Avelisar, Cathros, and Oderris…" he muses.

After Nythara fell, the remaining human kingdoms dwindled in strength. Avelisar is barely scraping by. I don't know how much longer the Southern Alliance will hold. Cathros is practically holding up the entire south on its own, our 'allies' infrequently helping us in return.

"When was the last correspondence with Erynthe?" he asks.

"I don't know—" The itch starts again, suffocating my breath and crawling beneath my skin. "Erynthe recently sent rations to Liora," he forces me to say.

"Why?"

"I have heard whisperings of a plan to seal the island off to outsiders, but they are rumors," I reply hesitantly, hoping the magic would let that one slide.

"Do you believe these rumors?"

"No." I shake my head. "What kingdom would be stupid enough to attempt to stand alone when you're thrashing about?"

I am walking right into Wrath's trap, giving him information about my kingdom in exchange for nothing. He can kill me after interrogating me and lay siege to the castle, ending us all in one fell swoop. I can't let that happen. Not to Lydia, or Eleanor, or Valentin.

"Thrashing?" His brow arches.

"I believe this is more than a few questions, King Wrath," I say firmly.

Wrath glances to his right, locking eyes with an Elvarran who looks similar to the king. The man has the same high cheekbones and grey eyes as Wrath, but is slightly more muscular and broader in build. He scratches at his beard absently as he stands leaning into one hip, his expression unamused. Long, pointed ears sprout from his black hair. The left ear is missing a large chunk close to his head.

"This is a terrible idea, brother," the Elvarran deadpans. "Kill her and be done with it."

"Always a stickler, Barnham…" Wrath's voice trails off as he turns back to me. "But *never* a visionary," he says under his breath so quietly that only I could hear.

"If you don't return me to the castle soon, every soldier in the royal army will be in these woods searching for me," I threaten.

Wrath makes a sound comparable to a low growl. "How many?"

"Five thousand."

"You will allow us to gain entry into Avelisar's castle and slay their king." Wrath refocuses on my original point. "Is that what you want? Do we have a deal?" He pulls off his right leather glove and extends his hand out to me.

Holding firmly, I keep my hands at my side. That was too easy… and yet, I have no other choice. If I refuse, they will likely kill me. Without Wrath, I am stuck with Olav.

"You must swear that no harm will come to me," I demand.

Wrath rolls his eyes. "You're insufferable, Princess."

"Your soldiers tried to kill me!" I remind him of our mutual distrust.

"Fine," he relents.

"Deal." I reach forward and take his hand in mine.

The moment Wrath's fingertips close around mine, something ignites between us. His magic seeps like fire under my skin, whispering shrouded promises directly into my veins. It violently claws up the length of my arm. My muscles tense from the searing pain. I try to pull away, but his grip only tightens.

The oath between us hums to life—an intense pull, a wicked temptation of fate. It feels as if he's staring straight into the darkest parts of my soul, seeing everything I've tried to hide. I'm drowning in his power—in him—unable to tell where his magic begins and I end. And still, my first instinct is to leap toward it, immerse myself in that power, and claim it like it belongs to *me*.

Wrath releases his hold, returning his arm to his side. A tendril of silver slithers under my sleeve. Pulling up the fabric, I watch the magic take root on the inside of my forearm—thin, wispy lines snake across my skin like streaks of starlight.

"Gods…" I curse under my breath, pulling my sleeve down to cover it.

"You cannot cross me. If you do, the magic will have consequences," Wrath explains. "Gilead, Stanik, take this stray back to where you found her."

CHAPTER FOUR

IT'S PITCH BLACK OUTSIDE. I'm unsure what part of the wall the Elvarrans tossed me over. I search for Timothy's body, my hands blindly patting around to find a path. As I turn the corner, I plow headfirst into a breastplate. I groan as I stumble back, and a strong pair of hands wraps around my shoulders to steady me.

"I found her!" the guard calls out. "Come, Princess." He beckons me to follow him.

The guard guides me through the darkness, and I'm now numb to the shrubbery scraping my skin and catching on the fabric of my dress. The castle eventually comes into view, and I realize we're on the southeast side of the inner bailey. He calls out for help as we ascend the stairs, my steps shaky as we walk inside.

My brother sprints down the hall. "Raelys!" He stops before me. "What happened?"

"Elvarrans… they came over the back wall." Tears well at the corners of my eyes as I try my best to play the role of the distressed princess. "They killed Timothy, and I ran away. They chased me, but I hid in hopes they would leave."

"Thank the gods you're safe." My brother hugs me. "Come, let's get you cleaned up." He guides me in the direction of my bedchamber. "Thank you, soldier."

"Of course, Commander." The guard bows, lowering his head to us.

"I want the entire castle grounds swept; Elvarrans could still be on the premises. Use the hounds if you have to." My brother barks out orders to every guard he sees. He's the epitome of strength and composure, never missing a beat as he works.

Opening the door to my chamber, Valentin and I walk inside. He forces me to sit on a nearby chair. "I'll call for Eleanor to draw you a bath. Do you need a healer?"

"I'm all right; thank you." I try to reassure him. "Just some bumps and bruises."

"I'll end every single one of them." He seethes with fury. "They will *never* touch these grounds again. It was a mistake ever letting them that close."

"Val—"

The door swings open, cutting off my protests. Lydia comes rushing to my side, her long, peach-colored gown trailing behind her. Her dark brunette hair flows in soft curls over her shoulders, framing her sun-kissed tan complexion. She crouches beside me, her hazel eyes wide with concern.

"I've got her," she says, taking my hand to comfort me.

"Thank you, Lydia. I must go and make sure the grounds are secure." Valentin quickly exits the room. I hear him barking orders to the guards on the other side of the door. He's furious—rightfully so.

"Are you okay, Rae?" Lydia asks.

"I need you to get something for me in secret." I ignore her question. My mind spins, grasping for the next move. Now that

I have a secret arrangement with Wrath, I must gather belongings to aid me in my travels.

"What is it?"

"A dagger, I think, or some type of small blade that I could conceal in my sleeve or dress," I explain. "Tonight has made me realize that walking around unarmed is foolish."

Lydia hesitates for a moment but nods. "Okay."

I sigh, pulling my right sleeve a little lower. There's a mark on my arm, a *permanent* mark. If anyone sees it, they will either lose their mind or accuse me of being a conspirator to the Elvarrans.

"You saw an Elvarran?" Lydia whispers.

"Three of them," I tell her. "They weren't at all like the tales people tell. They were human-like, and they had this… energy that pulled me in. It's hard to describe. But they were not monsters."

"I can't believe you encountered three Elvarrans and lived."

A tear falls from my lash. "Timothy didn't live, Lydia." I shake my head in disbelief that he's truly gone.

Lydia's arms wrap around my neck, pulling me into a hug. "I'm so sorry."

The door opens once more just as we embrace, and my father enters. Despite his tired appearance, his eyes burn with disdain as he glowers at me.

Lydia slowly releases me and stands. "Your Majesty."

"Leave us," Ulrik commands.

She does as she's told, giving the King a small curtsy before leaving. A tense silence settles between my father and me, a silent battle of wills neither of us is willing to lose.

"You are a disappointment to our house." Each word is severe.

"I almost died at the hands of the Elvarrans, and that's

what you have to say to me?" I feel anger rise within me as I stand. "I have begged you for years to let me hold court, send correspondence, and do anything I can to help this *house*."

For most of my life, I have heard my father complain about how insufferable it is to hold court. He would sit there and listen to countless requests, doing his best to help villagers without draining too many resources. They need him to pass judgment on trials or settle minor disputes, and people quarrel for countless hours.

"Duke Raoul Leonora holds court while I'm busy," my father counters. "You know this."

I know that Lydia's father holds court while Ulrik is not feeling well or absent, yet he still denies me when I express that I'd like to do it instead. It's as if he doesn't trust my judgment or intellect, despite having spent my whole life learning to navigate these things.

"All I have wanted to do is help you!" I raise my voice. "I can take some of the burdens off of you if you're not feeling well, I—"

My father cuts me off. "What makes you think I would let you have authority? You are incapable of having enough self-control even on a night as important as this!" Ulrik looks at me as if I am the grime beneath his boots.

"You've never given me a chance!" I implore him. "I know I can do it. Let me help while Valentin fights on the front lines to protect us."

"It is not your place to speak about my son." My father seethes, the scar on his neck flexing. "I'm talking about your insolence."

I roll my eyes, trying to mask the hurt. "I'm a horrible disappointment and a *stain* on this house; you remind me every chance you get."

It is no secret that Valentin is my father's favorite. His

golden boy. Heir to the throne. I never held it against my brother because he never treated me poorly. Despite my father's blatant favoritism, we remain the closest of friends.

"This is exactly what I'm talking about." Ulrik scoffs. "Have Margaret's lessons taught you nothing?"

"She hits me!" I hold up the back of my bruised hand in the air.

"She doesn't hit you *enough*." My father regards me as if I were rot in the gutter, something dirty to be discarded.

A tense pause hangs between us as I process his words. They break me on the inside, but I try not to show how much it stings. Between Margaret's abuse, my father's hatred toward me, and my looming deal with King Wrath, I feel completely out of place in this realm.

"You think that little of me?" My voice breaks.

My father only looks down at me, his gaze burning into mine.

"Why?" I demand. "What have I done for you to treat me this way?"

"Do your duty, Raelys." Ulrik's voice is deadly. "You want my approval? Marry the King of Avelisar and stop this nonsense."

I spent years earning a man's approval who never intended to give it. My father doles out kindness the way others trade coin—only when there's something to gain. I don't know why I still expect anything different.

"I will, and it still won't be enough for you."

CHAPTER FIVE

"I'm sorry about father." Valentin sighs, leaning against the banister on my balcony.

"It's all right." I pull my sleeves down over my bruised hands.

"It's not," my brother retorts. "No one has the right to speak to you like that."

"I don't know my place." I retreat further, the weight of my father's words casting a shadow over my thoughts. Maybe he's right. Perhaps I am an awful daughter. Impulsive, defiant, and too astute for my own good. I am the sum of everything Ulrik is not, and that infuriates him.

"Nonsense," Valentin says firmly. "Father was in a mood."

"When is he not in a mood?" I reply bitterly.

My brother huffs a laugh, knowing that I'm right. "I need your advice on this." He passes me a letter from his pocket, changing the subject.

I read the letter from the kingdom of Erynthe. King Francis demands a large payment from Cathros for not protecting their northern border, claiming we ruined their trade routes after the battle at Crossgate.

"I thought the rations were suspicious," I comment, realizing that the so-called 'rations' to Liora are part of a secret trade deal that bypassed our kingdom. "The fish they catch would never make it in shipment. So, what did they attempt to send north?"

"I'm unsure," Valentin replies. "Why send it that far west when Rykaris is closer?"

"Right?" I agree. "Rykaris is not aggressive either. Most of them are loggers and woodworkers."

"It's still an Elvarran kingdom. We can't fully trust them." Valentin runs a hand down the back of his neck.

"Are we to defend *every* border in the south?" I say in annoyance. "We have one army. You can't spread yourself thin trying to protect everyone."

"We have the biggest army," Valentin boasts proudly.

I wave him off. "If we protect the northern border, everyone else is supposed to supply *us* with gold or goods as payment."

"I know, but we need Erynthe," he counters. "The human kingdoms must remain united."

"The only kingdoms that have helped us are Oderris and Nythara. With Nythara gone, we are severely lacking in the hunting and fur trade. Father should be incredibly worried about the food supply," I rant, anger bristling in my tone. "Meanwhile, Avelisar siphons us dry with their demands, and we send our people to die!"

My brother takes the letter from me. "You're right."

"I know I'm right."

"If Wrath's Blade were to appear on our doorstep, we would have sent all our men away, leaving us vulnerable." Valentin's tone is severe.

"Exactly. Avelisar needs *our* army." I remind him, pointing a finger at his chest. "Not the other way around. Don't let them push you around when you're on the front lines risking *your* life."

"This is why I need you," he admits. "Snap some sense into me."

"House Valantis has not stood this long only to fail now," I urge, stepping closer. "You're the future king! They should respect *you*. You're the one who won Crossgate for the south, not them."

My brother nods, rubbing the stubble on his chin as he thinks. "I did. I restored all the land the Elvarrans captured and took control of the passage."

"Precisely," I assure him. "Avelisar's stonecutting and masonry have been of little help to us during this war. They would crumble without our support. And Erynthe is as reliable as a bridge made of glass."

Valentin paces across the balcony, crumpling the letter in his grip as he works out his frustrations. His chestnut brown hair sways slightly with each step, his thick brows furrowed in thought. He often did this when he worked out a new plan or strategy in his mind.

"Raelys?" Eleanor says as she enters my bedchamber.

"We're out here!" I call out to her.

"I'm here to pack your belongings for Avelisar." She walks toward my wardrobe and opens it.

"All right." Valentin nods, moving toward the door. "Let me talk to Father."

"Thank you." I am eternally grateful to my brother. "Just remember." I grab his arm, stopping him. "I am wholly loyal to you, no matter what. Avelisar may be where I end up, but Cathros is my home."

My brother's eyes burn with determination as he grasps my shoulders. "The same to you. I am loyal to you until the end, Raelys."

I nod. "Always."

He pulls me into a tight hug. I won't miss much about Cathros, but I will certainly feel Valentin's absence—his warm personality, sharp wit, and the kindness he always showed me. Tears gather at the edges of my eyes. The weight of saying goodbye is too much to bear. My brother leaves the room, taking a part of my heart with him.

I watch Eleanor fold up dresses and shawls, tucking them away. She packs my worn pair of slippers that I don't have the heart to throw away. My favorite wool gloves. Eleanor knows exactly which pieces to pack—those I like or those with the comfort of familiarity. She doesn't know that I won't have a need for most of the items. I don't intend to stay in Avelisar long, likely not even a day. After Wrath fulfills his end of the deal, things will return to normal, and I'll come home.

There is no turning back now. Our fates are bound together.

"Do you have a satchel, Eleanor?" I ask.

"You're a princess. What would you require a satchel for?" She folds another dress into a large trunk.

"That's enough things." I walk over and shut the lid.

"You need more than one trunk of clothes, Princess."

"Thank you, but I'll handle packing myself. Please get me a satchel so I may carry some books with me on the long carriage ride to Avelisar." The edge in my voice makes her flinch. I hate that rank is the only language she seems to hear.

"Yes, Princess," Eleanor replies quietly as she bows and leaves the room.

Pulling open the trunk, I remove several of my favorite gowns and pack the older and simpler ones for the trip. I replace some of my slippers with riding boots and swap a thin nightgown for a thick winter cloak.

I slowly open my door and peek out into the corridor.

There isn't a new guard at my door yet, as they are likely rotating for the afternoon shift. Exiting my bedchamber, I move through the corridors as quietly as I can toward Valentin's room. If he is out sweeping the grounds for Elvarrans again, it gives me a chance to steal a pair of pants from him.

I crouch down to peek through the keyhole. *Empty.* Twisting the knob, I open the door and slip inside Valentin's chamber. I open the wardrobe and rummage through for pants.

I hold the first pair I find up to my hips. Too big. I toss them back into the wardrobe. Holding up the next pair, I can see a large red stain. Too bloody. I keep searching until I find a third pair. It is a dark brown color and made of thick material. That will have to do.

I close the wardrobe, then fold the pants and tuck them close to my bodice, hoping I can conceal them as I exit Valentin's bedchamber. If all goes according to my plan, I must make the ten-day journey home from Avelisar on horseback. These pants will provide comfort and practicality while riding.

Upon my return, Lydia stands at my door, clutching something close to her body. A silk cloth wraps around the object, masking its shape from me. Her hazel eyes light up as she sees me, a smile forming on her lips as I approach.

"Lydia," I greet her.

"Hello." She gives me an impish look as we enter my bedchamber. "I got it," Lydia whispers, unraveling the small cloth to reveal a dagger in a sheath.

I pull the dagger free and examine the blade. It's strange, appearing to be made of black steel—the surface drinks in the light, not even a glint of reflection. The hilt fits perfectly in my grip, balanced and deadly without being too heavy and cumbersome.

"Where did you get this?" I keep my voice low in case anyone can hear us in the hall.

She has a devious look on her face. "I stole it from my father's collection."

"Lydia!" I say in surprise. She is never one for deception or trickery. "What if it holds significant importance to him?"

"Don't worry about it." Lydia pushes the dagger closer to me. "Take it! He has so many he won't even notice it's gone."

I hug her close. "Thank you, Lydia."

Lydia sniffles as she releases me, wiping a stray tear away. "I'm going to miss you, Raelys."

"I'll miss you more," I say softly. "There is no one like you in the world, Lydia. You are my dearest friend."

"Write to me as soon as you can."

"I will." I place my hand over hers, giving it a light squeeze. I can't tell her of my deal with Wrath, the promise to write hanging heavier than she realizes.

It's tempting to tell her what's going on, but I can't drag Lydia into this mess. This is my burden—mine to carry and mine alone. No amount of regret or second-guessing can change the path I am on.

"Goodbye, Raelys."

"We will see each other again," I vow.

With one last hug goodbye, she leaves, returning me to my solitude. I walk over to the trunk and hide the dagger wrapped in fabric inside one of my boots. I don't want to explain if Eleanor finds it while packing, or worse, if she takes it from me. Closing the trunk, I lock the hinges and take a step back.

A part of me cannot believe I am leaving my home. The halls I have walked since childhood will soon be behind me. I prayed to Itheon day and night for my freedom, and while granted, the circumstances were askew. I have always longed to see what lies beyond the castle walls—to experience more of what life has to offer. Now, that chance is finally mine, but braided within it is a dark power I'm forced to contend with.

A knock sounds at my door.

I open it to come face-to-face with a new guard. The soldier is stout and muscular, but I don't bother familiarizing myself with his features. To know him would be to admit that Timothy will not return. There's no room for grief, not for the friend who gave their life so I could keep mine. The world keeps dragging me forward.

"The King wishes to see you," he says, devoid of joy.

As I exit, the guard follows me down the hall like a shadow, not speaking another word. I enter my father's war room, watching him pore over maps on the large table in the center.

"You called for me, Father?" I ask, breaking the silence.

"Yes," Ulrik starts. I anticipate his reprimands. A hacking cough wracks through him, causing him to double over. I wait for his episode to pass, standing there in silence while I watch him.

"Have you calmed down now?" Another lecture is hot on his tongue.

"I'm doing exactly as you ask. Tomorrow, I leave for Avelisar." I try not to let the disgust fill my voice. My father is marrying me off to a man who is thirty-eight years my senior and sees no issue with that.

"You will do as told, Raelys," Ulrik commands, and I know if I make him any angrier, it will send him into an early grave.

I hold up a hand to reassure him. "I understand. I'll go to Avelisar, marry the King, and give him a son," I lie.

"Don't disappoint me," he warns.

"I'll miss you too, Father," I say with a hint of cynicism. It's difficult to shake the feeling that he won't miss me. In fact, he's probably pleased to be rid of me.

"We need this alliance." Ulrik reminds me. He treats me

like a wild animal that is a threat if released from my enclosure.

"I understand," I comply, pulling my right sleeve down a little more.

"This is very important. The fate of the realm depends on this."

I nod, forcing myself to stay still beneath the weight of his scrutiny. The deal I made with Wrath presses against my chest, tightening the air until it's hard to breathe. I wait for what comes next, knowing the rant is far from over.

"You are a Valantis, one of the longest-standing human houses. I have raised you to act with poise, dignity, and grace, lest you forget." Ulrik steps closer, pointing an accusatory finger at me. "And you will *not* ruin this for me!"

My father breaks into a haggard coughing fit as he doubles over in pain. His knuckles turn white as he grips the table's edge, his body trembling to steady himself—the once unshakable man, now brought low by an invisible force.

"Mother wouldn't have wanted this," I whisper.

"You dare bring Isla into this." Vemon fills Ulrik's voice. "You speak of her again, and there will be serious consequences."

"Just because you refuse to speak of mother doesn't mean she didn't exist."

I expect sorrow at the mention of her loss, but I only feel ire. It is a low blow, but I want to convey my point to him. She's been gone for so long, but the wounds have not healed—I'm unsure if they ever will.

"This is your duty. You get to be a queen, Raelys." He dismisses my point. "You ungrateful child."

CHAPTER SIX

THE JOURNEY from Cathros to Avelisar will take a total of ten days. I'm inside a small carriage, my body bouncing as we drive over rocks and other rubble on the road from the ongoing war. My home has long since disappeared over the horizon. I'm not used to traveling, and the dust kicked up by the wheels makes me sneeze.

On the second day, I finished reading *The Warlord Chronicles*. By the fourth, I'm practicing ways to use my dagger in case I need to protect myself. On the seventh day, I'm lying flat on the carriage floor with a bottle of wine in my grip, wondering if this journey will ever end.

Every time I look out the carriage window, the view remains unchanged. There is nothing but dreadfully dull grass in every direction, the barren fields empty as the silence around me. I take another sip of wine, attempting to stave off the chill of the rapidly approaching winter.

If this is what life outside the castle walls is, it is as dull as counting the stones on my bedchamber ceiling. I had hoped to feel a sense of excitement and intrigue when I departed

Cathros, but instead, I feel like a forgotten parchment blowing in the breeze. This can't be what true freedom is like.

The carriage thumps suddenly, rocking it from side to side. I sit upright quickly, brushing the stray hairs from my face. The carriage door flings open, surprising me. Someone nimbly steps inside while we are moving, sliding gracefully onto the bench across from me as they invade my space.

"Hello, Princess," he says, closing the door.

I lift the bottle of wine to my lips and take another drink, narrowing my gaze at the man before me. I study his features carefully: black hair, gray eyes, and olive skin. He resembles Wrath's brother. Something slightly masks his features, his pointed ears concealed beneath a helmet. He wears Avelisar's armor and crest, blending in perfectly with the rest of Olav's royal guard.

I couldn't remember his name. "Benjamin…?" I guess, unbothered if I got it wrong.

"Barnham," he corrects.

"That's right." I pick myself up off the carriage floor and sit on the bench across from him. "I was starting to think you wouldn't show."

"You're drunk."

"You would be too if you were stuck in a carriage for ten days." I point an accusatory finger at him. "I trust things are going according to plan?"

"They are."

"Good." I nod, taking another sip.

"Is there a specific point when you'd like us to engage?"

"Preferably before I have to say my vows." I grimace at the dreadful thought.

"Understood." Barnham nods, opening the door to my carriage and stepping out. The door slams with a heavy thunk, returning me to dreadful isolation.

As we finally approach Avelisar, I am struck by how far it is from a sight of grandeur. In fact, it looks quite downtrodden. The castle's so-called 'impenetrable walls' show signs of wear and age, with several cracks forming in the stone. Is this kingdom really secure? I pondered it for a moment before realizing it wouldn't matter for much longer.

As we approach, I expect to find streets or towns surrounding the kingdom—similar to Cathros—teeming with life. I see nothing of the sort. The gate opens, allowing the carriages to enter Avelisar.

I reach for the handle, but the door flies open on its own. The carriage driver holds out a hand to help me. I take a careful look at his features. He resembles the Elvarran named Stanik from the castle garden, but I am not entirely sure.

Several unfamiliar people swarm around me in the courtyard. Many offer greetings and blessings, hands outstretched in my direction. Some even stroke my hair, and I recoil instinctively. Others take my hand, sending panic up my arm wrapped in magic. I rip my right hand away and yank down my sleeve as I tuck my arms to my body.

"Welcome, Highness!"

"May the gods bless you!"

"Follow me. I'll escort you to your room!"

I ignore all of them, scanning the courtyard. Where are the Elvarrans? Why don't I recognize any of them? I can't identify a single face, and a faint unease coils beneath my ribs.

"Looking for someone, Princess?" I hear a deep voice.

Turning to my right, I see Olav hobbling toward me. He has a cane in his hand, using it to navigate the uneven stones. Each step is a struggle, and I wonder how he's managed to stay in power for so long. The closer he gets to me, the further my body recoils.

"I'm simply taking in the beauty of my new surroundings." I force a smile. "I never got to leave Cathros. Forgive me if I'm a little homesick, Your Majesty."

Olav barks a gruff laugh. He reaches out to tuck a stray piece of hair behind my ear, the feeling of his wilted fingers grating against my skin. "You will learn to love Avelisar." He wraps an arm around my waist as he guides me to the castle. "Come."

We walk through the tall iron doors and into the entryway. It's not as grandiose as the castle in Cathros. The halls are smaller, and the stone is unpolished. Hung on the wall are faded tapestries, the lanterns dim from low fuel. A middle-aged woman is standing in the main hall. Her brown eyes are blood-shot red as she holds back tears, her smile painted on. Her sadness grows when her gaze meets mine.

My heart sinks.

Queen Kathryn Friedrich. She wears a deep sapphire gown with a high neckline and long sleeves. She is beautiful, her brunette hair tied into an updo, a stunning crown of jewels adorning her head. Upon closer inspection, she has dark circles under her eyes, likely due to a lack of sleep. Her skin is pale and thin, like she hasn't gone in the sun for a while.

"Queen Kathryn Friedrich." I bow to her, lowering my head and keeping the poise and formalities of royalty. I must play the game and make it appear that everything is in order. There are potentially dozens of Elvarrans disguised as guards all around us.

"Princess Raelys Valantis." She curtsies in return.

"See?" Olav cuts in. "We can all learn to co-exist." His words drip with arrogance, a snide edge that makes my blood boil.

He leans close to Kathryn, conversing in short, hushed conversation. Kathryn turns and exits the hall immediately, leaving us alone. Olav hasn't seen his wife—his queen—in weeks, and he did not show any sign of affection towards her. I see red as I dig my fingernails into my palm to remain composed.

Olav returns his focus to me. "Tallulah will be your hand-maiden. She will help you to your chamber. We shall hold the ceremony tomorrow and move your belongings into my solar afterward."

"Yes, Your Majesty," I say softly.

He smiles at my compliance as he kisses my cheek before walking away. I can still feel his touch like filth lingering on my skin. The girl he called Tallulah approaches me. She looks young, no older than nineteen, with golden-blonde hair woven into a neat braid. Her warm brown eyes gleam with curiosity as they settle on me. A simple forest-green dress drapes over her slender frame as she folds her hands in front of her.

"Hello, Princess." She bows. "Follow me."

Tallulah walks gracefully up the main steps. Glancing behind me, I see three guards following us. I don't recognize them as Elvarrans. Sighing, I follow the girl through several maze-like corridors.

"Here we are!" Tallulah unlocks the door with a key, holding it open for me to enter.

I step inside, immediately noticing how vast the bedchamber is. In the corner is an oak wardrobe, a divider for changing, and a single wooden stool. The bed is larger than the one I had back home, the headboard eclipsed by pillows. There's a tall fireplace with a seating area nearby, the chairs covered with lush fabric. Two servants bring in my trunk of belongings and set it by the foot of the bed, leaving us alone.

Tallulah stands by my side, closely monitoring me. "Do you

need help dressing? Or perhaps a bath?" She doesn't take a breath. "Something to eat?"

"I'll call if I need something. Thank you," I say, moving towards the door. I must find Wrath or Barnham to get an update on the plan.

Tallulah sprints, slamming the door shut with a palm, entombing me inside. I hear the lock thunk closed on the outside, and a pit forms in my stomach. I am a rabbit caught in a snare, and Olav is my huntsman.

"The king has asked us to gather everything you need, Highness." Tallulah smiles.

"I can't go outside?" I ask suspiciously.

"We're happy to assist you with all that you ask." She presses her back against the door, blocking it.

"I've been in a carriage for ten days." I soften my voice, trying to convince her to let me out. "I need to stretch my legs, get some air—"

Tallulah cuts me off. "I completely understand, Highness."

"You're not going to let me out?" I deadpan. I am isolated among a court of people I don't trust—stranded in a kingdom miles away from my home. I realize the only person I can rely on for survival is myself.

"King's orders!" Tallulah laughs nervously, her smile twitching at the corner.

CHAPTER SEVEN

GUARDS PUSH open the doors to the main hall with a flourish, revealing a long hall with several rows of benches. The room falls silent as every guest turns to look at me. White rose petals flatten beneath my feet as I walk down the aisle, beckoning me to my fate.

My wedding dress trails behind me like a leaden chain. The skirt is heavy, layered with an excessive amount of fabric. I pull my overextravagant right sleeve down, an anxious habit developed to ensure the secret of my silver marking. The stems of my bouquet snap under my vice-like grip as dread swallows me whole. What is taking Wrath so long? Surely, they will arrive before the ceremony concludes.

Olav holds out a hand. I hate it when people touch my hands, let alone look at the scars that mar them. I begrudgingly take it in mine and allow him to guide me up the steps to the altar. His fingers linger on my skin for too long before he takes my bouquet and sets it aside. Olav's eyes rove over me as he takes in my appearance, a sinister grin forming on his lips.

"You look better than Kathryn in that dress," Olav whispers.

I bite the inside of my cheek so hard it bleeds. Holding my tongue and composure is far more challenging than I imagined. My gaze darts around for any sign of the Elvarrans, but there are none. A man in simple robes stands to my left. He opens a worn, leather-bound book in his hands, clearing his throat before speaking.

Itheon save me…

"Divine God Itheon, bless this union as two hearts bond into one. Guide their fates together and bless their union with warmth and peace. May honor bind their words under your watchful gaze," the cleric says aloud, starting the ceremony.

He holds a small cushion with two gold bands before us. Olav plucks the first ring, taking my hands in his as he starts his vows. "I, Olav Friedrich, vow to take Raelys Valantis as my wife from this day forward. To do my duty, till death do us part. May Itheon ordain, and therefore I pledge my troth," he announces confidently, slipping a ring onto my finger.

My heart hammers in my chest. Every nerve in my body is ablaze with panic as sweat forms on my brow. Like boiling water, the dread and anguish swirl around me, pulling me under the surface. Soon, I won't be able to hold my breath any longer. This wretched old man smiles at me, tightening his grip around my hands, as if he's pleased with my discomfort.

I want to scream.

Taking the second ring, I say my vows. "I, Raelys Valantis…" My voice trembles as I swallow the lump in my throat. *Itheon please.* Anything but this. "Vow to take Olav Friedrich as my husband from this day forward…" *I do not. I do not. I do not.* "May Itheon ordain, and therefore I pledge my troth," I say, my voice low and devoid of excitement as I slip a ring onto his finger.

"To be kind and obedient in bed and at home," the cleric corrects me.

Gods. I had completely messed up my vows because I am so flustered. Now I have to repeat them; my tribulation is never-ending. Olav strokes the back of my hand, a gesture of comfort, but it only makes my desire to crumple to the floor stronger, now from dread and embarrassment.

What is taking Wrath so *godsdamn* long?!

"I, Raelys Valantis, vow to take Olav Friedrich as my husband from this day forward." I start over. "To be kind and obedient in bed and at home, till death do us part. May Itheon ordain, and therefore… I pledge my troth." I repeat the hollow words.

The cleric nods, setting down the book. He pulls out a strap of cloth and binds our hands together. "I now declare in the eyes of Itheon that you are husband and wife."

Olav wastes no time, grabbing my face and placing his lips on mine. My entire body freezes, rooted in the spot, as I auto-matically tilt back. Luckily, Olav doesn't seem to notice as he takes our interlaced fingers and walks me back down the aisle. I flinch from the touch, recoiling from his tight grip. I stumble a few steps as Olav drags me from the room, a bolt of fear shooting through me.

I look around, up, behind, every corner imaginable for some cue or signal for help. None comes. Wrath made a fool of me. No one is coming to save me. This deal is some sick joke to him, and the silver bargain lingering on my skin is a farce.

Thinking quickly, I need to devise a plan to save myself.

"Perhaps my bedchambers?" I suggest. "I would be more comfortable there."

Olav laughs. "All right." His eyes rake over me, dark with anticipation. My skin prickles, instinct screaming danger, but there's nowhere to run. He looks at me the way a wolf studies its trapped prey.

I am no prey.

He opens the door to my bedchambers, slamming it behind us. I startle at the bang, surprised that someone his age could retain that much strength. Olav grips my shoulders and shoves me face-down into the bed, pinning me down. His fingers move to push up my skirt as he tries to sort through the layers of silk.

My hand darts underneath the pillow beside me.

"I promise I'll be easy on you… since it's your first time." He smiles, his teeth yellow as his rancid breath puffs against my cheek.

I close my fingers around the dagger's hilt, and I swing. The blade finds its mark, burying into his gut. Blood splatters over my face and the bedsheets as Olav roars in pain. I had kept Lydia's dagger under my pillow—a precaution now proven invaluable.

"You bitch!" Olav yells, the back of his hand meeting my cheek. "Guards!"

He knocks me to the floor, my body hitting the bedside table as I fall. Olav rips out the dagger, tossing it aside. The blade clatters to the floor and slides across the stone. I chase after it, running as fast as I can, but this damned dress is too cumbersome. Olav grabs a fistful of my hair, yanking me back towards him. I let out a cry of pain and pick up the stool that one of the handmaidens used to dress me to swing at him.

The wood hits him with a heavy thunk, causing him to loosen his grip on me. Pain shoots through my scalp as I tear myself free. I dash for the dagger, knowing if I don't get it, it will be the end of me.

"I'll have you hanged for this!" Olav yells at me, his bright red face matching the stain on his tunic. "Where are the guards!?" He pulls open the door, opening his mouth to call for help.

A sword soars through the air, sinking directly through Olav's chest. My breath catches in my throat from the gruesome sight. I watch as his body slumps to the floor, a pool of blood spreading across the stone. Nausea bubbles up in my gut. My hand shakes with adrenaline as I clutch the dagger in front of me. A black leather boot slowly steps over the corpse and into the room.

"My, my, Princess. I didn't think you had it in you." Wrath's voice reaches me as he passes through the doorframe.

"Took you long enough," I say in annoyance, lowering the dagger to my side.

"Does that mean you're eager to see me?" he asks curiously.

I scoff, storming across the room to my trunk and flinging open the top. I wipe the bloody dagger onto this hideous dress before sheathing it. I pull out my riding boots and cloak, knowing I have little time to get out of this castle, steal a horse, and ride back home to Cathros.

Everything would be back to normal before long.

"It seems like you're in a hurry. What for?" Wrath studies me closely. There's the invisible brush of his magic across my skin as he nears. I loathe the sensation.

"That's none of your concern," I bite out, ripping off my wedding ring and throwing it over my shoulder. It clatters to the floor in the distance, and I feel as though I've released myself from a handcuff.

"Surely you're not going to try to return home *alone*." Wrath's words make me pause what I'm doing. I give him a deadly gaze. "What will the seven kingdoms think when they discover the King of Avelisar's body dead in your chambers?"

"Then drag his body elsewhere!" I snap at him, reaching up to pull the adornments from my hair. I toss them aside as I free my hair from its updo. My waves fall to my waist, and I feel immediate relief across my scalp. "And it's more like five kingdoms now," I correct him.

I pull on the pants I stole from Valentin's room under my dress, realizing they're about two sizes too big. Striding over to Olav's body, I rip his belt free and loop it through my pants, buckling the belt on the tightest setting, and hoping it stays in place.

"It's unlikely they'll believe that the king died, and you escaped." Wrath is vexingly calm for having just ended a life.

"What are you suggesting then?" I race behind the divider, yanking the dress off. "Fake my death?" I pull on a tunic and tuck it into the waistband. Slinging my cloak around my shoulders, I fasten it in the front, preparing myself for a long journey ahead.

"That's a fair idea." He plays along. "Then where will you go?"

I circle the divider, braiding my long hair into three loose strands as quickly as possible before fastening the ends. Packing everything I can into the leather satchel Eleanor gave me, I sling it over my shoulder as I approach Wrath.

"You're not seriously suggesting that I go with you." It's my turn to laugh sardonically. "Does the destroyer of peace require a pet? I didn't take you for the companion type."

I expect him to get angry at my insult. That my outburst would end in him attempting to kill me once more. Instead, I see his lips quirk as he holds back a reaction, his eyes alight with challenge.

"I'm not suggesting." His tone is lethal as he leans close, invading my space.

My expression drops. "And what if I refuse?"

"Fine." He saunters from the room. "No one will trust you with magic on your skin."

I glance down at my arm, pulling it out of my cloak to examine it. It's still there. A shining silver sigil, reminding me I am bound to him. Why hasn't it gone away? We can be rid of one another now that our bargain is complete.

"Then remove it," I urge, taking long strides to catch up to him. "Our deal is finished, as agreed."

"I can't."

"You're the king."

"Magic is one-way. It's difficult to reverse," he explains. "You could always burn it off."

I huff in annoyance, shaking my head. "This isn't what I agreed to."

"It is," Wrath replies impassively. "I freed you from your marriage, and you haven't even thanked me."

"Why would I thank a scoundrel—"

Wrath halts mid-step, silencing me as he whips around. A chill runs down my spine as his stare cuts through me like a blade. I'm frozen in place, helpless under his commanding will. I've done it this time. He's going to kill me.

"Then take a horse and make the ten-day journey by yourself back to Cathros. See how long you last without food or supplies, *Princess*," he says through gritted teeth, rage emanating off him like steam from an oven.

I don't want to admit that he's right. I have no map and would soon find myself lost. Until recently, I haven't even left Cathros's castle, completely sheltered from the outside world. It is a fatal flaw in my plan. I became so fixated on surviving that I did not fully consider the logistics of returning home.

"You're taking me hostage." I cross my arms over my chest. "Is that what this is?"

"I'm offering you protection."

"And why would the most wicked king in Dratheria help me?"

"They've only taught you one side," he replies, voice low and accusatory.

He turns and walks away, heading toward the front of the castle. I don't follow immediately, stubbornly holding my ground. It's oddly quiet in the castle halls, causing suspicion to rise within me. I glance behind me, then to the front, and my left and right. Not a soul lingers in these halls. Wrath's footsteps are the only sound that echoes down the cavernous space, leaving me with more questions than answers.

On impulse, I surge after him.

"Where are all the guards?" I call out.

He doesn't slow down or wait for me to catch up with him. "There were only around a hundred men protecting Avelisar."

"That's it?" The words tumble from my lips before I stop them. "And what of the rest of the people?"

What happened to the guests at the wedding? What about Queen Kathryn, Tallulah, and the other handmaidens? What about the cooks, stable hands, and bird keepers? It's shocking to think they ended everyone that quickly. An entire kingdom wiped from existence in a single afternoon.

"It's best if you don't ask questions you won't like the answer to." Wrath levels me with a look.

He lives up to his name. I shouldn't be surprised that the most ruthless leader in Dratheria has an unsavory side. A heart untouched by remorse, moved only by its quest for power. Wrath is keeping me alive, and part of me is starting to believe he needs me for something.

The closer we get to the castle's exit, the less time I have to make a decision. For years, I begged Itheon to free me from the castle walls every day and night. And now, I am outside them, eagerly racing back to my father's captivity.

I ask myself what the warlord would do in this situation, how they would navigate such peril. They would use this advantage to infiltrate enemy lines and dismantle their kingdom from within. If I go to Khalessor, I can provide Valentin with valuable information.

"Make a choice, Raelys." Wrath cuts into my thoughts as we exit the iron doors and enter the courtyard below.

Dozens of Elvarrans move through the space, all armed to the teeth with weapons. I watch some pack up large satchels full of gold and other looted objects, plundering the castle for its riches. Others mount their horses and prepare to depart, their expressions calm and armor spotless despite the slaughter.

I count at least seventy Elvarrans, give or take. These soldiers have to be only a portion of Khalessor's army, yet they hold enough force to expunge the entire kingdom. These warriors are far more fearsome than anything I'd ever seen. There is no running from this situation.

"Fine." I scowl at him. "Take me with you."

I catch the corners of his lips turning upward as he turns. "Taryn!" he calls for someone as he approaches his horse. Wrath mounts the large brown steed with a dark mane and tail, and when he sits tall, he looks like a statue carved from stone.

"Yes, Your Majesty?" The woman with rich brown skin and short hair from the garden rushes over to us, two twin daggers strapped to her thighs.

"Grab a spare horse for Raelys. Make sure she doesn't fall behind," he commands.

"I know how to ride." I snap at him.

Wrath chuckles as he rides off, leaving us behind.

"This way, quickly." Taryn turns and strides across the courtyard.

She leads me to the stables. Taryn opens the door to a stall and brings out a black-and-white spotted mare for me, adjusts the reins, and then gestures for me to get on. I put my foot in the stirrup and swing my leg over smoothly, mounting the horse.

Taryn gets on a light beige horse beside me. "Ready?"

I nod and give the horse a light tap. I follow Taryn out the front gates, past the walls, and into the wide-open land. The sun is setting, the sky a brilliant shade of orange and pink. The open landscape stretches for miles in every direction, seemingly endless.

"We ride for five days until we reach Sinaia. We will cross the Northern Alps the following daybreak and return to Khalessor." Wrath's deep voice booms across the space, his horse at the head of the pack.

Someone rounds my left side, stopping their horse behind mine. It is Barnham, dressed in full armor with a spear in hand. He whistles up to Wrath, giving him a signal that everyone is here. The riders take off immediately, galloping quickly north.

Taryn rides beside me, keeping a close eye on my every movement. She likely suspects I could turn and run at any moment. The thought is tempting, but armed only with the dagger Lydia gave me, I wouldn't survive.

Shades of navy ebb into pitch darkness. My lower back and legs are sore from the fast pace. Despite my growing ache, I will not fall behind. I refuse to show the Elvarrans that I am weak. My stomach rumbles with hunger as I await our destination.

"Here." I hear a voice to my right. "Water?" Taryn holds out a canteen to me.

I take it from her, gulping down water to soothe my burning throat. "Thank you." I pass the canteen back to her.

"You kept up better than I expected," she comments, a playful gleam in her eye.

"Thanks...?" I say slowly, unsure if it's a compliment or an insult.

When I turn my attention forward again, I spot a fire and some tents in the distance. My heart leaps at the thought of rest. The cavalry slows as it heads into camp, transitioning from a gallop to a trot. I exhale a long breath of relief as I pull my horse to a stop, shaking out my sore hands.

Taryn stops at the camp, swinging her leg over her horse and dismounting. I do the same, releasing my foot and swinging my leg over. When my feet hit the ground, my legs wobble like a newborn foal. Pain and soreness creep into my muscles, and each movement feels heavy.

"I'm going to be sore in the morning…" I say under my breath.

"You'll get used to it." Taryn smiles at me, taking my horse's reins and tying it to a post.

She signals for me to follow her. We walk across the camp toward the large tent in the center. Taryn reaches up and opens the flap, allowing me to enter. She closes the tent behind me, sealing me inside.

I see Wrath and Barnham discussing something by the table, with several pieces of parchment and maps scattered around it. I avoid them, looking down to assess my hands. My knuckles are red from the wind. The bruises from Margaret's lessons are still lingering on my skin. It would be best to get some gloves to save my hands from more damage.

"Raelys."

Turning, my shoulder bumps into Wrath's chest.

"What is it?" His question is more of a demand.

"I'm—" I stop myself. I don't want Wrath to use his magic to force my words from me. "I need some gloves, that's all, and some food," I tell him the truth.

Wrath snatches my hand, pulling it close to inspect the damage on my skin. As his thumb lightly brushes my bruise, the mark on my arm ignites with a spark. It comes alive by his touch, as if calling to return home. Embarrassed by the scars that mar my skin, I quickly pull away, covering the back of my hand with my palm as I cast my eyes to the ground.

"I will make arrangements; food will be here soon." As he walks away, Wrath calls over his shoulder, "Then you should rest for tomorrow."

CHAPTER EIGHT

THE FOLLOWING MORNING, as I mount my horse and patiently wait for the caravan to take off, I hear the sound of approaching hoofbeats to my right. Wrath pulls his horse beside mine. His armor bears several marks, each a testament to the numerous battles he's survived. A heavy fur-lined cloak drapes over his shoulders, his left hand resting lazily on the hilt of his sword.

I am about to speak when he pulls off his leather gloves and extends them to me. The gesture catches me slightly off guard, and I stare at them momentarily before reaching out. "Thank you," I say softly.

His gaze lowers to my hands. A flush of embarrassment rips through me as I pull on the gloves. I know he's looking at the scars and bruises. Everyone stares at them. I hate the marks Margaret left on my skin; they are ghastly and decrepit. Once the gloves conceal my insecurity, I push out a quick breath of relief.

Wrath says nothing as he rides off, the army following in his wake.

The group maintains a swift and unforgiving pace, causing

the soreness in my legs from yesterday to resurface with a vengeful ache. As I endure the discomfort, I take in the surroundings, wondering where we are. The flat and open field looked identical to the previous day's passing landscape, leading me to believe we'd made no progress. I wipe the sweat from my brow, the sun's unforgiving rays beating down on us without the cover of trees. Taryn slows her pace to match mine, a smile on her face as she takes in my state.

"Hello, Taryn."

"How are we feeling?" she asks, seemingly more friendly than yesterday.

"Sore." I deadpan. "Where are we?"

"Still in the flatlands," she replies. "The lack of water makes it difficult to grow anything; the soil is dry, and the summers are quite challenging to shelter from. Humans abandoned trying to inhabit these lands a long time ago. Therefore, it makes a good traveling route for us."

"Interesting…" I say under my breath, looking at the land.

Taryn snickers beside me. "You've never traveled, Princess?"

"I have not."

She passes me the canteen of water. "Well, you'll see many things on our way back to Khalessor."

I drink, clinging onto the cool metal for as long as possible before returning it to Taryn. "You were in the gardens that night I spoke to the king."

"I was."

"You said you wanted to kill me when we first met, and now you're being kind to me," I continue, hoping she understands what I'm implying.

"I trust King Wrath with my life," Taryn says confidently. "He told me to guard you. Therefore, I will."

"Why?"

"I owe everything to him." Taryn's demeanor softens. "When humans raided my village near Corovya, I was only sixteen. They lit our houses with fire to draw us out, performed rituals to sever us from our magic, then slaughtered us." Her eyes burn with an intense fury. "My mother hid my sister and me in the food storage underneath our home while blood leaked through the floorboards and onto us for hours until the carnage ended."

"Taryn…"

"King Wrath found us three days later on the brink of starvation. I was too weak to walk. He carried us to the camp and insisted the healer save us when others said we were too far gone." She releases a deeply held breath. "I have devoted my life to serving him."

"I'm—"

She cuts me off. "Do not apologize. Simply observe and form your own opinions."

I consider her words. There are many things I don't know about the Elvarrans, as my father forbade me to learn anything about them. Ulrik raised me to believe they are my enemy, but it is clear I have much to discover about their way of life. I will never trust them fully, but perhaps I can delve deeper into uncovering why they fight this war.

"Why are you the only female in the royal guard?" I pivot the conversation.

"I killed the king of Nythara." Taryn attempts to hide her smirk, but I can see her beaming with pride.

I enjoy how spirited and passionate Taryn is when she speaks—a rare trait and clear indication of a true warrior. I admire her strength, how she was able to persist past the grief to blaze her own trail.

"Do tell."

Taryn's smile widens. "I scaled the keep and broke through

the window leading into the castle's solar. The king was attempting to flee into the underground tunnels when I arrived." She makes a noise of annoyance. "What a coward! You couldn't even fight honorably when so many others gave their lives to protect you?"

"I agree," I reply as we continue to ride. "How did you scale the castle wall?"

"I'm more of a scout than a soldier," Taryn explains. "The king usually sends me ahead to sneak into places and get a lay of the land."

That must be how they were able to infiltrate Cathros's castle.

The landscape around us shifts as we descend the hill. The trees are black and lifeless, their branches wilting, and the bushes are withered clumps of thorns, leaving a hollow and unsettling feeling as we pass. A pungent, metallic odor causes me to scrunch up my nose in displeasure; the scent is unfamiliar and unnatural.

As we travel deeper, I spot the remnants of an incinerated village. Pieces of ash still lay on the ground, stirring slightly from the breeze. I wonder if this forest burned recently, taking the town with it. Was it a human or Elvarran village? The destruction is devastating either way. People lost their lives, the wildlife of the forest destroyed, and still, war rages on.

Now more than ever, I realize the world is dangerous and vast beyond my wildest imagination. My father may have tried to protect me behind those walls, fearful of what may happen to me, but choosing to live in fear is a choice. Protection is a farce, stability an illusion, safety a false prayer we tell ourselves to sleep at night.

The veil has lifted, and no longer shall I remain in the dark.

My body sags from exhaustion as we ride into camp, begging for rest. I dismount my horse, pulling the reins over and patting the mare's neck a few times in my thanks. An Elvarran takes the reins from me and ties the horse to a post, allowing me to walk to Wrath's tent. As I enter, I see Wrath pluck a cork from a bottle of wine and pour himself a glass.

I move to the small cot, plopping down ungracefully to yank off my boots. With an exhausted sigh, I drop them beside me and roll my sore ankles out. I thoroughly enjoy riding, but the length of this journey is wearing me down.

"Raelys."

"Yes?" I glance up at him.

"Would you like some wine?" he asks, adjusting his sleeves lower.

I study him. For someone who spent all day riding, his appearance is immaculate—hair brushed back, a renegade lock over his temple. His black coat is smooth and wrinkle-free. Somehow, his boots are polished while mine are dusty and muddy. His offer surprises me. It could be a trick, but I'm too exhausted to care. A little wine would ease the soreness and help me fall asleep quickly.

"I would."

Pulling off my heavy cloak, I toss it to the side. I unweave my frizzy braid, untangling the long strands. Once I feel the relief on my scalp, I approach Wrath. He pours wine into a slightly dented tin cup and hands it to me. I take a long swig from it, trying not to let the displeasure show on my face. I now understand what Valentin meant when he said the wine he had while traveling tasted like piss. I am in no position to complain, though.

Wrath reaches out, taking my mother's pendant between his fingers. "Where did you get this?" he asks, running his thumb over the left wing on the crest. Wrath looms over me as we stand beside one another. I'm a bit taller than the average woman, but Wrath is still a head higher.

"It was my mother's," I reply pensively. A cold feeling spreads through my chest. The memory of her loss will forever haunt me.

"Your mother was House Izydor?"

I don't reply.

The itch of magic slinks at the back of my throat, snaking its way into me. "No—!" I protest, clenching my jaw together as I step back.

"No?"

"You will not use your magic to force me to speak," I demand. No matter what I try, I slowly succumb to the magic as I try to fight against it. I grit my teeth, press my lips together, and bite my tongue, but it's useless. "My mother is Isla Izydor," I say against my will, my chest heaving for breath.

"Your mother was the last of her line." Wrath's brows draw together. Intensity radiates off of him like a storm on the verge of breaking, striking fear into me.

I fight against it, shaking my head as I grip the table for stability. My lungs gasp for air that doesn't come. "I was born out of wedlock," I say, the magic wrestling my answer from me.

My father lost his first wife, Queen Thalia Valantis, to an infection and never remarried. He met in secret for years with Queen Isla Izydor of Rykaris, resulting in my birth. My veins carry royal blood from two great houses, but I am an illegitimate heir born outside of a union.

Valentin is my half-brother, but I love him just the same. My father forced me to swear an oath of secrecy. He did his best to make me appear as his second daughter, despite me looking nothing like Thalia, who had chestnut brown hair the same shade as Valentin's. We did share our blue eyes, but my pale blonde hair made me stick out compared to the portraits in the halls of House Valantis.

"This means—"

I cut him off. "Enough!" Irritation lines my voice. "You cannot rip my secrets from me against my will."

"House Izydor is an Elvarran line." Wrath ignores me, his face exasperatingly placid.

"Are you suggesting I'm half-Elvarran?" I ask impulsively, despite not wanting to know the answer.

The question gnaws at the edges of my thoughts, eating into one of the things I desire the most. I miss my mother every day. I cling to what little memories I have of her. If Wrath finds out how much I wish to know more about her, he will use it as leverage against me.

"You are."

"I don't remember my mother having pointed ears," I counter, recalling her features from memory.

"Your memory deceives you." He studies my face, scanning each feature as he tries to spot similarities to Isla.

"It doesn't change anything," I lie.

Wrath stole one of my deepest and most guarded secrets. I'm caught fast in his web, every thread pulled taut to remind me who holds the power. I am no person—just prey dressed in silk, struggling against the strands that tighten the more I resist. The familiar sting of helplessness rushes through me, burning beneath my skin.

"This changes everything," he counters.

"You do not get to dictate that." I cling to the fading remnants of my freedom.

"The magic does."

"I knew there were ulterior motives when you demanded I come with you." I slam my empty cup down on the table.

Turning, I move to walk away. Wrath catches my wrist in his grip, stopping me. A burst of magic shoots through my arm, igniting every nerve on my skin as it attunes to his will.

It sends chills down my spine as the world closes in around us.

"Raelys."

"I will never trust you," I snap.

"I don't need you to." His voice is low.

"Then what do you want from me?" I rip my wrist from his grasp. The sensation of his magic fades from the broken connection. I hate this mark. There must be a way to rid me of this shackle, or I will never be free.

Wrath doesn't answer my question.

CHAPTER NINE

"But how does it *work*?" I ask Barnham for the fifteenth time today.

Barnham and I have been riding together the past few days. Unlike Taryn, he converses with me very little. Five days of travel have worn me down. Fatigue creeps up on me from lack of sleep, as the Elvarran wake at dawn. My body feels slow, my mind dull.

He lets out an exasperated sigh. "You're not going to let this one rest, are you?"

"Come on, Barnham," I plead. "I've never even seen magic! Can't you make something disappear or shoot a fireball for me?"

"You saw magic when you made your deal with the king," he deadpans. "It's on your skin."

"That's not exciting magic," I counter. "We've been riding for *days* now. At least tell me how it works?"

"I'll answer your questions, Princess." A lively voice cuts in.

I turn my attention toward the sound. A man pulls his horse's reins back, slowing his horse to my left. He has tall ears that protrude from his golden, curly, blonde hair. The man wears dingy, tarnished armor that appears to have been through numerous battles.

"And who might you be?" I ask curiously.

"Knight Kieran Hale of Salasyr," he replies confidently.

"Please. You are a soldier, not a knight," Barnham says coldly.

"Barnham!" Kieran's blue eyes narrow. "The one time we get to travel with a beautiful woman, and you make her miserable the entire time."

He has a point.

"The only women who enjoy your company are those you pay with coin," Barnham taunts.

Raucous laughter erupts from up ahead. A man turns to the side on his horse, looking back at us. His dark eyes hold an air of quiet power. He has a long, jagged scar that cuts across his right eyebrow at an angle. His dark brunette hair is shorn short on the sides, revealing pointed ears. If I were not stuck in a court of enemies rooting for my downfall, I'd find him attractive.

"Well struck!" he calls out.

Much to my surprise, Barnham laughs. I didn't know he was capable of joy. He is always stoic and critical when speaking to me.

"Thank you, Marek," Barnham replies.

"Buncha bastards, you two," Kieran grumbles under his breath.

"Rank, my good fellow, rank," Marek reminds him, turning back around on his horse.

Kieran scoffs, kicking his horse and riding off. I watch him disappear into the pack, returning me to my isolation. What an interesting man. Bold, but a bit dense. Marek is correct. I am a princess, and he is a soldier. Our ranks do not allow such indulgences.

"There are three types of users: Verthari, Remedari, and Evokari. There, happy?" Barnham relents, finally beginning to answer my question.

"You're not going to tell me what they do?"

Barnham's eye twitches. "Verthari can manipulate various elements like fire, water, earth, and air. But can only specialize in one type."

"Are you a Verthari?" I ask curiously, wondering what type of magic he uses.

"Yes, water," he replies. "Remedari are healers. They can seal grievous wounds and take pain away from others."

"And the third one?" I push him for more, mainly to quell my boredom.

"Evokari is what the king does," Barnham explains. "They can bend people to their will, manipulate others' magic, and shape the energy around them."

My eyes widen in curiosity. That's how Wrath forced answers out of me when he questioned me. Even thinking of it sends the same chill down my spine.

"Now, will you stop asking me questions?" Barnham's tone is annoyed.

"Thank you," I say kindly, returning my attention to the landscape around us.

As we crest a hill, a small town comes into view. Every structure is abandoned, with broken windowpanes, sagging roofs, and weathered wood fences. I try to spot any townsfolk, but it is barren and devoid of life.

"What is that?" I ask.

"The town of Liora."

That means we are close to the northern border. Soon enough, we will be crossing into the Elvarran lands. My pulse thrums with the thought, the anticipation of the unknown sending a thrill through me. The south is dry and warm, so does that mean the north is lush and green?

"It's seen better days…" Barnham absently comments.

"What do you mean?" I tear my gaze away from the village.

"It looks like last winter was hard on them. There are fewer guards and fewer people in the fields, and some of their crops were wiped out due to the tainted water supply," he explains vaguely.

"Every winter gets more difficult for the humans," I reply. "We've sent rations to Liora for years, but I had no idea it was this… downtrodden."

"It's been difficult for the West this past year."

"Why—?"

An arrow flies directly into my horse, making it rear. I scramble, clutching my reins as I try to avoid falling off. It whinnies in pain as I try to keep her under control, my horse continuing to buck. Something hits my shoulder, a sharp burst of pain erupting as an arrow lodges itself into my skin.

The impact makes me lose my grip on the reins, as the horse throws me from its back. I hit the dirt with a heavy thud, the impact knocking the air from my lungs. There's no time to think. I rip the arrow free and roll to avoid the stomping hooves that threaten to trample me. I cry out in pain, my hand instinctively moving to cover the wound as blood coats my fingers. I have never been in battle, utterly helpless amid the chaos.

A figure approaches me, raising their sword high as they prepare to strike. Panic shoots through me like a lightning bolt as I roll quickly to the side. The sword sinks into the dirt beside my head, barely missing me. I try to stand, but the man shoves me into the dirt, causing my back to hit the ground once more. Pain shoots through my wound as my head snaps back, rendering me incapacitated. I try to get on my feet, but a hand closes around my throat, closing my airway with a forceful grip.

"Traitor!" He spits at me, moving to swing at me once more.

I can see the figure is clearly human… so why is he trying to kill me?

My heart is pounding rapidly in my ears, drowning out all else. I look around for a weapon, but there are none. I raise my hands in front of my face and prepare for the blow to hit me. A sword erupts through the man's chest, and a shower of blood rains down on me. Terror rips through me as the hot and sticky liquid coats my face and neck. The man falls dead to the ground beside me. My hand flies to my mouth, an attempt to push down the rising bile.

Barnham holds out a hand for me to take. "We have to move!"

He pulls me to my feet. I reach down to grab the sword from the man's lifeless grip. The blade is hefty, and I drop it before trying to pick it up again.

"You're not strong enough to wield a broadsword." He pulls out a small dagger and hands it to me. "Aim for the chest or the eyes."

I take it from him as more people rush toward us. A fist closes around my scalp and yanks at my hair. The pull is so intense I feel hair rip from my head, causing me to cry out in pain as tears well in my eyes.

"I done snatched the Princess!" he shouts, holding a blade to my neck.

The dagger cuts my neck slightly as he holds me, a trickle of blood running down my skin. I grit my teeth and swing my arm backwards, sinking the dagger into his side. He screams as I rip it free to do it again. The man moves to kill me. Marek plunges his sword through his chest, killing him instantly.

The man drops to the ground, nearly taking me with him. I bump into something—no, someone. They yank a bag over my head, plunging me into darkness. Panic fills me as I try to get away, swinging my dagger blindly through the air as arms try to restrain me.

"You bitch!" A man swears as I catch my dagger across something. "Human dick ain't good enough for ya, Princess? You like the taste of magical swimmers instead?"

His words make my stomach turn.

The man knocks the dagger from my grip with ease. Rough hands seize me and lift me into the air, my captor throwing me over his shoulder. He saunters away, taking me with him. I kick out my legs and squirm, but it's ineffective. The man tightens his grip around me even more.

"Help!" I scream.

"Quiet!" My captor yells, shaking me roughly.

My chest is heaving as I try to force air into my lungs. It's difficult to breathe with this bag over my head while upside down. "Let me go!" I yell, my voice hoarse.

He laughs. "The king's gonna pay heaps of gold for you."

Bandits? Is that who is attacking us?

I hear swords clashing as I fall to the ground once more, my body bouncing and rolling away in the grass. Reaching up, I pull the bag off my head, my eyes readjusting to the light. Standing before me is Wrath, his arm swinging gracefully as the black steel blade slices the head clean off of my would-be kidnapper. The severed part rolls towards me in the grass, stopping as it bumps against my leg.

I turn my body and plant my hands on the dirt as I vomit up the contents of my stomach, unable to hold it down any longer. I close my eyes and silently wish this is an awful dream —one I will wake from soon. Opening my eyes, I face the unfortunate reality that it's not a dream. Reaching out, I pat around until I find the hilt of a dagger. I close my fingers firmly around it and force myself to stand.

A man rushes toward me with a spear raised in the air, aiming directly at me. An arrow lodges directly into his eye, knocking the man to the ground. The spear tumbles from his grasp as Stanik's horse tramples him. The archer readies another arrow in his bow, letting it fly through the air at another target.

I sprint in Wrath's direction, desperate to get away from the chaos. Something wraps around my ankle, tripping me. I hit the ground again. Looking behind me, I see a bloodied man in the dirt who's missing a leg.

His lips curl up in a heinous smile, his teeth rotten and black, and the smell of decay wafts into the air. "Nighty night... *Princess*." He swings, cracking me across the head with a heavy piece of wood.

Everything suddenly goes dark.

CHAPTER TEN

When I wake, the world around me is a slow-moving haze. My head throbs so intensely that I think my skull might burst. My breaths are ragged and shallow, each rise of my lungs a struggle. I slowly open my eyes, trying to swim toward the surface I'm trapped beneath.

My vision adjusts to the soft glow of the candlelight, allowing me to see clearly. I am in a quaint cabin with wooden walls. It's a single room, with a kitchen and stove. A stone hearth warms the space around me.

Wrath sits on the edge of a bed, holding me close in his arms. My head rests against his shoulder. Sweat slicks his brow. A light smattering of dirt and blood coats his skin from the fight. Perhaps it is my head injury, but something causes me to reach up. My fingertips shakily close around the fabric of his tunic. It's as if a part of me refuses to believe it's real unless I feel something.

"Wrath?" I croak out, voice hoarse.

"You okay?" he asks.

My eyelids feel heavy. "It hurts."

He heaves a sigh, and in my current state of delirium, I swear I see worry etched into his features. I feel pressure against the wound on my shoulder. When I look down, I see Wrath pressing a cloth against my wound as he tries to stop the bleeding.

"How many did you lose?" I ask.

"Not too many."

Liora launched an attack as we approached, seemingly prepared for our arrival. I could have died at the hands of humans, rather than Elvarrans. It was shocking to realize that my own kind turned against me. I would be dead without Wrath and his troops protecting me.

I see now that bloodshed is a cycle neither side can break. It endlessly spins like a serpent devouring its tail, willing to destroy for so-called peace. I saw the hatred in those men's eyes as they attacked us. It is the same vitriol that greeted me when they hauled me into the Elvarrans camp that fateful night.

"I'm sorry," I say softly.

He remains silent. The words likely hold no meaning after many years of war. There are storm clouds in his gray eyes, allowing me a glimpse behind his battlements. It's a level of vulnerability I'm sure we'll never show each other again once this fleeting moment is over.

"Where are we?" I ask, trying to figure out how long I have been unconscious.

"The town of Sinaia."

"Weren't we supposed to cross the Northern Alps?"

He nods. "We will, once everyone has rested from their injuries. We're safe here. The humans won't cross the border."

I am in the Elvarran lands. It is a place few humans have seen, let alone traveled through. Wrath was right. I would never have made it home from Avelisar while traveling alone. I would have met my end swiftly, as I know nothing about how to defend myself.

Crossing into Elvarran territory feels like an invisible door closing. In that moment, I realize I may never return home again, the goodbyes I spoke more real than I could have imagined. I'd never be able to travel through Liora alone, not with those humans we faced lurking across the border. I am stuck in Khalessor for the foreseeable future, trapped among a court of people who want nothing more than my kingdom's ruin.

"What happened…" I ask.

"A group of men from Liora attacked us as we tried to cross the border." Wrath reaches out and tucks a stray lock of hair behind my ear, and unlike Olav, it doesn't disgust me.

"They called me a traitor. They tried to kill me—" I stop myself before I get upset.

"I know," Wrath says gently. It's a tone I'm not used to hearing from him.

He stands and slowly sets me on the bed. I pull the blankets up to my chest as I lie on my side, but my head throbs. Everything hurts, and the world feels like it's spinning. The bed dips as I feel Wrath lie beside me, tugging the blankets over him.

"Do you have to sleep next to me?" I hiss in annoyance.

"There's only one bed. You're welcome to sleep on the floor, Princess," Wrath replies, adjusting the pillow beneath his head and turning his back to me.

Sighing, I close my eyes to get some rest. Every time I try to settle, I can only see visions of the attack. It haunts me for hours. Tears threaten to fall, my mouth dry as I stare at the ceiling above. The warmth of Wrath's body and the steady rhythm of his breath provide an odd comfort in my state of duress. Eventually, it lulls me to sleep.

Although I'd never admit it to Wrath, sleeping beside him last night comforted me. When I woke up this morning, he was still asleep. Wrath usually rose before me in the mornings, leaving the tent to make travel preparations. I realize he likely hasn't slept since the attack, ensuring I was okay before relaxing himself.

I slowly unravel myself from the sheets and quietly move out of the room, grabbing my cloak on the way out. Closing the cabin door softly behind me, I sling the cloak lazily around the middle of my shoulders, holding it close like a blanket.

Stepping out onto the small porch, I take in my surroundings.

The Elvarran town of Sinaia is a collection of cozy log cabins at the base of a mountain range. Each mountain peak is capped with snow, indicating that winter is near. The morning sun combs through the pine tree branches that scent the air. Nearby is a small rushing creek, and I watch as two small Elvarran children dash across the bridge. They chase after one another, laughing as they play. It reminds me of Valentin—that childlike curiosity and search for trouble we shared.

I turn my attention away from the children and return it to the mountains. I am woefully unprepared to cross the Northern Alps after traveling across the flatlands on horseback. The only path through is a narrow, winding trail that climbs up a steep hill and disappears into the mountainside.

Feeling ravenous and unsure of how long it has been since my last meal, I wait patiently on the porch, hoping Barnham or Taryn will walk past so I can ask them for something to eat. Unfortunately, the only people to cross my path are farmers. One walks beside an ox that pulls a wooden tumbrel. A short moment later, I see an Elvarran woman carrying a crying child in her arms.

A footstep sounds behind me. I glance to my right as Wrath steps out onto the porch beside me. His dark hair is disheveled; I'm not used to seeing him in any state other than icy perfection. Wrath's eyes squint from the bright morning sun as they adjust to the light. He wears a loose long-sleeve tunic that he hasn't bothered to tie at the top, leaving his chest exposed. His pants hang low on his hips, accompanied by knee-high black leather boots, which he must have just thrown on.

Wrath inhales deeply, placing both hands on the wooden railing to stretch out his shoulders, rolling them out a few times. I watch as the sharply defined muscles in his chest move, a pure display of strength and discipline. Wrath has several scars and cuts on his skin, with four arrow wounds still open. One in particular appears to be on the verge of infection, the skin tattered and red.

"Something caught your eye… *Princess*?"

My spine stiffens. He caught me gawking. I knew last night's kindness was a farce, as Wrath is beyond bothersome.

"Shove it." I roll my eyes. "One of them looks infected."

He lifts a brow. "Are you worried about me?"

"I hope it goes to your blood and ends you." I make a poor attempt to get back at him after he told me to burn off the mark on my skin.

One corner of his mouth lifts. "I should have left you in Liora."

"You should have." I continue to play his games. "Letting me into Khalessor will be your greatest error."

"Is that a threat?"

"It's a promise." I refuse to back down.

"Now, now." A voice cuts into our argument. "I need my brother alive for the time being." Barnham walks up the front steps of our cabin, two steaming bowls of food in his hands. "Here."

I take it from him. I'm so hungry that I will eat practically anything. It is a strange-looking stew with a thick, dark broth that resembles gravy. Most of the vegetables are potatoes and carrots, with the occasional onion. It looks like something they scrounged together with the last of their rations.

CHAPTER ELEVEN

I WATCH the Elvarran soldiers mobilize the following morning while I silently stand on the porch waiting for instructions. They pack away weapons for a later battle, slinging large packs over their shoulders. A stir of light chatter hums among them.

"Ready?" I hear Wrath's voice behind me.

"Yes." I turn to face him. Wrath wears well-tailored, clean, dark clothing as he stands beside me, not a detail out of place. "Are we not riding?" I notice an absence of horses below.

"We are not," he replies vaguely, walking down the steps and disappearing into the crowd.

I reach the bottom of the stairs and find Taryn waiting for me. "You survived your first battle," she says proudly.

"I feel dreadful," I admit, my head still aching.

She pats my shoulder. "You'll get used to it."

"What do you mean by used to it—?"

Wrath's announcement cuts off my question. "My devoted royal guard, I am eternally grateful for every one of you. Your service has allowed us to return safely home, where you all will take a well-deserved break."

The soldiers erupt into cheers around me, some raising

their fists into the sky as they celebrate. Wrath's small squadron felled its second human kingdom, an accomplishment that would go down in history. With Nythara and Avelisar gone, I wonder if Wrath will continue his conquests after winter, still greedy for more destruction.

While I'm in Khalessor, I must study Wrath's tactics and determine what moves he plans to make next. Now that he knows Cathros has five thousand men, he may target Oderris next. If he intends to attack my home kingdom, I could send Valentin a letter and warn them of his plans, allowing him time to launch a counterattack.

The squadron hikes towards the base of the mountain, while my sore muscles scream in agony at the thought of climbing such a daunting path. It envelops my vision, and I crane my neck to see the peak. The trail ahead is narrow, a steady, winding incline into the trees. My boots slip on rocks, the loose dirt making my steps unsteady as I climb.

"Are we truly hiking *over* a mountain?" I ask in disbelief, watching the Elvarrans pass through the terrain with ease.

"Well, your brother controls Crossgate." Taryn's smile widens. "So... over the mountain we go!" Her voice is cheery, almost teasing.

I let out a noise of dismay.

There's a river up ahead. The only way across is a log. Ignoring my unease, I step onto it, wobbling slightly before steadying myself. I hold my arms out to the side to balance as I advance, one foot in front of the other.

Taryn snickers behind me.

"You find this amusing?" I ask, my voice trembling.

My steps are slow, knees shaking as I do my best not to slip. Although the water doesn't appear deep, I don't think I could survive the embarrassment of taking a plunge. I'd much rather let the waves sweep me away than face Wrath sopping wet.

"You're like a bumbling doe." Taryn torments me, pushing me from behind. "Hurry up! You're holding up the line."

"Taryn!" I cry out, stumbling forward as she lets out raucous laughter.

"Come on, Raelys!" she teases. "A snail can pass you at this pace."

I whip my head around to glare at her, but as I do, I lose my footing. Gasping, my arms flail wildly to keep my balance. Taryn's hands grab my tunic, yanking me upright before I plunge into the river.

"I won't let you fall," Taryn insists. "Now, *go*."

Sighing, I turn and quicken my steps across the log, rushing to the end. My boot touches the dirt, and I feel my shoulders relax. How humiliating, to be nearly bested by the small task of crossing a log. Every lesson Margaret taught me is useless here. I was never allowed any physical training; they believed I didn't need it as I always had a guard. Sure, I could play a fugue on the pianoforte, or recount every historical figure in Dratheria, but I am helpless to protect myself.

"You can drop the prim act, Princess." Taryn bumps her shoulder into mine, sending me into a nearby bush. "Have a little fun."

"I wasn't allowed much fun in Cathros," I tell her, clawing out of the brush and back onto the trail.

"Lemme guess," she says. "You need to be a *lady*." Her voice drips with sarcasm.

"Something like that," I reply, picking a stray branch from my hair.

"Sounds boring." Taryn huffs. "You royals are a bunch of schmucks."

"I heard that." Wrath calls out from ahead of us.

"Especially you!" Taryn yells across the trail, and Wrath's

laughter echoes in return. She turns back to me, seemingly boundless with her energy today. "So—"

"Gods," I say under my breath, unsure of what she's going to ask next.

Taryn laughs, clapping a hand on my shoulder. "Oh, come *on*! I'm not going to hurt you." She gives me a scrutinizing gaze. "You're more fun to torment than my little sister."

"Glad I can be of entertainment," I huff, turning my attention back to the trail.

At the base of the mountain is a large opening, a deep tunnel carved into the stone. Elvarrans disappear into the dark, each one seemingly unfazed by what lies inside. As we approach, I feel my spine straighten in apprehension.

What if there is a bear? Or a wolf? What if—?

"Goddess above, Raelys, are you afraid of everything?" Taryn loops her arm in mine. "Come on!" She surges ahead, yanking me with her into the dark as she drags me along.

"I'm not—" My words stop mid-sentence as we plunge deeper into the cave, eyes adjusting slowly to the lack of light as we descend. All around us are blue, glowing stones that light the path. "What is that?"

"Nithite crystals. They glow in the dark."

"And if you mine them?"

"They still glow," Taryn explains, leading me quickly through the humid tunnel. "I wouldn't recommend keeping them, though. The light will keep you up all night long."

The small passageway eventually expands outwards, into a tall cavern with thick stalactites hanging from the ceiling. Below us, a pool of turquoise water stretches through the cavern, illuminated by the stones. Thousands of tiny blue stars surround us, the crystals twinkling as we pass.

"Whoa…" I whisper, stunned by the beauty.

Before I can process the scene, my gaze lands on a tall

stone arch, the group of travelers stopping at its entrance. I
don't understand why we need to pass through an empty arch.
I can see through it to the other side, which looks identical to
this one.

Wrath presses his palm to the surface of the arch, and a
ribbon of silver light races along its inner edge. The space
ripples, warping as the magic cinches tight, then splits open to
reveal a passageway. I tilt my head to get a better look and see
forest shimmering on the other side. The soldiers file into the
magic arch, disappearing without a trace.

"Come on, then." Taryn surges forward, pulling me along.
"Keep your eyes forward. The magic can be a little *mischievous*
sometimes."

"What do you mean?" I ask in confusion as Taryn walks us
through the opening. We step through a long tunnel of light,
the surrounding area shimmering with vibrant colors. I hear
faint voices around me, the magic whispering in my ears.

"Long live the queen…"

"My mortal star…"

"Cursebreaker…"

The voices make my head turn. It sounds familiar, but I
can't place who is speaking. My gaze searches to find the
source, but I don't see anything. Everything around us is too
bright, like the world stripped raw.

Taryn tightens her grip on me. "Eyes forward." Her voice
is deadly. "Now."

I return my head forward, focusing on the exit in the
distance. The voices grow, all talking over one another until my
ears ring. Each voice beckons me to the edge of the passage,
waiting for me to fall right off, into the bottomless abyss of the
magic. The sensations are terribly overwhelming. I close my
eyes and inhale sharply, spine locked straight, fighting to keep
myself anchored in the flood of chaos.

"*Traitor…*"

"*Liar…*"

"*Deceiver…*"

"No," I whisper, praying for the end.

A thousand voices shriek in my ears. No matter how much I try to block it out, the ghostly whispers take root in my mind, tormenting me with slander and malignance. My heart skitters in my chest, unable to function among the chaos.

As quickly as the voices flooded in, they became silent.

My eyes fly open. Taryn is beside me, holding me close as she walks us away from the arch. Glancing over my shoulder, I watch Wrath lift a hand to the stone. The strange gateway seals shut, leaving an empty arch.

"What was that?" I turn back to Taryn, completely frightened.

"You've got a lot to learn, Princess."

I'm about to press Taryn further when I realize where we are. My breath catches in my throat in disbelief, eyes darting from left to right as I take everything in. My feet carry me forward of their own volition as I drop Taryn's arm and surge forward.

Khalessor.

The Elvarran kingdom unfolds around me like a masterfully crafted painting. The trees are tall, with thick trunks and branches densely covered in green foliage. Soft moss grows on nearly every surface, climbing up the trees and covering almost every stone. I see small clusters of colorful mushrooms and thick tree roots beneath my boots as I walk, beckoning me to continue exploring.

There are tiny bugs with lights on them. They illuminate the forest with a golden glow as they flit happily around us. Every corner of Khalessor seems to be straight out of a fairytale. Dozens of white flowers bloom in the bushes, their petals glistening like starlight in the sun.

I lean down to smell them—

"Don't smell those!" Taryn yells.

"Why?" I startle upright, my cheeks heating.

"Those are Dormishade." She strides over to me. "If you inhale the scent, they'll put you to sleep."

"Really?" I say in disbelief, looking back at the flowers.

She nods, walking alongside me. "You can crush the dried petals and make tea with them when you can't sleep, though."

"Interesting." I hum a note of acknowledgement as we descend.

The dirt path transforms into cobblestone as the city around us takes shape. The roads are wide and arranged in neat rows, with large homes and shops standing on each side, built from dark wood and arched stained-glass windows. Between each building lay a narrow alley, begging for someone to get lost in it.

There is a constant hum of chatter and activity all around me. Merchants set up their booths to sell goods, while farmers carry carts full of fresh produce. Several Elvarrans return home from the mines, carrying pickaxes and shovels, their faces smudged with thick, black soot.

The Northern Alps are home to a plethora of mines, providing Khalessor with an abundance of natural resources such as salt, crystal, stone, and ore. The small amount of these resources that reach the south are incredibly expensive and rare; Cathros always experienced steel shortages, making it difficult to craft enough weapons.

A streak of long, curly brunette hair flashes across my vision. A woman nearly leaps into Taryn's arms, hugging her close. She's beautiful—warm brown skin, freckled cheeks, tall ears. I notice how similar they look, nearly a mirror reflection.

"I've missed you!" Taryn releases the woman. "Come. We have much to catch up on…" her voice trails off as they depart, walking in the other direction.

I watch as more Elvarrans rush to greet the soldiers. Others trail off, disappearing down different roads and alleyways. Every time Valentin left for battle, I had no idea if he would return home. All I could do was wait for a letter or try to overhear gossip in the castle. It was agonizing. The Elvarrans must endure the same hardship, never knowing when their family will return.

"So?" A deep voice rumbles beside me.

I glance to my right and see Wrath. He has a smug expression on his face. My focus was so captivated by my surroundings that I did not notice him walking alongside me. I wonder how long he was watching me wander from place to place.

"It's quite beautiful here," I tell him.

To say anything else would be a lie. Khalessor is one of a kind, a kingdom that lives harmoniously with nature. It's far more beautiful than Avelisar, which felt like it was holding on by a thread. Everywhere I look is something I've never seen.

"Thank you," he says graciously.

I turn my attention back to the road and nearly stop in my tracks at the sight of the castle. The facade is stunningly ornate, each arch and pillar masterfully carved from white stone. A large circular window sits in the center, with detailed tracery resembling lace. Several tall, slender spires shoot out from the top, crowning each buttress with gilded details.

The beauty of Khalessor is so surreal that it feels like a dream I might wake from at any moment. My only anchor to reality is the reminder that I am walking alongside Wrath's Blade, and this is *his* kingdom. How could remaining within the castle walls have been best for me when a place this majestic existed all along?

We reach the castle's front steps and ascend towards the large front gates. Two guards flank either side of the door, allowing us entry. As I step into the main hall, tall, pointed arch ceilings and elaborate stained-glass windows that shift in the light hang above us. There is an invisible energy swirling around me, almost as if the castle breathes with magic.

"Raelys," Wrath says. Hearing him say my name makes my spine stiffen. "You should rest. Your body may take some time to adjust to the altitude of the north. The air is thinner up here. You may feel dizzy when exerting yourself."

"All right." I observe him, still unsure whether to trust him.

"Barnham will take you to one of the guestrooms."

"Thank you."

Without another word, he walks away. I glance behind me, realizing Barnham is standing close by. He guides me through several passageways before leading me down a small corridor and unlocking a door for me.

Handing me the key, he says, "If you're plotting anything—"

I cut him off. "You seem to forget that his magic binds me not to cross him."

"Doesn't mean you can't still wreak havoc." Barnham's tone is deadly, a clear warning to avoid strife. He walks away, and all I can hear are his retreating footsteps, leaving me in the silent and empty corridor.

I push open the wooden door and step into a small, dimly lit room. It has the necessities: a small bed, a woven rug on the floor, a trunk for belongings, and a small private washroom. Closing the door behind me, I set the key down on the bedside table. I yank off my riding boots, cloak, and satchel, tossing them lazily to the floor.

I flop onto the bed and fall right to sleep.

CHAPTER TWELVE

I sɪᴛ in the tub for hours, picking dried flecks of blood out from beneath my nails. The sweat and blood that coated my skin were so thick that I thought it would never come off. My legs and hips are sore from riding for days, and my head is still tender. I soak in the bath long after the water turns cold, not wanting to move. I eventually will myself to stand and dry my skin. I pull on a light linen dress, the only clean piece of clothing I have left.

Traitor. They called me a traitor in Liora.

A soft knock at the door startles me. I open it to find a tall, slender woman carrying a woven basket against her hip. A few stray pieces of black hair frame her round face, the rest pulled into a long braid. Her blue eyes flow like endless ocean waves, contrasting her thick, dark brows. Her features remind me somewhat of Wrath's, but I can't precisely place them.

"Hello there," I say hesitantly.

"I am Rowena Bainbridge of Myragos. I am a seamstress. Would you like me to make some gowns for you?" She smiles warmly at me.

"Yes." I blink in surprise at the woman. "Thank you."

Rowena steps into the room, sets down her basket, and pulls out a notebook. I close the door and face her. "Did—"

"The king told me to visit you," she replies. "What colors do you prefer wearing?"

I don't reply at first. A few moments of quiet pass as I watch the woman work. I often had a tailor in Cathros, but I realize I won't be wearing the red and gold of House Valantis. I will appear as a traitor to the Elvarrans if I don those colors; I wonder if I should wear their colors instead.

The woman turns over her shoulder. "Princess?"

"What do you think will look best?" I ask.

"We can start with a few colors—forest green, black, silver… perhaps a slate blue?" Rowena digs through her basket and pulls out a few fabric swatches. "Come, please."

Walking to her side, she places the swatches over my shoulder. "Too bland," she says under her breath. She swaps to a new color, a walnut brown. "No…" Then another, a slate blue. "Lovely." Another swatch, this time a dark mauve. "Yes, I think these are best to start with."

"Agreed." I go along with her suggestions.

Rowena appears confident enough to make anything look good. If she is the king's tailor, she can be mine. She smiles, puts her swatches away, and writes notes in her notebook. Tucking it away, she pulls out a dark forest green gown with silver accents on the long sleeves from her basket.

"I prepared this before your arrival without knowing your measurements ahead of time. I will have to make some adjustments," Rowena says. "Hopefully, it will fit you."

"Of course." I nod, stepping closer to her. I am accustomed to tailors taking my measurements.

Rowena quickly measures parts of my body, writing them down as she goes. I change into the dress, and Rowena pulls the laces in the front to tighten the corset. I huff a breath as she yanks one last time, the bones closing around my ribs. Stepping back, Rowena adjusts the fit on my sleeve, her fingers moving nimbly and confidently as she works. She doesn't make any mention of the mark on my arm, which I'm grateful for.

"Has anyone ever told you that you look like the king, Rowena?" I ask curiously.

She giggles. "He's my cousin."

"Really?" Surprise fills me. "He never told me that."

"I'll make sure to scold him for not informing you," Rowena says playfully.

The dress is quite beautiful. The thick, dark brocade fabric hugs my body before flaring out at the bottom. The silver embellishments are surprisingly detailed, and I can only imagine how long it must have taken her to complete. After some alterations, Rowena helps me into the gown one last time. Stepping to the side, I look at the dress in a tall mirror leaning against the wall. I must commend Rowena on the precision in her work, not a detail out of place.

"Perfect," she breathes, standing before me.

"Thank you, Rowena."

She gives me a polite curtsy. "The pleasure is mine, Princess." Rowena gathers her things and packs them away in her basket.

"Please call me Raelys." I smile at her.

I hold no titles here. No one needs to address me in such a manner. While in this unfamiliar kingdom, I need every friend I can make. Rowena is perfect. She is close enough to the inner circle to share some gossip with me and keep me informed on what is happening in this court.

Rowena smiles at me. "What about Rae?"

"Only if I can call you Ro."

"It's settled, then."

I feel downright pathetic as I struggle with the simple task of making my bed. I've rotated the blanket several times, one end longer than the other, but I can't figure it out. My pride won't allow this to continue much longer, so I yank the messy sheets across the top and cover it with the blanket, tossing the feather pillow at the headboard. With an annoyed sigh, I grab the one dress that Rowena thankfully gave me and put it on. I walk out the door, on the hunt for food.

I turn down the small corridor and try to backtrack my way to the main halls. Each passage confuses me more than the last, so I start keeping track of the paintings on the walls to ensure I don't double back to the same place. The castle's labyrinthine corridors seem to twist and turn with every step I take, as if mocking my attempts to find my way. As I turn the corner, I bump directly into someone. Strong hands clasp my shoulders, steadying me from falling over.

"My apologies." I quickly step back.

Standing before me is a man. He is broad-shouldered, with a slim yet powerful physique. I can see the outline of his corded muscles through his finely tailored coat, the shining buttons matching the gold rings on his fingers. His skin is smooth and sun-kissed, and his eyes are piercing sage green. Pointed ears peek through medium-length hair that cascades in waves of warm brunette to his cheekbones.

"Who are you?" His voice is light like a fresh summer breeze.

"My name is Raelys."

"Lady Raelys." He repeats my name like a prayer. "Sebastian Black of Ashvarin."

"It's nice to meet you." I smile, finding him quite charming. "Do you know where the kitchens are? I seem to be lost."

"This way." He gestures to a small corridor, waiting for me to go first.

It is foolish to ask a stranger for help, but I desperately need something to eat. If I don't get something soon, I fear I may faint from starvation. I walk alongside the Elvarran and see if I can gather some information from him.

"First time in the castle?" Sebastian asks curiously.

"Yes," I reply. "Are you a member of the king's guard?" I know the answer is no; he's too well-dressed. One thing I've learned growing up in a castle is that men love to explain how their rank works.

"No, I'm a duke," he says without a hint of ego or pride in his words.

"A duke from Ashvarin…" I muse. "I've never been there. What's it like?" I stroll effortlessly alongside him.

"You'll have to visit sometime." Sebastian gives me a saccharine smile.

I giggle. "Now, now, Sebastian," I reply sweetly, wondering if he is attempting to flirt with me.

His face lights up, and I take note of how my words affect him. Sebastian can prove useful in this court of adversaries. If I want to survive, I need people in my corner.

"What are you doing here in Khalessor? It's nearly snowfall." I pivot the conversation.

"I'm working on brokering a peace treaty for Dratheria," he explains. "My king has tasked me to speak with Wrath first, as he's the primary aggressor."

I nod. "Why is that?"

"I heard he recently killed the King of Avelisar." Sebastian's expression turns sour. "A senseless loss of life."

News travels fast around here, as it did back home in Cathros. The highest currency available is information. It is worth more than gold, jewels, or land. Those with power wield information as a blade, using it to strike at the correct time to get ahead.

"So you recently arrived?" I linger with an open end on my question, hoping he will help me fill in the blank.

"About three weeks ago, but the King has been away until two days ago." Sebastian slows his steps. "When did you arrive?"

"Today." I lie, hiding my identity for now.

Sebastian gestures to a door. "Here you are."

"Thank you, Your Grace," I say with a small curtsy.

"Of course, my lady."

He departs, and I open the door leading into the kitchens. A wall of scent hits me: roasted meats, freshly baked bread, and fragrant herbs. I see several women moving quickly throughout the space, kneading bread, stirring large pots of stew, and washing newly picked berries. They all work in perfect sync, holding a light conversation among the chaos.

"Need something?" A tall, muscled woman with pointed ears asks as she walks past me, carrying a tray of pastries. She has a bandana around her head, her curly red hair tied in a low bun at the nape of her neck. The Elvarran wears a white tunic and taupe pants, covered by a stained apron.

"Do you have anything I could eat?" I ask, unsure of why I feel hesitant.

"Here." The woman shoves a small bowl into my hands as she strides past me.

I look down at the contents. "Do you—" She plops a fork into the bowl as she passes. "Thank you," I say graciously.

"Bryn Eldrin of Myragos," she says, walking over to me and stopping. "And you are?"

"Raelys."

She crosses her arms over her chest. "It's impolite not to offer your full house."

"My apologies." I quickly try to rectify my mistake. "Raelys Valantis of Cathros."

I look down at the food. It's a meat pie with a flaky crust and well-seasoned vegetables. My stomach growls at the sight of it. It looks delicious. After eating stale rations while traveling, I will devour any hot meal.

"Hmm..." Bryn's gaze narrows on me. "The King told me about you."

"He did?"

She nods, taking something out of the oven. "Any food preferences? Things you dislike?"

"Oh." I blink in surprise. "That's very thoughtful. I'll eat most anything except for venison."

Bryn nods. "Anything else?"

"Would you happen to have any pumpkin scones?"

She plucks something off the steaming tray, tossing it at me. "We got those comin' out of our ass."

I grab it, the piping-hot pastry burning my hand. I suck in a breath, trying to hold it, but eventually give up and sit in the bowl before my skin starts to blister. *Score.* I haven't had the delight of a pumpkin scone in years.

"Thank you, Lady Bryn," I say with a curtsy, moving to leave.

"Just Bryn." She corrects me with a slight scowl.

CHAPTER THIRTEEN

I'M LOST in the castle. Again. Three days have passed, and I have only managed to figure out how to navigate to and from the kitchens. Everything else has left me wandering around like a lost puppy. I crave some fresh air and perhaps a new book to read, but I am unable to locate the library or castle gardens.

It is strange to roam freely without people following me around like a shadow. I keep turning around expecting to see someone, but no one is there. Back home, my days were predetermined and monitored closely. What I did, where I went, and whom I could speak to, all out of my control. I never experienced what it is like to have a day, or several days, without any schedule. I found myself at the castle's main entrance, an area I have been unable to find since arriving in Khalessor. My footsteps slow as I approach the castle doors, and I tightly clutch the strap of my satchel as I glance behind me.

I could… leave? No one is going to stop me?

Pushing the door open, I step into the sunlight. I see Marek and Kieran posted outside the door. They both nod at me but say nothing as I descend the grand steps. I look behind me one last time in disbelief before disappearing into the crowd. For once in my life, no one knows who I am. Is this what freedom feels like? Moving about freely without a glance from anyone is strangely unfamiliar and... liberating.

My gaze catches sight of a table with handmade jewelry. Several crystal necklaces sparkle in the sunlight, accompanied by thin silver bracelets featuring intricate patterns. I pick up a band to examine it closely. We don't have anything of this style in Cathros, delicate and vine-like.

"The bracelets are five silver," the woman informs me.

Then it dawns on me. I don't have any money. I've never had to carry coins. Items and belongings appeared at my will in Cathros. Whatever I asked for would arrive. I'll probably have to find a way to make money in Khalessor. I place it back down on her table and look at the merchant. She has beautiful, curly brunette hair that falls past her shoulders, with part of it braided on the side of her head. Her brown eyes and freckled cheeks smile at me, and her warm, tawny skin radiates.

She looks familiar, but I can't quite place her.

"I feel like I've seen you before," I comment, hoping she will know what I'm talking about. "With Taryn."

"Taryn's my sister!" She smiles at me. "I'm Zinnia Darragh of Corovya."

"Raelys Valantis of Cathros," I return my name.

Zinnia nods. "Are you two friends?"

"I think so...?" My brows lower, unsure if Taryn likes me after heckling me throughout our journey.

She giggles. "That sounds like Taryn. If she likes you, she's usually a little rough with her words."

I smile in return. "Then I guess she considers me a friend."

"Well, if that's the case..." She plucks the bracelet and places it into my palm, closing my fingers around it. "You should have this!"

Surprise fills me with her generosity. "Are you sure? This is so nice, I—"

"I insist." Zinnia nods confidently. "A token of our friendship."

A warm feeling spreads through my chest—a friend. I miss Lydia so dearly that it nearly brings tears to my eyes. She probably thinks I am dead at the hands of the Elvarrans, and I wonder if she grieves over my loss. I wish I could send her a letter to tell her that I am okay, but I have no idea if that is possible in Khalessor.

"Let me size it for you." Zinnia slips the cuff onto my wrist, arcing her wrist above the metal. As Zinnia's fingers move, I watch it tighten to the perfect size so it won't slip off. I am transfixed by the magic, eyes wide in fascination.

"There." She lowers her hand.

"Thank you. I will find a way to repay your generosity," I say, holding it up to the light.

Zinnia smiles. "No need."

I realize now that I need money. It's not about shiny bracelets or new leather boots. Money is the only language anyone listens to. With enough of it, I can pay for secrets or buy silence. I could ask Wrath—he'd probably give me whatever I asked for—but that would tip my hand. I can't risk letting him sense even a whisper of my plans. The only issue is that I've never worked a job, never lifted a finger, or even had to cook a meal. If I want money, I'll have to find a way to earn it.

"Do you know of any places looking for help?" I ask. It's not as though I'm short on time. Wrath leaves me alone so often it borders on suspicious. Part of me fears I'm being stored, like a weapon he plans to unsheathe only when it suits him.

"Hmm…" She taps a finger against her cheek as she

thinks. "I believe the tavern has trouble keeping people for long. It's called The Whispering Willow, but it's a far walk east." Zinnia points to the left down a small road. "It's that way."

"Thank you, Zinnia." I smile at her.

"Of course," she replies, her personality bright and warm.

Giving her a small wave goodbye, I continue onward. I turn down the street Zinnia pointed to and walk for quite some time. My eyes dart between signs as I try to find the place she spoke of. The sky turns grey, and the air grows cooler. A water droplet hits my cheek, causing me to flinch as I walk. I keep going; it can't be that much further.

Drop. Drop. Drop.

I duck under a small awning as it starts to pour. "Gods..." I curse under my breath, waiting to see if the cloud will pass, allowing me a moment of reprieve to head back to the castle.

It never comes.

The sun lowers as dusk approaches. Khalessor seems relatively safe, but I don't want to walk the streets alone at night. I take a deep breath and step out from under the awning into the heavy rain. My slippers soak through. Wet strands of hair cling to my skin. I hug my arms close, trying to keep myself warm despite my chattering teeth. I ascend the castle steps like a wet rat, my clothing thoroughly drenched. The two guards at the front snicker at me as I enter the castle. I ignore them. I look to my left, then my right, trying to figure out the path back to my room.

Why can I never remember which way it is?

Turning to my right, I trudge back to my room as water droplets fall from my clothes and pool at my feet. I circle a corner, sure of my surroundings, only to find myself at the servants' quarters. Sighing, I turn and go in the other direction.

I grow so frustrated that I open random doors and look inside. It isn't that late at night… so why can't I find anyone?

The next door I try leads me into a large, cavernous room. It shuts behind me, sealing me into the dark space. Heading to the tall floor-to-ceiling windows, I pull the thin gossamer drapes open, flooding the space with moonlight. I try to see which part of the castle I am in, but all I see is a view of some trees and shrubbery. As I turn, I bump into a large object covered in a thin white sheet. I wince from the impact, my hand cradling my elbow as it stings. A faint ringing emanates from the object, and as I circle it, I realize what it is.

Pulling the thin cover free, I see a stunning pianoforte.

I huff, turning my chin to the ceiling. "If I play you a song, will you stop changing the corridors on me?" I call out to an empty room, questioning my sanity. A few days in Khalessor has reduced me to talking to walls.

Pulling my soggy satchel over my head, I plop it beside the bench. I carefully open the lid, looking inside to determine the instrument's age. The strings seem in good enough condition. I hike up my heavy skirt and sit, placing my damp slippers on the pedals. Gathering my bearings, I pluck a few chords, checking the tuning.

Then, my fingers move, playing a tune from memory—one that I practiced a million times in front of Governess Margaret. For every mistake I made, she would strike me and force me to start over. I play it perfectly, the song carved into my bones against my will. My fingers slow, and I stop playing halfway through. I don't feel whole. I hate that song, hate the woman who turned my passion into a dreadful plight. I sit there and stare blankly at the keys, the pouring rain my only company.

Why do I feel so hollow?

I start again, this time with a different song: Flight of the Silverbird. Margaret never let me play anything she did not consider a classic, constantly scolding me that a princess would never play something so unrefined.

The song echoes through the quiet room, the melody comforting me like an old friend. My hands move faster, pouring unspoken frustration into the music until the world beyond the keys ceases to exist. Each note gathers a fragment of the self I lost to perfection. Perfect daughter. Perfect speech. Perfect manners. Perfect choices. I shaped myself into what everyone wanted until nothing real remained. I played the part so long I forgot the sound of my own voice.

What do I even want?

I continue. Playing song after song until it heals a part of me that I did not know was broken. My fingers ache, but I don't stop. I don't know how much time passes, but as the last note lingers in the air, I feel something I haven't felt in years… *solace*. Standing, I turn to exit the bench.

I am not alone.

I startle back with a gasp, my hand clutching my chest as I bump into the pianoforte. "How long have you been standing there?"

Wrath's tunic is neat, his pants sitting low on his hips. He leans against the back wall, hands tucked into his pockets. Wrath's black hair is preposterously smooth and styled. He is the living embodiment of composure. Would it kill him to have a single flaw?

"A while."

I huff an annoyed breath, collecting my discarded satchel from the floor. I sling it over my shoulder, then close the cover and lid to protect it from dust. Part of me longs to return to this room, to touch the keys again and rediscover the joy that once lived in every note.

"You play quite well," Wrath says.

"I think that's the first time you've complimented me," I comment, knowing he will say something irreverent in return.

"Would you like me to praise you more?"

My jaw clenches. It's not what I expected Wrath to say, but I won't allow him to get a rise out of me. I cross the room to where he's standing, stopping before him. Wrath is a figure carved from moonlight and shadow, the scar on his jaw catching in the faint light. His magic coils around me like a snake waiting to bite. I hate the sensation. Wrath watches me with a quiet intensity in return, and I catch the subtlest glint in his gaze as it lowers.

"Why are you damp, Raelys?" he asks, voice harsh.

"I got caught in the rain," I admit.

"You went outside the castle?"

A bolt of panic shoots through me. "Am I not allowed?" I ask meekly, knotting up my hands in front of me.

"Who told you you're not allowed to go outside?" He pushes away from the wall, standing upright. I preferred it when he was leaning, as now he looms over me.

I anticipate his anger at my insolence, hesitating for a moment. "No one…" my voice trails off. Wrath's magic prickles up the back of my neck, causing me to squirm. In my discomfort, I continue rambling, "Back home, I was forbidden to leave the castle walls. So I just assumed—"

"Ever?"

"Yes…" I reply reluctantly.

Wrath's brows draw together. "You're telling me that when Gilead pulled you over the wall, that was the first time you had ever left?"

I nod.

The silence between us is deafening. I regret revealing that about myself. Wrath will only see me as the weak and sheltered princess who is too much of a liability to set loose. I grow restless under his scrutinizing gaze, feeling utterly inferior.

"You think less of me because of it?" I speak, unable to take the quiet much longer.

"I think more of you."

I falter at his words. My lips part to speak, but nothing comes. The King of Wrath has no reason to be kind to me. He's playing some twisted game. This is a trick to gain my trust or get me to do a favor for him in return. I can sense it.

"You don't mean that." I step away, desperate to escape the sensation of his magic.

"I do," he replies firmly. "You can go wherever you like, Raelys. You are not bound to these walls."

"Why would you say that?" I push open the door and exit into the hallway. I don't believe his words. "When I am your prisoner."

My mind reels at the thought that someone handed me freedom so easily, as if it meant nothing. I've fought for it for so long, desperate for the tiniest sliver of independence, and now it's been given to me by the man I loathe. It doesn't make sense. None of this does. I should be planning my escape from the North, not cozying up to the king. What am I thinking? His game is obvious. Wrath wants me to let some information slip —something he can use against the South.

Wrath follows me. "If you were a prisoner, you'd be chained in the dungeon," he challenges. "It's fifteen days to Crossgate. Twenty to Grimhold Crossing. If you can manage to open the keystone arch and travel back through the mountains, I'd be impressed." Wrath rattles off the travel routes with ease. "Therefore, you wandering around the town doesn't worry me."

"Because I am trapped here," I reply bitterly, hating this feeling of always being a tool to control.

"You came on your own volition, Raelys," Wrath reminds me. It wasn't a real choice, though. I would have never made it home from Avelisar by myself. He knew that and leveraged it against me.

"I had no other choice."

"There's always a choice," he counters. "Like the choice you made to enter that room."

"I got lost on my way back." I huff in annoyance.

"Are you implying my castle is more grandiose than yours back home?" he taunts.

"No." I scoff. "It is like the magic changes the corridors as I walk." I turn my head and speak to the walls directly, gesturing to them as if they can hear me.

"It does no such thing."

"Then maybe I require a map to get around," I comment under my breath before changing the subject. "If it isn't magic in the castle, what is it?"

He hummed. "It's magic, but not all of it. It's a shell of what it once was, an ember slowly burning out."

Confusion washes over me. "Your magic is dying off?"

"It's a curse that limits us from accessing our full powers," he explains.

"How do you know it's a curse?"

"You passed your room six doors ago," Wrath points out, ignoring my question entirely.

Halting my steps, I turn and look behind me. Sure enough, my room is down the hall. I glance back at the king, a dozen questions still lingering on my lips. I don't ask them.

Instead, I simply reply, "Goodnight."

CHAPTER FOURTEEN

"You even know what kinda place this is, girl?" A burly man stands before me, his forearms thick as tree trunks, wiping the surface of the bartop. He has thick, curly reddish-brown hair and a scraggly beard. The man's dark brown eyes hold a serious gaze that sends a bolt of nervousness down my spine.

Behind the man are several stacked wooden barrels, each with a spigot protruding from the wood. They bear a worn and slightly rustic appearance. Some of them leak onto the floor, causing my boots to stick.

"Umm…" I glance behind me, taking in my surroundings one last time.

The tavern is dim, illuminated only by a few oil lanterns. Groups of men and women fill several small clusters of tables scattered around the space as they eat and drink—the scent of ale wafts through the air, accompanied by a strange undertone of… piss.

Two men fight nearby. They yell obscenities at one another, slurring their words. Blood streaks across their knuckles as they throw fists. One picks up a barstool, slamming it across the back of the other to knock them over. The tavern erupts in cheers as the patrons thoroughly enjoy the spectacle. Others place bets on who will win, sliding coins back and forth to one another.

"I need a job…" I say hesitantly, tearing my focus away from the fight and back to the man behind the bar.

The barkeep is seemingly unfazed by the chaos. He huffs, grabbing something and tossing it at me. "See how you fare for an afternoon."

I catch the stained apron in my hands and unfold the mess of fabric. I've never worn an apron before. Pulling the cloth over my head, I tie the strings behind my back and adjust it over my dress.

The warlord would establish a favorable reputation. If people discover who I am, their trust in me will erode. This means I must create as many positive associations as possible so that people will come to my defense.

"Ale and wine cost one bronze. A plate of roast is one silver. Vegetable pottage is three bronze, got it?" He spouts a list of prices to me. "When folks leave, clear off the table and wipe it down so others can sit there. And if anyone tries skippin' out without payin' you, come get me."

"And you are…?"

"Alastor."

"I'm Rae." I smile, shortening my name to hide my identity. While most Elvarrans likely don't know who I am, it's best to take as many precautions as possible to blend in.

He grunts before walking away to help someone on the far side of the bar. I turn to look at my surroundings. The fight between the two men comes to an end, and everyone returns to their conversations.

"You, halfling girl! I need a refill." A voice shouts from across the room.

Glancing over, I see an older Elvarran raising their tankard at me. I pause for a moment. Halfling girl, not human girl. The distinction jolts me. Many Elvarrans must have assumed that I am a halfling already. Do they really believe no human would ever cross the Northern Alps and settle in Khalessor? Maybe that assumption will work in my favor. Let them keep calling me that.

I walk over to him, pluck the empty cup, and return to the bar. After Alastor fills it, I drop it off at the table, and he hands me a bronze piece. This isn't so hard... perhaps having employment is easier than I thought.

"What can I get for you?" I make a round to a patron who has recently arrived.

"Vegetable pottage." An older woman says, passing me three coins.

"Of course." I smile, picking up the coins. I return a few moments later with her bowl, setting it on the table. Grabbing a rag from the bar, I wipe down a dirty table. I accidentally overhear the men talking beside me, three soldiers likely unwinding from a long day.

"This bloodshed is unnecessary," one of the soldiers says, slamming their tankard on the table with a thud. He has unruly, dark hair and brown eyes. "Another king dead. And yet we still can't access our magic."

"I heard whispers of a resistance forming against the blade," the second soldier says in a hushed tone. He has short black hair, deep umber skin, and ice blue eyes.

My body freezes. A resistance... against the King? If the other Elvarrans didn't want him to kill the humans, then I must find out what is happening. Rumors are often more potent than the truth, and an excellent one can turn the tide in any court.

"I heard the curse is the King's fault," the third soldier whispers before leaning back in his seat. He's young, with blonde hair and blue eyes.

"I heard the king of Rykaris is threatening to stop defending the Grimhold Crossing if he doesn't comply," the first soldier replies.

Desperate to hear more, I keep wiping the same table. Grimhold Crossing is one of two travel routes between the north and south. Crossgate is the other. Many battles and squabbles break out over these two mountain crossings, as whoever controls them could control the flow of humans and Elvarrans across the border.

"Woman!" One of them calls for me.

"Yes?" I stand upright, turning to face them with a smile.

"Another ale." He pushes his empty tankard towards me.

"Right away." I pluck it from the table and move to the bar.

Carrying food and drinks to patrons in exchange for the whisperings of the townspeople is more valuable than any money Alastor could give me. I need to find this resistance and determine their plan. If I help them take down Wrath, I can finally be free.

"Raelys?" I hear a voice call my name.

I set the drink down at the table and turn to see who it is. Standing in the entryway is Sebastian, dressed in a crisp navy coat with silver embroidery. His brown hair is slightly disheveled from the wind, yet his expression is relaxed.

"Hello, Sebastian." I cross the room to him.

"You work at the Whispering Willow?" Sebastian asks suspiciously.

"I do," I reply vaguely. We don't know each other well enough to have a detailed conversation with so many people around us. "Do you visit often?"

"It's a peculiar place," he comments. "I'll enjoy it more now that your beauty graces it."

His coquetry makes me giggle, and I let his dashing looks

captivate me for just a moment before refocusing on my work. "Enjoy your evening, Sebastian."

"You as well," he replies, sitting at the table with the three gossiping soldiers.

Moving around to each table, I check in on the patrons. Some make small talk with me as I work. The rumble of activity dwindles as the fast-paced rush slows. I pick up six empty tankards and carry them to the bartop for Alastor to clean.

"You ain't so bad," Alastor grumbles.

"Truly?" I say with excitement.

"Come back in two days at noon," he replies, placing three coins on the bartop and sliding them over to me.

Plucking the coins from the surface, I tuck them into my satchel. "Thank you!"

Alastor grunts in place of a response.

Turning, I leave the Whispering Willow with a newfound sense of accomplishment. Having some money will allow me to bribe people, forming an elaborate web of knowledge. I don't know exactly how I'll use the information yet, what quiet uttering will become my golden ticket, but I do know that what is happening around me is vital to my survival.

The east side of town is more scrappy and arduous than the streets near the castle. A foul stench lingers in the air. In a nearby alley, I see two cloaked figures with thick black hoods over their heads. They speak in quiet tones and exchange something between them in the shadows.

Someone cuts off my path, stepping in front of me. "You! Halfling girl." Their raspy voice startles me. "Lookin' for a cursed object? Or how 'bout an elixir?"

The man has one eye, the other covered with an eyepatch. He sneers at me. His clothing is ragged, frayed at the edges. Behind him is a worn-down cart filled with strange-looking objects and trinkets, glowing crystals, and various glass jars with swirling liquids.

"No... I don't need to curse anyone," I reply hesitantly, stepping away from the peculiar merchant.

A nearby tent opens, and a woman saunters out. She wears a rumpled dress, her hair a mess of tangles, as she wipes the corner of her mouth with the back of her hand. Her eyes meet mine, and I can see a quizzical expression on her face as she watches me.

She is beautiful, like a dangerous seductress. Dark brown eyes. Long brunette hair. Cheeks dotted with dozens of freckles that complement her pale skin. Her bodice and dress hug every one of her curves, a ruinous temptation from every angle.

"That ain't for you." The merchant blocks my line of sight with his body. "Less you lookin' to make a lil' extra coin... awfully pretty for a halfling."

A strike of fear shoots through me. I nearly sprint away, needing to flee as soon as possible. I get a short distance down the street before a little girl approaches me, holding a dented tin cup.

"Got a spare coin... lady?" the little girl asks. She is frail and unkempt, her thin frame barely filling out the tattered clothes that hang loosely around her. Strands of frizzy brunette hair frame her dirt-smudged face as she begs for money.

"How old are you?" I ask softly, placing my hands on my knees and bending down to look at her closely.

"Twelve," she replies, still holding the tin out for me.

"What's your name?"

"Violet."

"You quit talkin' to me daughter!" someone yells at me from across the street.

Standing, I turn and look for the source of the voice. An old man sits on the ground with his legs crossed, equally downtrodden in appearance. He's doing nothing, while his small daughter begs for coins in the street. Another girl sits beside him, this one slightly older. She has tears streaming down her cheeks, wiping her face with the heel of her palm.

"Father, please—"

"Quit yer sniveling!" He reaches out, backhanding the girl. "And make me some damned money."

Unrelenting rage fills me as memories of Margaret's abuse flood to the surface. She left permanent scars that won't heal, no matter how much time passes. My fists clench at my sides, nails biting into my skin as I do my best to control myself.

"Get lost, halfling cunt!" the man yells at me.

I snap.

"What did you call me?" My voice booms throughout the street as I surge forward, taking elongated strides toward him as I pull my dagger.

The older girl beside him screams, dropping to her knees and burying her face in her hands. As she bends over, the scars on her back come into view—deep, brutal lines that someone must have left with a whip.

I raise my blade to strike when the man bolts from his place, scurrying off like a rat. He leaves his two daughters behind, turning down a small alley and disappearing. Stopping my approach, I slowly lower the dagger to my side. The street around me is deadly silent, and the onlookers stop as they watch with bated breath.

Sighing, I put my weapon away.

So much for developing a good rapport with the locals; there will be rumors circulating the castle by dawn about how the halfling girl almost slaughtered an Elvarran. This gossip will stay with me for quite some time, harming the reputation I'm trying to craft.

The girl is still on her knees, shaking with fear. "Please don't kill me," she cries.

"I'm not going to kill you," I say softly. "What's your name?"

"Aurelia." She raises her head to look at me, eyes rimmed in red.

"How old are you?"

"N-nineteen…"

My chest aches. What an awful existence these poor girls are living. I take two of the three coins from my shift and hand them to her. "Here. Try to get an inn for the night or some food."

Aurelia shakily reaches out, taking them from me. She wears a pale, tattered dress that is stained and thinning at the hem. Her brunette hair is unkempt, and her skin is sallow and malnourished.

The younger one, Violet, hugs my leg. "Don't leave us, nice lady."

I hesitate, unsure of what I have gotten myself into.

CHAPTER FIFTEEN

"Morning, Bryn," I say as I enter the kitchen for breakfast.

"Hello, Raelys," she replies, plucking a bowl of food from the counter and passing it to me. The fragrant smell wafts up, making my stomach growl in excitement.

"Thank you." I take the bowl from her. "I have a question. Do you have a moment?"

Bryn wipes her hands on a rag. "What is it?"

"Do you need any extra help here in the kitchen?" I start. "There's a girl I met in the eastern part of town whose father is abusing her, and I want to help her."

A crease forms in her brow. "All employment has to go through the king's justiciar."

"And that would be...?"

"Barnham Bainbridge."

"Wrath's brother?" My eyebrows raise in surprise.

Bainbridge. The king's house name! I wonder why Wrath is so secretive about his namesake. He must be hiding something. I should research his family's history and potentially uncover if he is hiding anything. That is, if I can find the library in this labyrinth of a castle, which I am constantly getting lost in.

Bryn nods. "You gotta ask him."

"Much appreciated." I smile up at her. "Could I—"

She waves me off. "Take as many scones as you'd like."

Plucking a few extra scones to take with me, I wave my goodbyes and head back to my room. As I turn the corner, I notice a petite servant girl waiting by my door. She wears a clean, simple blue dress with her pale blonde hair pulled back into a bun.

"Hello there," I greet her.

Her sorrowful brown eyes don't lift to meet mine. "The king asked me to deliver this to you." She hands me a rolled-up piece of parchment with a small piece of twine around it.

I take it from her, wondering what it might be. The servant girl curtsies before silently walking away. Closing the door, I set down the parchment and pull the string. As I unroll it, a castle map reveals itself before me. Wrath got me a map—how thoughtful. I did not think the King was capable of kind acts, let alone attentive enough to hear a small comment I'd made.

Taking a large bite of my scone, I let out a small sigh of pleasure, reveling in the warm, sticky-sweet pastry. I continue to eat my breakfast, my fingertips tracing the castle's corridors as I study the map. That's when something exciting catches my attention—the gardens. After seeing the Dormishade on our way into town, I wonder if there are more unique flora here in the North to discover.

Rolling up the parchment, I tuck it into my satchel in case I need it later. I set down my empty breakfast bowl, plucking my copy of the Warlord Chronicles from the bedside table as I exit my room. After wandering around for some time, I find the gardens.

The air is crisp with a slight chill, a sign that snowfall is imminent. The oak trees are tall and mighty, their branches thick with leaves, providing ample shade. Walking along the path reminds me of the last time I went wandering around in a garden—the night the Elvarrans captured me. I sit on a shady bench beneath a tree, opening my worn copy of the Warlord Chronicles right to my favorite chapter.

Someone approaches me, and I startle at their footstep. My gaze meets Sebastian's, and I give him a polite smile as he stops before me. His warm, brunette hair billows in the breeze. He wears a loose tunic that hangs comfortably over his frame, the fabric wrinkled somewhat as if he threw it on in a hurry.

"Sebastian," I greet him. "We seem to be running into one another quite a lot."

"I'll admit I purposefully sought you out today," Sebastian replies. "Will you take a promenade with me?"

I hesitate, then accept. "Sure."

Closing the book, I tuck it in the crook of my arm as I stand. The two of us walk down a path that leads deeper into the gardens. I scan the space to ensure no one is watching us together. The last thing I need is a rumor spreading of my involvement with a duke.

"You'll have to forgive me, Raelys, but it's strange to find one of the King's guests working in a tavern that... unsavory."

My brows lower. "I'm not sure what you mean."

Sebastian's steps are leisurely as he glances sidelong at me. "There are whispers of your house name floating around the castle."

A thread of apprehension shoots through me. Sebastian's usual lighthearted demeanor toward me has shifted into apprehension. I wonder what has changed since the last time I saw him.

"I belong to House Valantis," I tell him forthrightly.

"Then you are the sole survivor of the attack on Avelisar," he points out. "Which means you are still the queen."

My heart nearly skips a beat. It is something I haven't given a second thought to in weeks. I am technically a queen, but there is no point in being a queen of an empty castle.

I redirect his attention with a lie. "Ah, that would be true if the King hadn't launched his attack in the middle of the ceremony. We did not complete our vows."

"Then why did the King keep you alive?"

I give him a lazy shrug. "Perhaps he is using me as a negotiation piece with Cathros. I'm not mistreated if that concerns you."

Sebastian grows quiet beside me. I can see he's deep in thought as we stroll through the lush gardens. There are several things I need him to explain to me, so I steer the conversation away from me and towards him.

"Now that I've told you something, you must tell me how your negotiations with the King went." I lighten my tone, stepping closer. Our shoulders accidentally brush against one another.

He releases a heavy sigh. "He will not listen to any of my king's requests. If this continues for much longer, Erynthe may ally with Rykaris. If that happens, it could leave your kingdom as an easy target for The Blade."

That information is exactly what I need to inform Valentin about. The only issue is sending a letter without getting caught. Wrath may let me roam freely, but I am about to push the boundaries of our agreement.

I lean close and say, "I've heard whisperings of a rebellion."

He chuckles. "You are well informed."

"What makes you say that?" I ask curiously.

Sebastian gives me a quizzical look as we stop at the garden's entrance. "Good day, Princess."

Taking note of his rather cold departure, I nod, lowering myself into a curtsy as he departs. If there is a limit to my intrusive questions, I found it. Sebastian's usually friendly demeanor turned as soon as I inquired about the rebellion.

I reenter the castle, poking my head into one of the dimly lit rooms I discovered while wandering around. It's empty. I slink inside and rummage through old drawers and shelves, causing specks of dust to stir into the air. I pull brittle parchment from the desk. It's a little rough, but it will work. I open the cabinet behind me, and the hinges creak so loudly I flinch.

My gaze snaps to the door as I tensely wait to see if someone discovers me. When no one enters the room, I continue my search, finding nothing but empty ink bottles. My frustration grows with each empty shelf until, at last, I see what I am looking for—a quill with a fresh bottle of ink. Grabbing it, I swiftly exit the study and return to my room.

Placing the parchment on the bedside table, I dip the quill into the ink and write in my family's cipher. I can disguise the coded message as a shipment update of livestock, so that it wouldn't be apparent to the naked eye, but my brother would understand. I plan out each word carefully so I can weave the message into the page, my pen flowing quickly across the parchment.

The inside of my right wrist burns like a brand, as if the magic is thwarting me directly—the muscles in my hand contract. I let out a pained cry as I grip my wrist with my left hand, forcing myself to continue writing through the pain. My fingers shake as wobbly letters form. The mark is like a snake coiling tightly around my arm, moving upwards to my shoulder. Eventually, it constricts so tightly that I lose feeling in my arm.

I drop the quill, unable to take the excruciating pain. Sharp jolts of pain shoot into my fingertips like tiny lightning bolts as tears gather in my lashes. My breath is ragged as I wait for the sensation to fade, swallowing the lump in my throat.

I cannot betray Wrath, not directly, no matter how veiled my attempts. Swearing under my breath, I take the parchment and toss it into the hearth to burn. I must be more creative with my plans if I want to find a way out of Khalessor.

Pushing my frustrations aside, I pack the pastries and work apron away. I sling my satchel over my shoulder and head out for the afternoon. I exit the castle and stroll down the busy streets, making a stop to deliver the pastries to Zinnia on my way to work.

She gasps. "For me?"

I smile. "Yes. They made extra at the castle. I brought you some."

"Thank you!" Zinnia takes a bite. "I *love* scones." She lets out a sigh of approval while she chews.

"Me too. Especially the pumpkin ones."

"I'll have to bake you some of my blueberry scones. I have the best recipe," Zinnia insists.

"I'd love that," I say with a smile. "Hope you make lots of sales today!" I call out to her as I walk away.

"See you!" Zinnia waves.

Making my way to the Whispering Willow, I open the door and enter. A throwing knife flies across the space, narrowly missing my nose. I jerk back out of instinct as the blade lodges itself into the wood. Drawn on the opposite wall is a poorly shaped target with three rings. Six other knives are buried in the wood, proof they've been at it for a while.

I inch around the target practice by pressing my back to the wall and slowly slinking around the perimeter of the tavern. "Hey, Alastor," I say as I reach the bar, pulling my apron over my head and tying it in the back.

"Afternoon," he replies, unfazed by the knife throwing.

"Girl! I need a refill now!" someone calls out from across

the room. Glancing in the direction of the voice, I see an older Elvarran sitting at a table.

I walk over and pick up his tankard to refill it. Walking the empty tankard to Alastor, he fills it to the top. I return to the old Elvarran, who tosses me a bronze coin. I fall into a rhythm —picking up tables, filling glasses, and avoiding wandering hands from drunk men.

Dropping off a tankard, I see the beautiful brunette woman who accompanied that elixir peddler now sitting on a soldier's lap. Her dark eyes meet mine, and a smile forms on her plush lips. She slides off him, and the soldier leans back with a scoff, drumming his fingers against the table.

"I wasn't done—"

"One moment." Her voice is melodic, laced with sensuality as she glides a finger underneath his chin. "Good boys get rewards when they're patient."

A flush spreads across the man's face, and he quickly clears his throat, drowning his fervor beneath his ale. The woman circles the table, elegant fingers untying my apron and pulling it over my head.

"What are you...?" I watch her fold it in half, rolling it slightly before reaching around me.

"You're never going to make any tips like this," she mutters under her breath, tying the apron low on my hips.

She unties the front laces of my corset, pulling it low before re-tying it, pushing my breasts together. She yanks my dress down, hiking part of the skirt up into the apron, revealing one of my legs.

"There!" she says confidently, stepping back to examine her work.

"Thank you?" I blink in confusion.

She sweeps my long hair over my shoulder. "My, you have lovely hair." The woman adjusts my corset one last time, making sure my breasts are even more exposed. "Men should pay you silver to gaze upon you. You're a halfling, too—so *exotic*."

"What's your name?" I ask her.

"Kaia," she replies warmly.

"Rae," I tell her. "I saw you with that... peddler. He's not—?"

Kaia snorts a laugh. "Oh, 'ole Renwick? He's harmless. You live over two hundred years and see how solid *your* mind is." She shrugs. "I do that sometimes to make a bit of extra coin on the side."

"What do you normally do?" I ask, drawn to her confidence and charm. She is so effortlessly bold and sharp-tongued, an amplified version of qualities I pride myself in—the version I might have been if it wasn't trained out of me.

"A little bit of this, a little bit of that," Kaia replies vaguely. "I have lofty aspirations."

"I see..." My curiosity piques. "I think we're going to be excellent friends."

CHAPTER SIXTEEN

I FIND myself reading in the gardens again, tranquil beneath the tall oak trees. I grow increasingly accustomed to my new schedule as each day passes. There are no more tedious lessons with the governess, no more lectures from my father. I wonder how furious Ulrik will be if he learns I am here in the North.

Someone rips my book from my grasp.

I gasp at the sudden invasion. Wrath stands before me. I didn't even hear him approach. He flips through the pages with a leather-gloved hand, scanning its contents with a meticulous gaze.

"What book are you constantly reading?"

"It's none of your business," I say bitterly, standing from my seat.

We haven't seen one another since the night I played the pianoforte. My days are calm without his imperious presence, and I breathe easier without him near. I don't move to take the book back; I know I won't be quick enough.

"You're reading the Warlord Chronicles?" His brows draw together. "It's so tattered and worn, I barely recognize it. You've scribbled in nearly every margin."

My cheeks heat. Tamping down on the embarrassment creeping through me, I lift an open palm and wait for him to give it back. "Are you insulting my reading choice?"

"No." He closes the cover and hands it back to me. "I have another copy in the library, if you want it."

"Really?" My tone lightens.

"Yes." Wrath turns and sets off in long strides. "Come."

I tuck the book in the crook of my arm, rushing to catch up with him. Even his steps infuriate me, each one a graceful sweep across the path. We fall into a tense silence as we walk alongside one another. I refuse to look at him, keeping my focus ahead.

"I received the map." I acknowledge his gift, hoping he'll share more about his intentions.

"Are you finding your way a bit better?" he asks plainly.

"It's helpful. Thank you."

Wrath doesn't reply. We enter the castle and walk toward the west wing. I rarely venture to this side; the guards patrol it like ants on a carcass.

Then I remember. "I have a request."

"Do you now?" A hint of curiosity creeps into his voice.

"There's a girl whose father is abusing her on the eastern side of town. I asked Bryn if she would hire her in the kitchens. She told me to ask Barnham," I explain.

"Did you ask Barnham?"

"No…" I reply hesitantly.

"Tell him to draft it, and I'll approve it for you." Wrath leads me down another corridor.

"Truly?" I ask.

That was surprisingly easy. I twist my head to look at him, trying to catch any insincerity. I immediately regret my choice. Grey eyes meet mine in return—two piles of smoldering ash that make a flush burn across my cheeks. It vexes me that I notice such details about him. He is a monster. He is a scoundrel. He is a killer, lest I forget.

"Yes," he replies.

"Thank you."

"You're inclined to help an Elvarran girl," Wrath points out. His keen intellect never misses a detail. He likely suspects I have ulterior motives—I do not—and is investigating me.

I lower my gaze to the floor. "I know what it's like to have an awful father," I say, my voice distant.

Wrath doesn't push further, dropping the subject. He stops before a tall door. I notice the embedded gemstones in the handle that shine as he pulls it open. We walk through a short corridor before the library expands into a large, central atrium.

The room soars three stories high. Each level is lined with tall pillars, evenly spaced between railings carved from dark wood and etched with intricate patterns. To my right, a pointed arch blooms into a domed ceiling, with windows that stretch from floor to vault, their stained glass panels casting shards of color across the space.

Beneath the dome stands a tall statue of a goddess, clad in thick robes, carved from dark purple stone with veins of silver running through it. Her left hand holds a scale that is tipped to one side, while her right hand holds a long staff topped with a crescent moon.

It is the most beautiful library I have ever seen. I could spend months here, and wouldn't be able to read even a fifth of the volumes lining the endless shelves. Everywhere I look, there is another piece of art, each detail accounted for with ornate precision. Below my feet are mosaic tiles adorned with the same crest as my mother's necklace—a sword with two wings on either side.

Above us is a faded mural on the ceiling. It depicts Elvarrans gathered around a small, glowing spring, as if in some type of celebration. The water is an almost unnatural shade of blue, the surface adorned with unique, constellation-like patterns.

"It's Elderaneth," Wrath says.

"What?" I tear my attention away from the ceiling.

"It's said that humans jumped into the spring's waters and emerged with pointed ears, gaining the ability to wield magic." He absently pulls down the edges of his sleeves.

"It's depicting the first Elvarrans?" I glance back up at it.

"Yes."

"Does the spring still exist?"

"About a three-month journey north into the mountains," Wrath replies.

Surprise fills me. I never even thought to question how Elvarrans came to be, the story revealing a side of them that is more complex, more... human. After being raised to hate them, it's quite a shift to discover that we are all, essentially, the same—only the use of magic dividing us.

"Have you gone?"

"No. It's difficult to access and is guarded by a guild whose members vow to devote their lives to protecting it," he explains. "The last person to visit was Isla Izydor."

A tense pause stretches between us—my mother. I knew Wrath wanted something from me, but now the object of that desire is beginning to come into focus. Maybe my relation to Isla would somehow help them regain their magic, given her association with the spring. I am a tool to him, I realize—a means to an end, nothing more.

"You worship Itheon in the South, correct?" Wrath asks.

"We do." I nod, turning my attention back to the goddess statue. "I've never seen a depiction this beautiful of Seluna before."

"We believe that Seluna created the heavens and the earth, and Itheon created the humans and the animals," he replies.

"Really?" His story differs from what I learned in history lessons. Humans believe that Itheon created all life, the heavens, and the earth, while Seluna manages the underworld and the spirits, guiding people when they pass to the afterlife. Perhaps the true story lies somewhere between the two, each a variation of the same tale.

"Seluna took a human lover and gave birth to Krateus Izydor, the first Izydor." Wrath recounts the mythos to me. "When her lover died, she cried so much in the mountains that it created Elderaneth."

"Is that why no one is allowed to visit?" I ask curiously.

"It's the source of all of our magic," he replies. "It's very sacred to the Elvarrans."

"That seems like important information for you to be sharing with the enemy." I get slightly suspicious of how open he's being with me.

Wrath shrugs. "I don't think you understand how important the Izydor's are."

He is right. I don't understand anything about my mother's side of the family. After she disappeared, my father forced me never to speak of her. If Wrath speaks truth, what does that mean for me?

"You believe it's connected to the curse?"

"Not the spring," Wrath corrects me. "But your mother."

"Why would I be willing to help you?" Irritation frays my nerves.

"I need you to tell me the details of your mother's death." Wrath walks between two towering shelves of ancient tomes.

"I was a child. Maybe ten?" I follow him closely. The aisle is dimly lit and far too narrow for my liking, making me slightly uneasy.

"How often did you see her?" Wrath scans the shelves, fingertips brushing along the spines.

"Only in the summer, for a few weeks." I am not sure why I'm speaking so openly. Maybe it is because I know if I don't, he'll only force my words out with his magic. I don't want to feel that pain again. Beyond that, though, I think a part of me wants to seek to learn the truth about my mother's fate, even if I have to share pieces of it with Wrath to get it.

"Do you know where or how she passed?"

"No." I shake my head. "One summer, the time had come to visit with her, but she never came. I was then bound to the castle walls and forbidden to speak of it."

"No one else knows?" Wrath plucks a thick leather-bound book off the shelf. He holds it out for me to take.

"Just you and my father," I reply, taking the book from him.

It's unbelievable that they have a copy in such pristine condition. Mine has missing pages, tattered edges, and a broken spine. Wear has erased the letters from the cover and spine, keeping me from knowing the author's name.

"Raelys, I strongly suggest you continue to hide your lineage," he urges.

Our bodies are nearly touching in the narrow aisle, close enough that I can feel his breath brush against my skin. The air thickens with tension, neither of us daring to look away. Unspoken words stretch between us, fragile as a bridge suspended over a canyon.

"You think I would trust anyone enough to share that with them? You should know, as you were the one who ripped the secret from me," I remind him.

Ire ripples across his features. I pushed him too far, and now I will face the consequences. I need him to provide me with more information about the Elvarrans, so that I can inform Valentin—that is, as soon as I discover how to reach him.

"This could end the war," Wrath says, voice deadly serious.

"A war that you started!"

"A war I see no issue in continuing."

We face each other in a silent battle of wills. Neither of us yields, both too stubborn to give into the other's demands. For the first time, I feel the weight of someone else's resolve pressing back against mine.

Wrath and I will surely be the end of each other.

"Thank you for the book." I turn on my heel, exiting the narrow corridor.

Anger thrums in my veins. A faint trickle of magic runs up my arm, setting my nerves ablaze. The air hums between us, tight and trembling, ready to snap. I press forward without looking back, exiting the library and putting as much space between us as possible. I glance down at the new copy of the Warlord Chronicles. Twisting the book to glance at the spine, I read the author's name for the first time.

C. V. Bainbridge.

I read it again.

Bainbridge— the King's house name. Did his father write the book? Or maybe an uncle or grandfather? My mind races over every possibility as I take the book to my room. I set it down and scour every page to ensure I don't miss a single detail.

A knock at the door breaks me out of my studies. Rowena walks into the room with a flourish, carrying a large garment bag. Kicking the door closed behind her, she brushes past me and flops the heavy bag onto my bed, the mattress dipping under its weight. She unzips it, revealing a pile of beautiful gowns nestled inside.

"Hello, Rowena," I say, genuine excitement blooming at the prospect of new clothing.

"Good afternoon, Raelys." She sorts the outfits. "Sorry for the delay, but I had to wait for some fabrics to arrive from Corovya. You must be sick of rotating between a few things."

"It's all right," I reassure her. "Tailoring can be time-consuming."

She sighs. "Indeed. I am quite busy with Lunithia and Noctalis quickly arriving." Rowena continues to pull out clothing. "Eight new dresses, a riding outfit, and…" She holds up the most stunning gown I've ever seen. "…in case you need something elegant."

A small gasp leaves me as I reach forward to touch the fabric. "Rowena!" I exclaim, tracing my fingertips over the embroidery and beading. "This must have taken you days."

"It did." She giggles. "Could you put this on so I can check the hem length?"

I pull the new formal gown over my body. "What's Lunithia?"

"The autumn festival!" Rowena bends down with a needle and thread to hem the length. "You should come! The entire town is celebrating the final harvest and showing gratitude for the bounty. There are crystal candies that are so sweet your eyes water."

A small laugh leaves me from her enthusiasm. "I'll have to attend then."

Rowena pulls the last stitch, knots it, and cuts the loose thread. Then, she stands and moves to hem the other dresses.

"What is Corovya?" I circle back to her earlier words.

"It's a city outside Mysatre, to the southwest," she explains. "Lord Horatio Thorne's territory."

Timothy had mentioned Lord Horatio—the duke who abandoned Crossgate and allowed Valentin to take control of the passage. I know very little about the different territories and regions of the North. I resolve myself in that moment to study a map so I can understand the territory better.

"You said you were from Myragos, yes? What is it like?" I ask curiously.

Rowena lets out a dreamy sigh. "It's stunning, Rae. Full of flowers that bloom with every color imaginable. Natural springs that have warm water to bathe in. It is one of the most secluded and peaceful places to the north of here."

"Who is the duke there?"

"Duke Roderick Bainbridge, of course," Rowena explains. *Wrath's father?* It must be. He has to come from a high-ranking house to take the throne. If Roderick is Wrath's father, then who is C. V. Bainbridge?

"I'll have to plan a visit sometime." I smile.

"You must," Rowena insists, packing away her sewing supplies into a small basket. "I'll see you at the festival then?"

"Only if you promise to show me around." My hands trace over the soft details of my new dress, taking in its beauty. "Thank you for everything, Ro!"

"Don't thank me, thank Wrath." Rowena winks playfully at me before heading out the door.

CHAPTER SEVENTEEN

"Here." Barnham slides a wax-sealed envelope across the desk. "Give this to the girl the King spoke of. It will allow her to gain entry into the castle." He sits back at his desk, folding his hands in front of him.

I pluck it from the surface, looking down at the crest of a serpent breathing fire. "Thank you, Barnham."

Without another word, I exit the room. Making my way onto the streets of Khalessor, I start my search for Aurelia. I haven't seen her or Violet for a while. It leads me to believe that their father has moved his so-called business elsewhere.

I begin with the neighborhood near the Whispering Willow, focusing on the more rugged and downtrodden parts of the city. When I don't spot them, I walk in the other direction, searching the small alleyways and shadowed corridors. I move through the maze of narrow streets, my eyes scanning every corner for the two girls as hours pass, the sky slowly darkening.

Then I spot the little girl covered in dirt and soot, holding a dented tin cup as she begs strangers for coins. I hide a few paces away out of sight, pressing my back against the wall of a nearby alley. Leaning around the corner, I wave to try and grab Violet's attention.

She doesn't see me as she walks between people on the busy street. Crouching down, I pick up small pebbles and throw them toward her. By my tenth pebble, Violet notices, picking up the rock and looking around. Our gazes meet, and I silently beckon the girl towards me with my hand.

Violet runs over to my side. "Hello, nice lady."

"Hi, Violet," I whisper, ensuring no one spots us. "Where's your sister?"

"In the tent." She frowns.

"When she comes out, come get me, okay?" I tell her. "Is your dad there?"

Violet nods.

"Does he hurt you?"

She nods again.

"I'm going to help you." I try to give her a reassuring smile. "Now go before your father spots me." I gently guide her back to the street. Violet runs off, and I hear her father yelling at her, his voice echoing down the narrow street.

I dig through my bag and unsheathe my dagger. Their father had run off once before in the wake of my weapon; I'm sure I can get him to do so again. Aurelia and Violet must carry the letter to the castle to break free from his clutches. The sky darkens further to the warm hues of sunset, the day fading rapidly. Violet is making me wait a long time, and a part of me hopes she won't forget. I stay, hoping I can make my move soon.

Violet turns the corner. "Sissy is back."

"Okay." I nod. "Tell Aurelia that when I come around the corner, she needs to take this letter from me." I show her the letter. "Then, you two need to run to the castle. Don't stop for any reason, okay? Run as fast as you can. Do you understand?"

Violet nods along as she listens to me. "What 'bout you?"

"Don't worry about me." I smile. "Now go tell your sister without your dad hearing."

The child runs back out onto the open street. Standing, I lean around the corner and watch as she approaches Aurelia and whispers in her ear. Aurelia's expression turns to confusion, but Violet points in my direction. Her gaze follows the path until she sees me. I nod at Aurelia, hoping she understands the plan. Aurelia nods, wrapping her fingers around Violet's wrist as she stands.

"Where do y'all think you goin'?" their father asks.

I dash out of the alley toward the girls. When she sees me, Aurelia takes off, dragging Violet behind her. "Take this!" I shout, holding out the letter for her to take. She snatches it from my grasp, the paper crinkling in her fist as she takes off down the street.

"Hey!" her father calls out, quickly standing from his seat. "You best tell me right now where you be takin' my daughters!"

I turn on my heel to follow the girls, when I bump directly into a broad chest. A hand clasps my shoulder, and I look up to see a burly Elvarran sneering down at me.

"Get that halfling girl!" Their father points at me.

Shit.

I quickly move around the burly man. I only get about two steps away before the Elvarran closes a hand around the strap of my satchel, yanking me back. He reaches to grab me, and I swipe my dagger in an arc at him, causing him to step back.

"Don't come any closer!" I yell, hoping someone nearby will hear the commotion.

The two men laugh. A hand hits my cheek, knocking me into some crates on the side of the street. My heart pounds furiously as I try to think of a way out. I am not a fighter, and do not know how to use the blade I am holding. Even if I did, I am not strong enough to take on a man three times my size. There has to be a diversion somewhere.

The burly Elvarran closes a fist around my scalp, yanking me toward him. I swing the blade, but he grabs my wrist, grip tightening as he twists. Pain shoots through me, bones cracking from the force as I cry out. The dagger tumbles from my grip, clattering to the ground beneath us.

"I ain't never had halfling pussy," the man sneers. "Wonder what it feels like."

A strong gust of wind blows through the street, knocking the man off his feet. I stumble from the gale, my hair whipping wildly around. Turning, I see a silhouette of a man running toward us in the dark.

"Sebastian?" I catch sight of him in the faint light.

"Quite the trouble you're in," he says, rushing to my side.

The burly Elvarran has my dagger in his hand as he rushes toward Sebastian. I back away quickly. "That's my dagger!" I call out as the two spar in a blur of fast-paced movement.

Aurelia's father reaches me, his wilting hands closing around the front of my dress. "You tell me where my daughters are!" His breath smells of alcohol.

"Get off me!" I shove him back.

He falls back onto the stone. I run to the opposite side of the street, watching Sebastian brawl with the other Elvarran. Each step is precise, like a well-trained warrior. Sebastian disarms the man in three swift motions, the blade flying into the air before he effortlessly catches it. His arm is quick, pinning the blade to the man's throat.

"Leave. Now," Sebastian commands.

The man scoffs, pushing Sebastian's arm away before taking a few sloppy steps back and walking away. Aurelia's father rises to his feet, his hands curling into fists at his sides as his jaw tightens. His eyes burn into me, a silent promise that I will come to regret this day.

"You'll pay for this!" he yells, shaking his head as he walks away.

Adrenaline thunders through me like a storm. I hate fighting. Sebastian holds out his arm, returning my dagger to me. When I reach for it, pain shoots up my arm. Sucking in a sharp breath, I cradle my right wrist in my hand.

"What's wrong?" Sebastian notices my distress.

"My wrist." I breathe through the pain.

"Come." He nods in the opposite direction.

I follow him, the two of us walking a short distance to a small wooden cabin on the south side of Khalessor. Sebastian unlocks the door, opening it for me to enter. Inside, I walk towards the hearth for warmth and sit on a wooden chair. On the small table beside me is an envelope and a stamp that bears the symbol of a broken sword emitting rays of light.

Still holding my wrist, I look down at the damage. The skin is bright red, but there are no surface wounds. Every time I try to move it, the ache grows.

Sebastian places another log on the embers to re-ignite the flame. He takes a knee before me. "Let me see," he says gently.

Holding out my hand, Sebastian tests the joint by moving it slightly, causing me to wince in pain. Sebastian takes a long strip of cloth and wraps it tightly around my wrist, stabilizing the joint. My nerves begin to steady as his presence anchors me against the chaos of my evening. His steady breaths sync with mine as he works, and the frantic beat of my pulse begins to slow.

"I didn't take you as the fighting type, Raelys." Sebastian breaks the silence.

"That's the first time I've been in a fight," I admit, embarrassment flushing my cheeks.

"And did you cause this trouble?" He eyes me with suspicion.

I frown. "I did." Sebastian laughs at me. "I can explain!" I quickly say.

"Explain."

"That man was abusing his daughter! Using the little one to beg for coins in the street while he sat on his ass and drank all day!" I tell him, fury filling me. "I helped them escape."

"That's quite noble of you." He returns his attention to my wound, moving his hand to check the scrape on my left arm.

"Did you manipulate the wind?" I ask, curiosity getting the best of me.

He smiles. "Yes. It's a simple form of magic."

"How?" I blink in disbelief.

"Magic is like breathing. Most Elvarrans source it directly from the earth, wielding the elements around us," Sebastian explains. "But for the last thirteen years, it's been limited... strained."

"Because of the curse?" I ask, desperate for information.

He nods. "They call it a curse. I'm not sure I believe that theory either. It's like the magic was purposefully sealed off."

"Who would do such a thing?"

Sebastian sighs. "We don't know who would commit such a heinous act."

Silence falls between us. I don't press him further. He is the first person to discuss the curse with me openly, and I don't want to push the issue. The subject seems sensitive, as if the Elvarrans have lost a part of their soul without the full force of their magic.

"I have something I could use your help with," I say.

"Yes?"

"Could you write a letter to Cathros...?" I nervously ask.

"I'm not sure my brother knows I'm still alive, and I—" I get choked up for a moment. "I want him to know I'm okay."

The intensity of all I've been through bubbles up for the first time. In a few short weeks, I traveled to two different kingdoms, watched one of them destroyed because of me, stabbed a man in Liora, and potentially took my first life. Now, I realize that while most Elvarrans are kind to me, there are still dangers I need to look out for.

"I cannot."

"All right." I deflate, sitting back in the chair.

"I'm sorry," he replies coldly. "I cannot contact the South. That is going against my king's wishes. Your brother likely won't believe a letter from an Elvarran kingdom anyway, even if I were to send one when I return to Rykaris."

"You're leaving?" I say in surprise.

"I'll be gone for about two weeks." Sebastian stands. "I must sort out some issues with my lands, meet with my king, and then I'll return."

He moves to the other side of the room, stoking the fire and adding another log. The space slowly warms, the soft crackle from the wood comforting my frayed nerves.

"You should stay here. It's late." Sebastian pours himself a drink. "I'll sleep in the chair. You can take the bed."

I turn my head away from the fire to look at him. "I cannot impose—"

"Then I'm going to have to walk you back to the castle in the cold." He shrugs. "Your choice."

"I can walk on my own."

"Are you always this stubborn?" Sebastian chuckles, the sound melodious. "If you insist on walking alone, then you must let me teach you how to disembowel a man properly."

A sigh leaves me. I have no idea what I am doing in a fight.

Some training could prove helpful if someone were to target me again. "You'll teach me?"

"Yes." He sets his empty glass on the counter, picking up my dagger and tossing it to me. "Catch."

My hand reaches out, but I quickly pull it back in fear I'll end up slicing my fingers. It hits the side table next to me, the blade sinking into the wood with a loud thunk. I wrap my fingers around the hilt and pull. I have to shake the table a few times to free the dagger.

"That's a very interesting blade, by the way. Where did you get it?" Sebastian asks curiously as he watches me struggle.

"My dearest friend gave it to me before I left Cathros," I reply, freeing it from the table. "Why?"

"It's made of Umbraferr… or more commonly called shadow steel. The ore can only be mined here in Khalessor," he explains. "And the handle is wrapped in hide, an Elvarran technique."

Lydia told me she stole it from her father's collection, but I have to wonder why he had an Elvarran blade at all. It may be a family heirloom, or maybe he traded with someone during his travels. I wonder how rare it is.

I stand from my seat. "I see…" I hesitantly glance between the blade and Sebastian a few times in confusion. "What if I hurt you?"

Sebastian's lips quirk up. "Are you worried about me?" He pushes the small table to the side, clearing space for us to spar, unfazed by the prospect of me swinging at him with a blade.

He waits at the ready, knees slightly bent as he braces for me to attack him. I step closer, trying to figure out how to hold it, when Sebastian swiftly disarms me, the blade slipping from my grasp as he takes it.

"I wasn't ready!" I exclaim.

"There's no such thing as ready in battle." He flips the

blade around in his fingertips, holding the handle out for me to take once more. "Now, try to strike me. Aim for the heart, eyes, or ribs. If you puncture a lung, it will take a man out."

I strike, but Sebastian stops my advancement. "You must strike with your whole body, not just your arm. Put force behind the blow." He steps behind me to adjust how I hold the blade.

Using the closeness of our bodies, I strike again. This time, I catch the fabric on Sebastian's tunic. He swears under his breath, and a wicked grin forms on his lips. "Again."

CHAPTER EIGHTEEN

I PRACTICE with Sebastian all night long, going over different techniques. He's patient, and he reassures me every time I get frustrated. Unlike Margaret, who used brute force while teaching, Sebastian gently corrects my mistakes and explains what I am doing wrong.

My leg kicks out, causing Sebastian to topple over. His hands close around the fabric of my dress, and I fall with him. His back hits the floor as I press the blade to his throat, pinning him to the ground. Our chests heave in tandem, faces close as we watch one another.

"Well done, my lady," he praises.

I pull the blade away, quickly rising. Heat flushes across my skin, and I turn my head away so Sebastian won't see. Sebastian gracefully rises to his feet, brushing his pants clean of dust with his palms.

"Sun's up." Sebastian parts the curtains over the window, allowing some light inside.

"Thank you…" I say sheepishly, picking up my satchel and pulling it over my shoulder. I tuck the blade away, feeling more confident in my abilities.

"Get home safe, you hear?"

"Thank you for saving me," I say truthfully.

"Of course," Sebastian replies, opening the door for me.

I exit the cabin and make my way through the streets of Khalessor as they come to life for the day. Merchants set up their stalls, while others make their way to the mines for work. I walk up the castle steps and trudge my way toward my room as exhaustion settles into my bones. I can't wait to rest; my muscles are sore from fighting.

A small servant girl crosses my path, causing me to stop.

"The King wishes to speak to you," she requests. I recognize her as the girl who delivered the castle map to me and wonder if she directly assists with Wrath's tasks.

"What's your name?" I step out of the way, allowing her to lead me.

"Serafina," she replies.

"How long have you been working at the castle?"

"Since my parents died."

Serafina may have lost them due to the war. If she orbits Wrath closely, I must earn her trust. That means patience, careful words, and sincerity to lower her guard.

"Do you like working here?" I ask gently.

"I'm grateful for the King." Her words are empty, eyes still cast down, refusing to look at me.

I don't press her further, allowing us to stroll down the halls until she stops at a door and gestures for me to enter. Standing guard outside is Kieran, who smiles warmly at me. I step inside to see Wrath and Barnham having a discussion. The space is similar to the war room my father uses to hold meetings with the other lords. Unlike my father's war room, however, Wrath's is immaculate. Everything is perfectly organized, from the chair and the bookshelves to each piece of parchment or map. For someone who sheds so much blood, he's quite neat and orderly.

"Raelys, why do you smell like ale and piss?" Wrath's eyes travel down, taking in my disheveled state. The lower he gets, the more I see annoyance course through him. I am a stark contrast to his pristine standards, and it clearly irritates him.

"I just returned from work." I lie, hoping the magic won't wrestle the honest answer from me.

"You have a job?" Barnham cuts in. "Where?"

My focus turns to him, my patience dwindling. "You think that because I am a princess, I believe honest work is beneath me?"

"Barnham, leave us," Wrath snaps.

Barnham shakes his head, sauntering from the room to leave us alone. I can tell Wrath is turning over the thought of me having a job in his head. It is part of my plan to thwart him, of course, but I cannot allow him to discover it. After spending years studying the warlord's tactics, I will at last put them to use—ready to play war with Wrath as my opponent.

"Are the gowns not up to your standards?" Wrath asks bitterly.

My spite drops immediately.

"No." I shake my head. "Rowena is far more skilled than any tailor in Cathros." I hesitate for a moment, choosing my following words carefully. "If you spent your whole life locked within castle walls, wouldn't you try to experience what it's like to have an *actual* life? To have people speak to you without preconceived notions of your rank?"

"We are royals. There is no break, no escape from the expectations that bind us." Wrath's response sounds more habitual than true—exactly like something my father would say to me.

"So, have you brought me here to *brighten* my day with your lectures?" I sass him, placing my hands on my hips.

A muscle in Wrath's neck twitches in response to my comment, causing his scar to flex. He plucks a square object from the table and plops it into my palm. "Hold this."

I examine the stone closely. It's lightweight and carved from a smooth material. Each side has a different emblem, one with a phoenix, a crashing wave, a shooting star, a feather, a mountain, and... the last one is hard to distinguish. Bringing it closer to my face, it looks like an eclipse over the moon.

"What is it?" I ask, flipping it over to study each side. The shape on the left lights up, casting a very weak glow. Turning it over, I look down at the phoenix shape. It's beautiful and free, wisps of flame emitting from its wings as it flies.

"Fire," he says plainly. "Isla was a fire user."

"I don't understand."

"It's a Sorstone." Wrath holds out his hand. I place the stone into his palm, and the eclipse lights up with a brilliant, blinding glow. "It tells you what magic the one who holds it specializes in."

"I'm a Verthari?" I ask in awe, recalling the few details Barnham shared with me about magic while traveling.

"Do you believe me now when I say you are half-Elvarran?"

Wrath puts the stone back in my palm, and the phoenix sparks to life. It's not nearly as bright as the light it gave off when Wrath held it, but it's there. It is a sign that faint traces of magic flow through me—proof that something more lingers in my blood.

"Partially..." I reply hesitantly, staring at it for a moment longer.

"Suit yourself." He plucks the stone and turns away, setting it back on the table. "I need you to open something." Wrath holds up a thin leather book for me to see.

"What is it?" I ask, walking over to the table to stand beside him.

"Isla's journal."

Disbelief fills me. "Where did you get that?"

"I stole it from Rykaris." He sets it down on the table in front of me.

Grabbing the journal, I attempt to open it, but an invisible force fuses the pages shut. I pick it up, trying to pry the covers apart with all my strength. When that doesn't work, I resort to shaking it.

"You can't open it by hand." Wrath watches me struggle. "She used her magic to seal it."

"Why would I help you take my mother's secrets?"

"Don't you wish to know the details of your mother's death?" His tone is severe. "She did not die of natural causes. She should still be alive."

"Are you implying my mother was murdered?" I set the journal back on the table, giving up on trying to pry it open.

"You're the one who said she stopped visiting," he reminds me. "Don't you find it strange that she wed Gottfried and died without any heirs?"

He is right. It is a reality I don't want to face. My father brushed everything under the rug so quickly, rendering my mother as a distant memory. Isla was a queen from one of the oldest houses. She wouldn't have gone down without a fight— her throne was taken from her.

"Yes, that's oddly suspicious." I cross my arms over my chest. "But I'm not helping you."

"Try it once," he insists.

"No."

"If I don't find a way to break this curse, there will be no magic in Dratheria," Wrath says harshly.

"That sounds like a *you* problem." I won't allow him to pressure me into helping him.

"Goddess above, you're stubborn," Wrath comments under his breath.

My scowl deepens. I stand my ground and refuse to give in. I won't break the curse, not while he's imprisoning me here. It may be a different kingdom, but the walls remain the same.

"Are you done taking your revenge out on me?" he asks.

"Not necessarily."

"Fine." Wrath steps closer. "Since you like nefarious dealings—"

"I am not nefarious!" I lower my hands to my sides.

"You are undoubtedly a menace, Raelys." Wrath's keen gaze studies me.

"Well, *you're* a scoundrel," I remind him. "You keep speaking as if you have something to offer me."

I try to throw him off. To make him question where I might be heading. No one will keep my freedom from me. Those kings who keep me as a pawn will learn I am the hand that topples them.

Wrath raises a curious brow at me. "Then what do you want?"

"Money."

"Money?" he repeats in disbelief.

"*Gold*," I clarify.

Wrath reaches forward, hooking a finger around the chain of my necklace. He yanks roughly on it. I stumble, my neck craning forward as the space evaporates between us. His scent fills my nose. *Bergamot.* It's not at all the smell I'd imagined on him—light, aromatic, and a bit citrusy.

"And what would my pretty princess do with gold?" His deep voice rumbles against my skin like the purr of a cat. Wrath traces his thumb over the crest, not releasing the tension on the chain.

"Princess things," I say sweetly, denying him any type of honest answer.

Wrath lets out a gruff laugh. "Do you even know what this crest means?"

"No."

"Legend says that Krateus Izydor had wings," he explains, releasing his hold on my necklace, letting it fall. "Many people saw him as a savior. A *god*."

I give him a mercurial look, tucking the necklace back into my dress. "Like a bird?"

He smirks. "Yes. Like a bird."

"Sounds lame." I shrug, leaning away from him.

"Tough crowd."

"Tell me he could at least do something cool, like… rewrite time or something." I ponder the thought of what a god is capable of. "Or shape the continent."

"So destructive, Princess," he says derisively.

"Why are you talking about a dead guy?" I place my hands on my hips.

"That dead guy is your lineage," Wrath reminds me. "How about this—you try to open it for today. If you can't, you can return to your peasant job."

I seethe at his insult but try not to let it show. My job at the tavern is a peasant job, but he doesn't know that. He has no right to act all high and mighty just because he's the king. Those 'peasants' are his hardworking subjects, the ones keeping the kingdom alive.

"What do I get out of it?" I counter.

"I'll let you read what's on those pages," he says. "She

likely wrote entries about you. Don't you want to read them? To hear her thoughts?"

"I want *money*," I insist. There is a plan I want to try that requires an investment larger than what I make at the tavern.

A tick forms in his jaw, his patience reaching its limits. Wrath's hand dives into his pocket, pulling out a small pouch. He grabs my wrist, turning my palm open and plopping the pouch into my hand with an annoyed sigh. Coins clink together as I close my fingers around the leather, a sense of satisfaction filling me.

"Okay, I'll help you." I slide the pouch into my satchel and step over to the journal.

"Place your palm on the cover." Wrath stands behind me. His palm moves to cover mine. I pull away, covering the back of my hand instinctively. I don't want him to touch my scars, let alone see them.

"Do you have to touch me?" I ask, my voice shaky.

His brows lower. "Does the thought of my touch repulse you?"

"No!" I gasp out, realizing my mistake. "I... I have these disgusting scars on my hands."

"Do you find my scar disgusting?" he asks calmly.

My gaze lowers to his left jaw, trailing down the elongated scar. The longer I look, the more I realize there's something undeniably magnetic about it. "I do not," I reply softly.

"I do not see yours that way, either."

Something stirs in my gut. I push away the sensation as I slowly uncover my hand and lower it to the journal. Wrath's hand covers mine, eclipsing my scars with his palm. I can feel his breath against my skin as he steps closer. The mark on my arm flares to life as magic flows between us.

"Try to will it to open," Wrath instructs.

"What do you mean?"

"Close your eyes." His lips hover above my ear. I do as told. "Breathe."

Drawing a deep breath, I exhale through my lips, letting the tension in my body ease. It's hard to focus with Wrath so close. I try to sense the magic around us, searching for something... anything to hold onto, but I only feel the leather under my palm.

"What if I light it on fire?" I whisper.

"Shhh..." Wrath shushes me softly. "What do you feel?"

"Your hand."

"*Obviously,* you impudent woman," he replies. "What else?"

Inhaling another deep breath, I try to find something. Wrath's magic spreads across my skin like wildfire, igniting every nerve in my body. It takes hold, slowly beckoning me toward a source.

"Power," I whisper.

"Now harness it."

I silently will the book open in my mind. Channeling the power I feel in my veins, I push. A white light erupts from my palm, the force so strong it blows me off my feet. I hit the cold and unyielding stone floor with a heavy thump, the air huffing out of my lungs.

"You overcharged," Wrath says as he shakes out his right hand. Tiny wisps of silver magic flow from his fingertips and dissipate into the air.

"I'm supposed to know what that means?" I grumble in pain.

"If you try to seize too much at once, the magic backfires because of the curse. Instead, you need to focus on drawing it from the earth," he explains.

"That would have been helpful to know beforehand!" I declare, pushing my palms into the stone as I stand. Adjusting my dress back into place, I try to compose myself.

"I wanted to see if you could do it at all." Wrath shrugs.

"That was magic?"

"I channeled a significant amount of my power into you. But yes, you can *technically* use magic," he replies reluctantly.

My lips quirk up in a slight smile at the realization. I wielded magic… *real* magic. The thrill of the unknown beckons me. If I stayed in Avelisar, I might never have learned I could do such a thing.

"You seem excited for someone who wants to live as a simple village girl," he taunts me. My excitement fades faster than a candle snuffed of air. I narrow my eyes at him, and his mouth tilts—not quite a smile, but close enough to make my pulse jump again. "Try again, Princess."

Walking over to the book, I set my hand on the cover again. Wrath's rough palm brushes against my skin as he laces his fingers with mine. Closing my eyes, I take steady breaths and strengthen my resolve.

The book will open. It will open. It's going to open.

I try to source it from the ground this time, but all I feel is Wrath's aggravating presence. The magic bursts again, sending my body flying back. I twist, attempting to break my fall as I hit the ground.

"You didn't listen."

"Of course I listened!" I snap at him, standing upright. It is hard to focus when his magic makes my mark sing for him like a songbird—the traitor.

"I think you can try once more before you reach burnout."

"What's burnout?" I ask.

"It's the amount of magic one can wield before you become drained," Wrath explains.

"What happens after that?" I keep pushing him for answers, wanting to learn more.

"Most commonly, you'll fall into a deep slumber for a few days as your body replenishes. In rare cases, death."

My eyes widen. "You can die?"

"It's a nasty curse," Wrath says. "You won't die, though. I'll flood you with my magic before that happens."

"How benevolent of you." I lighten my tone, almost teasing him. Of course, he needs me alive—for this journal, for the curse. I am a tool for him to get what he wants.

"Careful, that almost sounds like you're being nice to me," he warns.

I stifle a laugh. "You're right. Can't have you thinking I enjoy your company."

His lips twist wryly, but Wrath refuses to smile. I wonder if he thought that was amusing. Placing my hand back on the book, I try to unlock it one last time. He places his hand over mine. My mark runs down the length of my arm and into my fingertips to meet his touch, which infuriates me to no end.

I close my eyes and try to draw power from the earth, not Wrath. I take my time, trying to feel through the shadows for something to come to me rather than trying to seize it. It lingers in the air around us, the walls, and the stone beneath my feet. I wait for it, then leverage the power. Something pops under my palm, and my eyes fly open in surprise. As soon as I look down, I lose focus, and control slips through my fingers.

The magic sends me backward, directly into Wrath's chest. His hands grasp my shoulders to steady me. We are a mess of limbs and hands as we clamber to stay upright. Wrath stabilizes me, and I apprehensively glance over my shoulder at him. We stare at one another for a tense moment, his hands still clasped around my shoulders. I jump out of his hold like a cat dropped in water, trying to hide my flustered state.

"Did I do it?" I open the cover of the journal. On the inside, written in a thin script in the top corner, is my mother's name. I try to flip to the next page, but they remain bound together.

"You opened one page."

"That's farther than you got," I point out.

"Yes, congratulations," Wrath says indifferently. "We'll try again in four days. Don't exert yourself too much so the magic can replenish."

When I gather myself, I feel the wave of exhaustion, but still, I stand an inch taller. I wielded magic and didn't die, which is a great success in my book. What other things could I learn to use magic for? It's strange to see myself as one of them after being raised to hate them.

I likely don't have that much in my veins compared to a full-blooded Elvarran, but it is an interesting prospect. The power I'd been taught to fear tasted nothing like evil as it moved through me. If anything, it felt like possibility. Could I turn it to my advantage?

"Who said 'we'?" I challenge.

"You did. You asked for money, and I gave it to you. We will continue until the journal is open," he replies firmly.

"In four days, then." I accept his challenge, closing the journal's cover.

CHAPTER NINETEEN

THERE IS a soft knock on my door, so faint I almost miss it. Moving across the room, I open it to find Aurelia. Like the other kitchen staff, she wears a soft cream dress, an apron, and a bandana around her hair.

"Aurelia!" My heart leaps. "Come in."

Widening the entrance, she slips past me. Shutting the door, I glance back at the young girl. She struggles to hold herself together, her hands tightly wound in front of her, and the edges of her eyes water slightly. Underneath her right eye is a large purple bruise that is beginning to fade. I wondered how many times he'd struck her over the years.

"I-I wanted t'say thank you." Her voice wobbles, emotion flooding to the surface.

"Are they paying you enough to find another place to stay?" I ask.

She nods, her fingers tightening around the fabric of her apron. Aurelia's eyes shift around the room, unable to hold eye contact for long.

"You're safe here now," I reply calmly, reaching out and placing a hand over hers. "He can't hurt you anymore."

"Really?" Aurelia finally meets my gaze.

"Yes." I smile reassuringly. "He won't find you here."

She shakes her head, tears threatening to fall. "I don't want to go back…"

I feel her agony in every fiber of my being. Margaret's voice echoes in the back of my mind, tormenting me in my dreams. *You are as untrained as an alley cat*, she would say as I balanced a stack of books on my head and walked to fix my posture. If the books fell, she would make me start over. *Fortunately, you have beauty; that wit of yours will get you nowhere.* She often degraded me like this, leaving a permanent mark on my soul. *Your handwriting is worse than your pianoforte; it is as if you strive to be inadequate*, she scolded. Every cruel word is still engraved into my marrow. Margaret tore me down so many times over the years that I lost sight of who I am.

"I won't let him." I strengthen my resolve to keep the sisters safe.

"Thank you." Aurelia inhales a shaky breath, her lashes slick with tears.

"I need your help, Aurelia." I lower my voice, ensuring that no one can hear us in the hall.

"With what?"

"I'm new here at the castle," I explain. "If you hear any gossip or anything suspicious floating around, please tell me. And before you do, I want you to use this phrase: 'The birds are lovely today, Princess.'"

Aurelia's eyes widen. "Why?"

"It's so we can ensure no one is eavesdropping on us."

Women are often overlooked by men of high status, disregarded. I know this from firsthand experience growing up in a castle full of lords and captains who spoke boldly, as if they had no regard for the privacy of information. Aurelia will be helpful for such a task. No one will hold their tongue around a simple kitchen girl. If I were more informed back home, I might have known of my father's plans to marry me off. I may have avoided it by speaking with him before his rash announcement.

I will not make the same mistake twice.

"I understand." Aurelia nods.

"Very good." I move towards the door. "Come find me if you need anything."

Waving goodbye, Aurelia departs from my room. I will check up on her in a few days to ensure she is settling in and can find a safe place to keep Violet off the streets. I exit shortly after her, retracing my steps to the library. I do my best to slip by the guards unnoticed, cracking open the door and slinking inside.

The dim glow of candlelight from within welcomes me, and the familiar scent of old leather fills the air. I scan the space for others, but the library is so vast that it's difficult to tell if it's empty. Hoping the shadows will hide me long enough, I search for the history section.

My footsteps echo all too loudly, causing me to curse under my breath. I pull off my slippers and hold them as I walk barefoot. I pluck a book at random off the shelf, opening it to a detailed drawing of pox. Stifling a gag, I quickly close the book and return it to its place. This section is about medicine and disease. Turning the corner, I pick a different row to browse. I pluck a smaller book and open it. As I read, I notice a variety of Elvarran herbs and their uses. Not what I need. I slide the book back into place and continue my search at the back of the library.

A lone text on a stone dais catches my attention. The pages are half-filled with ink, the story seemingly incomplete, so I flip to the front of the book. There is an image of a woman clad in armor. Her long, pale blonde hair flows behind her as she rides a horse into battle. Hundreds of arrows darken the sky, but the woman charges forward, flames erupting from her palms and devouring everything in her path.

Underneath the depiction, it reads: '*Queen Isla Azur Izydor of Rykaris, the battle for Grimhold Crossing*' My eyes widen, lips parting in silent shock as I reread the words once... then again... and again.

My mother.

I read on immediately, drinking in the words about my mother like holy water.

After suffering heavy casualties, Queen Isla Izydor rode into battle with a remaining fleet of 300 Elvarrans. The kingdom of Erynthe, which marched on the border, outnumbered the Elvarrans four to one. Isla's magic reached unexplainable heights of fury, leading to the surrender and peace treaty offered by King Ulrik Roderick Valantis of Cathros to end the war. Due to her bravery, fifteen years of prosperity passed between the North and South.

Tears well at the edges of my eyes. Here is the truth of my mother's past I was forbidden to learn. She was a queen who went to great lengths to protect her kingdom, even if it meant fighting until her last breath. I ache to know more, to hear the tales I was robbed of.

I cast so much suspicion on Wrath when he told me I was half-Elvarran, but it is true. Proof bleeds from the pages like an open wound. I must choose to patch it up or leave it to scar my already broken heart. This is a part of me that Ulrik hid, not Wrath. While I don't trust him, I want to know more about Isla, so I need his help for now.

Returning the book to the dais, I continue my search on the shelves lining the library's back wall. Rows upon rows of ancient tomes fill each shelf, my fingers trailing along the spines as I search for one name in particular: C. V. Bainbridge.

I spot an encyclopedia, its leather cover cracked with age.

Dust clings to my fingertips as I pull the heavy volume free. The book slides out halfway and comes to a stop. I yank on it again, but it doesn't release. The bookshelf beside me rumbles, and a passageway opens.

I gasp.

Cold air rushes from the tunnel, blowing the stray hairs away from my face. A deep, musky scent invades my senses, the smell slightly foul. My curiosity gets the best of me... I take a hesitant step forward and lean in to get a better look. Below my feet lies a small stone staircase leading down into a tunnel. The bottom steps disappear into the darkness below. The deeper I peer, the more my nerves twist up in fear, as if the tunnel is trying to swallow me whole.

Not today.

Stepping out of the entryway, I return to the encyclopedia and pull it again, hoping the passage will close. The mechanism grinds together, and the tunnel closes with a thunk. Breathing a sigh of relief, I allow my shoulders to relax as I step away.

That's when I hear the faint echo of a voice.

"We have received word that human troops have attacked the border near Ashvarin several times. Stanik intercepted a pigeon stating that the humans expect to attack again before the first snowfall." Gilead fires off the information in rapid succession, their voice growing louder.

My breath catches in my throat as I slip into the next corridor, pressing my back against the towering bookshelf. Footsteps echo against the marble floors, and my heart pounds with suspense. Every muscle tenses as I pray the shadows will hide me from view.

"Let Sebastian defend his border." Wrath's voice echoes throughout the library. "We're not leaving with this so-called *resistance* running amok." The word resistance is laced with venom. "Rykaris can send troops."

I press myself tighter against the shelves, wishing I could merge into the books and disappear. Holding my breath, I try to silence myself completely as they stop in the aisle beside mine. Wrath's magic bristles against my skin, causing me to tremble from the sensation.

"They're after Raelys," Gilead says. "Just give the human princess back."

"I will not." Wrath refuses. "I would rather burn Dratheria to the ground than give her back."

Shock coils in my chest at his words. Wrath has no intention of letting me go. The King sees me as a key to breaking the curse. If I fail—if I prove useless—what then? Will he cast me aside, discard me like a broken tool no longer worth keeping?

"Yes, Your Majesty," Gilead replies. "What of the plans to cut off trade to Oderris before winter?"

"We're moving forward with it."

"Anything else?" Gilead asks.

"Write to Duke Nikolas Sterling of Thalvar," Wrath commands. "Tell him I've got a deal for him."

The echo of Gilead's footsteps fades in the distance. Every nerve in my body fires at once, yet I stay frozen. I don't move, don't breathe—not until the library door creaks open.

"How long are you going to stay like that?"

I let out a yelp in shock.

Whirling, I see Wrath behind me. He eyes me with intrigue as he crosses his arms over his chest. I watch his corded muscles flex beneath his tunic. It is the kind of strength gained only from years of relentless combat. It infuriates me that I allow his physique to catch my eye.

"You scared the *shit* out of me!" I say in dismay, keeping my voice low.

Wrath laughs. Actually laughs. His lips part, the scar on his jaw pulled tight. It's the first time I've seen him truly smile. It catches me off guard, my anger waning. I didn't know Wrath was capable of any emotion behind his cold, stoic exterior.

"Why are you barefoot, Raelys?"

"No reason." I toss my slippers down and slide my feet into them.

"Snooping around, are we?" Wrath says in amusement, knowing he's caught me.

"No." I huff, paying him no heed. I turn down the previous aisle. "I was reading this book about my mother." I pluck the text from the dais, holding it up and pointing at the page.

"The battle for Grimhold Crossing," Wrath says. "A classic."

"Were you there?"

"That battle was nearly thirty years ago. How old do you think I am?" His lips press into a thin line.

My words must have struck a nerve. I keep the conversation lighthearted to distract him. "I don't know. Don't Elvarrans live forever... or something?"

"We have slightly longer lifespans than humans, but we are not immortal. About two to three hundred years," he explains, not elaborating further.

"So... how old are you?" I ask curiously.

"Thirty-four," Wrath replies. "I think you reading ancient Elvarran texts counts as snooping, Princess."

"What are you going to do? Lock me in the dungeon?" I taunt, returning the book to the dais.

"I'm considering it." Wrath's eyes glint with amusement.

I continue to mock him, making a sweeping gesture. "I

hereby sentence you to the crime of reading! Head on a pike, immediately!"

"That's a great idea," he says smugly.

Wrath takes a step closer to me. The space between us closes. I feel the brush of his magic against my skin once more, my mark tingling in response. Something shifts as the air charges with a surge of magnetism. When I'm around him, every breath feels sharper—as if the world is amplified tenfold.

"I can only read one book so many times before growing bored," I reply sweetly, tilting my head to look up at him.

"How many times have you read The Warlord Chronicles?" Wrath asks curiously.

I shrug. "Hundreds?"

"Hundreds?" Wrath repeats, his interest piqued. "What's your favorite part?"

"Understand yourself. Understand your foe. For the enemy of my enemy may become my ally." I quote the book perfectly.

"Trust in this truth, and you may find unexpected strength in unlikely places," we say in unison. "The sharpest blade is wielded not by a steady hand, but with cunning, patience, and wisdom."

CHAPTER TWENTY

I AM WOEFULLY unprepared for how vast Lunithia is. Nearly every street in Khalessor is teeming with life. Everywhere I look, I see Elvarrans drinking, chatting, and dancing in the streets, all of them exuding merriment. Small children run past me, carrying small sticks that sparkle on the ends. The smell—gods, it is divine, the air carrying the scent of rich spices and wine.

Rowena walks beside me, arm looped through mine as we enter the festival. Her black hair is styled in a half-updo, a golden crystal pin sticking from the back, catching the light like dewdrops on leaves. The rest of her long hair cascades down with loose, small strands framing her face. She wears a forest green gown adorned with simple pearls, the patterns weaving up the sleeves like intricate vines.

At Rowena's request, I wear a sapphire-blue gown with silver stars embroidered into the fabric. The silky fabric is smooth against my skin, the bodice hugging my curves snugly. With each step I take, the skirt sways like tree branches in the breeze. The lower neckline is different from what I'm used to wearing, but it feels modish.

"It's so enchanting," I tell her, unable to focus on one thing for very long.

"We must make an offering at the Eldertree," Rowena starts. "It's an Elvarran tradition to honor the earth that gives us our magic," she adds. "We will get many glasses of wine and drink until we're fuddled. After that, we will cast our gazes among the fine men of Khalessor."

"Are you married, Ro?" I ask, recalling that she's never mentioned a husband.

"I am not." She sighs in relief. "My mother is a tyrant, demanding that I give her grandchildren, as it is my duty as their only child. Wrath has been hiding me here in Khalessor for four years now, helping me avoid my mother's fury. Being away from my parents has allowed me to pursue my passion for sewing."

"I understand completely." I frown, knowing what it feels like. To face your parents' scorn for not obeying they're every command. A pit forms in my stomach every time I think about what my life in Avelisar would have been like, a fate I am happy to have escaped.

"If you see any vendor selling crystal candies, we must stop to try some," she insists. "We can play a game of Mystic Runes."

"A game of what?"

"It's a card game," Rowena says, her tone exasperated. "Honestly, Raelys, do the humans do *anything* fun in Cathros?"

"Plenty." I smile. "I grew up playing a game with a mallet and ball… but I don't remember the name."

"We have that as well!" She pulls me down a road. "This way!"

Rowena points to a large tree in the distance. Its branches are so tall they touch the clouds, casting a large canopy over the town. The leaves are bright green and pointed, branches rustling softly in the breeze. The closer we get to the tree, the more I can feel it radiating magic from the twisted roots that burrow deep into the earth.

"That's the Eldertree?" I ask, tilting my head back to take in its majesty.

"Yes." She stops at the base of the tree.

"Where did it come from?"

"They say that Krateus Izydor planted this tree to represent his life," Rowena explains. "And when it speaks to you, it's Krateus who speaks." She pulls a strip of ribbon from her sleeve, her fingers trailing over the small handwriting on the fabric. Then, she reaches up and ties it to one of the branches.

Rowena kneels, pressing one hand on a tree root and the other over her heart. She bows her head and closes her eyes. Her lips move in a silent prayer, but I can't hear what she's saying. With a deep breath, she opens her eyes and stands, returning to my side.

"Oh no!" She gasps. "I completely forgot to tell you to bring an offering!" Rowena frantically scans the space around her. "Does anyone have a spare piece of parchment?" she calls out to the crowd.

"I do," someone says in return.

She rushes off, speaking in hushed tones to an Elvarran before returning with a bottle of ink and a small parchment. "Many people write their offerings and place them inside one of the hollows."

"Thank you." I bend down, using my knee to write as Rowena holds the ink bottle for me.

Dear Eldertree,

Please reconnect me with enough of my mother's

magic so I may open her journal. I miss her more with every passing year, her absence a wound that refuses to heal. Guide me. What path am I supposed to take?

— R

Once I finish writing, Rowena dashes off to return the ink to the man who lent it to us. Folding the paper a few times, I close my fingertips around it and press the parchment into my palm. I try to commit the words into my skin before reaching up on my toes and dropping them into one of the tree hollows.

I press my palm against the tree trunk, feeling the cool bark under my skin as I close my eyes. Instead of praying to Itheon, I try to speak to the tree, feeling the magic flowing beneath the surface.

"Receive my humble petition and bestow upon me the Eldertree's blessings and share in her bounty if I am worthy," I whisper.

Not even a heartbeat later, the tree whispers back to me. "*Long live the queen…*"

I gasp, my eyes flying open as silver wraps around my right hand and surges into me. I feel the Eldertree's magic flow into my fingertips and up my arm. A light erupts from my palm as I pull away in shock. The tree branches quiver, as if they've caught a chill. Every Elvarran falls silent around me, the weight of their stares pressing against my skin, heavy with disdain. A hand wraps around my wrist and pulls me away from the tree.

"Time to go!" Rowena's cheerful voice cuts through the silence as she guides me back to the busy streets.

"Ro, what happened?" I say in a hushed tone as we disappear into the crowd.

"The Eldertree spoke to you." Rowena smiles. "It used to speak to all of us before the curse. So you'll have to forgive everyone for being a little surprised."

"Is that a bad thing?" Worry fills me. "Did I take it away from someone who needed it?"

"Don't be silly! The tree thought you needed it." Rowena stops at a booth and hands two bronze coins over to a merchant. "Elvarrans love connecting with nature, protecting it, and finding solace in it. Before the curse, we could communicate directly with trees, rivers, and mountains."

"You can talk to a mountain?" I blink in confusion. "What does it say?"

Rowena laughs. "It doesn't say *words*, silly. You would connect your magic to nature and feel it flow back to you. Since we draw our magic from the earth to wield, we sometimes give it back in thanks."

The vendor passes us two wooden sticks coated in brightly colored candy. I have never seen a sweet like this back home. It is slightly jagged and hard to the touch.

"Try it!" Rowena urges me, already chewing.

Taking a bite, I chew the hard candy as it slowly dissolves into a sweet liquid. It assaults my senses, causing my left eye to twitch and water up. I cough, trying to clear the sensation, but the sweetness persists.

"See!" Rowena exclaims, taking another bite. "It's the one I was telling you about! It makes your eyes water," she says with her mouth full.

"It's quite sweet." I swallow the candy, shaking my head. "Gods, I need something to wash that down."

"Come on! We'll get some wine," she loops her arm through mine, pulling me along.

I watch in awe as Rowena wolfs down her entire candy by the time we make it back to the main road. We circle the corner and cross under the lanterns, stopping at a booth that sells wine. Before Rowena can pay, I pass the merchant two bronze coins.

"No fair!" she calls out.

"You can get the next round," I tease.

Rowena picks up her glass and holds it aloft. "Hear! Hear!"

"May the wine flow." I clink my glass against hers, taking a long sip. It's delicious, with a sweet berry and clove flavor.

"Tell me, what do the beaches look like in the South?" Rowena urges me, taking another drink.

"Do you not have beaches or shores in the North?"

Rowena shakes her head. "I am only familiar with the mountains and forests of the North." She sighs. "We have some tall cliffsides, but that hardly counts when the water is frigid."

I know the feeling. Up until recently, I have never left my kingdom, either. The North is far more beautiful and lush than the South, but each has its unique beauty. Khalessor is a marvel. There is no doubt in my mind about that, but even its splendor can't quiet the ache for home.

"I wasn't allowed to leave the castle walls, but many people told me that the sand was soft to the touch, and the water was excellent to swim in during the summer months. From my balcony, I had the best view of the sea that stretched across the horizon, and during sunrise, the water would glimmer," I explain.

"Does it snow there?"

"Yes, but only a few weeks out of the year. The rest of the time, it's quite hot," I reply, wondering if I will ever see my home again.

She gives the man two more coins, and he refills our glasses to the top. Rowena and I drink and talk and wander until the world grows a little hazy. My skin flushes with warmth, and my body relaxes. The sound of a lively melody carries through the street as an Elvarran plays a lute somewhere in the crowd.

"That one is handsome." She points at a man with curly, brunette hair and thick brows as he passes by.

"I like that one." I point to the black-haired man lost in his music—the source of the lively melody.

She giggles. "He looks like Wrath."

"Rowena!" I gasp. "Don't you dare!"

My outburst only makes her mischievous smile grow. "I'm kidding! Though you're turning quite red, Rae."

I hide my flush behind my glass. "It's the wine."

"That one can do whatever he wants to me." She points at the tall Elvarran with dark hair and a scar across his cheek.

"You mean Gilead?" I look at him across the street. "From the King's army?"

She sighs longingly. "We see one another around the castle all the time. He's the captain of the royal guard. But he usually keeps his distance."

I inhale a playful breath. "I'm going to tell him."

"Raelys!" Rowena hisses under her breath, making me burst with laughter. "I will never speak to you again if you do that."

"I'm kidding," I tease.

"If you're not going to eat your candy, can I have it?" Rowena plucks the treat from my grasp.

"Of course." I smile, enjoying the sight of her devouring the sweet in one go.

A searing gaze cuts through the lively festival from afar, and a familiar prickling sensation creeps up the back of my neck. Turning away from Rowena, I glance up the street and lock eyes with Wrath. He wears a finely tailored black coat, a high-collared vest of deep plum, and polished boots. In typical Wrath fashion, he is faultless.

Perhaps it is the wine, but tonight he looks... otherworldly. Divine power coils beneath the surface as he stands, and it steals the breath from my lungs. His eyes hold such intense desire and yearning that it makes me question if he is gazing at someone other than me. People surround the King, all vying for his attention, but he ignores them to watch *me*. Unable to hold the weight of his gaze much longer, I turn back to Rowena. She is busy drinking another glass of wine, her attention on the crowd of people dancing.

"Is the King always so..." I consider my words. "Fickle?"

Rowena stifles a laugh with her hand. "Whatever do you mean, Rae?"

"Sometimes, I am unsure if he loathes me or is enraptured by me," I tell her truthfully.

"My cousin is *such* a curmudgeon." She shrugs. "Don't take it personally."

"I won't—" I see the glint of a dagger as a figure rushes toward me. I recognize the man as Aurelia and Violet's father —we are in danger. "Rowena, look out!" I push her out of the way, covering her body with mine as we fall.

CHAPTER TWENTY-ONE

THE DAGGER WHISTLES through the air so quickly that I lose track of it, wondering if I will meet my end. I brace for impact, hands moving to cover my face. A sudden gust of cold, icy air shoots past me as Rowena and I hit the dirt with a heavy thud. Glancing up, I see the man's body covered in a thick piece of ice—his blade frozen inches from my gut. A bolt of terror shoots through me as I scramble back, unable to regain my footing.

"Raelys," a voice calls out. Hands grab my shoulders, steadying me enough to turn my head and meet Wrath's gaze. "Are you all right?" he asks.

"I'm fine," I say between ragged breaths. "Rowena?" Pulling out of Wrath's grasp, I quickly turn to face her. Rowena is lying on the dirt beside me, but she's no longer moving, her body still and lacking color. I shake her shoulder. "Rowena?!" I start to panic. "Why won't she wake up?"

"She hit burnout." Wrath circles us, bending to pick Rowena up in his arms. "Can you walk?"

I nod and stand, brushing the dirt off my dress. Wrath places a gloved hand on the ice, shattering it into tiny fragments. The man's remnants disappear into the breeze. I watch Aurelia's and Violet's father melt away into nothingness. How am I going to tell Aurelia? Should I tell her? I debate whether she will feel relieved or mournful.

"Come, Raelys." Wrath walks away.

I follow him up the castle's steps, examining Rowena's condition. "She froze him to save me?"

"Yes."

Disbelief fills me. I didn't know Elvarrans could produce ice from their fingertips. Sebastian can manipulate the wind... so what else are they capable of? Wrath and I enter the castle, rushing through the corridor. At the end of the hall stands a massive door, flanked by guards on either side. Their hands rest on the hilts of their weapons as they wait, unmoving from their post.

"Call for a healer," Wrath says to one of the guards, opening the door and stepping inside.

I follow him, suddenly realizing that I'm in Wrath's bedchamber. Every detail speaks of wealth and luxury; not a single item is out of place. The thick velvet curtains frame the doorway to the large balcony overlooking the garden. In the center lies a plush bed. To my right are tall mahogany shelves filled entirely with books. A tapestry hangs from the wall, bearing the crest of a serpent breathing fire—the crest for House Bainbridge.

He gently sets Rowena on the bed and presses two fingers into the inside of her wrist. Wrath releases her, stepping away. "She'll be okay."

A sigh of relief leaves me.

"You pushed Rowena out of the way in place of yourself." Wrath never misses the slightest detail. "Why?" he demands.

"I consider her my friend," I reply. That answer isn't good

enough because I feel the magic creep up my throat. "I knew he was after me anyway," I say against my will.

"What do you mean?"

"Must you always wrestle my words from me?" My voice slightly rises.

"Answer my question," Wrath commands.

"That was the father of the girl I requested you to employ. When I freed her from his clutches, he swore that I'd pay for it." I tell him the truth.

"You are lacking self-preservation skills, Raelys." Wrath scolds me as he walks away. He pushes open the double doors to the balcony, putting some distance between us as he steps outside. "You would have been killed if Rowena were not there."

A gust of crisp night air flows into the room, sending a chill across my alcohol-flushed skin. It sends a spark of confidence through me, leading me to follow him. If he wants to quarrel with me, fine—I'll unleash my pent-up fury on him.

"I'm still alive, aren't I?" I counter. "That must mean I have excellent self-preservation skills."

"Says the woman who made a deal with me," he says derisively.

"A deal requires two parties," I remind him. "You only care if I breathe or not because you need me to break the curse."

Anger flashes across Wrath's features. "You can look me in the eye and tell me Rowena deserves to suffer like that? She will stay in that state for weeks, all because she used her powers to save *your* life."

"You're acting like I wanted this to happen."

"Answer me," he demands.

"Aren't you going to force it out of me anyway?" I return fire at him, not willing to back down in this battle.

"I had sympathy for your situation. I still do, even now. I

wouldn't want that for Rowena either." Wrath steps closer. "I see that sympathy was misplaced."

"You don't know *anything* about me," I seethe. "How can you judge me when the townspeople whisper such atrocities about you?"

Wrath's gaze darkens—the scar on his neck flexes. I can feel him holding back his temper. I struck a nerve, good. I enjoy rustling his feathers, as he completely frays mine. We are like two vultures circling the other, waiting to strike our prey.

Part of me still aches when I think of the events in Avelisar, unable to fully move on, knowing I recited empty vows that I wouldn't keep—and to a man I loathe. If I could wipe that night from my memory, I would. The humiliation of having to parade around in that dress, the fear of having Olav nearly force himself on me, and the guilt of knowing it is my choices that led them all to their deaths—it all weighs so heavily on my soul.

"You have no idea how humiliating it was to go through that ceremony. To know that I belong to that wretched creature, that I still do—"

"You do not belong to anyone, Raelys."

"We said our vows." My voice is firm as I try to keep my emotions in check. "I am technically still the Queen of Avelisar."

"And you would still be in Avelisar if it weren't for *me*."

I don't respond immediately, still feeling as if my head is under the surface, and I'm afraid to breathe. I no longer know what's up or down, right or wrong. Wrath freed me, but he also took my deal to use me.

"Did you purposefully wait until I said my vows to utilize Avelisar?" I accuse him.

His nostrils flare. "What use do I have for an empty castle, Raelys?"

"You couldn't open one of those magical arch portals to go through the walls?" I challenge him. "Why did it take you so long?"

"How large do you think a personal guard is? I managed to sneak in six Elvarrans. We had to get the rest through the wall while the ceremony was taking place. I came to get you as soon as I could," Wrath explains, each word with a sharp edge. "And no, I cannot open portals. Those are tied to keystone arches. Which are only in the North."

Six guards. That isn't many. They opened the gates and allowed the rest of the soldiers to invade the castle. With the siege underway, Wrath searched for me. His story is likely valid, but I refuse to acknowledge it.

"As soon as I got to Avelisar, they locked me in that room and wouldn't let me leave. They claimed I would run…" I inhale a shaky breath. "…and in Cathros, I spent my *whole* life behind those walls. You said it yourself. I'm trapped here, too. It's the *same* cage in different forms."

"That is how you see me…" Each of his words drips with ire. "I am the villain for freeing you from your arranged marriage and giving you the freedom to go wherever your heart pleases. All I ask in return is your help before our magic is sealed off for *good*."

"That's not freedom, Wrath; that's an assignment!" I shout at him, reaching my breaking point.

"Then what do you want, Raelys?" Wrath is maddeningly calm in the face of my anger.

"I want this damned mark off my skin!" I push up my sleeve, showing him the silver lines etched into my skin.

"Is it because I added to the ones you can't remove?" he asks, low and careful, his eyes tracing the scars on my hands.

Glancing down, I assess the state of my hands. The bruises and cuts have faded, but the scars remain. Even now, Margaret haunts my dreams when I'm kingdoms away. I wonder if I will ever be free of the damage she inflicted, her wounds seemingly permanent.

I return my focus to Wrath. My emotions are so weary and broken that I don't know what's right or wrong anymore. His grey eyes watch me with a careful reverence that makes me question everything. They remind me of the moon that hangs above us, gentle and unyielding.

"Don't you dare bring that up." I quickly lower my sleeve in shame.

"I'm trying to understand," he says gently.

I swallow the lump in my throat, shaking my head and turning away. It is far too much to bear. I can face anything this realm has to challenge me with… but not that, anything but my scars.

"Wait!" He grabs my wrist, stopping me from leaving.

"Don't," I whisper.

"Those who seek to unmake me may conjure flame, but I shall not be reduced." He recites a line from the Warlord Chronicles perfectly. "Tell me what's next. I know that you have it memorized," he urges.

"Those who seek to unmake me may rise with blade, but I shall not be stricken." I finish the quote, growing suspicious that he mentioned the book again.

He's the last person I'd like to discuss this with. This part of me has been under lock and key for so long that I'm not ready to face it. My abuse is sealed away in a place so far away that I'm not sure I can even reach it anymore. I can't bear the weight of his judgment for much longer.

"I want, for once in my godsdamn life, to not be treated like an *object* to be owned." I release the last of my heaviness.

The door opens behind me, interrupting our bickering.

"You called for a healer, Your Majesty?" an unfamiliar voice calls out.

Murderous intent flashes across Wrath's features. He begrudgingly releases his hold on my wrist, and I feel the mark fade from the broken contact. Wrath tears his gaze away from me, turning his attention to the healer, but he doesn't move away from me.

I turn and leave without another word.

CHAPTER TWENTY-TWO

PLOPPING down two empty cups on the bar top for Alastor to wash, I sigh, turning back towards the tavern. It is a slow night, with only a few tables full. The usual lively atmosphere is exchanged for dull and quiet. Perhaps everyone is hungover, recovering from the festivities.

"Slow night, huh, Alastor?" I make small talk with the grumpy bartender.

"Seems like it." He huffs, polishing a glass with a rag.

The door opens. A few lively soldiers, chatting amongst themselves, walk inside. I recognize them from the night I first worked here at the tavern, as Sebastian went to sit with them after spotting me.

This is my chance.

Walking over to the table, I smile at the three men. "What can I get for you?"

"Three ale," one says, sliding some coins across the table.

I pluck the coins from the surface, moving across the tavern so Alastor can fill some tankards with bubbling, dark-colored ale. Taking all three in my grip, I slide them across the worn table toward them.

"I don't mean to be impolite, miss," one of the men starts. "But are you a halfling?"

My gaze turns to the one speaking. He is young, perhaps in his early twenties, and has wavy, medium-length blonde hair. His armor is made of bronze, not steel, and lacks dents and scratches.

"Yes, I'm a halfling," I reply warmly, keeping up the facade.

"Really?" His bright blue eyes hold a spark of curiosity.

"Yes." I nod. "And you are from?"

"Ashvarin… my lady," he stammers nervously, and I take note of his stare as it lowers.

I style my dresses the way Kaia has shown me: the corset pulled down, the apron low on my hips, and my skirt hiked up. To my surprise, I am making far more tips, but attracting the wrong type of attention. Many men stare at my breasts, while others have wandering hands that grasp at my backside as I pass. I've seen enough of men's lust to know exactly how ugly it is, yet somehow it still manages to disgust me every time. Nevertheless, I didn't know much about Ashvarin, so I used the conversation I overheard between Wrath and Gilead to learn more.

"I've heard the humans have been attacking in recent weeks." I frown, appearing distressed. "Is all well over there?"

He nods. "We just returned from defending the border. It seems like they were searching for supplies before snowfall."

"I'm glad everyone is safe," I reply sweetly. "So you're a part of Sebastian's forces?"

"Yes." His brows raise in surprise. "Do you know him?"

"I am acquainted with him, yes."

"My name is Hans." The young soldier offers me his name. "And you are?"

"Rae."

"This is Gavriel," he says, pointing to the Elvarran with short black hair, umber skin, and ice blue eyes. "And Lucio." The second Elvarran is tan with curly, dark brown hair. A faint scar runs along his jawline, cutting through his stubble.

"It's nice to meet you all." I step away, hoping to ask more questions the next time they return. "Enjoy your evening and let me know if you need more ale."

All of the information I collect at the Whispering Willow will be useless the minute Wrath tears it from me. My plan rests on his moods. He can't know what I'm doing. I need to find a way to beat him at his own game.

If someone feeds me false information, could it throw him off? Or there is a way for me to resist his pull, safeguarding my mind. If I act fast enough, could I pretend to be distressed from the magic and slip in a lie before he can get the truth?

Moving around the tavern, I try to pick up on stray pieces of passerby conversations as I fill empty glasses, wipe down tables, and carry plates of food to the guests. The mindless and simple tasks are my favorites, as they allow time to pass quickly without hassle.

When the grandfather clock strikes, it signals the end of my shift. I untie my apron, pulling it over my neck and folding it into my satchel. Grabbing my cloak from behind the bar, I tie it around my shoulders and brace myself for the cold outside.

Alastor slides me a few silver coins, and I take them from him. "Thank you."

"See you in a few nights."

Exiting The Whispering Willow, I tuck my cloak closer to my body, noticing the chill in the wind. I only get a short distance away before Renwick hobbles in my path, his lips curling upwards to reveal a toothy grin.

"Ello, halfling girl."

"Hi, Renwick," I greet him. "No, I don't want an elixir."

He frowns. "How do ya' know my name?"

"Kaia told me." I smile. "Do you know where she is?"

I have waited for Kaia to turn up at the tavern again, but she never does. We have much to discuss, as we can mutually benefit one another if she is interested. If our ambitions align, then we can be excellent partners.

"One moment!" I hear a lilting voice call out nearby.

"How 'bout a cursed object?" Renwick gestures to his cart, plucking a crystal ball and holding it close to me.

I sigh. "I don't need any curses..." Then an idea suddenly pops into my mind. "Hey, you wouldn't happen to know who C. V. Bainbridge is?"

Kaia told me that Renwick is nearly two hundred years old. Maybe he knows something about the author of the book, as he's likely lived through several generations.

"It'll cost ya!" Renwick holds up a finger.

I reach into my satchel, pulling one silver coin and handing it to him. "Here."

"That's Casimir Vaelric Bainbridge."

"And who might that be?" I ask.

Before Renwick can reply, Kaia emerges from a nearby tent. A man follows shortly behind, buckling his trousers as he strides off. Her brown eyes meet mine, and a devious smile forms on her lips. She adjusts her dress as she strides over to us, running her fingers through her long hair to push it out of her face.

"You're not my usual customer," Kaia teases.

"Can I speak with you?" I ask.

"It'll cost you!" Renwick quickly cuts in.

Kaia places a hand on his shoulder, leaning down to kiss his cheek. "Oh, come on, Rennie. Be nice to *pretty* girls," she coos.

He grumbles, but eventually relents. "Fine."

"You should close up shop; it's getting late." Kaia drops her arm. "Go find a nice tree hollow to sleep in, or you'll catch a cold."

Renwick doesn't reply. He turns to close the cover on his cart. With a triumphant humph, Kaia saunters down the street, seemingly unaffected by the cold.

I follow her. "So, these 'lofty goals' of yours."

"Yes?" She raises a curious brow at me.

"How lofty?"

"Quite," Kaia replies confidently.

"How close are you to court?" I continue my vague questioning.

"What an intriguing question," Kaia muses. "I used to service many highborns while at the premier house, but alas, the Madame is wretched and keeps most of the fees."

Interesting. There are many ways to manipulate someone to get what you want, but no influence is as strong as seduction. I know little of this tactic. Kaia does. That's why she fixed my dress at the tavern.

"What if I could assist you in starting your own premier house?"

She gives me a knowing sidelong glance. "I knew I liked you," Kaia says smugly. "You want something in return? A percentage?"

"A web."

Kaia giggles. "And who are we trapping in this *illustrious* web?"

I glance around us, ensuring no one is within earshot. "The crown."

"I love shiny things," she says sweetly. "It's costly to rent the kind of building we'd need on the nicer side of town."

"But you know enough girls to… staff it?" I ask hesitantly.

"Please," she huffs. "I know most are ready to leave that

wretched Madame. Take the best girls, and the *clientele* will follow."

"How much is the rent?"

"Hmm…" Kaia taps a finger to her lips. "A hundred silver at least."

"Here." I palm her the small leather pouch full of coins Wrath gave me. It is close to that amount, give or take a few dozen coins. "How long will it take?"

Kaia pockets the pouch of money. "A few weeks. I'll start talking to the girls. Find a place and get the right furniture."

"All right," I say plainly, hoping my investment will pay off.

CHAPTER TWENTY-THREE

A PLUSH BLANKET of snow covers the entire kingdom of Khalessor. Icicles hang from the eaves, glistening in the morning sun, while frozen windowpanes shimmer with the warm glow from within. I didn't think the castle gardens could get any more beautiful, but I was wrong.

A snowball hits me in the shoulder, causing flecks of snow to spray on my face. I laugh warmly, throwing a snowball back at Rowena. She lets out a slight yelp of surprise before bursting with laughter. We chase after one another, our boots crunching against the icy snow. Rowena raises her hand into the air, flicking her wrist in a quick circle. All the snow from the oak tree's branches falls on me, burying me under the snow.

"Ro!" I cry out, wiggling as I try to unearth myself. The weight of the snow is immense, and I kick my feet out as I struggle to move.

A hand closes around mine as she pulls me free, snow clinging to my eyelashes and hair. My breath curls in the frigid air as I stand and try to brush myself off, piles of snow falling from my lap.

Rowena clutches her middle, doubled over in laughter. "Sorry, Rae."

I giggle. "You win, okay?"

"I didn't think it was going to be that much." She wipes a stray tear from her lashes, unable to control her laughter.

"It's all right," I reassure her. Rowena is back to her usual self. She has fully recovered from her burnout, and that's all that matters. "So you can wield ice?" I ask, brushing the snow from my cloak. I've been eager to hear more about her powers since the incident.

"Yes, but it's rare. When two Verthari with different powers have a child, sometimes their offspring possess the ability to combine both their powers. My dad is a water Verthari, and my mom is an air Verthari. So, I can wield ice," Rowena tells me.

"That's so interesting."

"Some earth and fire babies can manipulate metals, while some fire and air users can use lightning," Rowena explains. "But usually, the child will take after one or the other parent's ability."

We begin walking on the path back to the castle, my boots slipping several times on the ice. Rowena grabs hold of my arm, trying to steady me, but both of us end up fumbling around. I hold my arms aloft, wobbling until I find my footing. Our gazes meet, and we holler with even more laughter.

I can't remember the last time I had this much fun.

"What about the other two..." I try to remember what Barnham told me. "Evokari and Remedari?" My growing curiosity gets the best of me.

"Those are just as rare." Rowena doesn't seem to mind filling me in. "Rather than focusing on the elements, their magic focuses on the physical. They are kind of... counterparts, offshoots of one another. Evokari can manipulate things to their will, whereas Remedari bend themselves to get the desired result."

"I see…" My mind drifts to Lunithia. "Is that how the King made the man you froze disappear?"

Rowena giggles. "You catch on quick, Rae. Yes, Wrath can make people disappear into nothingness. Evokari are known for being destructive," she adds. "Most Remedari are healers, making them invaluable because they're scarce."

"Fascinating," I reply, walking under the large archway as we enter the castle.

Dropping Rowena's arm, I push open the large wooden door for us to enter the castle. A rush of warm air greets us, a relief from the weather outside. I tap my boot against the ground, trying my best not to track snow through the halls before we walk.

"I love the cold." She frowns. "I wish I could be back home in Myragos. The hot springs in the snow are the most *divine* experience."

"You should go. I'm sure your father misses you," I tell her as we stroll through the castle.

She shakes her head. "I cannot. If I travel home now, my mother will surely force me into an arrangement."

"Ah, yes. The lovely Natalia Bainbridge." A voice cuts into our conversation. "She is… a force."

Glancing back, I see Barnham approaching us. He wears a long, thick coat with a fur-lined collar, brown trousers, and knee-high boots. His thick beard has grown fully for the winter, and he scratches at it absently as he yawns. I still want to know about the chunk missing from his ear.

"Hello, Barnham," I greet him.

"You're putting it lightly, cousin." Rowena lets out a defeated huff. "My mother is a tyrant."

"I was trying to be kind." Barnham chuckles. "Raelys, the King wishes to see you."

Dread fills me.

"All right," I reply sweetly, trying to hide my apprehension.

"Chat soon, Rae." Rowena waves goodbye and departs.

Barnham and I stroll down the corridor together. It completely slipped my mind that I agreed to help with my mother's journal. The days after the festival have been a blur of work and checking in on Rowena, my focus elsewhere.

"I saw you push Rowena out of the way in place of yourself," Barnham finally says. "Although I don't fully trust you, you have my thanks."

"Are we turning over a new leaf, Barnham?" I tease, a smile forming on my lips.

"That's a stretch."

Barnham holds the door open, letting me step inside before he closes it again, sealing me in. Wrath sits at the head of the table, eyes scanning over a letter as he reads. As I take a few more steps into the room, his gaze lifts to mine, and I can immediately sense him growing weary from my appearance—disheveled once again.

"Raelys, why are you covered in snow?" he asks, exasperated.

It's the first time I've seen him since the festival. After what occurred on the balcony, I took different routes across the castle and spent more time in my room, successfully avoiding him until now. Wrath doesn't seem any different—back to his usual brazen self, which I suppose I should be grateful for.

"Rowena buried me with her magic."

Wrath says nothing in return as he places my mother's journal on the surface for me. I put my right hand over the cover and try to remember the proper technique. Wrath steps behind me, pressing his palm against mine.

"You're manipulating my magic with yours? Is that how it works?" I ask, closing my eyes as I try to steady my breath.

"Who told you that?"

"Rowena."

"It's more shaping… than manipulating."

I stifle a laugh. "Isn't that the same thing?"

"It's the intention." Wrath's lips are above my ear. "Magic is fickle. Shaping is like guiding it. Manipulating is more of an attempt to control it, which it doesn't like."

"Okay. Shape, don't take," I repeat the mantra.

Drawing a deep breath, I feel the magic around me and try to shape it. Wrath's magic feels different today—more consuming. It surges through me like a violent tide, swallowing my thoughts and breath until all that's left is *him*.

I claim to loathe this man, but our intermingled magic says otherwise each time our skin touches. No matter how much I try to resist, I react the same—skin flushed, racing pulse, breath hitching in my throat, and a deep need for release. I'm too embarrassed to ask if Wrath also feels it, so I suffer in silence.

Lost in thought, I hit the ground, not realizing that I accidentally overcharged.

"You're not listening to me." Wrath's tone is abrasive. "You have to focus."

"I am focusing!" I huff as I stand.

"No, you're not." He narrows his gaze at me, adjusting his sleeves lower.

"Well, maybe if you weren't standing so close—"

"Flustered, Princess?"

I roll my eyes, smacking my hand against the cover with a bit more attitude than I intended. Pushing away all my conflicting emotions, I focus solely on the book. Wrath's steady breaths sync with mine as he floods me with his magic once more. I close my eyes and inhale a deep breath, trying to source it from the earth around me, remembering how I felt when I touched the Eldertree.

I think I'm finally doing it right when a void opens up and swallows me whole. Everything instantly turns black. I can't tell if I'm floating or falling, caught in something untethered from reality. The occasional jolt of pain strikes through my veins like tiny lightning bolts. When I try to move, it only makes it worse, plunging me into a haze.

"Raelys." I hear someone calling my name repeatedly. "Raelys!"

"Gods…" I murmur, still completely numb to my surroundings.

There's something warm spreading across my skin, the center of my chest reverberating with a strange sensation. It feels like serenity, like safety, with a soft familiarity I can't place. It almost feels like… home.

Am I dying?

My eyes crack open slowly as I groan. I try to take in my surroundings, but my vision blurs with painful streaks. Every pulse in my veins causes an aching throb to shoot through my temples, making my head feel impossibly heavy. Wrath studies me with a worried expression, searching my face for signs of life. He has one hand pressed above my heart, the other cupping my cheek as he gently holds my head upright.

"Wrath?" I croak out.

"You're okay." His tone is so gentle that it takes me by surprise. "I've got you."

"Did I die?"

"You hit burnout," he replies. "That's what it feels like."

As I attempt to lift my head, the ground shifts beneath me, the world spinning in rapid circles. The dizziness makes my stomach flip as nausea coils in my gut. I blink to clear the fog from my vision, but it makes Wrath's outline blur even more.

"Do you understand why I'm trying to fix this?" Wrath is nothing but anguish. "My people are suffering. This curse is torment and agony like you've never felt."

I can't figure out what's up from down. My eyelids droop as I fade again, only somewhat attuned to my surroundings. Wrath easily hoists me into his arms, and I fold into him, unable to pull myself above the surface.

"Where are you taking me?"

"To your room so you can rest," he replies coldly.

His heart beats steadily in his chest, anchoring me to this reality for a bit longer. Despite how safe I feel in his arms, I know it's a farce, the magic playing tricks on me. But in this moment, I don't want him to let go.

"You hate me," I mumble, in a state of complete delirium. My head seeks comfort on Wrath's shoulder. I wish I could keep my eyes open to look at him as he carries me down the hall, but they feel so heavy.

"You think I hate you?"

"Yes…" I flicker between consciousness and awake.

Because I can't do anything.

My father's words echo in the back of my mind. All of his mistrust and lectures come flooding to the surface. I'm a liability. It's why I deserve to be locked up. It's for the realm's good. I only make things worse. All I do is leave a path of destruction and chaos in my wake, just as my father has always said.

"You make me feel many things. Hatred is not one of them," Wrath says as I drift away.

CHAPTER TWENTY-FOUR

I FEEL *a sharp pain across my hand as I write, causing the quill to scratch across the page. Before I can brace myself, Margaret strikes me again.*

"Start over!"

Flipping over the parchment, I start at the top. Even though I had nearly finished the last page, something erased all my progress. Sighing, I write again, but this time the quill in my hand has iron barbs that dig into my skin and cause my fingers to bleed.

"Start over!" She strikes me again.

I can't see the parchment—the desk is slick with my blood. With my left hand, I drag through the liquid, searching frantically as panic rises.

"No, no, no…" I whisper, knowing this torment will never end unless I find that page.

"Start over!"

I gasp, startling awake. My eyes dart around the dark room, looking for danger, but there is none. I glance down at my hands, expecting bruises and blood, but they are clean and dry, only the scars to remind me. I sit up, taking a few slow, frazzled breaths as I wait for the fear to subside.

A nightmare.

The last thing I remember is Wrath carrying me after I hit

burnout. How long have I been out? It took Rowena a week to wake up after the festival. Every muscle fiber in my body complains as I lower myself back down.

I lie in silence, staring at the ceiling to steady my breath. The walls inch nearer, closing in like a vise as panic threatens to swallow me whole. I stand and toss my cloak around my shoulders like a shrug and slide into slippers to enter the hall.

When I had nightmares back home in Cathros, I would go out on my balcony to get some fresh air. The view of the sea always calmed me down, and although there isn't any ocean here in the North, perhaps a view of the mountains could ease my weary soul.

I open the door to a random balcony, closing it softly behind me. It's dark outside, and I have no idea what time it is. Above me, stars glitter against the mountain peaks like tiny spectators. It is a sight I never tire of. Khalessor looks carved from a dream, every color too vivid to belong to the waking world. It's snowing, a light dusting of flecks falling from the sky around me.

The frigid air makes my nose run, and my body has a slight chill that won't go away no matter how tightly I pull the cloak around me. Using my pointer finger, I draw swirls and other small designs on the frosted railing to distract myself. Despite my shivering, I can feel my body relax. Small flecks of snow cover my hair, the waves still flowing loose down to my waist from sleep.

The balcony door behind me opens, causing me to glance over my shoulder. I see Wrath dressed in a thick black coat with a fur collar. His face is slightly displeased by the cold as he steps out to join me. Snowflakes nestle in Wrath's dark hair like glittering stars. His magic skates across my skin, and I realize how accustomed I've grown to the sensation of it.

"You're awake," he comments.

"How long was I out?" I ask.

"Three days." Wrath's eyes scan my scrawlings. "How do you feel?"

"I can't sleep."

"Why?"

"Thinking," I reply plainly, inhaling a deep breath. "I know, dangerous."

His brows lower. "Who said you're not allowed to think?"

I shrug, not necessarily in the mood to explain the details of my father's retributions. If Ulrik had his way, I would have never spoken in his presence. Maybe then I'd be a perfect daughter. Not a person, but a blank canvas for him to paint.

"What are you thinking about?" he asks.

"Aren't you going to force me to answer anyway?" I counter, not in the mood for repartee. I may be used to the feeling of his magic, but the violence of pulling words from my mouth will never be familiar or welcome—nor is it conducive to my plan.

If I can't get Wrath to respect my boundary, then all of the information I collect will be for nothing. His mood dictates how far I'm able to plan, but he won't know what to believe if I can find a way to outsmart him at his own game.

Wrath doesn't respond right away. His shoulders are rigid, as if he can't quite relax around me. He studies me like a riddle he can't solve. "Not tonight," he finally replies.

"The Eldertree spoke to me during Lunithia," I tell him, changing the subject. "Rowena told me it used to speak to everyone."

"The last person it spoke to was me, nine years ago." Wrath pulls down the edge of his right sleeve.

"What did it tell you?"

"You must rule." His voice is low, as if the memory haunts him.

"You've only been King for nine years?" Surprise fills me. The other rulers of Dratheria have held their thrones much longer. "Who was king before?"

"Someone who believed the curse was a good thing."

"You overthrew the King?" I ask, completely intrigued.

Wrath takes a deep breath, waiting for a moment before speaking. "My father pulled many strings in the shadows," he says vaguely. "After that, I was installed as king."

I pause, considering his choice of words. *Installed.* Wrath made it sound like he was selected, rather than a choice. He was forced into the role by his father's expectations, rather than born into it.

"You didn't want to be king?" I pick up on his hesitation.

"Our lives are threads woven along an unseen path—one whose reasons we may never fully understand." The edges in Wrath's voice have all softened. He avoids answering my question, which leads me to believe this role is not what he wanted.

"The tree told me, 'Long live the queen.'" I hope he can decode the message for me.

"Interesting…"

"I don't feel like a queen," I say truthfully.

"I don't feel like a destroyer of peace," he echoes.

His admission surprises me. During the battle in Liora, I saw firsthand the skilled and savage warrior he is, and yet, he doesn't resonate with such a title. Did he force himself to be that way just to fit a mold? Or is he manipulating me to feel pity for him?

"Then why do they call you Wrath's Blade?" I ask, returning to my drawing now that enough new snow has piled up.

"Is that what's keeping you up at night?"

I let out a soft laugh. "Of course not."

"It started as a tale after we killed the King of Nythara.

Everyone called me that, and eventually I stopped correcting people."

"I thought Taryn killed Arthur?" I ask, recalling the tale she told me while traveling to Khalessor.

"She did." Wrath nods. "Most don't want to credit her because she was only nineteen at the time."

The soldiers' pride must have been wounded, losing their chance at glory in favor of a young girl. Taryn seems proud of her accomplishment, and despite people wanting to take it away from her, Wrath acknowledged it without question.

"Do you feel like you deserve such a title?"

"Do you?" he counters.

I ponder his question for a moment, considering the person in front of me versus the tales people tell about him. While a bit abrasive and ferocious at times, Wrath is a king who cares for his people and fights for them on the front lines. We may not see eye to eye, but I can recognize his tenacity and effort as a ruler.

I shrug. "The humans blame you for breaking the treaty."

"Do you want to know why we attacked Nythara?" Wrath's question is soft. I expect him to get defensive or angry in response to me, but tonight he seems… introspective.

I glance up. "Okay."

"They kept traveling through Crossgate and attacking the Elvarrans in Corovya," he explains. "They almost wiped out that entire territory before I finally stepped in. Did Taryn tell you what happened to her?"

"She did." The Kingdom of Nythara was known for its hunting and fur trade. I wonder if that made its inhabitants equally skilled hunters of the Elvarrans.

"She is one of the lucky ones." Wrath's gaze darkens. "If you remember, there was little to no bloodshed for about five years after that."

I think back to those years. Valentin wasn't off in battle as much as he had been before I left. We would race horses in the gardens, sneak around the castle halls, and stay up all night playing games. They were some of my most cherished years, the ones I always look back upon when I feel homesick.

"Those were peaceful years," I admit.

"It's because we controlled Crossgate and kept it closed most of the time," Wrath says. "Until your brother recently took control of it."

"Yes, that was recently. Maybe five months ago?" I nod, remembering that Timothy and Valentin were away for quite some time at the beginning of the year.

"Since then, humans have been traveling to the base of the Northern Alps, poisoning the roots of the trees and rivers. It kills off the natural wildlife, so we have less to hunt, and it taints our water supply." Wrath's words feel hollow, almost haunted. "We had to burn it away. That's why it's destroyed."

"I see."

I remember what the lands surrounding the base of the Northern Alps looked like. It is scorched and devoid of all life. Liora is equally downtrodden and ghastly, like they were struggling to survive. It is likely why they always requested more supplies and aid from my father. If there are no animals to hunt, they would need a constant supply of rations. They were so desperate for money that they attempted to kidnap me, descending into madness.

"Is that why you traveled to Cathros?" I ask curiously.

When Gilead, Stanik, and Taryn came across me in the gardens, they were scouting for something. The three stealthily scaled the back wall just as I had reached the clearing, killing Timothy with ease. What were they looking for?

"No."

"Then why?"

"Why do you think?"

"I don't know!"

"That's not an answer," he challenges.

"You wanted to find out why the King of Avelisar had traveled to Cathros?" I say the first thing that comes to mind.

"Come on, Raelys." He sounds almost disappointed in me. "You know why."

I don't want to come to terms with it, but deep down, I know the truth. Yet, I feel so foolish, playing right into Wrath's hands. He accepted my deal too easily, binding me to him, leaving this damned mark on my skin.

"Me?" I say softly.

"Yes."

"You knew as soon as you saw my necklace," I state the obvious, still wary of him. "Then why not take me right there? Why accept my deal?"

"You needed to come with me willingly."

"So you could manipulate me into thinking you're some type of savior?"

"I am *desperate*, Raelys," Wrath says despondently. "You are my last hope."

"I'm no one's hope," I whisper, feeling the weight of all of my defeats and disasters compounding into one.

"You're mine."

I'm stunned into silence. The way he looks at me sends a flutter through my chest, but I push it away, denying the desire. I tell myself that it's only the mark that makes me feel this way, yet whenever we're alone, I see a side of him that makes me doubt it.

"Now that I've answered your questions." He reaches out, completing the swirl I made in the banister earlier. "You must answer one of mine."

"What is it?"

"Why do you have those scars on your hands?"

My palm moves to instinctively cover my scarred flesh, even though I know he's seen them. The weight of this burden drags me down like an anchor across the sea floor. Maybe it's best to let go and float to the surface for air. Maybe, by the grace of Itheon, he'll understand that we are both trying to survive in this court of curses and crowns, bound by the expectations around us.

"My governess enjoyed using physical punishment during my lessons," I say vaguely, finally admitting what happened to me.

"How long was she with you?"

"Since I was ten."

"Your governess harmed you for over a decade?" His anger is palpable.

I nod, trying my best not to let my emotions show on my face. It is strange to talk about this with anyone, let alone Wrath. I am ashamed that I was too weak to stand up for myself—that I let Margaret get away with it for all those years.

"I'm sorry." Wrath's words feel sincere. "You are not weak; you are resilient. Your pain will never be a measure of who you are, nor dictate your path."

I built walls so high to protect myself that I forgot what it felt like to see past them. And yet Wrath found a way to break through, gentle where others were ruthless. His compassion runs deeper than anything I've known, and still, I can't help but feel I don't deserve it.

"Thank you…" I lower my hands, no longer shielding them.

Wrath's tender gaze sends a burning flush across my skin. Everything around me suddenly becomes attuned to him. Something stirs in my chest the longer he watches me. My pulse quickens as my gaze drops to his plush lips, wondering what it would feel like to kiss him. The thought sends a shiver down my spine, replacing all common sense and logic with desire and want.

Get a hold of yourself, Raelys.

Wrath's head tilts slightly, as if sensing my thoughts. A silky lock of his hair falls, brushing against his cheek. Wrath's expression is unreadable as an invisible string slowly pulls us together. I go still. He is so close I can count every eyelash. Something curls in my stomach from anticipation as he nears, yet I don't pull away.

The door opens suddenly, and Kieran steps onto the balcony. "Your Majesty?"

My breath catches, and I jump back slightly. Embarrassment scalds me like boiling water. I search for reprieve, my eyes darting to the floor, the mountains, the sky, anything. I was about to kiss Wrath. My adversary was a moment away from shattering the careful restraint we both held.

The urge to flee fills me, and panic slowly consumes all logical thought. My conflicting feelings send me into a tailspin of mortification. What am I doing, pining over the king? I must still be exhausted, my mind not yet back in order from the burnout, nothing more. I am surely misinterpreting the situation. There is not a chance in the seven kingdoms that Wrath would ever kiss *me*.

"Goodnight, King Wrath." I leave the balcony without another glance.

CHAPTER TWENTY-FIVE

I OPEN my door to depart for the day and find Serafina on the other side. Her brown eyes always hold a distant sorrow, and her shoulders slump slightly forward. Her fingers tremble around the slender, leather-bound folio in her grip.

"Serafina," I say in surprise. "Hello."

"The King asked me to deliver this to you." She holds out the folio to me.

"Thank you." I take it from her.

Serafina bows and walks away without another word. I step back and close the door, examining the delivery with curiosity. Untying the thick cord that binds the covers, I flip it open and see a thick stack of sheet music.

Wrath got me piles of sheet music to play on the pianoforte. A sweet gesture—his thoughtful nature beginning to feel more habitual than surprising. Over the past few weeks, I visited the pianoforte, cycling through the same ten or so songs I had memorized, pining for new material. Although I am eager to dash across the castle to play these, I promised Aurelia and Violet a visit this afternoon.

Setting down the folio on top of my copy of the Warlord

Chronicles, I head for the castle's exit. As I descend the front steps, I see Aurelia and Violet waiting for me. Violet is bouncing with uncontainable joy, her face alight with a smile.

They appear far healthier than when I found them, no longer scrawny and sullen. Aurelia's face has regained a healthy warmth, the earlier pallor gone. Violet's hair is no longer scraggly and tangled, now neatly pulled into a bun at the nape of her neck. Both radiate with newfound purpose, and although the scars of their past may never heal, they're on their way to fading.

"Hello, nice lady," Violet greets me.

"Her name is Raelys, Violet." Aurelia corrects her.

"Raewees?" she repeats.

"Close enough." I laugh, holding out my hand for Violet to take.

We walk past the stalls, taking in the assortment of crystals, baskets, and clothing on display. The market is busy today as people move in every direction around us. I appreciate it more than usual, having been in my room resting a lot since I hit burnout.

"Yesterday I saw a squirrel," Violet says excitedly. "It took a loaf of bread out the window."

I laugh. "The whole loaf?"

"It was too heavy, so it dropped it." Violet smiles. "Then it started eating on the ground."

"I bet it was happy," I reply, glancing between the merchant tents.

Zinnia smiles at me as we pass, her curly brunette hair braided atop her head in a crown. She looks busy this after-noon; several patrons surround her booth. We exchange a brief wave before she returns her attention to her work. I need to visit her soon, as the last time we chatted was when I dropped off some extra bottles of wine Alastor gave me.

"We've been busy at the castle," Aurelia starts. "Many guests are visiting from other courts over the next few weeks for some type of ball. I've heard some things, but I'm not sure if it will help you or not."

"Like who?" I ask curiously, wondering what the event could be.

"Duke Nikolas Sterling of Thalvar. Some Elvarrans from Salasyr... I don't know their names. And Miss Penelope Thorne of Corovya."

"Who is that?" I am unfamiliar with the name.

"She is the Duke of Corovya's daughter."

I only recognize Nikolas' name from the time Wrath mentioned him. For the rest, I will have to figure out who they are. "I'm unfamiliar with her. Anything else?"

"I see Master of Coin Harlan Cary walking the halls late at night recently," Aurelia whispers, leaning in close to me. "They've been whispering that he miscounted over ten thousand Platasia from the treasury."

That is some good hearsay. I'll have to keep an eye on it in case the story develops. He may be stealing money to keep for himself, which could lead to more rumors spreading.

"Thank you. Update me if you hear anything else," I say graciously.

"Raelys." I hear someone call my name.

Glancing, I see Stanik and Marek as they walk past us. "Hello." I smile and give them a friendly wave. "Out on afternoon patrols?"

"Yes," Stanik replies, but he isn't focused on me, his gaze glued to Aurelia. "Lovely day out, isn't it?"

"Indeed..." I glance between the two of them. Aurelia's hands fold neatly in front of her as she nervously smiles at him, but she doesn't speak.

"The King lets you outside?" Marek's gruff voice cuts in.

"Yes, Marek." I lighten my tone. "I'm not a prisoner."

"I jest." He chuckles. "You're not so bad for a human."

I laugh. "Only the finest of compliments." I glance back at Stanik, who won't stop gazing longingly at Aurelia. "Well, enjoy the rest of your afternoon!"

"You too." Stannik nods, walking in the opposite direction from us.

Continuing our stroll, I watch Aurelia's cheeks flush as she stares at the ground. I know she's incredibly shy, but her crush is unmistakable. I'm about to ask Aurelia if she and Stanik know one another when Violet cuts in.

"I wanna berrybun!" She shakes my hand a few times to get my attention.

I frown. "I don't even know what that is."

While staying in the North, I encountered many new types of food and sweets, which were quite delicious. However, what I miss most about the food from home is the sea salt. It is our main export in Cathros; it makes everything taste delectable.

"No, Violet. No sweets before supper." Aurelia sighs. "I'll bake some tomorrow."

"Sissy!" Violet whines.

I watch them squabble with one another and can't help but see myself and Valentin. I can't even imagine how he felt when he received the news that Avelisar had fallen, likely thinking that I was gone. Once his grief subsides, he will be fuming, ready to take retribution on the Elvarrans. I wish I could somehow let him know I am still alive and well.

A soft breeze unexpectedly brushes across my skin, drawing my attention. That's strange... it hasn't been windy all day. I glance in the direction of the wind and meet a pair of emerald green eyes watching me.

"Aurelia, I—"

She cuts me off. "Our hostel is a block away. Thank you for allowing Violet to see you. She has been begging me nonstop."

"You leaving?" Violet whines as I bend down to her level.

I hold out my arms. "We'll see each other again soon," I reassure Violet, hugging her close.

"Goodbye, Raewees," Violet replies.

"Listen to your sister for me, okay?" I tell her, standing upright.

"Okay," she relents.

"I'll see you at the castle." Aurelia waves as they depart.

I cross the street towards Sebastian, his smile broadening as I approach. He has this carefree presence today, body relaxed as he leans against the wall. The top laces of his tunic are undone, showing off a part of his muscled chest. His brunette hair is artfully disheveled, the waves brushing his cheekbones.

"Hello, my lady."

"I haven't seen you in a while," I say playfully.

"Are those the girls we had to scuffle in the alley for?" he asks curiously.

I nod. "The very same."

"Then it was well worth it."

"Indeed." I glance back, watching them disappear down a nearby street. "I'm glad I could help them." I turn my attention back toward Sebastian. "How were your travels?" I inquire.

The last time I saw him, Sebastian told me he would be leaving for two weeks, but it has been almost a month. I nearly forgot that he was returning to Khalessor. Dukes are quite busy, so maybe there was more to handle at home than expected.

He lets out a long sigh. "Nothing more riveting than paperwork." Sebastian steps closer to me. "Promenade with me?"

"Sure," I reply warmly, strolling down the street alongside him. "How long have you lived in Ashvarin?"

"All my life. When Gottfried ascended to the crown in Rykaris, he gave these lands to me," Sebastian explains. "I am very grateful to him."

I must tread carefully. "He sounds like an honorable man."

"Very." Sebastian beams. "You shall meet him one day."

That is an interesting statement. It sounds more like a demand than a friendly suggestion. Sebastian acted cold toward me when I asked for favors and inquired about the rebellion, likely due to a lack of trust. I need to bond with him more to encourage him to open up.

I redirect the conversation. "Do you have any siblings?"

He shakes his head. "I am an only child."

"Really?"

"Yes. My mother was a…" he hesitates for a moment. "Courtesan."

If his mother isn't high-born, then how did he manage to rise to the rank of a duke? His father must be an Elvarran lord or perhaps well-connected to Gottfried. It is worth trying to see if he knows anything.

"She must be proud of how high you've been able to ascend." I smile, passing no judgment.

A warm radiance and pride fill his gaze. "Very. This rank has allowed me to take care of her, so she no longer has to work." He folds his hands behind his back. "Your mother is no longer with us, correct?"

I frown. "Yes. Thalia is no longer with us."

My heart breaks slightly at the lie, but I must keep up the appearances of my heritage. No one can know about Isla. The secret must remain hidden at all costs. If people find out, they could see me as the true heir to Rykaris and force me onto the throne. Others may try to ransom me off like those bandits in Liora. If that happens, I may never truly be free. I need to keep moving and find a way to escape these chains that bind me.

"I'm so sorry."

"It's okay." I smile. "It sounds like you're close with your mother."

Sebastian nods. "We are very close. She means the world to me."

"My brother and I are the same." I give him a sidelong glance.

He pauses for a moment, something lingering on the tip of his tongue. I can tell he's choosing his following words carefully. "My king has taken an interest in you," he finally says.

"Is that so?" I reply curiously.

My pulse quickens in my veins, but I keep my mask of indifference on my features. I have this gut instinct that Gottfried knows something. These were the games of court, after all, a constant grab for power and ascension, and perhaps he wants to separate me from Wrath.

"I know you said your ceremony in Avelisar was interrupted, but he's offering you refuge in Rykaris if you're being held here against your will," Sebastian explains.

"Your king's grace is boundless," I lie, a tight smile on my lips. "I can see why you speak so highly of him."

"Thank you."

"As I've said, I'm not being mistreated here." I look around at the piles of snow. "And I'm not sure this is the best time to travel as winter settles."

"Of course." He nods. "I'm merely extending his offer."

"Is there a timeframe by which he needs a definitive answer?" I ask, knowing that his urgency will determine Gottfried's motives.

Sebastian shrugs. "Not necessarily. Once you're in Rykaris, you can send word to your brother."

How dare he hold that over my head.

"Yes, my brother will be pleased to know I'm still breathing," I comment, pivoting the conversation once more. "I do wish we could put this war between the North and South behind us. My time here in Khalessor has made me realize we're not so different after all."

His expression softens. "We're not. We've allowed those in power to convince us we are enemies. It's why I'm drawn to you. You are very open-minded compared to most humans."

"Thank you," I say gently, noting his choice of words. "And your king? What are his beliefs when it comes to humans?"

"The East is known for its leniency on tradition. We have many halflings living in Rykaris," Sebastian replies, dodging my question about the King. "It was once the most popular Elvarran kingdom to reside in."

"What happened?"

"They lost their beloved queen."

My mother. A knife of unease twists in my gut. My mother passed, the curse began, and shortly after, the war broke out. It didn't explain the sudden exodus of the population from Rykaris to Khalessor. People fled Gottfried. Due to laws, taxation, or beliefs, they left him in droves.

They left him for Wrath.

"Do you know what happened to her?" I ask hesitantly, putting our trust to the test. If Gottfried had a hand in killing my mother, then I am going to get to the bottom of it.

"No. All I know is that it was very sudden and unexpected," he replies coldly. "She was incredibly beloved. Rykaris has truly never felt the same."

There's something Sebastian isn't telling me. I can feel it—his previous caution exchanged for a warm willingness to help me escape. Why the change of heart so suddenly?

"Do you think they were in love?" I push him further.

Sebastian's smile wanes. "Sometimes, royals do not get the luxury of marrying for love. You know this firsthand."

I give him a slight chuckle. "Trust me, I know." We turn the corner, stopping at the base of the castle stairs. "How long are you in town for?"

"Until Noctalis."

I nod. "I'll consider his offer."

"Of course." Sebastian bows, striding off.

I can't leave Khalessor yet. If I do, I'll lose all the progress I've made. Aurelia has already proven useful, gathering some gossip in the castle halls for me. Kaia is working on our new business venture. I've swayed many minds at the tavern, blending seamlessly among the townspeople.

I'm ready to take the kingdom down.

CHAPTER TWENTY-SIX

I PLACE a bubbling mug of ale on the table, sliding it toward a cloaked figure. Where I expect a coin in return, a thick black iron key stealthily glides in my direction. Reaching out, I pluck the key from the surface, wondering why someone would give it to me.

"To the back door of our new business. Figured you might not want to be seen going in the front," a familiar, melodious voice says. "It's located on the northwest side of town, next to the lodge."

Tilting my head, I see beneath the hood a pair of dangerous brown eyes and freckled cheeks coming into view. Kaia. Surprise fills me. She followed through and didn't steal my money. Though I'm unsure why she's gone to such lengths to be stealthy.

"I'll stop by as soon as I'm done."

Kaia nods. "See you soon," she says quietly, standing and quickly slipping from the tavern's exit.

I turn to continue my work, trying my best to focus on serving the patrons, but my mind spins with the possibilities. I drop off more drinks, swapping full tankards for empty ones as soldiers and townspeople fill the tables around me. We've been busy; many northerners drink as a way to stave off the cold, warming their bodies from the inside before braving the snow.

As I wipe off a table, my gaze catches on someone as they enter: Gilead. He shakes the snow off his boots, walking to a small table in the corner of the tavern. He leans back in his chair, weary from a long day, still clad in armor.

"Anything to drink?" I ask with a smile, approaching him.

"Raelys?" His brows draw together at the sight of me. "What are you doing here?"

"Yes, I work at the Whispering Willow." My tone is exasperated. "Why is everyone so surprised?"

"Have you looked around?" He huffs a laugh. "It isn't the finest of establishments."

"I like it." I giggle, attempting to loosen his gruff and hard exterior. "So, what are you drinking?"

"Just an ale." He slides a coin for me to take.

Grabbing his drink, I return to the table and slide him the tankard. "Here you go."

"Thank you." Gilead takes it. "And Raelys?"

"Yes?" I whirl, turning back to face him.

"Sorry for almost killing you in the gardens," he says abashedly.

I laugh, not expecting his apology. "I'm not taking it personally." I step closer. "You and I didn't get to chat too much while on the road."

"That's because Taryn can't shut her mouth to take a breath," he says in a snarky tone. "She'll chat your ears off. I'm surprised you could handle it for that many days in a row."

I giggle at his grumpy mood. "I dunno. I kind of like her spirit," I reply. "Where are you from?"

"Valneth," he replies.

Unfortunately, I am unfamiliar with that territory. "Who is Duke there?"

"Duke Leander Vaughn," Gilead replies. "But I grew up there long before he was selected."

"How old are you?" I ask curiously. "You don't look a day over thirty."

Gilead lets out a bellowing laugh. "You're too kind. I'm nearly a decade over that."

I huff a laugh in return. "Well, holler if you need anything else," I say sweetly. "See you around."

"Will do." He nods.

Turning, I cross the room to straighten out some tables that got moved during the last brawl. The patrons slowly dwindle, allowing me to clean up the last of the empty plates and scattered mess.

"Rae, you can take off. It seems like things are slowing down for the night," Alastor says as I drop off a few empty dishes.

I take the coins he slides across the bar top, tucking them into my satchel. "Night, Alastor."

I wave goodbye, turning to exit the Whispering Willow with a mix of excitement and apprehension. As I step out into the cold night, I follow the route Kaia laid out for me. My eyes scan each building on the street as I look for the lodge, wondering which building it is.

Eventually, I come across a manor with a tall wrought-iron fence woven with dense ivy to conceal the building. The tall stone pilasters frame the carved pediment above the door, the ornate details catching my eye. I try to peek inside to ensure I am in the right place, but the windows are covered with thick curtains, blocking my view.

Standing in front of the manor are two guards, each well-dressed and polished. They carry an air of menace to them, as though either could snap me in two with their bare hands. Kaia likely hired them to protect the manor and the women inside, a good choice to keep everyone safe. It doesn't make me any less nervous to approach.

"I'm here—"

"Welcome, Madame," one says, opening the gate for me to enter.

I walk inside, weaving through the thick, maze-like hedges that circle toward the back of the courtyard. I see a small metal door among the brush. Moving toward it, I try the handle, the lock rattling as I attempt to pull it open. I grab the key, fitting it into the lock and twisting it open.

The door thunks behind me after I enter, and a thick wall of scent hits me. Incense and rose assail my nose, alluring and heady. It will cling to my clothes long after I leave. As I walk deeper into the manor, I notice the red velvet settee and luxurious gossamer curtains, each surface designed to encourage indulgence.

As I take in the opulence of the manor, confusion fills me. Surely, a hundred silver did not pay for all of this. Unless Kaia had a secret stash of gold lying around, this is far beyond what we can afford. My only hope is that she did not go into debt to take on such a large business.

Then I hear it.

Soft moans and breathy begs. Lilting laughter and murmured desires. I pass a room, accidentally peeking through the curtains to see a man on his back, a woman bouncing happily on his length. My cheeks flush from the provocative sight, and I quickly tear my gaze away.

"Hello…"

Turning, I see Kaia dressed in an ornate plum gown. Her long bell sleeves drape elegantly at her sides as she clasps her hands in front of her. Draped across her neck is a sparkling jeweled necklace.

"Madame," I greet her warmly.

"Here." She takes my hand, plopping the leather pouch I gave her in my palm.

It's a decent weight. I hear coins clinking around inside. "I don't understand. How did you—?"

"I don't think you realized that was *not* silver." Kaia snorts a laugh. "It's Platasia, a special Elvarran metal mined here in the North. Similar color, but worth about ten times the amount of gold."

I blink in shock, realizing I gave Kaia coins worth around ten thousand. Even more shocking, though, is that Wrath gave me that pouch. When I asked him for money, I didn't think he would give me *that* much.

"Oh," I say in surprise, tucking away the pouch. "Of course," I reply, trying to play off my foolishness.

Kaia loops her arm through mine as we stroll down the hall. "That's your first cut. I suspect we'll make back half of your investment within a month once the rest of the girls arrive."

"Excellent," I muse. "Take good care of them. Ensure they are getting good pay and have breaks."

"Indeed." She nods. "This is real work, and I treat my girls well." Kaia radiates confidence as she walks me through the manor. "Now, about this web…"

My focus on Kaia is easily distracted by the sounds of pounding flesh and loud moans. Everywhere I look is a provocative sight. One has his head between a woman's legs, her head thrown back in ecstasy with her hands lost in his hair. I wonder what that feels like, to be worshipped like that with tongue and fingers.

"Have you never lain with a man?" she asks curiously, noticing my stare.

"A few times…" I reply, feeling a flush cross my skin, still unable to avert my gaze.

"Well, I have plenty of girls who can show you how to please a man—"

"I'm fine." I snap my attention back to her as I try to compose myself. "Is there somewhere less… *stimulating* to speak?"

She snickers at my unease, leading me upstairs. Closing the door behind us, Kaia strides over to a table and plucks a crystal decanter of wine from the bookshelf. She pours us each a glass before leaning lazily against the desk in the center.

"Cheers." Kaia raises her glass in a toast to mine, the glasses clinking together.

"To lofty goals," I reply.

"Indeed." She sips from her wine, her long lashes fluttering closed briefly as she savors the taste.

I take a long pull, noticing the unique taste. It is herbal, with an undertone of spice that is hard to place. It has notes of cinnamon or anise, and the more I drink, the more it grows on me. "There are a few things I need to sort out." I start, swirling the wine.

"Of course."

"Do you know who Casimir Bainbridge is?" I ask curiously.

Kaia hums a soft note, losing herself in thought. "That name doesn't sound familiar to me."

"That's all right." I pivot elsewhere, not wanting to spend too much time on that for now. "There's whisperings of a rebellion going around. I need to find out who leads it." I waste no time telling Kaia exactly what I require. "If Master of Coin Harlan Cary stops by, convince him to divert more funds away from the treasury. He recently miscounted ten thousand silver, so I'm sure he can make a few more disappear."

"*Lofty*," Kaia replies with a saccharine grin.

"There's a ball coming up at the castle. Do you know what it is?" I ask her.

"Yes, Noctalis. It happens every year."

"How many people arrive for this event?"

"Usually all the important *lords* and *ladies* of the land," Kaia says in an almost mocking tone as she takes another drink from her glass. "Highborns love a good party."

"See if you can scrounge up any whispers or secrets for me."

"What kind of secrets?" She raises a sly brow at me.

"Reputation ruiners." I take another drink. "Or blackmail material," I tell her. "The King called Duke Nikolas Sterling of Thalvar to make a deal with him, but I don't know the details. Is that something you can find out?"

"He's not the finest gentleman." Kaia huffs, refilling my glass. "I'm sure he'll stop by eventually."

"Do you know which lord handles the harvest?" I ask. While court is busy partying, I'll have the harvest delayed or sold elsewhere. Causing a famine would be difficult, but if done correctly, it could cause widespread trepidation among Khalessor.

"I'll chat with my girls to see what they know."

I nod, scouring my mind for anything else that could forward my plot. Sipping my wine, I move to my next thought. "Do you know anything about the Duke of Ashvarin?" I ask.

Kaia lets out a dreamy sigh. "Now that's a man who can have his way with me." She stares off in the distance. "Those green eyes and strong arms…"

"Kaia!" My brows raise. "I'm surprised."

"He's a bit too honorable to stop by a place like this." She shrugs. "All men have needs eventually."

"He's taken a sudden liking to me, but I don't trust it. Nor his king," I tell her the truth.

Kaia giggles. "Then we need to practice your seduction skills." She sets down her wine glass, reaching out and untying my corset in the front, pushing my breasts together. "You did much better than that prudish girl I first met at the tavern." Kaia tucks in my dress. "But you can *always* do a bit more."

"What kind of seduction skills?" I stand still, letting her work.

She huffs a laugh. "You think I sit on men's laps for fun?" Kaia steps away. "I pickpocket them! One well-placed kiss, and I'm sneaking off with all of his coin."

"Is that what you meant by a little bit of this, a little bit of that?"

"You're a quick learner!" She smiles. "Men don't fall for you. They fall for what you become in their presence. Some want you to fawn, others dominate, but *all* men love it when you boost their ego," Kaia continues. "So praise their brilliance, then ask them a question, feigning confusion. Men *love* explaining things."

I nod, taking in her advice. I'd seen the evidence of this already at the tavern. A well-placed sigh of dismay could make a man want to help. In comparison, others will ramble on nervously while you remain silent.

"You may think that physical touch is essential right away, but you should *never* give them too much. That's how you lose your advantage," she continues. "Desire is quiet. So look at one eye, then drop your gaze to his lips, then lift your gaze to the other eye. Let their need grow so agonizing that they *must* have you. Make them chase. Make them crave what you haven't given them. That is how you gain control over them."

Kaia smiles. "Then, when they're starving and hollow with need... they snap, finally giving in. And you let them. Let them kiss you, touch you, fuck you until they're brainless." She sips from her wine. "Then you leave. Disappear for days or weeks and let them *burn* in your absence until they can't handle it any longer. Then you have them wrapped around your finger. Because they'll do anything to have you again."

She's right. I am wasting time trying to get Sebastian to trust me when I could be mindlessly flirting with him. Wrath and I have been at each other's throats when I could be swaying his mind with salaciousness. Instead of arguing, I could disarm him.

Kaia opens a second bottle of wine. "Shall I continue?"

"Yes."

CHAPTER TWENTY-SEVEN

I'M PISS DRUNK.

The last time I was this intoxicated was when Lydia and I stole four bottles of wine from the castle kitchens one night. We drank in the gardens under the maple tree so Ulrik wouldn't catch us. We eventually fell asleep under the stars, Valentin waking us early the following morning. The memory left me feeling wistful, missing my closest friend. The longer I ponder things, the more I realize that I don't miss Cathros. I miss the people who live there, like Lydia, Valentin, and Eleanor.

I stumble up the front castle steps, nearly falling as I hold my arms out to steady myself. Glancing up, I see Kieran and Marek, both attempting to stifle their laughter as they watch me. Frowning, I hurry into the castle to save myself from any more embarrassment. I rush through the halls before anyone else sees how inebriated I am.

My eyelids feel heavy. Keeping them open is a struggle— how late is it? Sleep is whispering sweet promises in my ear with each step. The world around me is a haze as I turn the corner, bumping directly into someone. I stumble, grabbing fistfuls of their jacket as I try to stay standing. Their hands grasp tightly around my shoulders, steadying me so I don't fall.

Glancing up, a pair of gray eyes meet mine.

"*Hey*..." I greet him, using all my effort to keep my tone casual.

It is time to put Kaia's advice to the test. Instead of arguing, I will throw Wrath off by flirting. Then, I can ask questions while he's distracted, setting up my game pieces in the shadows.

Wrath assesses my state as he releases me. "Are you drunk, Raelys?"

"Are you *sober*, Wrath?" I mimic, words slurred. Of course, he's able to tell I'm intoxicated simply by looking at me. Nothing ever gets past him.

One corner of his mouth lifts. "Unfortunately, yes."

"That *s-sucks* for you, then..."

"Is that so?"

I shift in my boots. The wine coursing through my veins gives me boundless confidence. I focus on Wrath's lips, unsure of why they look more inviting by the second. Something about his hair is enticing me to run my fingers through it, and I try not to think too deeply about the impulse.

"You know..." I point a finger at his chest. "For the most wicked king in Dratheria, you sure do get me a *lot* of gifts." I step closer. "It's... it's like you *like* me... or sum'thin."

Wrath's hand wraps around the back of mine, causing my skin to heat from his closeness. It's one of the rare times he's not wearing gloves. "You're counting?" he muses. "That must mean you like me, Princess."

I roll my eyes. "Don't flatter yourself."

"I wouldn't dream of it," Wrath replies, his breath grazing across my skin.

"Did... d-did you mean to give me that much coin?" I ask boldly. "It starts with a P... *Plalala*, or something?"

"Platasia," Wrath corrects. "And no, I accidentally gave you an entire year's worth of feudal dues."

I stifle my laugh. "Well... *thank you*."

"You spent it all."

"On *pretty princess* things," I coo.

Wrath steps closer, closing the space between us. "Well, you *are* a pretty princess."

A thrill runs through my body from his gruff voice, but I try not to let it show. His smell is intoxicating, as leather and bergamot invade my senses. Every part of Wrath holds a dangerous edge, like a wolf cloaked in shadow. His magic sweeps across my skin, sending a chill down my spine.

"Are you flirting with me, Wrath?" I raise a brow at him.

"You'd know if I was flirting with you, Raelys."

"That's exactly something a—" A burp escapes my chest, and I feel the familiar burn of alcohol in my throat. "S-something a *scoundrel* would say."

"And what is my menace up to tonight?" he asks gently, thumb slowly running across the back of my hand.

The sensation sends me into a tailspin. No one touches my hands. *Ever.* Wrath passes over every divot and scar with a tender caress. I struggle to remain composed as I go breathlessly still. He does it again. I had aimed to throw Wrath off with flirtation, but now, with only a touch, he is the one catapulting me off a cliffside. Wrath's body is warm as it eclipses mine, all corded muscle and broad chest silently beckoning me to press against it.

"Oh, you know..." I shrug lazily. "Just another day of bringing *r-ruin* to your kingdom..."

A roughish grin forms on his face. It's the second time I've seen him smile. "It's still here. Are you sure your master plan is working?" Wrath taunts.

"The Warlord always says… that victory is not in the clash of s-swords—" I waver on my feet, stumbling slightly. "But forcing y-your enemy to kneel by willpower and… prestige—or something."

"It's willpower and unseen influence," Wrath corrects me. "But close enough."

"*Riveting,*" I reply, unimpressed that he also knows the lines. Someone with his family's name wrote the book—I'm not sure who—so of course, he's familiar with its contents.

Pride shines in his gaze. "You truly have the whole book memorized."

Neither of us drifts away from the other, locked in a battle of wills. I study his features, looking for a crack in his facade so I may slip inside. His dark lashes lower as he slides his hand down, looping his thumb between my pinky and ring finger. It's not a complete handhold, yet the touch feels so intimate that a small breath escapes my lips.

"So do you," I point out, dropping his hand and walking away. My room is a few corridors away, if I could make it on my own without succumbing to the wine. "Why do you have the pages memorized?"

Wrath follows me. "You think my only skill is slaughter?"

I laugh. "You're right, the destroyer of peace must mean something else."

"Where did you find a copy of that book?" he asks.

"I stole it from Cathros's library." My steps are uneven. "When you're trapped within a castle… you end up having a *lot* of free time."

"And now you have busy days?" Wrath's question holds a quiet triumph.

"Yes," I huff. "I have a job, friends, and this Elvarran king who keeps finding himself in my presence." My gaze narrows at Wrath to emphasize my last point.

He hums. "Where do you work?"

"The Whispering Willow…" I sigh, awaiting his scrutiny.

"An interesting choice of employment."

"That's putting it lightly."

"On average, how many fights do you see a night?" Wrath asks curiously.

"I only pay attention when t-they t-take their tunics off," I admit boldly, the alcohol giving me unfiltered assurance.

He raises a brow. "Hiding that salacious side, are we, Princess?"

I erupt in a fit of giggles. "W-wouldn't *you* like to know?"

"Just be careful on the eastern side of town," he warns.

"Why?" My lips quirk up. "Are y-you *worried* about me?"

Wrath ignores my question. I notice he's trailing a step behind me, prepared to catch me if I trip over my own two feet again. My steps slow, and I turn to face him, stopping my advancement.

"Why are you following me?" I ask.

"I'm making sure you get to your room after you nearly toppled me in the hall," he replies plainly, standing before me.

"The King of Khalessor taking time out of his busy night for me?" I say playfully as I turn and continue walking. "You must not be *that* important, then."

"Well, I am a scoundrel." Wrath follows me.

"You accept your fate." I feel a sense of triumph in getting him to admit it.

"Oh, *Princess*," he purrs. "I think it's you who needs to accept your fate."

"What fate?" I sass him.

"That you enjoy it here."

It may be the copious amounts of wine, but at this

moment, he's right—I am thoroughly enjoying my time in the North. I would never give Wrath the satisfaction of knowing that, though. Our banter is like a duel, each line a scheme for the other's surrender.

My smile widens. "Then you've fallen for my plan."

"Your plan to fool me into thinking you enjoy it here in the North?" Wrath muses. "And then what?"

"It's no fun if I tell you—" I stumble while walking down a small step, my arms shooting out to stop my fall as I anticipate hitting the ground.

Arms wrap around me, stopping me mid-air as Wrath bends down and picks me up. "Come on, Princess. Let's get you to bed."

"Careful, too many altruistic deeds... and people might think you're not soooo... *wrathful*," I mumble, my body liquid in his grasp.

"Noted."

My eyelids feel heavy, the world spinning slightly as I drift away in the safety of his hold. I reach up, smoothing a hand down his coat to steady myself. My mark excitedly flares from his touch—the traitor. In my drunken state, I inhale deeply, taking in his delicious scent.

Something crunches against my left hand, and I notice a piece of parchment sticking from his coat pocket. If I distract him, I can take it. There may be something to learn, an important letter to intercept. I must get it from him without him noticing, but how?

Wrath impressively holds me with one arm as he twists the knob, opening the door to my room and walking inside. As he bends down to set me on the bed, I reach up and press my fingers on the very place that would cost someone a hand if they touched—his scar. I gently brush down the length of it, moving closer while my left hand lowers to his pocket.

"Raelys," Wrath warns, his voice a low growl. His body goes rigid as he restrains himself from moving. I trail lower, past his jaw and onto his neck. His breath catches in his throat from my caress.

"Yes?" I whisper, tilting my chin up slowly, inching closer to kiss him.

Wrath pulls back suddenly, the parchment slipping from his pocket. I crumple it in my palm to hide it, lowering it to my side. Wrath's eyes go wide. I've never seen him this visibly shaken before. He clenches a fist at his side. A tick forms in his jaw, the air thickening with unspoken tension.

"Go to sleep, Raelys," he commands in an abrasive tone, storming from the room and slamming the door behind him.

My lips press into a thin line as I take note of his flustered state, feeling slightly dejected. Why didn't Wrath want to kiss me? Is it because I'm a human? It's not like I *wanted* to kiss him. Yes, I simply needed a distraction to take the note, I tell myself. So why do I feel the sting of rejection? Huffing an annoyed sigh, I roll onto my back and unfold the crumpled parchment to read.

King Wrath,

We sincerely appreciate the gift you sent to our Salasyr residence. My Lady Lydia Leonora has expressed gratitude for our union's faith. May Khalessor hold strong with Salasyr's support.

- Duke Alec Wulfstan of Salasyr

I gasp.

"Lydia!" I whisper to myself in disbelief.

Lydia married the Duke of Salasyr? She's here in the North? My mind races with every possible outcome, but I can't figure out why an Elvarran duke would want to marry a human girl. It is possible that Lydia and I have something in common that we never realized? Would she accept me if I told her I was a halfling?

There must be more to this.

CHAPTER TWENTY-EIGHT

My head throbs as I try to remember the details of last night. The sun's blinding rays are my mortal enemy. I rub my face with my palm, trying to clear the fog from my mind, but it's no use. How did I manage to get to bed last night?

I left the manor and then—"oh gods," I say aloud, the breath stilling in my chest. *Wrath.* I don't remember everything I said, but I do remember him carrying me. My gaze lands on the parchment I took from his jacket, and I let out a groan of anguish.

Lydia! Well, at least I made one important discovery.

Getting up is a chore, my head still pounding. I get ready for the day, only having patience to pull on a simple dress. Sliding my shoes onto my feet, I race out the door. I promised Zinnia I would stop by today, but I am unsure how long I've slept in. Hopefully, she will forgive me for being late.

"The birds are lovely today, Princess."

My steps immediately halt.

Quickly turning, I see Aurelia standing behind me. She knots up her hands in front of her as she nervously smiles at me. Aurelia wears her usual kitchen uniform, her hair braided in a way that makes her tall ears poke out.

"Indeed, they are," I reply confidently, scanning the halls around us for anyone of importance. "Come."

Aurelia strolls beside me. "Uhm. I have heard whisperings that Duke Leander Vaugn and Duke Roderick Bainbridge have arrived at court."

Wrath's father.

"Anyone else?" I ask quietly.

"A few other lords, perhaps?" Her voice is unsure as we walk to the front of the castle.

"Do you know if any of them handle the harvest?" I inquire.

"Yes, Lord Cerian," Aurelia whispers.

"Excellent, thank you." I lighten my tone, eyes still scanning to make sure no one is within earshot. "As you were," I dismiss her.

Aurelia bows, turning to return to the kitchens. I walk in the other direction, exiting the castle and heading into town. I pass through a few busy streets and stop at Zinnia's quaint cabin, knocking on the door.

"Come in!" I hear her call from the other side.

I open it to see Zinnia stirring a batter in a bowl. "There you are!" she huffs. "I almost made my blueberry scones without you!"

"I'm so sorry," I say apologetically, moving quickly inside and closing the door behind me. "I got in far too late last night."

"Here, stir this together while I pull out the bread." She hands me the bowl and spoon. Her brown hair is tied up lazily atop her head, and her stray curls hang down to frame her features.

I try to mix with a large wooden spoon, but my hand

shakes against the thick batter's resistance. No matter how I hold the bowl, it slips away from me, my struggle blatant. Zinnia promised to teach me how to cook, but I didn't think I'd be so awful at it from the start.

"Honestly, Raelys, I thought you were joking when you mentioned you've never cooked anything." Zinnia frowns as she watches me. "But now I can see that you were serious."

She plucks the spoon from my grip and sighs. "You should try holding it like this." Zinnia places the spoon in my hand, adjusting my fingers around the handle. "And using more of your wrist."

I do as told, folding the batter with the spoon as I mix. Zinnia drops several handfuls of fresh blueberries into the batter before turning to pull her bread from the oven.

Growing up behind castle walls, I never learned the tasks most do every day. Cooking is entirely foreign to me; this is my first attempt at preparing anything. Cleaning has been another challenge. I only recently managed to make my bed without it looking like a storm had passed through. Now that winter has come, I need to learn how to start a fire. The small hearth in my room has remained cold and unused, leaving me shivering through the nights.

"Rest assured, my governess thought it was pertinent that I learn mathematics before cooking," I say jokingly, getting a warm laugh from Zinnia.

"I can't believe you grew up in a castle!" Zinnia says in excitement. "What was it like?"

"I am very aware of the luxuries that accompanied my upbringing," I start. "For many, your parents raise you to do the tasks your life requires. My father was preparing me to be a king's wife. It is a different skill set. Neither one is more valuable than the other, in my opinion."

"Yes, but what was it *like*?" Zinnia presses me further.

I shrug. "It was quite boring. I had my lessons and waited for my brother to return home from battle."

Her brown eyes go wide. "You never left the castle?"

A smile forms on my lips. "No. Not until I was engaged and shipped off to Avelisar."

Zinnia takes the spoon and bowl from me. She dusts the wooden counter with a light sprinkle of flour before moving the batter from the bowl onto the surface. I watch in awe as her hands gently shape the batter into a round disk with speed and grace.

"And now you're in Khalessor," Zinnia points out. She spreads a thin layer of melted butter over the top and dusts it with sugar. Grabbing a knife, she slices the dough into several triangles and places them on a tray.

"Indeed, I am in Khalessor... for now." There's a hint of hesitation in my voice.

Zinnia slides the tray into the oven, stands upright, and wipes her palms with a towel. "You seem so happy here, though," she replies, cleaning up the dirty surface with a damp rag.

I help her clean, moving to wash a few bowls and spoons in the sink before setting them on a small rack to dry. Zinnia's words sink in further the more I think about them. During my time in Khalessor, I have experienced many things, and my eyes are opening to new possibilities, changing how I view the world.

"Well—"

A knock at the door cuts off my response. Zinnia walks quickly across the room, discarding her cleaning rag with a slight toss. She opens the door and lets out a squeal of excitement.

"Taryn!" She tosses her arms around her sister and hugs her close. "What are you doing here?"

"I was on my way to the castle," Taryn replies, stepping into the cottage as a rush of cold winter air sweeps into the room. "Raelys?" she asks in surprise as she sees me.

"Hi, Taryn." I smile at her, stopping my cleaning.

"What are you doing here?" Her brown eyes narrow.

"Zinnia is teaching me how to make blueberry scones," I explain.

"Come. Sit. I'll make some tea!" Zinnia dashes across the room. "Raelys, have you ever made tea before?"

I consider her words for a few moments. "Hmm... I don't think so."

Zinnia giggles. "I'll teach you." She fills a worn kettle with water, setting it on the stove to boil. Then, she turns and plucks fresh rosemary sprigs from the plant on her windowsill, mixing them with lavender and other crushed herbs.

"How do you two know each other?" Taryn asks suspiciously.

"Raelys is one of my good friends. She brings me extra pastries from the castle and bottles of wine from her shifts at the tavern," Zinnia says, grabbing three cups from the cupboard.

"Does she now?" Taryn crosses her arms over her chest. "I didn't think royals had compassion."

"Taryn!" Zinnia frowns in displeasure.

Taryn laughs, moving from her spot near the door to sit at the table. "I'm kidding. Raelys isn't so bad."

Zinnia huffs, rolling her eyes at Taryn. She pours the hot water into the container with the herbs to steep. I watch her closely, trying to memorize the steps she takes so I can recreate them later.

"And how do you two know each other, Taryn?" Zinnia checks on the scones in the oven.

"I helped escort Raelys across the flatlands to Khalessor,"

Taryn explains. "I'm surprised you're still here. I thought you would've been shipped back to Cathros by now."

"You and me both," I say jokingly, knowing Wrath would never risk that when he still needs me to break the curse. I spoon some honey into the tea and mix it.

"Annoyed with the king yet?" she asks with a devious smile.

I chuckle. Annoyed? Yes. Wrath irks me to no end because the rest of the world fades into insignificance when I'm in his presence. There are these fleeting moments where I catch a glimpse beneath the surface and see who he truly is. The more we quarrel, the more I understand him. It's annoying how well we see one another. But I wouldn't dare say anything about this aloud.

"The blade isn't as menacing as I thought," I reply, pouring the tea into cups and setting them on the table.

"Then you haven't truly seen the blade," Taryn says ominously as she sips her tea. "You don't think he's infatuated with you, Raelys?"

I choke on my tea. The hot liquid burns my nose and throat as I cough and gasp for relief, my hand covering my face. "Of course not!" I scoff, shaking my head. "Don't be absurd."

"Now, that's something I would pay to see." Taryn laughs, relaxing back into her chair.

"How's work been recently, Taryn?" Zinnia asks sweetly.

Taryn rolls her eyes. "Awful! Goddess above, that Penelope woman is a spoiled, arrogant, imperious little—"

Zinnia cuts her off. "Now, now, Taryn. Be nice."

I recognize the name—one of the figures Aurelia had mentioned. A highborn Elvarran woman. I don't know much about her and wonder if I will encounter her at the castle.

"If I have to escort her one more time from Corovya, I will

quit the king's guard," Taryn threatens. "She acts all high and mighty, but she has no idea that her father is *broke*."

My eyes widen. This is my chance to gain some vital information. "No." I mock a dramatic gasp. "Do tell."

"Ten thousand Platasia in feudal dues he didn't pay." Taryn releases her frustrations. "It left hundreds of soldiers without pay for weeks! The Duke of Thalvar had to cover the costs." She runs a hand through her hair. "Don't tell anyone I told you that!"

"I would never tell a soul." I hide my smile as I take another sip of tea. Setting down my cup, I open the oven and check the scones.

"Oh!" Zinnia exclaims. "They look done." She folds a rag to grab the tray from the oven, then sets the steaming pastries on the counter to cool.

Leaning over, I inhale the sweet air from the scones, savoring the lovely scent. "Zinnia, these are exquisite!"

"Thank you!" Zinnia smiles. "It's my recipe."

I pluck a scone from the sheet, blowing on it a few times before taking a bite. It is delicious, flaky, and tart from the berries. I sigh, feeling the tension in my shoulders ease, as the soft, comforting warmth of the pastry fills me.

Taryn stands, taking a scone from the tray. "Good to see you, my dear sister." She wraps her arms around Zinnia's shoulders and hugs her close. "See you around the castle, Raelys."

CHAPTER TWENTY-NINE

"Lord Cerian?" Kaia muses. "Why didn't you say so!" She moves to a drawer, rifling through some parchment and whipping one out. "This is his tab."

My brows raise. "Three hundred gold?!"

"He's here nearly every night." She shrugs.

I'll write a letter and threaten to expose this to his wife if he doesn't accommodate my demands. Aurelia will know which room in the castle he's staying in and could slip it under the door for me. The people of Khalessor will be hungry without food, while the royals party lavishly in the castle, causing resentment to fester.

"Excellent," I reply, grabbing a quill and beginning to write. "Do you know his wife's name?"

"Felicity," Kaia replies. "He's mentioned her to me a few times in passing."

"*Foul,*" I comment under my breath. If a man is unmarried, he can do what he pleases, but to have a wife and spend that much on courtesans is revolting.

"I did try to extort the Master of Coin, but he told me that money was to pay off Thalvar," Kaia explains.

"So I've been told. He covered Corovya in secret," I reply, recounting the gossip I heard from Taryn. "Does that mean Corovya is in financial trouble?"

"It would appear so."

"I wonder why…" I muse, setting down the quill and folding up the letter, sealing it with wax by spreading it across the seam with my thumb.

If I can find a way into Noctalis, then I can observe the highborns directly rather than relying on secondhand information. I can ask Wrath for an invitation, but he will likely find my request suspicious. If this is a sacred event, will the presence of a 'human' sully it?

"Any news of this rebellion I keep hearing of?" I ask her, moving to my next topic.

"No." She shakes her head. "But all rumors are rooted in a bit of truth, so there must be something out there. We're just not looking in the right place."

That is excellent advice.

"You're right." I agree with her. "Where should I look?"

"If the tavern and the manor aren't working, perhaps the castle? Or the gambling hall?" Kaia suggests.

"They're more secretive than that," I counter.

"Hmm…" Kaia hums beside me, tapping her pointer finger to her lips. "Have you ever tried wandering around alleys at night?"

"That's an excellent way to get killed," I deadpan.

She laughs. "Well, shady dealings happen in secretive spots." Kaia is right. I need to gain access to covert places. "Is your web weaving around your target?" she asks curiously.

"Slowly," I reply.

After destabilizing the North, Valentin can launch an advantageous attack when spring arrives. Maybe then, I'll finally be free. If he wins the war, Valentin could conquer the entire continent, forcing the other monarchs to bend the knee.

All of this will be over soon.

Standing, I slip the letter into my sleeve and gather my things. "What time does Lord Cerian usually stop by?"

"Very late at night," she replies. "Around the hollow hour."

I nod. "Thank you."

"See you." Kaia winks as I leave.

Exiting out the back of the manor, I make my way back to the castle. It is about midday, meaning Aurelia is still around. The halls are significantly busier than I've ever seen them, many new faces passing by. My steps are brisk as I make my way to the kitchens, weaving through the crowd. Opening the door, I see Aurelia stirring a large pot of stew, while Bryn and the other girls work on cutting various pieces of freshly butchered meat.

"Hello, Princess, did you need anything?" Aurelia asks warmly.

"Stop by my room after your shift," I tell her, taking a bowl of food with me.

"Of course." She smiles, returning her attention to her work.

Heading back to my room, I kneel beside the hearth, stacking a few dry logs into the center. I close my eyes, trying to feel the magic around me as I open my palm. Inhaling a deep breath, I command, "Fire."

Peeking with one eye, I see no fire emitting from my palm.

I wave my hand from left to right, surging my palm towards the logs. "Fire," I repeat. Nothing happens, causing me to let out a groan of annoyance. "Come on, fire! I'm freezing at night!" I sigh, dropping my arm back to my side.

"Okay... shape, don't take. Shape, don't take." I repeat the mantra over and over as I try to focus. Trying my best not to overcharge, I will the magic into my palm exactly as Wrath taught me.

Several silent moments pass, but then, I feel something. A slight heat creeps across my skin. I squint to look at it. There's a tiny spark forming on my fingertips, but no flame. It fades instantly. Sighing, I open my eyes and drop my hand.

"Think... think..." I tell myself to keep going, refusing to lose motivation.

Picking up a small piece of kindling, I hold it between my fingers as I try to summon the sparks again. I close my eyes and steady my breath. Shape, don't take. Draw from the earth into my fingertips. I feel a fiery spark between my fingers, slowly growing into something hot.

I open my eyes, and the spark fades immediately.

"This is so difficult!" I whine.

The space around me is so quiet, so still. It reminds me of all the time I spent locked in my room back home in Cathros, lying on my back as I counted the stones in the ceiling. It is one of the ways I coped when Valentin was gone. Winter was the one time of the year we got to spend together, the one time my isolation was bearable. Even though we were within the walls, his company made them seem far less constricting.

I flop on my back, holding my right hand into the air above me, aimlessly snapping my fingers as I try to imagine sparks shooting from my fingertips. Since arriving in Khalessor, I have been far from alone. Yet I still feel unfulfilled. What is my purpose? My place? When I'm finally free, I might be able to learn those things. I barely know who I am; my sole focus was on surviving Margaret's abuse and fulfilling the roles my father expected of me. I enjoyed playing the pianoforte and eating pumpkin scones, but didn't dwell on much beyond that.

The longer I think about who I am, the more blank my mind becomes. Like my favorite color, or what season I enjoy the most. I feel like a shell sometimes. Alive but hollow, breathing but not prospering, conscious but never *happy*. All that kept me from hurling myself over my balcony's railing in Cathros were the few good memories with Valentin and endlessly re-reading The Warlord Chronicles. Those pages were my only comfort in the loneliness.

I snap my fingers absently one more time, my palm shifting from hot to cold as a flicker of heat and flame sputters to life in the blink of an eye. It vanishes as quickly as it appeared, my body shooting upright as I gaze at my open palm in shock. Magic, however small and fleeting, emitted from my hand.

There's a soft knock at my door. I stand and open it to reveal Aurelia, who steps inside. She appears tired, her eyes a little weary, but she still radiates a friendly warmth.

"Is there something you need, Princess?" Aurelia asks.

"Do you know where Lord Cerian is staying in the castle?"

She ponders my question for a brief moment, tapping her foot a few times. "I think I've delivered food to his room once before."

"Confirm which room he stays in and slip this under the door for him." I pull the letter from my sleeve and hold it out to her. "When you do, leave as quickly as possible. Do not let anyone catch you, understand?"

Aurelia nods, her brown eyes wide as she takes it from me. "All right."

"This is very important, Aurelia. You must do this soon," I urge her, my voice unwavering.

"Yes, Princess," she obeys.

"Thank you," I say softly. "You've been a great help." I dig through my satchel, pulling out some of my pay from the tavern and handing it to her. "Here."

She shakes her head. "I can't possibly take that much. That's a whole week's pay—"

I take her hand in mine, turning it over and dropping the ten silver coins into her palm. "For Violet."

"Thank you so much, Princess!" She bows. "I'll handle this right away."

"One more thing–!" I call out, stopping her from leaving. I have been purposefully avoiding this for weeks, trying to find the right time to explain her father's death.

"Yes?"

"Your father..." My voice trails off as I try to find the confidence to tell her. "He's no longer with us."

The edges of Aurelia's eyes water. "Thank Seluna." She inhales a shaky breath. "That's a relief."

CHAPTER THIRTY

THE DOOR to Wrath's war room flings open, slamming against the opposite wall with a loud bang. A booming voice fills the space. "Begone. Now." Wrath's voice echoes down the hall, stopping me in my tracks.

"Y–your Majesty—" A voice trembles as a man backs out of the room.

"Hold your tongue. I tire of your voice." Wrath steps out into the hall, homing in on his prey. "She is *mine*. If you ever bore me with such trivial matters again, you'll lose your tongue."

"Yes, Your Majesty." The man takes off, brushing past me as he retreats.

Wrath's jaw flexes, his scar pulling tight. His gaze follows the man down the hall, ensuring he's left. As his focus lands on me, my spine straightens in apprehension. His magic coils like a serpent from his anger, ready to strike.

His expression softens. "Raelys."

"Hello…" I reply hesitantly, trying to pretend that I hadn't witnessed the scene that took place.

"Do you need something?" Wrath asks.

I shake my head. "Just on my way to the gardens."

"Come, then." He enters the room once more, leaving the door open for me.

I glance at Kieran, who stands guard as I pass by. I step into the room. Wrath sits at the table, his workspace tidy as ever. His pen flows with an elegant script across the page as he writes. I notice a coat of arms hanging on the wall, the shield stamped with his family's crest.

"I won't impose if you're busy," I say, wondering if he isn't in the right mood for my antics.

"I figured you'd want to read this." Wrath gestures to an open book. "Since you keep sneaking into the library."

"It was one time," I rebut. Striding over to the table, I study the ancient text. Parts of the ink have faded, leaving me to fill in the gaps. A name sticks out as my fingers trace over the page.

King Ivar Izydor's reign lasted nearly sixty years, bringing forth the Dawnlight Era. Ivar was slain by Duke Warrick Wulfstan of Salasyr, who laid siege to the crown. He was successful, sitting on the throne for eight days before being killed by knight Balthazar Bainbridge. Isla Izydor was crowned queen at sixteen.

"Who is Ivar Izydor?" I ask.

"Your grandfather."

"And Balthazar Bainbridge?"

"My grandfather. His actions ascended my house from common-born to high-born. He was given those lands in Myragos by Isla," Wrath replies, and I glance up from the book to see if there's any sign of jest, but he's serious. "That is what brought on the Age of Blood and Ruin—the previous war of the seven kingdoms."

If Roderick is Wrath's father, and Balthazar his grandfather, then who is Casimir? While my copy of The Warlord Chronicles is battered and worn, the one Wrath gave me did not appear that old. It must have been written within the last decade, as the writing style is more in line with present-day speech.

I'd had the thought before—could Wrath himself be the author? Is his real name Casimir? I don't want to believe that and have been denying the possibility altogether. He's playing tricks on me, a well-crafted plot to get in my head. He wants me to admire him, knowing that I'd spent my whole life studying that book, so that I'll help him break the curse. It is a clever ploy, but I won't fall for it.

"Ivar's death brought on that much outrage?" I ask.

Wrath nods, standing to join my side. "House Izydor was the most beloved house among the Elvarrans. People did not take kindly to the slaughter of an elderly king."

"And Isla's death caused this war?" I continue with my relentless questions, my quest for the truth growing with each new finding.

"It wasn't her death. It was when Nythara attacked the North," he replies, eyes scanning the pages. "The events line up. The curse happened shortly after your mother's last journal entry. She said you were about to turn eleven, and the curse has been in place for thirteen years, making you twenty-four years old, correct?"

"That would be correct," I reply, waiting for him to elaborate.

"I think Isla sealed the magic off out of revenge... or maybe spite," he theorizes. "We simply need to figure out how to reverse it."

Why would my mother do such a thing? What little memories I have of her are all filled with her kindness. She's not a vengeful woman. There's something we are missing, a piece to this puzzle that we're not seeing.

"Is there ever a time when you do not think logically?" I ask, trying to crack that composed mask of his.

His jaw flexes at my insolence. "There are very few times when I do not think logically, Raelys, and every time you seem to be involved." Wrath closes the ancient text, sliding it over and replacing it with my mother's journal.

My brows raise in surprise. Perhaps I get under his skin more than I think I do, as Wrath certainly gets under mine. We clash like hammer and steel, the two of us constantly trying to outmaneuver each other.

"Not this again…" I mutter, pulling off my glove and pressing it into the cover.

A lot of time has passed since my last training session with Wrath. I'm wary of using magic like this again—scared that I'll hit burnout like last time. Worse, I acted like a drunk idiot around Wrath the last time I saw him. I still only have a hazy sense of what happened between us. Nevertheless, he places his hand over mine, causing my mark to ignite. And if I'm being honest with myself… it ignites me too.

"You're nervous," Wrath comments. How he detects the minute shifts in emotion, I'll never know. I feel as though he has a map to navigate me, while I'm left with a blank page.

I pull my hand away as I turn to face him. "Yes, I'm nervous."

"The magic won't work if you're afraid of it," he replies, lowering his arm to his side. "I know burnout hurts. You can't let your fear of pain control you."

"I'm never going to be able to do this." My shoulders slump in defeat.

"Yes, you can," Wrath counters. "You opened the first page."

"I'm just a half-blood—"

"Halfling," he corrects me. "You're a descendant of Seluna. Don't diminish your flame."

Wrath told me the tale of Seluna a while ago. To be honest, I didn't give the story a second thought. If the goddess's power truly runs in my veins, shouldn't I have already been able to open the journal?

"The Warlord would silence their doubts long before the enemy ever could. Right?" Wrath reminds me with yet another word-for-word quote.

"Yes…"

"Nothing is scarier than being an Evokari," he says coldly. "Trust me."

"Why?"

"Most Evokari try to siphon magic from others to gain more power, but end up hearing voices and having surges of uncontrollable emotions," Wrath explains. "Too much manipulation of others can cause mental loops, where the user hears certain phrases or words repeatedly. It causes psychosis and insanity."

"You've experienced that?" I ask softly.

He nods. "The majority don't live past the age of eighteen. It's too grueling to master; they end up taking their own lives."

His sudden admission shocks me—a small glimpse of vulnerability that few could see. It is a testament to his mental fortitude. Do people fear Wrath for his command of this erratic power? They are subservient but always wary, never getting too close to the one who could turn them inside out on a whim.

"Do you feel as if Remedari are more beloved?"

"Remedari have it worse. They take on the pain they heal, many shortening their lifespans on accident if they give too much of themselves trying to heal someone." He sighs. "They often get phantom pains, even though no physical harm is present."

"That's so awful…" I have long viewed magic as mystical and fantastic, but now I see its equally complex dangers.

"You are lucky that you are a Verthari," Wrath says, his voice distant. "Try again."

I return my attention to the journal and press my hand to the leather. Wrath's hand covers mine, now a strange comfort I've grown accustomed to. Closing my eyes, I take a deep breath to focus.

"Attune yourself to the earth first, power second," he guides me. "Find the source."

By source, I assume he speaks of Elderaneth, the well of all magic. I sift through the noise and try to find the spring. My palm erupts, and the magic pushes me back. I go completely rigid as I anticipate hitting the ground. Arms wrap quickly around me as I slam into Wrath's chest. He caught me. I look up at him, our faces close as I search his features for the incoming reprimand or anger.

It's not there.

"It's okay," he reassures me. "You can try again."

"Okay," I whisper.

Walking back to my spot, I try again, letting the magic flow through me as it did last time. My fingertips tingle as energy pulses beneath my skin, seeking connection. A deep hum of energy vibrates through the air as I focus on the journal beneath me.

"You're going to overcharge." Wrath's words snap me out of my trance. "Relax."

I open my eyes, breaking the focus and returning to square one. Wrath is right. I am too eager, trying to grasp too much. That is what's causing me to overcharge. Clearing my throat and adjusting myself, I try again. Searching through the shadows, I let the magic come to me before shaping it.

Wrath's fingers lace between mine, holding my hand. I relax into Wrath, and much to my surprise, he wraps a hand around my waist, pulling me flush against him. His thumb makes slow circles on my hip, and I nearly combust from the touch. Wrath's chin lowers, and I feel his breath hot against my skin. A soft sigh leaves my lips, one of pleasure mixed with contentment as I completely lose track of where I am. Wrath's power caresses every nerve in my body. For a fleeting moment, I surrender to the sensation, utterly *his*.

The book unlocks.

My eyes fly open as I gasp, startling out of Wrath's grip. The journal cover flies open with a thunk, and the pages flutter like a ghost flipping rapidly through them. I stare at it, stunned by the spectacle as the journal moves on its own.

Then, it suddenly stops on a specific page.

Wrath and I both lean over the table slowly to read the journal entry.

10th of the Month of Sunbloom

Today is the happiest day of my life. My daughter was born, Raelys, and she is my light, the very breath in my lungs. Holding her in my arms feels unreal after trying for so long, but Seluna has blessed me with her grace. Raelys is now the reason my heart beats with purpose, and all of my magic flows within her now.

Gottfried is covering for me in Rykaris. My

court is furious with my absence, and I am
unsure of how much longer I can stay. There is
not a day that passes that I do not want to be
parted from Raelys and Ulrik.

Tears well in the corners of my eyes, threatening to fall at any moment. "Fuck," I swear under my breath, stepping away from the table as I try to control my emotions. Sniffing, I shake my head and refuse to let any tears fall.

I will not cry.

I will not cry.

Not in front of Wrath.

"Sorry, I—"

"My mother died giving birth to Barnham," Wrath says distantly. "I never knew her." He plucks a stack of letters from the table. "I have to drop these off. Stay here and read the journal. I'll… return in a few hours."

And then he leaves.

Stunned by his empathy, I wipe the stray tears away with my fingertips. I never knew Wrath's mother was gone. Their father raised them on his own. I pick up the journal and flip through a few more pages.

3rd of the Month of Harvestcall

Raelys is six years old today. She has all the
fire of an Izydor—intelligent, curious, and bright.
I see the strength of Seluna in her, and one day,
she will be the most beloved queen. I want to bring

her back to Rykaris, as I know she'll fall in love
with the kingdom.

My heart aches. She never got to take me. I keep going. I flip to
the very end of the journal, searching for clues about her
death. When I finally find where the entries stop, I read.

25th of the Month of Springsong

My daughter is nearly eleven. The older she
gets, the more she begs me to stay or wails to have
me take her with me. It's raising too much suspicion around the courts, and people are beginning to
whisper. I can only travel to Cathros so many
times under the guise of the peace treaty now that
the war is over.

I have two loves in life, both of whom are in
Cathros. Sometimes, I wonder if my crown is
worth the cost of the time lost with them. I asked
the guild to grant me passage to Elderaneth in
search of answers.

That is her last entry. I set the journal down, bury my face in
my hands, and cry. The Eldertree granted my wish, giving me
enough magic to open the journal and get the closure I so
desperately craved. My thoughts and emotions clash within
me, tangled in a battle I can't seem to win, leaving me with
more questions than answers.

CHAPTER THIRTY-ONE

I'VE NEVER SEEN The Whispering Willow this busy. A full band plays lively music as people dance and sway in the aisles. Every table is brimming with people, the majority of them playing Mystic Runes. Whenever someone loses a round, they have to finish their drink, leaving many patrons devastatingly drunk.

I weave between the busy rows as I slide ale to different tables, dodging flying fists every time a fight breaks out. Some men pull off their tunics and wrestle, a sight I'm not unpleased to witness. When someone loses, they start slinging magic at one another, occasionally singeing the corners of the furniture or the walls with fire.

A strange man is sitting at a table in the corner. His hooded cloak casts a shadow over his eyes, and a scarf wraps tightly around his nose and mouth, concealing his identity. Hints of brunette hair poke out from under the hood, a stark contrast to his deep brown eyes that pierce through the shadow.

"Anything to drink?" I ask, my words catching slightly in my throat.

"No, thanks." His voice is raspy, worn down.

"Oh…" I take in the man slowly, scanning for weapons. Two daggers. A blade hidden in their sleeve. "Any food?"

He reaches out, sliding a gold coin across the table to me. "Give that to Alastor for me."

I pluck it from the table, studying the coin in my palm. I have never seen a gold coin in Khalessor before, and I wonder if it is of incredibly high value.

"What's your name?" My curiosity gets the best of me.

"Zev," he replies calmly.

"It's a pleasure to make your acquaintance." I nod, turning to walk away.

"Yours?" Zev calls out.

"Rae." I smile warmly.

Zev doesn't reply, turning his attention elsewhere. I take the coin to Alastor and slide it across the bar for him to take. "The man in the corner told me to give this to you," I say vaguely, hoping he will fill in the cracks for me.

Alastor takes the coin. "That's a Shadow Weaver."

"What is that?" Confusion fills me. "Like an assassin?"

"They can provide any service you want," Alastor replies. "They only accept payment in secrets, though."

My brows lower. Payment via secrets? I suppose Zev sold the information in return or used it to blackmail people. If Zev gave Alastor a gold coin, did that mean he sold a secret to the Shadow Weaver?

"Interesting…" I glance back at Zev.

"I recommend steering clear of any Shadow Weaver you come across." Alastor notices my gaze. "Best not to get involved in the web of secrets."

"Of course." I nod, giving him a reassuring smile as I step away from the bar. Making my way around the tavern, I stop at the tables playing Mystic Runes. The men usually guzzle their drinks quickly during rounds of the game.

"Another round?" I walk up to one of the tables.

"You're cheatin'!" Kieran yells as he takes his eighth drink of the night, slamming down his cards.

"It's not my fault you're useless at this game, Kieran," Stanik replies, leaning back in his chair. His pale blonde hair is messy, his sleeves rolled up lazily as he holds his cards close.

"Raelys?" Stanik takes notice of me.

"Hello, Stanik," I greet him warmly.

Stanik stands quickly from his seat, tossing his cards on the table and clutching my shoulders tightly. "I need your help," he says with hushed urgency.

I recoil from his sudden closeness. "With what?"

He releases me, stepping back and running his fingers through his hair as he paces around the tavern. Stanik's skin flushes momentarily as he opens and closes his mouth a few times.

"I—you see..." He stumbles over his words. "There is a lady who has caught my eye. Lady Aurelia."

My brows raise from his sudden admission. Before I can reply, Kieran bellows out a loud laugh, slamming his fist on the table a few times as he clutches his side. Stanik shoves Kieran, who nearly falls from his seat.

"Shut it, you bastard." He returns his attention to me. "She won't speak to me."

"She's very shy," I tell him. "She likely also believes that your rank is above hers and is trying to be polite in her role."

"I've seen her with you a few times. Is she your friend? Can you ask her?" Stanik requests.

The things Aurelia endured at the hands of her father are difficult for me to stomach. She's only just learning what freedom feels like. I would hate for her to feel obliged to settle down so quickly.

"Well..." I pause to contemplate things. "She has a sister,

Violet, who is twelve. They can never be separated. They have no parents, and Aurelia is her sole caretaker."

Stanik nods. "I understand."

"I'll think about it," I reply, not fully turning down his request, but not fully accepting either. "Give me a couple of days." I know Aurelia wouldn't be confident enough to speak up for her needs, so I will on her behalf.

"Of course." Stanik returns to his seat at the table. "Thank you, Raelys."

"It's nothing." I smile. "Now, another round of ale?"

"Yes."

I take their empty cups to the bar so Alastor can refill them. Making a quick round to drop them off, I wipe down a nearby sticky table with a rag, straighten out some tables, and gather up the scattered tankards left behind by the night's more rowdy patrons. The scent of spilled ale mixes with faint traces of perfume and sweat from the evening's festivities, a smell I've actually become quite fond of.

"There she is." I hear a voice behind me.

Turning, I see Sebastian. "Hello," I greet him, and can't help the smile that spreads across my face.

"Hello, darling." Sebastian's arm circles my waist, pulling me out of the line of fire as a stone sails across the room, hitting the wall beside us. Someone lost a game of Mystic Runes.

"Were you traveling?" I ask, taking note of his thick cloak and layered clothing. Bits of snow are stuck in his hair, slowly melting from the heat.

Sebastian lets out a sigh. "Yes, and it was more difficult than imagined. A snowstorm caused us to delay our return for about four days," he explains. "That's not why I sought you out, though."

"It's alright to admit that you missed me." I shamelessly

flirt, knowing it will get a rise from him, practicing Kaia's advice.

"I missed you dearly." Sebastian beams, his touch still lingering on my waist. "How have you been?"

I frown. "I must say, I'm not a fan of this cold."

He chuckles. "I can imagine, considering you're used to the South." Sebastian leans in close, whispering into my ear, "Have you considered my offer?"

Sebastian is growing bolder. Gottfried truly wants me separated from Wrath. Based on my mother's journal, I believe that there is no ill will between them. I still don't trust anyone in the North, especially the nobles.

"Sebastian?" I fawn, placing a gentle hand on his chest.

"What is it?" His brows lower, a gloved hand covering mine. Concern fills his features as he steps closer to me. "What's wrong?"

"You wouldn't happen to know anything about Noctalis, would you?" I give him a petulant look.

"It's tomorrow night," he replies.

It's now or never. I must gain entry into this party to see if my blackmail of Lord Cerian was successful. Second, I need to find Duke Alec Wulfstan of Salasyr so I may learn of Lydia's whereabouts. Third, I think it would make Wrath covetous to see me with another man, and I find that highly entertaining.

"That's a shame." I pout my bottom lip. "I'm not invited. I do love a good party."

"Nonsense. You're coming with me," he says without hesitation.

"Are you sure? It won't hurt your rank to be seen with a human?" I pretend to waver, but this is precisely what I want.

"I don't care what anyone thinks." Sebastian gives me a confident smile. "I'll fetch you tomorrow evening." I'm about to speak when Sebastian's eye catches on someone behind me. "Is that a Shadow Weaver?"

I follow his gaze until I reach Zev. "It is," I reply simply, waiting to gauge his reaction.

"Goddess above," Sebastian swears under his breath.

"Have you worked with one?"

Sebastian shakes his head. "Never. I suggest you don't either."

"Why?" I ask, trying not to sound too eager.

"Because they start using your secrets against you." His voice is deadly. "Then you'll find yourself doing things for them to keep your secrets from getting out."

"I see…" My voice trails off as I glance back at Zev. The table is empty, as though he were nothing more than a ghost conjured by my imagination.

"I must depart, but I'll see you tomorrow." Sebastian drops his hand from my waist, moving toward the exit of the tavern.

Sebastian appears a bit shaken from the presence of the Shadow Weaver, and his abrupt departure makes me wonder if he's chasing after Zev. Does Sebastian have a personal experience with the dark exchange he'd warned me against?

Shrugging, I turn back to my work, moving throughout the tables to pick up discarded cups and clean off tables. By the time Alastor lets me go for the night, my eyelids are heavy and my steps slow.

Leaving the Whispering Willow, I turn west and head toward the manor. Kaia may know something about these Shadow Weavers. I'd spent weeks at the tavern, and this is the first time I'd seen or heard of one. I don't like being out this late at night alone, the streets barren and quiet. My steps are quick, the hood of my cloak pulled high to conceal my face. Weaving through the hedges, I open the back door and head upstairs.

I find Kaia pressed against the bookshelf, a man's hand reaching underneath her dress, the two of them passionately kissing. Her fingers thread into his hair as she tilts her legs further apart to give him more access.

"Oh Gods—sorry!" I gasp, quickly slamming the door shut.

I hear Kaia's laughter on the other side. "Come in, it's fine!" she calls out.

Hesitantly opening the door again, I see Kaia smoothing out her dress with her hands, a broad smile on her lips. "Now go be a good boy and finish your guard shift," she coos.

"Yes, Madame," he obeys, passing by me to leave.

The door closes, and I do my best to regain my composure. What am I here for again? *Gods*. Maybe I need to take my pent-up aphrodisia out on a man.

"You know, Lord Cerian is downstairs." Kaia's words break me out of my thoughts.

"He is?" My eyes widen. "Dress me up like one of the guards, quick!" I say urgently, rifling through my satchel for Lydia's dagger.

"Here." She plops a garment bag on the desk for me. "He's in room six."

"Do you have something to cover my face?" I reply, quickly pulling on the pants and coat.

I pull my hair back as much as I can, tying it into a low bun at the base of my neck. Kaia hands me a strip of black cloth, and I tie it around the lower half of my face, just like Zev's had been. Pulling on my cloak and hood, I slip leather gloves on, grab the dagger, and dash for the door.

"Have fun!" Kaia says playfully.

Racing downstairs, I scan each room until I find the one labelled six. Flinging open the door, it slams with a loud bang, startling the people inside. In three long strides, I'm across the room, pressing the dagger directly into his cock.

This is the most deranged thing I have ever done.

Cerian screams. The two girls run from the room, taking armfuls of clothing with them. The door slams behind them as they flee, leaving us alone.

"You didn't heed my letter," I say, then suddenly realize I'm supposed to be a Shadow Weaver. I clear my throat, lowering my voice as much as I can. "Where's the shipment?"

"I-I sent half of it away—"

I press the dagger harder, drawing a small droplet of blood onto the blade, causing Cerian to yelp in pain. "Do you know who I am?" My voice nearly cracks as I try to growl my words fearsomely.

"Y-you're a Shadow Weaver." Cerian's voice shakes. "Look, whatever you have on me isn't true."

"Make it all go away," I demand, forcing my voice to sound baritone. "Send it south to the town of Karnys if you value your *life*."

"That would cause a famine in the North," he replies hesitantly.

I dig the dagger deeper into his cock. "I guess you won't be needing this."

"Wait!" he cries out.

Then I smell something, sharp and pungent. My nose crinkles behind my mask. The scent is unmistakable. "Did you just *piss* yourself?" I say in disbelief, glancing down and then back up to meet his gaze.

Cerian only whines in response.

"What in the—"

"I'll do it! P-please don't hurt me," he sobs, eyes darting between his member and me.

"Make it go away by tomorrow or Felicity *dies*." I give him an ultimatum.

"Not my wife!" His eyes widen in horror. "Please, she's innocent."

"Swear to me!"

"I'll do it." He nods. "I swear it."

I lift the blade, holding it out as I slowly back toward the door. Cerian stays put, a hand protectively cupping his length. My left hand darts out, turning the knob, allowing me to slip out of the room.

CHAPTER THIRTY-TWO

SLIPPING my hand into Sebastian's, I allow him to guide me down the steps and into the castle ballroom. I wear the formal gown Rowena made for me, infinitely grateful for her foresight.

My gown is stunning, the color of rich, fine wine. It has gold sparkles woven into the silk, like tiny bursts of wildfire. The long, off-the-shoulder sleeves hide my mark, draping elegantly across my decolletage. With each step I take, I feel the full skirt sweep across the floor. The tight bodice hugs the curves of my waist. Sebastian slips a gloved hand across the small of my back, guiding me through the crowd.

"Not a single star in the sky burns as brightly as you this night," Sebastian whispers in my ear.

"Sebastian," I say his name with a salacious tone. "Tell me more."

"Every river has emptied itself, thirsting for your beauty."

I giggle, taking him in. I admire Sebastian's brunette hair, elegantly swept back, spotlighting his features. He wears a red capelet fastened at the shoulder with an ornate gold clasp. Beneath it, a long dark coat accentuates his frame. Sebastian radiates pure confidence as we walk, beaming with pride to have me by his side.

"You're excellent with words," I compliment him.

"That's not the only thing I'm excellent with." Sebastian gives me a devious look.

I laugh again. "Now, now, Sebastian."

Sebastian's amorous conversation is a sign that Kaia's lessons are working. It's the friendliest we've been with each other over the past few weeks. I need to focus; nearly every prominent member of Khalessor's court is here tonight. This means I need to appear a certain way, carry myself with a level of grace I've been practicing my whole life, and perform on a gameboard of political chess.

I'll try to blend in, make conversation, and hopefully extract some useful information in the process. My eyes scan the room, and I note each lord and lady locked in performative small talk. Their expressions appear polite, but they are masks. I catch sight of stolen glances in our direction, and conversations turn to hushed whispers.

"It seems my presence is causing a stir," I tell Sebastian.

"Good," he says confidently, his gaze fixed ahead. "Let them look."

I spot Wrath conversing casually with two dukes across the room. One of the Elvarrans holds a dangerous edge, amber eyes gleaming like firelight on a blade. He is tall and lean, with short black hair and a thick beard. He wears a finely tailored coat and pants, his boots polished so brightly they reflect the light.

To his side is a shorter Elvarran, his belly round from too much ale. His brown eyes dart between Wrath and the other duke, trying to cut into the conversation, but his comments often go unnoticed. His golden blonde hair is short, paired with a thick beard.

A short woman with golden-spun hair stands beside Wrath, her arm looped through his. She wears a peony-colored gown with a full skirt cinched at the waistline. Atop her head is a gold tiara with an opal at its center, which catches the light as she moves.

Every time Wrath speaks, she sighs longingly at him, fluttering her lashes and pouting her plush lips. Wrath doesn't acknowledge her as he continues his conversation with the two men, his features an unreadable mask.

"Who is the King speaking to?" I ask quietly.

"Duke Nikolas Sterling of Thalvar and Duke Horatio Horne of Corovya. The lady is Penelope Horne, his daughter," Sebastian says above my ear, stopping me at the center of the room as we turn to face one another.

"I heard about Corovya's financial issues." I rest a hand on Sebastian's shoulder, waiting for the next song to start.

"I have heard whispering of a misplaced bag of Platasia, but it is a rumor," Sebastian replies, leading me into a waltz.

I suddenly put two and two together— the money Wrath accidentally gave me. He blamed his blunder on the duke, refusing to take responsibility for the lost bag of coins. Perhaps he does not like House Horne or value their allegiance.

Without replying, I step forward and allow Sebastian to spin me before returning to his arms. I know this dance. I've practiced it with Margaret so much that every step lives in my muscles. I did not think the North and South would share the same traditional dances, but I am relieved to be able to follow along. My dress swishes at my ankles with each move, precise yet effortless.

I focus on the music, counting the beats in my mind to keep time so I don't distract myself with all the gawking from the crowd. I step away, twirl, and reach out my left hand for him to take. Sebastian grabs it with his right hand, and we move in

opposite directions as we circle one another, weaving between
the other dancers. We return to each other's arms. I feel Sebastian pull me toward him, closing the space between our bodies.
He leads me effortlessly through the dance, the two of us in
perfect sync, rising and falling like the rhythm of ocean waves.

"You're an excellent dancer, Princess."

"So are you, Your Grace." I smile as we dance, and my
gaze darts between his eyes and lips, exactly as Kaia told me
to do.

Sebastian must sense my feigned desire, because he grips
my waist even more tightly as we dance. Although he is
wearing gloves, I can feel the searing heat of his touch on my
skin. Lifting my hand, Sebastian pulls me to him as the music
draws to a close and dips me in a graceful arc. Rising, I spin
one last time and step back, bowing in a low curtsy. Sebastian
places a gloved hand across his chest and bows to me in return.
Smiling, I offer my hand to him once more and allow him to
lead me off the dance floor.

Every pair of eyes is on me.

"Now we've definitely caught attention," I whisper.

"Focus on me," he replies. "No one else matters."

"Sebastian." A voice cuts in.

Stopping, we turn as a tall man with short red hair and
pointed ears approaches us. He has sharp features with angled
cheekbones and precise brows. His blue eyes fix on us with a
piercing gaze, sharp and unyielding.

"Alec." He gives a slight bow of his head. "Raelys, this is
Duke Alec Wulfstan of Salasyr."

I curtsy as well, following Sebastian's lead. "Your Grace."

Is this Lydia's husband? I glance down at his left hand to
see a wedding band around his ring finger, then quickly return
my attention to him. I desperately want to ask, but I know this
likely isn't the right time.

"Lady Raelys." Alec places a hand on his chest and bows his head.

"I heard you got married recently," Sebastian says, flowing effortlessly through the appeasement of socialization. "Is she in attendance tonight?"

Alec shakes his head. "She has come down with some bouts of morning flu. If she is with child, I have no wish to make her travel."

Sebastian gives him a dazzling smile. "That's excellent news. I'm delighted at the potential expansion of your family."

Lydia is pregnant? So soon? About three months have passed since I made my deal with Wrath, and my father shipped me off to Avelisar. Her duty as my lady-in-waiting is complete, leaving her to find a marriage of her own.

"Thank you," Alec says graciously. "Are you traveling back to Rykaris shortly?"

"I recently returned," Sebastian replies. "Is there something I can assist you with?"

"Tell your king he's got a deal." Alec's tone is cold. "Salasyr has had enough of this current regime."

"Of course." Sebastian nods. "I send my correspondence every first day, but if you prefer things not to be in writing, I can send a messenger."

"A messenger is preferred," Alec replies. "If you have time, I'd also like to ask you how you collect tax on the…" his voice fades into nothingness as their small talk continues.

I feel a gaze on me. Without turning, I know who it belongs to—that fierce, unmistakable presence presses against me like a held breath. It prickles down the back of my neck, making it difficult to focus on the conversation.

I relent.

Glancing at the source of the tension, I lock eyes with the person who burns through my restraint in seconds. *Wrath.* He looks at me as if I am his every desire, the air pulling taut between us. It makes the vast space of the ballroom constrict tighter than the corset caging my lungs.

The only color in his black ensemble is a streak of sapphire in his vest. Every hair, thread, and button is in place. I expect no less from him. Perfectly pristine. Unfairly unblemished. Breathtakingly beautiful. He is the embodiment of brilliance itself.

It's the first time I've seen a crown on his head, the thick spires a symbol of sovereignty and dominance that suit him far too well. It is a reminder of who he is, a king whose force shapes the fate of the realm at every turn. I have gotten far too comfortable, too complacent with allowing him into my battlements.

Penelope's arm is in his, and Sebastian's looped in mine. Neither of us focuses on our partner as time slows, allowing several moments to pass. It is wistful—forbidden—both of us locked into our arrangements but craving only one another.

Penelope moves to say something in Wrath's ear, but his gaze does not falter from me, and he says nothing in return. She turns, trying to find the source of his yearning, her gaze eventually locking in on me. She scowls as she yanks on the sleeve of Wrath's jacket. Penelope's lips are moving, but the string quartet drowns out her words.

"Raelys." Sebastian's voice snaps me out of my trance.

"Yes?" I say softly, returning my focus to him.

"Would you like some wine?" he asks, gesturing to the servant with the tray.

"I would." I reach out to grab a glass. "Aurelia?"

"Hello, Princess," Aurelia whispers, holding a tray. "I'm not allowed to talk to the guests."

"As you were, then." I dismiss her, not wanting to get her in trouble.

Taking a sip, I turn my back to Wrath; I do crave his presence, but it's not what I'm here for tonight. Despite my best efforts, I can't ignore his magic lingering in the air. It slithers toward me and brushes against my skin like a caress of silk.

"A productive chat," I say vaguely to Sebastian, missing most of his conversation with Alec.

"Indeed, it was," Sebastian replies. "Are you hungry?"

"Slightly."

"At Noctalis, supper is served at midnight to honor Seluna," he explains.

He slips a hand around my waist, tugging me closer to him. Sebastian's fingertips glide lower across my hip. The gesture is possessive, taking me by surprise. I lift my gaze to Sebastian and watch him study every part of my features as if he's trying to drink them in.

I'm sure Wrath is seething.

There goes my vow of not thinking of him.

"I'll send a letter to your brother, Raelys," he says quietly.

Sebastian told me that sending a letter to Cathros was going against his king's wishes. Now, he's willing to do it to sway me to take his king's deal. It is suspicious, yet I have to play along.

"Truly?" I feign surprise. "Thank you, I'll be forever grateful."

"Of course."

Sipping my wine peacefully, I watch the royals around us converse and move through the room. Strangely, I miss this atmosphere now that I've been away from it for so long. Playing games of court at an event like this has made me realize that I thrive in this environment.

Footsteps approach me, and I turn to see Rowena striding toward me. A smile forms on my lips as I step away from

Sebastian to greet her. She's wearing a large emerald green ball gown with silver embroidery and long sleeves.

"You look stunning, Lady Rowena."

She smiles. "Me? Look at you!" Rowena steps closer. "You look like goddess divine."

"Only due to your craftsmanship." My tone is light as I give her a spin.

Rowena nods, taking in the dress. "Truly one of my best."

"Rowena, this is Duke Sebastian Black of Ashvarin." I introduce the two, causing Rowena's gaze to flick to Sebastian.

"Your Grace." Rowena curtsies.

"Lady Rowena. It is a delight to meet any friend of Raelys." Sebastian nods his head in greeting. "Allow me to depart for a few short moments. I will return shortly."

Sebastian walks away, leaving me alone with Rowena. I drain my glass of wine, handing the empty glass to a servant as they walk past.

"You didn't tell me you were… *acquainted* with the Duke," Rowena whispers, keeping perfect composure on her features.

"I am," I say quietly. "Is there an issue?"

"No, no issue," Rowena deflects. "He's quite handsome."

"There is an issue," I deadpan, keeping my posture perfect.

"Ahem." I hear someone loudly clear their throat nearby.

Turning, I see Penelope Horne standing before me. She is significantly shorter than I am, and has to tilt her head back to look at me. Her jaw clenches so tightly that I see a vein pop out in her forehead. It feels as if she's sizing me up as her opponent, but I don't exactly know why.

"And you are?" I ask blankly.

"Lady Penelope Horne of Corovya," she declares proudly.

"It's a pleasure to make your acquaintance," I reply, my tone light. I'm very familiar with the placations of court. A well-placed smile, or a casual chat, is usually all it takes. Most highborns want to be acknowledged or respected.

My politeness only makes her ire grow. Penelope's brown eyes narrow at me. "I saw the way you looked at him," she accuses.

"At who?"

"The king." Penelope's voice is venomous. "We're set to be engaged soon."

I don't know why, but that stings more than it should. An ache spreads in my chest. My smile wanes. How foolish of me to think Wrath and I were growing closer. That my irritation was fading into fondness, and maybe there was a small part of me that wanted him to feel the same.

"I'm doing *you* a favor by letting you know," she sneers.

The benevolence withers away inside me. Everyone is always hunting for blood, waiting for you to slip up so they can publicly scrutinize you. Penelope is a lady, but sometimes, it is better to bite back.

"I'm not sure how that's possible with no dowry money," I point out.

"My father is a duke," Penelope snaps, clenching her hands into fists at her sides.

"Oh, you didn't hear?" I mock disappointment. "Your father's broke. Ten thousand Platasia, to be exact."

The corner of her lip twitches. Her gaze darts from left to right, checking to make sure no one heard my remark. Penelope steps closer. "He will never love you!" she hisses, her voice low.

I have to stop myself from bursting into laughter. "Gods, you are simple-minded if you think this is about love," I say in disdain. "Love does not stop blades from sinking into flesh or kingdoms from falling to ruin."

"That's enough!" A booming voice cuts into our conversation. "You will not speak to my daughter that way." Horatio storms across the room to where we are standing.

"The Duke of Corovya. Still running from abandoning your post at Crossgate?" I announce loudly, drawing the attention of nearby Elvarrans.

"That's a lie!" Horatio's voice rises.

"You lost control of the passage the moment you chose to abandon it for the sake of your pregnant mistress," I say with scorn. "All of your men died because of *you*."

"You will not accuse me of such things!"

"I don't deal with cowards," I hiss. "Let alone broke ones."

A whip of magic lashes out in my direction in the form of a vine. It strikes across my cheek with a harsh snap, my head snapping to the side—a loud gasp ripples among the crowd. The music ceases. My jaw is agape in shock as I lift my fingertips to my cheek and press into the sore skin. I pull away to check if there's any blood, but see none.

In my rampage, I failed to realize that the Elvarrans have a clear advantage against me with their magic, but I never expected one to hit me with it. The vine slithers back into a nearby floral arrangement, the vase nearly tipping over. The entire ballroom watches the scene with bated breath. A body steps protectively in front of me—Sebastian.

"Only a coward strikes a woman," Sebastian growls. "Leave. Now."

CHAPTER THIRTY-THREE

Horatio looks like he's about to burst. A mixture of humiliation and fury runs through his features before he storms out of the room. Penelope grasps her gown in her hands and quickly dashes after her father. The doors slam shut, their echo the only sound to disturb the stillness. Sebastian takes my hand and pulls me in the opposite direction. He walks me out of the ballroom and into the main castle corridors.

"I leave for one moment to take a piss, and you're out there waging war with one of the great Elvarran houses!" he scolds me as we continue down the hall.

"Sorry… I got a little irate," I apologize.

"A little?" Sebastian scoffs, stopping his advancements as he turns to face me. "Raelys, you have to trust me." He takes my face in his hands and pulls me close.

"I do trust you," I lie. I don't trust anyone in the North.

"Let me take care of you," he says gently. "I can keep you safe, if you'll allow me."

His words stop me cold. The revelry drains from my body, leaving a raw quiet in its wake. I spent my entire life behind walls being told, and sometimes believing, that safety could keep me whole. But safety is nothing more than a gilded lie when we are at war. What I want now is to show my full fire: plans to topple those who keep me small. Never again will I be a fragile piece of crystal kept in the curio cabinet.

"What do you mean?" I ask softly, placing a hand on his chest. I notice his heartbeat quickens beneath my touch.

Sebastian's gaze fills with longing. His gloved thumb runs along my cheek. The gesture is soft, as if he's worried I'll shatter in his grasp. "That I would do anything for you," he replies gently, tilting his face towards mine.

He's going to kiss me. I have to play the part and smooth things over with him after slandering Horatio. It will continue to build trust with him, allowing me to utilize him later. I slowly tilt my head toward him. Sebastian doesn't hesitate, his lips brushing against mine.

Booming footsteps echo down the hall.

Gasping, I startle away from Sebastian, my head whipping around. My body already knows who it is, adrenaline coursing through me, my heart hammering in my chest. Sebastian steps in front of me, as if to shield me from any approaching danger, but there's no protection from the wrath that's coming.

Wrath turns the corner with two guards at his sides— a predator closing in on its prey, measured and deliberate. He clenches his jaw tightly, holding back a fury of words. Wrath's fingers twitch at his side, as if he's itching for a blade to sink into Sebastian's chest.

"Escort the Duke of Ashvarin out of the castle," Wrath commands.

"Wait!" I call out, defensively raising my hands.

Wrath lets out a sinister chuckle. "You and I are going to have a chat, *Princess*," he seethes.

Glancing back at Sebastian, I see the sorrow of the kiss that was stolen from us. He opens his mouth to speak, but the guards reach him first. They press flat palms against his chest and shoulders to force him back. Sebastian goes willingly, sighing as he turns the corner, their footsteps fading down the hall.

"That's a high-ranking member of your court. You can't throw him out; that's bad decorum," I point out, hoping he'll put an end to this. "He didn't do anything!"

Wrath—who is currently living up to his namesake—stops before me. He is a dagger cloaked in velvet, dangerous yet alluring. Wrath's magic rips through me so painfully that I cry out, my hands going to my throat.

"Gottfried wants me in Rykaris," I say against my will.

"I knew it."

"I want to be free!"

"You can't. My magic is etched into your skin," he says, voice deadly. "Doesn't matter where you go in Dratheria, Raelys, my presence will cling to you like shadow to a flame."

I hate that my skin flushes. Hate that I falter even for a moment, because it shows him how much those words affect me. They're possessive, claiming—no one has ever spoken to me like that before, as if I were already his. And gods help me, maybe part of me wants to be.

"If you insist on keeping me here, I will bring ruin to Khalessor," I challenge.

Wrath gives me a wolfish grin. "Do not play the games of war with me, Raelys. You will not like the outcome."

"Is that a threat?" I ask furiously.

"It's a promise," Wrath replies, repeating our discourse from our time at the cabin in Sinaia.

That memory feels like a lifetime ago. The naive, sheltered girl I once was has since brought ruin to a great Elvarran house —with nothing but her words. A remarkable feat for someone once taught to stay silent. We hold each other's gazes, neither yielding to the other as we wage a silent war of wills. Wrath's lips press into a thin line. His posture turns rigid to maintain control. I wonder if he sees the same in me—the fire burning behind my carefully composed exterior.

"Are you jealous?" The realization dawns on me suddenly. "Go back to Penelope, your *fiancée*."

"She's not my fiancée and will *never* be my fiancée." Wrath brazenly corrects me. "You have no idea what that man you were with is capable of."

"And you're the pillar of honor and veneration?" I counter. "The most wicked king in Dratheria has the nerve to critique *my* sense of company?"

"You're one to judge." The scar on Wrath's neck flexes. "When you traded an entire kingdom to save yourself."

His words strike true, hitting the part of me I've repressed since leaving Avelisar. What's worse is that I don't feel a single ounce of regret for my actions. All of those lives were lost so I can be free… and I'm still chained.

I turn, taking long strides away from him as I surge down the hall. My anger boils over as I reach a breaking point. Wrath and I are like wildfire, ready to consume anything in our path, including each other. If we keep going much longer, one of us will burn the other to ash.

"Raelys!" Wrath's voice calls out as he surges after me. It's the closest I've heard him to yelling. His fingers wrap around my right wrist, stopping me in place.

Magic flares up my arm, the mark beneath my sleeve sending a tinge of heat throughout my body. I whirl quickly, ready to unleash my fury on him, when my gaze catches on something. With his arm outstretched to grab my hand, Wrath's sleeve rides up, allowing me to see the inside of his right wrist.

On Wrath's skin is a silver mark that matches mine.

I move in the blink of an eye, shoving up his sleeve before he can stop me. All the air leaves my lungs as I try to make sense of what this means. I trace my thumb over the skin, the magic jumping to life at my touch. It moves closer to greet me, the same way mine moves when Wrath touches me. A realization crashes over me.

I look up at him and feel his heavy breath brush my cheek. "What's this?" I whisper. "Why do we have matching marks?"

"We're bonded," he says in a voice equally low.

I pull away. The tingling sensation immediately fades from the broken contact. Wrath's eyes darken as he watches me, standing deadly still.

"I'm bound to protect you. You're bound not to cross me." He reminds me of our deal. "When you're in extreme pain, I feel it," Wrath reveals, sending a shockwave through me.

"You certainly didn't mean to do that... did you?"

Wrath inhales a sharp breath. "When we made our deal, and we touched hands, the magic within you reached out and took root in me."

Wrath made a mistake—a severe one. That's why he doesn't want me to return home to Cathros. He is trying to figure out the nature of the bond between us. It is why I feel the magic call out to him. His power flows through me, and mine in him—a bond neither of us can break.

"You probably can't think of a worse fate than being tied to me," I say softly, feeling pensive.

I remain suspended in the intensity of his gaze as I wait for his response—two twilight skies of gray, the dawn to my every day and the dusk to my every night. The two of us are a cycle of ruin, a curse with no end. He is the culmination of everything I am not: composed, distinguished, and controlled. Yet he is the source of my every undoing, and the sum of every ache my soul carries.

"You have invaded my kingdom, my thoughts, and my sanity. I have fought many wars, but the one you wage seeks to destroy everything I have worked for." He steps closer, closing the space between us. "You are the bane of my existence. And no matter how fiercely I try to resist, you are everything I desire."

My breath catches in my throat. Every nerve in my body becomes attuned to this moment, to Wrath, as he waits for my response. The world around us slowly melts away, and the magic in the castle walls holds its breath alongside me.

"If I am the bane of your existence, then you are the *plague* of my peace," I counter, losing all sense of logical thought. "Because when our skin touches… I burn for you. I know it's the magic that makes me feel this way, but sometimes it's not—"

"I can do this no longer." Wrath's lips crash into mine.

He takes my face between his palms and kisses me like I'm the air keeping him alive. The kiss is commanding and wild, tempered only by the faintest trace of tenderness. The world narrows to this—his hands, his mouth, the breaking of every wall between us.

I reach up, wrapping a hand around the nape of his neck as I thread my fingers through his hair. Wrath's arm circles my waist as he pulls me through a doorway. Slamming the door behind him, he pins me to it with his hips. Our lips meet once more as he grips my body tightly. Wrath's jaw is smooth against my palm as I cling to him, desperately craving more.

"Wrath…" I whisper his name, trying to get his attention. "We shouldn't be doing this."

"Then stop me." His mouth finds the pulse jumping at my throat.

I tilt my head back and release a soft moan of pleasure.

"Wrath," I repeat his name in a poor attempt to stop this revelry. Secretly, I don't want him to stop—I want to *indulge*.

"Casimir," he murmurs against my neck, breath fanning across my skin.

"What?" I ask in a haze of lust.

"My namesake."

"Casimir…" My brows lower as I scour my mind for the reason why that sounds so familiar. "Casimir… *Bainbridge*?"

"Yes, that's my name."

Then it hits me.

I jolt backwards out of his arms, stumbling over my dress. "You!" I gasp.

Dread fills me. I knew it. I was in denial for so long, refusing to believe what was right in front of me. What I thought was a clever ploy ended up as the truth, and now I've *kissed* the Warlord. Itheon is likely laughing at the irony of my anguish, Seluna, too. And if I could, I would let the castle walls swallow me whole to avoid the mortification I feel.

He gives me a bewildered look. "I what?"

"The book." My breaths turn ragged. This corset feels all too tight, too constricting, too stifling as it cages my lungs.

"What about it?"

"You wrote it."

"I know, that's why I gave it to you," Wrath—no, Casimir replies. "I thought you understood immediately. Isn't that why you stormed out of the library?"

"Is this all some game to you, Wrath—Casimir, whatever your damned name is?" I slowly back away, my dress weighing me down like an anchor.

"Raelys, we've been quoting the lines back and forth to one another for weeks. It was so blatantly obvious, I thought you knew the entire time." Genuine confusion flickers across his features. "I wasn't trying to trick you. It's—"

"I live my life based on those words." My hands tremble at my sides as I come to terms with this newfound discovery.

"I know you do," he says gently. "You and I are two sides of the same coin, Raelys, bound to one another by our oath. Your soul's desire for power and vengeance is a mirror to mine. And you have no idea how beautiful, how bold, how *spellbinding* you are to me."

My heart skips a beat.

"Don't play the games of war with you," I repeat in disbelief. "Is that what you meant? Because you're the warlord? That I couldn't possibly win against you?"

His gaze darkens. "Yes."

My mind is trapped in an endless cycle of doubt as I agonize over every interaction I've had with the King. Each lingering look and fleeting touch replay in my mind over and over. How could I not have seen it sooner?

You are everything I desire.

I would rather burn Dratheria to the ground than give her back.

She is mine.

Wrath's words echo in my mind, taking on new meanings each time I recall them. He has taken root in every part of my mind. It is maddening how my thoughts twist around him like a tunnel with no exit, trapping me inside.

"Raelys."

"I have to go—"

Casimir steps in my path, stopping me from leaving. "Wait." His eyes fill with something I've never seen—anguish. "I know you. You are a viper waiting to strike in the shadows. There is a part of you that reads that book every damned day because it's what you *aspire* to be," Casimir says ardently. "You can release that darkness, Raelys. It is not a flaw. It is your strength."

"You only need me to break the curse," I challenge, my whole world spinning.

"No." Casimir shakes his head. "The curse can go on for an eternity for all I care. I will wage this war until my very last breath before I live in a world without *you* in it."

His words steal the air from my lungs. I've never been desired like that, so completely that it terrifies me. I can't trust it. He's the Warlord, and I'm nothing more than a piece on his gameboard.

"I must go." I head for the door.

This time, he doesn't stop me.

CHAPTER THIRTY-FOUR

CASIMIR BAINBRIDGE.

Casimir *Bainbridge.*

Casimir Bainbridge.

I try to cope with the shock and anguish this revelation brings. My slippers hit the stone as I run, the sound of my footsteps echoing down the corridor. Opening the door to my room, I slam it shut behind me and press my back against it like a barricade.

"I can't breathe." Panic shoots through me as I pace around the room. My fingertips rub at my temples to ease the tension. "I can't—what am I supposed to do now?" I whisper to myself in a frenzy, my mind spiraling. "Think… think…" I repeat, but no ideas come to mind.

The walls feel like they are closing around me. No matter which corner of the room I walk to, it restricts me more. Walking faster, I trip over my gown, my arms flinging out as I try to break my fall. A cry of pain leaves me as I hit the floor, my chest so constricted that every breath is painful.

Tears sting my eyes as I push myself upright, the heavy skirt engulfing my legs and torso. My fingers fumble behind me, clawing at the corset strings. The fabric bites into my skin as I tug and twist, my breaths coming shorter with every failed attempt. Panic rises, hot and choking. I twist harder, nails scraping against the laces, until, at last, one gives way, and the air rushes back into my lungs. Standing, I pull off the dress and stay in my chemise, the cold air settling across my skin. I tuck the gown into the tall wardrobe and step back slowly, trying to calm my racing heart.

It isn't even about the book—the fact that he wrote it. It is this undeniable urge neither of us can resist, drawing us to each other. I should want him gone, should be able to expel him from my desires... but I can't. Instead, I find myself craving the sound of his rugged and baritone voice, desperate to feel the way his hands caress my skin. He worships my body perfectly—rough and unrestrained—and I can still feel his touch lingering on my skin.

I lie down to rest but end up staring at the ceiling. Wrath—Casimir—saw the parts I keep so hidden that even I have forgotten they are under lock and key. He broke past every barrier and unchained my embered soul. He saw my darkness and matched it with his own—neither afraid nor repelled but drawn to it.

The light trickles through the curtains in my room, dawn inching ever closer. I can't shake the realization that I have met *the* warlord. He is real, not some figment of my imagination that I spent years studying. There is a man behind those words on the page—and it's the man I am magically tied to, perhaps permanently. I give up sleep, get out of bed, and dress myself. My eyelids feel heavy, my mind numb from racing in circles. There is no point in wallowing anymore; I must formulate a new plan.

I scan the map Casimir gave me until I find what I'm looking for—the dovecote. I exit my room, quickly heading towards the west wing of the castle. I'm vigilant in the corridor, trying to find an exit. I spot a gate, pushing it open and heading toward a small building at the edge of the inner bailey.

I step inside, looking around for someone who can help me. I notice an older Elvarran, his skin dotted with age spots and hair white as snow. His brown eyes meet mine, and he smiles at the sight of me, a pigeon perched on his right hand.

"Hello, Princess," he greets me warmly.

"H-hello." I blink in surprise, wondering how he knows who I am. "And you are?"

"Irving Kinley of Myragos." He bows politely. "How can I be of service?"

"Pleasure to make your acquaintance," I reply graciously, eyes scanning the room for any sign of Sebastian's seal stamped on a letter. "Did you receive any correspondence from the Duke of Ashvarin?"

Sebastian said he dispatches letters every firstday, which would be tomorrow. His letter will send my brother's fury into a tailspin, and I know he will march north immediately to free me from my captors. I don't want to make him fight an unnecessary battle, not when I'm planning to escape the North soon. If I can swipe the letter from the pile, that will prevent Valentin from knowing my location.

"Unfortunately, I am not allowed to share that information with you, Princess." Irving pets the bird before setting it down on a perch.

"Of course." I give him a friendly smile. "And if I wanted to send something myself?"

"The King has to approve it," Irving replies. "With his seal."

Damnit.

"Thank you." I nod my head. "Have a lovely day."

I turn, exiting the dovecote and returning to the castle. There are a few stray servants and guards who pass by me in the halls, but I pay them no mind. How can I prevent that letter from reaching Valentin now? It isn't as if Casimir will let me send a letter to my brother directly, not when he has made it clear that he wants me to stay here.

That's when it comes to me.

Aurelia.

Heading straight to the kitchen for breakfast, I open the door to see Bryn kneading a large ball of dough. Aurelia cuts vegetables, humming a soft melody to herself. She appears joyful despite the early hour, her attention fixed on her work.

"Morning," I greet them warmly. My gaze scans the crates of food, wondering if Lord Cerian did as I demanded.

"Morning, Raelys." Aurelia smiles, picking up a bowl and filling it with porridge for me. "You're up earlier than normal."

"Thank you." I take it from her. "Yes, I've come to speak with you. Do you have a moment?"

"Me?" Aurelia's eyes widen in fear.

"You're not in trouble," I reassure her, taking a bite of food. "It's a good thing."

"Quickly now, I need her to prepare for the upcoming banquet," Bryn cuts in.

"What banquet?" I ask, curiosity filling me.

She wipes the sweat from her brow. "The dukes are returning to their kingdoms after Noctalis. It's the final sendoff."

"Thank you, Bryn. I won't take any more of your time," I reply before walking out the door and into the hall.

Aurelia follows, her hands folded in front of her. "Is everything all right?" she asks softly. "From the ball…?"

"Yes, everything is fine. Don't worry." I smile reassuringly at her. "Are you familiar with Stanik?"

She nods. "From the king's army?"

"The very same."

"I've done something to displease him?" Worry crosses her expression.

"The opposite!" I place my hand over hers to calm her. "You've captured his eye. He wants to court you. He told me he's tried approaching you before, but you didn't speak with him."

"That's because his rank is far higher than mine." She sniffs. "I was following the rules."

"And you're doing an incredible job." I pat her hand before leaning back. "I told him I would ask you, but the decision is yours. Stanik knows that you and Violet cannot be separated, and he agreed."

Aurelia thinks carefully about my words. I can see the wheels turning in her mind as she considers the offer. "I'll do it!" she says.

"Really?" I say in disbelief.

She nods fervently. "Perhaps I can get Violet an apprenticeship somewhere with his rank. He has a salary much higher than mine, which means we can leave the hostel we are staying at."

"You should let him court you first. There's no need to rush into anything," I tell her.

Aurelia surges forward, hugging me close. "Oh, thank you, Raelys! You've done so much for me. Now I get to marry the lieutenant of the royal guard?"

I laugh softly, my hand rubbing her back. "It's nothing."

She releases me, excitement twinkling in her eyes. "I must return before Bryn is displeased with me."

"Of course." I nod. "Do you know where Alec Wulfstan is?"

Aurelia frowns. "I do not, I'm sorry."

"No need to worry," I reply. "We'll chat again soon."

"Of course." Aurelia smiles as she opens the door and returns to work.

Taking my food back to my room, I promptly eat, sling my cloak over my shoulders, and freshen up before exiting the castle with purpose. I weave through busy streets, heading right for the royal army's training camp.

CHAPTER THIRTY-FIVE

It takes some time to walk to the castle barracks, where I hope I may find Stanik. I walk to the outer bailey, approaching a large stable. Some Elvarran soldiers sneer at me as I pass. Strangely, I don't feel like I'm in danger. Wrath—Casimir—will end any man who lays a hand on me. The knowledge sends a strange confidence surging through me.

"Raelys?" A deep voice calls out.

I stop and see Marek sparring with another soldier nearby. His brunette hair is messy from training, his face smudged with sweat and dirt. He sheathes his longsword into its scabbard as he approaches me.

"Hi, Marek." I smile at him.

"What are you doing here?" His eyes narrow at me.

"I'm looking for Stanik."

"Why?"

"It's personal." I shrug.

Marek walks me to the main building. Pushing open the door, he guides me inside. Barnham and Stanik discuss something with each other, the two of them leaning over the table.

"Why are you here, Raelys?" Barnham eyes me suspiciously.

"I need to speak with Stanik."

"Why?"

"It's about the… offer," I say hesitantly, unsure if I should divulge such private matters to Marek and Barnham.

"I asked for Lady Aurelia's hand," Stanik explains.

"The kitchen girl?" Barnham deadpans.

Stanik nods. "A short promenade, Raelys. Then I must return."

"Sure thing." I clasp my hands in front of me.

We exit the building, strolling through the barracks. The soldiers around us hone their skills with swords and bows despite the freezing temperatures. I wonder if they use the winter season to improve their skills, rather than to rest.

"And?" Stanik asks nervously.

"She has accepted." I smile, watching him light up beside me. "Aurelia hopes you could help her sister find an apprenticeship somewhere to learn a useful craft. She is happy to move into your residence."

"Today is the greatest day." Stanik sighs in relief.

I chuckle. "May the gods bless you both."

"Thank you, Raelys." He stops at the edge of the barracks, turning to face me. "You have done me a great service—one I will not forget."

"I have a task that requires your expert bow," I tell him quietly.

"What is it?"

"You see, someone is sending a pigeon to my brother. I need to intercept it," I tell him the truth, hoping my mark won't burn. "It's supposed to go out tomorrow."

"Then you must wake before the sun rises and meet me at

the castle's west side in the forest," Stanik replies in an equally low tone. "Before they send the morning rounds."

I nod. "All right."

"One favor," he says seriously. "Then we are even."

"Understood." I nod, exiting the barracks.

Entering the castle, I turn left and walk through the busy halls. Due to the number of guests staying for the festivities, the castle is far more lively than usual. I scan each group, straining my senses to hear any side conversations or hushed whispers on my way back to my room.

I spot two dukes in the hall. I recognize them both from Noctalis. The taller, red-haired one is Lydia's husband, Alec Wulfstan of Salasyr, and the menacing, amber-eyed one is Nikolas Sterling of Thalvar. Their conversation quiets as I pass, Nikolas turning to take notice of me. I need to speak with Alec privately, as I'm desperate to know more about Lydia's whereabouts.

"Pardon me," Nikolas speaks.

I stop walking. Nikolas steps closer, his tall form looming over me. He's trying to intimidate me; I see it in the measured stillness of his stance, in the smile that doesn't reach his eyes. But I won't fall for that.

"Your Grace." I give him a slight bow out of courtesy, playing the game.

"You're a long way from home, Princess," he taunts.

"Undoubtedly," I reply plainly, not giving him any information he can use against me.

"All of Avelisar is gone, but you've remained." Nikolas insinuates that something suspicious occurred.

"Really?" I lighten my tone to feign surprise. "I hadn't

noticed." I skirt around every one of his tactics, knowing precisely what he's trying to get out of me.

Nikolas chuckles. "Tell me why the blade is keeping you here."

"I'd like to have a word with Alec." I deflect his question.

"Oh, do you? Sebastian didn't fuck you well enough?" Nikolas sneers. "He's married, concubine."

I bite down on my tongue. He's purposefully trying to get a rise out of me, and I won't allow him to see me squirm. Nikolas is likely taking retribution out on me for when I destroyed Horatio's reputation at the ball, or perhaps I got in the way of one of his plans. Either way, I abhorred this man simply because of the way he talked down to me.

"That's enough, Nikolas," Alec pipes up, stepping closer to us.

"Until next time, *Princess*," he mocks, sauntering away.

"This way." Alec walks in the opposite direction. "You wish to speak with me?" he asks curiously.

"Yes." I walk alongside him. "You wouldn't happen to be married to Lady Lydia Leonora, would you?"

He nods. "I am. Are you acquainted with her?"

I'm in complete disbelief. "She was my lady in waiting back home in Cathros. Lydia is one of my closest friends. When you return to Salasyr, can you tell her I miss her dearly?"

Recognition dawns on Alec's features. "You're the Princess of Cathros?"

I nod.

"Lydia has spoken to me in great detail about you. Her father, Raoul Leonora, is one of my longest trade partners in the South." Alec smiles. "I did not realize who you were when I met you at the ball. Lydia grieved your loss for weeks. I thought there were no survivors from the attack on Avelisar."

My brows raise. "I'm the sole survivor."

"Well, you're very fortunate," Alec remarks.

No one knows about my deal with Casimir.

"Is Lydia happy here in the North?" I pivot the conversation. I care deeply for Lydia. If she is close, then I need to find a way to contact her.

"Very much so. Lydia is soft and kind." Alec's blue eyes grow distant as he thinks of her, radiant even. "I am deeply in love with her."

"I am very pleased to hear that," I reply, relieved she's well taken care of. "Her happiness means a great deal to me."

"You are an excellent friend. Lydia speaks very highly of you," he continues. "I wish I could do more for Cathros. I'm quite fond of the South."

"You are?" I ask in surprise. "Is that why you are pledging your house to Rykaris?"

"I am torn." He sighs. "I am trying to make right for my predecessors' past transgressions. The Wulfstans have a history of being... bloodthirsty."

I nod, slowly taking in his words as I remember the history book I read with Casimir. Warrick's thirst for power caused a war among the Elvarran kingdoms, and Alec has likely spent most of his days trying to repair his family's name.

"If Erynthe allies with Rykaris, that will leave Cathros vulnerable," I explain. "If Cathros falls, then Dratheria is done." I argue my point, hoping he will come to my aid. Perhaps with Lydia on my side, we can sway Alec to protect our home.

"I agree with you," Alec replies. "I have tried to stay neutral for as long as possible."

"I'm working on the King and my brother," I tell him. "Don't decide until spring if you can. I will correct this."

Alec hesitates for a moment, but then relents. "All right."

"Thank you," I say graciously.

"You've got that Valantis fire, I'll give you that." Alec chuckles. "I'm sure Lydia will be begging me to visit you as soon as she knows you're alive and here in Khalessor."

I smile. "I await the day we are reunited."

CHAPTER THIRTY-SIX

DAWN HAS YET TO BREAK, still nearly pitch-black out as I trudge through the deep snow, my boots soaked through. The air holds a biting cold, each exhale accompanied by billowing puffs of white as I traverse through the forest. I step forward, and the snow gives way beneath me, sliding down the small hill in a rush. My feet go out from under me, and I land with a muffled plop.

I groan.

The snow soaks my back within seconds, adding to my misery. I wish to be inside, sitting next to a warm fire with a steaming bowl of soup right now… but I chose this fate instead. Pulling myself upright, I see a glint of sunlight crest over the mountains, and a feeling of relief washes over me. There is nothing like this in the South—no forests teeming with wildlife or winding rivers with tall trees.

"Ready?" I hear a voice.

I startle, nearly tripping and falling again. My head snaps up, and I see Stanik approaching me with a longbow and a quiver full of arrows. He appears to be completely unfazed by the cold, dressed in a simple long-sleeve tunic and pants.

"Yes." I breathe, brushing the snow off my clothing.

"Let's go."

We trek deeper into the thicket, weaving through dense bushes and ducking under low branches. I hear the sudden fluttering of wings overhead, then a loud thunk.

Stanik lowers his bow. "Find it," he commands, notching another arrow into his bow as he waits for the next pigeon.

Turning, I search through the brush for the bird, trying to spot it among the snow. I follow it, circling a tree until I spot it. I bend down and see the king's seal stamped into the wax, a serpent breathing fire. I quickly tuck it into my satchel before returning to Stanik.

"Was that it?" he asks me.

"No." I shake my head.

Stanik lets loose another arrow, and a second bird falls. Blood brightly stains the snow where it lies in stillness. I quickly grab the letter and look at the seal. Stamped into the wax is a lion holding its paw up inside the outline of a shield. I don't recognize the symbol, but take the letter anyway. Before I can ask Stanik what the seal is, another pigeon falls. As I walk to it, the bird flails in the snow, struggling to stay alive.

"Sorry, little one," I whisper as I pull the scroll from its leg, unsure of how much longer I can handle watching these inno-cent animals die in front of me. I see Sebastian's seal—a broken sword emitting rays of light. This had to be it. I recog-nize the symbol from his cottage. "Got it," I tell Stanik, tucking the letter away.

"Good." He nods. "Don't get spotted on your way back."

"Thank you," I reply, trudging back toward the edge of the forest. I skirt along the brush, doing my best to stay hidden as I take the long route back to the streets of Khalessor. Now that I no longer have the cover of darkness, taking a direct route is too risky.

I walk through the quiet streets as a few villagers begin their mornings in the bitter cold. Shopkeepers lift their shutters as the scent of fresh bread wafts faintly through the air, my stomach growling involuntarily. Frost clings to every surface, making the stone pathways slightly slippery as I stroll to the castle.

Entering the main hall, I stop in the kitchens for breakfast. Aurelia rushes over to me, eyes alight. She wears a newer-looking peach-colored gown, her hair braided in a crown across her head.

"Raelys, you've done it!" she whispers in excitement.

"Done what?"

"I am to marry Stanik!" Aurelia giggles.

I huff a laugh. "What happened to courting you?"

"We are! I mean... he is," she replies quickly, stumbling over her words. "I accepted, though. Which means we will be wed in the spring. You'll come to the ceremony, won't you?"

"Of course." I smile at her. Aurelia bounces excitedly before turning and grabbing food for me. "Thank you." I take the plate and pluck a few pumpkin scones from the pile to take with me as usual.

I sit on the edge of the bed, balancing my plate of food on my knee as I rifle through my satchel with one hand. I start with the letter bearing the king's seal. Opening it, I see a long string of numbers spanning the parchment.

A coded message.

I feel the rush of a thrill. I *love* ciphers. I wrote and updated Valentin's cipher several times to ensure no one could thwart his war plans. Pulling out a piece of parchment, I create a chart with letters and numbers. I begin with a fundamental shift cipher, where each letter and number shifts one position forward in the sequence. Casimir would likely never use such an easily cracked method, but I have to check it first. Then, I try assigning each number to a letter and shifting it three down, but that doesn't work either.

I draw four squares on the opposite side of the parchment, filling in the numbers with the usual assigned letters. *Nothing.* Taking bites of my food between scribbles, I think of more advanced methods. What would Casimir use as a keyword? Or did the letters need to be mapped to symbols and then to numbers second? I tap a finger across the parchment as my eyes scan the numbered code. I have to be missing something… a pattern, a name, a word hidden in plain sight.

Grabbing my copy of the Warlord Chronicles, I flip through my annotations in the margins. I pore over the code for hours, trying every method I've learned.

Warlord, wrong. Myragos, wrong. Wrath, wrong. Blade, wrong.

I groan in annoyance, my body growing weary as the day slips into night. With every failed attempt, I crumple up the parchment and throw it into the fire, ensuring there are no remnants for someone else to find. I don't sleep. I flip through every chapter of Wrath's book to look for something to use.

Then, for the sake of it, I try my name. That is also wrong.

Princess.

P-r-i-n-c-e-s-s.

I shift the cipher eight letters to the right and then assign each to a corresponding number. Then, I subtract the set of numbers from the ones on the page, leaving me with a smaller string of numbers. Using the new set of numbers, I reassign them to the shift cipher and convert them back into letters, a process that takes me several hours to complete.

The message transforms slowly under my fingers, each new character revealing a portion of something larger. It's tedious work, but I press on, pulse racing as the jumbled text begins to form words.

"Of course, it's fucking princess," I swear under my breath as I read the message.

> As requested, the camp will move to Thalvar in two weeks. They will stay until winter's end and continue through Crossgate to defend the border.
>
> — C.

Although I cracked Casimir's cipher, I am not sure if it will help me. I can share my findings with Sebastian, but I don't want to reveal that I know the code. If I ever need to send Casimir a secret message, I can use this code to do so—that may be useful. I toss all my scrawling, along with the letter, into the fire and ensure every last bit is ash. I move onto the next letter, tearing open the wax seal with the lion stamped into the center, and to my surprise, it is a message from Nikolas Sterling of Thalvar.

> Send the money from the master of coins directly to Rykaris. Kill the soldiers as soon as they arrive.
>
> — Duke Nikolas Sterling of Thalvar

My eyes widen in shock. Casimir is going to send soldiers off to their death, and what's worse, Nikolas is going to extort money from him as well. I should be thrilled by the prospect, but I'm not. I have grown close to Taryn, Gilead, Stanik, and heck, even Barnham. If they go to Thalvar, it will be their end.

Then, when Casimir is vulnerable, Nikolas will kill him. He

is ready to strike and claim the power for himself. He must be the leader of this rumored rebellion! A horrible feeling of dread creeps into me at the thought of someone like Nikolas sitting on the throne. He's arrogant and cruel and would likely be far more monstrous than Casimir.

Finally, I open Sebastian's letter, expecting to see the message to Cathros. As I read each word, the ground seems to vanish beneath me. My chest tightens, breath catching as I read it again... and again. Two times. Three. Four. I keep hoping the meaning will change, that I somehow misunderstood something. No matter how often I read it, the truth is right there in ink. Everything I thought I knew shatters like a mirror, leaving behind only fragments of deceit.

I will not make the same mistake twice.

Folding the letter up, I formulate my next plan—every word burned in my memory, fueling the fire in my chest. Whatever is left of my benevolence and virtue slowly wither away inside of me, as something far more sinister takes its place. The last of my kindness vanishes, replaced with a vengeance that will make everyone regret the day they ever underestimated me.

I tuck Sebastian's letter into my sleeve, straighten my posture, and turn toward the door. If he believes I will break, he is wrong. He will feel my fury long before I fall, and I'll drag him down into the flames with me.

I exit my room and quickly search for a place to hide the letter. It is too risky to keep it in my possession, but I may need it later. I know the contents, the words already committed to memory so I may never forget these transgressions.

As I leave the room where I hid the letter, I hear hushed voices and a slight struggle around the corner. The sound of shuffling feet and a muffled plea makes me press my back against the wall and lean just enough to see.

Nikolas has Serafina pinned against the wall. A hand clamps around her throat as he forcefully yanks up the hem of her dress. The young girl struggles to breathe, tears streaming down her cheeks as she shakes against his hold.

Against all better judgment, I know I must do something.

"Is there an issue?" I turn the corner and boldly announce myself.

Nikolas freezes, his head snapping in my direction. He releases his hold on Serafina's throat, and I grin at his terror being interrupted. Serafina immediately runs off, brushing past me as she flees, sobbing uncontrollably.

"Ah, the Princess of Cathros," Nikolas says with malice. "This is a rather curious hour for creeping about, don't you think?"

"Cancel your deal with the King," I demand, standing my ground.

His expression turns to one of curiosity as he steps closer to me, his amber eyes piercing in the dim light. "I don't think so. I'm making quite a fortune off this deal."

"I know exactly what you are."

"Oh?" Nikolas stalks closer to me. "Do you now?"

I nod. "The rebellion will not succeed."

"Is that so?"

"I will make sure of it."

Nikolas chuckles. "How cute." He nudges my chin with his hand. "Thinking you can play the games of war with men. Better luck next time, *Princess*."

The lines drawn between us mean one thing—this is war.

CHAPTER THIRTY-SEVEN

RACING down the front steps of the castle, I head west, pulling the hood of my cloak further over my face. The frigid air makes my toes curl in my boots, and my breath puffs in large clouds of white fog. I glance behind me a few times, feeling the sense that someone is following me, but in the dark, I don't see a soul.

It's close to the hollow hour, a time when I'd much prefer to be asleep, but I need to speak with Kaia about Nikolas. Instead of going through the back, I pass the guards at the front, one of them opening the door for me to enter. It's so late at night that I don't worry about anyone seeing me.

I'm halfway down the hall when the front door closes again with a thunk, signifying that someone has entered. There's a familiar prickle of magic that drips down my spine, making me shiver. My steps immediately halt, and my head instinctively whips around out of paranoia.

A pair of grey eyes meets mine.

Oh. *Fuck.*

Turning on my heel, I dash, running as fast as my feet can carry me toward the back door. Casimir's booming footsteps echo down the hall, and his magic wracks through me. I turn the corner and get a few more steps before Casimir's arms tangle with mine. Casimir's palm wraps around my throat, pinning me to the wall. His other hand slams to the wall beside my head, boxing me in with his body. Neither of us speaks right away as we catch our breath, the tension between us ready to snap.

"If you're going to put your hand there, at least tighten your grip—" I start, but Casimir's hand closes, cutting off my airway.

I let out a soft moan as he chokes me. I've never had a man's hand around my throat, and *gods*, I like it. Like the way his body staves off the cold. Like the way I unravel his control despite the indignation on his face.

His gaze flickers with lust as he squeezes again, leaning closer. "You drive me to a level of madness no one else has dared to reach." His patience reaches its limits. "What the *fuck* are you doing here?"

"I could ask you the same thing." I point out, my voice strained.

"Don't make me force it from you," he replies, loosening his grip slightly so I can take a breath.

"What do you think I spent all that money on?" I insinuate, sparing him the details of how I own half of this brothel.

Casimir lets out a haughty laugh. "Such a menace…"

"And what is my scoundrel doing here?"

"*Your* scoundrel…" he purrs. "I was looking for my pretty princess. She left the castle at a rather *suspicious* hour."

"Maybe I wanted you to follow me." My voice is enticing.

"You look good with my hand around your throat." Casimir tilts his head, and our lips brush together.

Casimir kisses me with unbridled need, biting down on my bottom lip and dragging it between his teeth. His tongue sweeps inside my mouth, twirling with mine in a maddening rhythm, his grip tightening around my throat.

Tilting my head, I part my lips and allow him deeper. The world falls away, leaving only the press of his mouth and the air we share between us. I reach up, threading my fingers through his impossibly soft hair. My fingertips graze those tall ears as I steady myself against him, and he shivers in response.

Footsteps echo around the corner, and a sudden rush of ignominy fills me. Someone is going to see us. I turn my head to see who's approaching. Casimir lowers his head, biting down on the hollow of my neck, seemingly unfazed that someone is about to spot us.

"Cass," I whisper. "Someone will see."

"Good." He releases my throat, both hands making quick work of my corset. "Maybe that's what you need. For me to take you against this wall and make you ache the way I ache for you." His words are so provocative that they leave me breathless. "Is that why you led me here?"

Kaia rounds the corner, her footsteps immediately halting at the sight of us. "Whoops!" Her eyes widen at first, but then her lips turn up in a wicked grin. "Don't let me interrupt." She turns and saunters off in the direction she came from, leaving us alone.

Casimir gently pulls down the front of my dress, my nipples pebbling against the chill in the air. His fingertips rub slow circles across my breasts, sending me deeper into a state of lust. My eyelids flutter closed as he pulls and pinches the gentle peaks, a needy moan tumbling from my lips.

Heat spreads through my body as my mark sings from his touch, setting every nerve alight. The aching desire to have him grows stronger by the moment, and I wonder how I denied myself for so long. Casimir's presence is so commanding that it makes my pulse stutter, my body aching to yield. Every touch between us feels like a contest—two forces locked in battle, neither willing to surrender.

"More…" The word tumbles from my lips before I can stop it.

Casimir lets out a low noise of approval. "Say that again…" his voice is like satin across my skin as he trails a fingertip up my thigh, pushing the hem of my dress up.

"*More*," I plead as Casimir lingers over my center, pushing my undergarments to the side and exposing me.

"You're soaked, Princess." Casimir's voice is heady as he trails a finger up my center.

I inhale a shaky breath as I resist pressing my hips toward him further. "Are you going to do something about it?" I provoke him in return, my eyes not leaving his.

Casimir's lips turn up in a wicked grin at my words. "If you ask nicely." He makes slow circles over my clit, teasing me. "Tell me what you want," he commands.

A loud gasp leaves my lips when he plunges a finger deep into me, making me tighten my grip around him. "I need you," I whisper, desperate.

"Louder."

"No."

He lets out a dark laugh. "Oh, you're going to scream for everyone to hear." Casimir pumps his fingers into me, curling them deep.

"Please!" I cry out, my body aching for relief.

"That's my girl," he purrs, quickening his pace.

Casimir adds a second finger, pumping in and out of me at a maddening pace, curling his fingers and reaching *that* spot. I run my palm across his trousers, cupping his hard length. He elicits a growl of pleasure, biting down on my nipple in response. The mixture of rapid sensations quickly brings me to the edge, his fingers filling me to the brim with each steady movement.

"Casimir…!" I loudly cry out his name—waves of pleasure coursing through every nerve in my body as I climax.

He draws out my pleasure with his fingers, moving them in a dizzying rhythm that makes me want him even more. Casimir doesn't stop. He has me gasping and crying out so loudly that I'm sure everyone in the manor can hear.

Casimir removes his fingers from me, lifting his hand to his lips and sucking each of his fingers clean. The sight steals my breath from my lungs, wanting even more. My chest heaves with uneven breaths as I wait to see if he will pull away. He doesn't. Casimir holds me close to him, arm banding around me, my back still pinned against the wall.

I've never felt like this before. And I don't want to stop now.

I slowly unbuckle Casimir's belt, his gaze darkening as I free his length. I lower to my knees, wrapping my fingers around his base and licking from length to tip before taking him in my mouth. I've never met a man I wanted to please so completely, but with Casimir, surrender feels like desire itself.

A slight shiver runs throughout his body as I continue sucking and licking, moving my head up and down his impressive length. I rub his thigh with my left hand as I squeeze his base with my right, feeling his cock tighten in my mouth.

"Fuck…" Casimir's voice is rough, and his hands get lost in my hair. "Raelys."

I glance up at him, his gaze meeting mine as he takes control, quickening the pace of his thrust. His length hits the back of my throat repeatedly. The edges of my eyes water as Casimir pulls me from length to tip, relentlessly fucking my throat with speed. I moan around his length, my hands gripping his thighs to steady myself.

Casimir pulls me to the hilt and holds me there, his hot release running down my throat as I take all of him. He lets out a delicious moan, eyes never leaving mine as his grip tightens around my hair. I lift my head, my mouth leaving his cock with a pop as I lean back and swallow.

Casimir's chest heaves as he catches his breath, his grip tightening at my scalp. Something inside me stirs at how I am affecting him, the King of Wrath losing control over my touch. I slowly rise to my feet, watching as he yanks up his trousers, buckling them. Then, he fixes my dress, covering my breasts and re-tying the strings. He smooths my skirt with his hands, too, the gesture almost possessive, as if he can't bear the thought of anyone else seeing me like this.

He takes my cheek in his palm and kisses me sweetly. It's a real kiss, one that makes my heart flutter in my chest and my stomach coil with excitement. I place a hand on his chest, and his fingers wrap around my wrist. Casimir's fingertips trace the mark on my arm, sending a chill down my spine from the sensation.

He cups my chin between his forefinger and thumb, gently tilting my head to meet his gaze. "Remember this feeling, Raelys. Hold this desire you feel for me into the very core of your body." He trails a slow thumb over my swollen bottom lip. "Because the next time you let another man touch you… you'll realize that no one else can make you feel this way but *me*."

And then he leaves.

I lean against the wall for support, my knees still weak. Lust and need tingle in every nerve, begging for more of his touch. *He's still the warlord.* I remind myself, and I'm magically tied to him in this game of curses and crowns. He is my greatest desire, and yet, he is my greatest downfall.

Kaia comes back around the corner. "What did I say?" she says proudly. "So agonizing that they *must* have you."

CHAPTER THIRTY-EIGHT

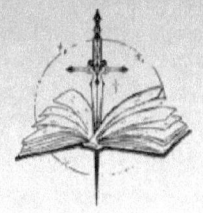

"Hey, Zev." I smile, leaning against his table at the Whispering Willow.

"Rae," he greets me calmly. His features are darkly shrouded as they were previously, his brown eyes piercing through to study me closely. Zev's posture is relaxed as he lounges in his chair, but he is unmistakably alert.

"Business going well?" I ask cheerfully. Zev only stares at me, the air taut with tension as silence stretches between us. "You wouldn't happen to know where I could get something to put in someone's drink to send them into a psychosis but not fully *kill* them… would you?" I lower my voice so only he may hear.

"I do."

"Perfect." I smile at him.

"You know I only accept payment in secrets."

"Well, I have a secret for you…" I whisper. "Duke Nikolas Sterling of Thalvar is extorting money from the King and plans to kill the troops once they arrive in his kingdom."

"Do you have proof?" Zev's raspy voice is barely audible over the noise of the tavern.

I slip the letter from my sleeve and slide it across the table for him to read. Zev's eyes scan the parchment with a scrutinizing gaze as he deciphers the contents. He folds the letter and tucks it into his coat pocket.

"Here." He slips something into my palm. "Scorpion's Haze."

"Many thanks." I smile at him, walking away from the table as I return to work.

Tucking my hand into my satchel, I put the vial away without looking at it. I clean off some tables and bring empty mugs to the bar. Alastor is preoccupied, dragging a man out of the tavern by the back of his tunic and throwing him out the door for not paying his tab.

Hans and Lucio sit at a nearby table, the young soldiers dressed casually as they indulge in lively chatter. Walking over, I smile at the men. "Anything to drink?" I ask warmly.

"Hello, Rae." Hans smiles at me, sliding some coins across the table. "Two ales and beef pottage."

"Sure thing." I nod, then pick up the coins and walk over to the bar. "Two ales and beef pottage," I repeat the order to Alastor.

"We don't have any pottage tonight. There appears to be a lost food shipment," he replies, pouring two ales for me.

That means Lord Cerian heeded my threat, disappearing along with the harvest.

"I see…" I wait for him to pass me the drinks. I did it. Truly did it. Now I can leave the North, flee this place once and for all. I can *finally* be free. All my hard work will soon pay off.

Picking up the tankards, I carry them over to Hans, along with his change. "Sorry, no food tonight." I hand them their drinks. "I believe there's a shortage."

"I heard about that." Hans bristles. "Can you believe that?

While highborns party in the castle, we're here, cold and hungry!"

I nod in agreement. "It's egregious! The audacity to continue festivities while people go hungry."

My plan is working.

"You wouldn't happen to know who Thalvar is allied with… would you?" I pivot the conversation to get some information from Hans.

The warlord—*Casimir*—always says to weaken the pillars that hold your enemies upright. When you chip away at the foundation, the thrones crumble to dust beneath them.

"Thalvar and Valneth are in an alliance," Hans replies, filling in the last piece of the puzzle I need.

"Thank you. Let me know if you need anything else." I walk away.

Gliding effortlessly between tables, I plant seeds of doubt in the hearts of Khalessor's people. Every smile I've offered and every favor I've granted has laid the groundwork for me to unravel the kingdom at my fingertips. It will already be too late when they realize the roots of mistrust have taken hold.

"I heard Horatio is unfaithful to his wife," I tell the soldiers from Corovya. "I saw him pinning a servant girl against the wall at the castle."

Horatio's reputation is already in shambles after Noctalis, but I can't help myself; it's too fun. I feel a sudden rush course through me, a thirst for more power. For the first time in my life, I am the warlord dominating the realm.

The soldiers let out a collective gasp, muttering words of disapproval under their breath. "The nerve after he lost all that money," one soldier comments. "Why bother with this job?"

Moving to the following table, I find my next target. There's a table of young men all playing a game of Mystic runes. "Have any of you heard about the rebellion?" I ask quietly.

One of the young boys nods. "They wear bronze armor and the colors blue and gold. Their banners fly a wolf."

"Thank you." I pat him on the shoulder as I walk away, empty cups in tow.

Moving to the back of the tavern, I make bets with the thieves who frequently throw knives at the makeshift targets on the wall. "If you make this, I'll tell you how the Duke of Thalvar cheats his taxes," I say, causing the men to sneer in excitement. The knives both sink into the bullseye, hitting the mark perfectly.

"Pay up." The rugged Elvarran demands.

I lean in close. "He's got blackmail on several collectors. The treasury is probably overflowing with gold. Sounds like an easy target for looting if you ask me."

The two men eye each other deviously, the wheels turning in their minds as they consider my words. I watch as they flick the knives between their fingertips, itching for the next strike.

"Have fun," I muse, walking away.

The air hums with quiet resentment, every conversation edged like a blade. All of it is my doing. My plotting. My plans. I am the hand that topples kings and brings ruin to courts. The banquet tomorrow will be the final piece; the Scorpion's Haze will end my adversary.

The grandfather clock strikes, signaling the end of my shift. As I leave the tavern, I notice the number of people in the street. Many are wrapped in scraps of long cloth and various blankets to keep warm in the snow, their palms outstretched as they beg for a coin.

"You there, halfling girl!" I hear someone call out.

Turning, I see Renwick hobbling over to me. His wrinkled hands wrap around the front of my cloak as he yanks me forward. Renwick's one eye looks weary and desperate as it meets mine.

"You have to help me," he begs. "I'm starvin'."

Sighing. I pull out two silver coins from my satchel and give them to him. "Here." I place it in his calloused palm.

"T-thank yew." He closes his fingers around the coins. "I haven't eaten in days."

"Are all these people starving?" I ask, already knowing the answer.

Renwick nods, not saying another word before he scurries away. I glance around at all the people on the street as I pass, wondering how they are going to sleep in the snow. The weather is getting severe, and the snow is piling up thickly on the roofs.

I did this.

A pit forms in my gut, but I push it quickly away. I have to bury this remorse temporarily, because if I falter now, all of this will be for naught. We are at war. There are always blades sharpening on the sidelines, ready to strike and claim power for themselves.

I ascend the castle steps, moving quickly through the entry-way. I turn down the corridor that leads to my room, tired from the lack of sleep I got the night before. My body is beckoning for rest with every step, my eyelids heavy.

There's an echo of voices carrying down the hall, and as I round the corner, I see Casimir and Gilead walking towards me. I slow my steps, turning subtly in the other direction to avoid the King. We haven't spoken since our tryst, mostly because I've been battling with my conflicting feelings of lust and deceit.

"Raelys, wait one moment," Casimir calls out to me, causing me to freeze in place. He speaks in a hushed tone to

Gilead, who nods and walks away, leaving us alone. "Where are you headed?"

"Back to my room," I reply, still feeling slightly tense in his presence.

"Then let me walk with you." Casimir closes the distance between us, stopping at my side.

"All right," I relent as we stroll beside one another.

"About last night—"

"You regret it…" I say softly, a crack forming in my chest.

Casimir's hand wraps around mine. "Never."

I catch myself blushing like a fool as Casimir releases me. Even worse, I wish he had held on a little longer. My gut flutters with excitement at the thought that he wants me, causing the warring between my head and heart to grow.

"I… I wanted to make sure you didn't feel pressured," he finally says.

I give him a saccharine smile. "The only pressure was your fingers in my—"

"Raelys," Casimir warns, stopping me from finishing my sentence.

I giggle, enjoying the sight of his shoulders going rigid. It is fun to throw him off, to poke holes in his stern and calculating exterior. I like the way I affect him, but I hate that he also affects me in turn.

My body moves on its own, lingering closer to him as we walk alongside one another, our shoulders gently brushing against each other. There's the familiar sensation of his magic skating across my skin, which is starting to feel less like a prickle of thorns and more like a caress of silk.

"Are you happy, Raelys?" Casimir asks out of the blue.

My brows draw together, my smile waning. "What do you mean?"

"In Khalessor."

The air suddenly pulls taut. My lips part slightly as I shakily inhale, unsure of why I'm hesitating. This is my chance to pull the wool over his eyes. I can use his vulnerability to advance my game pieces. Unfortunately, I can't bring myself to do it.

"It's far better than staying locked inside castle walls," I admit truthfully.

His expression softens. "You're welcome to stay."

My confusion only grows. "I wasn't aware I was leaving."

"I do not wish to cage you," Casimir explains. "The choice is yours when spring arrives. I want you to stay, but I won't force you."

"What about the curse?" I ask in utter disbelief.

"I meant what I said at Noctalis."

I recall the words Casimir spoke to me the night of the ball. I haven't put too much thought into them after finding out he is the warlord. My brother may think that I'm being held captive and march north to attack.

"Won't my staying cause more war?"

"I'd go to war for you."

I stop in my tracks. If I thought I was the one throwing Casimir off, I am wrong. He's completely flipped my world upside down, resetting the hourglass of my reality. I know he means it, too, and that makes my pulse race even more. He's the first person who's given me a choice for my freedom, knowing how much it means to me.

"Don't give me that look." Casimir's voice is low and sultry, stirring something in my gut. "I am no stranger to war, Raelys."

Neither am I.

"Did you send your forces to Thalvar?" I ask quietly, glancing around to make sure we are alone.

I planned to keep the information I learned from the letters to myself, but after our conversation tonight, I decided to share it with Casimir. Nikolas is the leader of the rebellion and is a direct threat to the throne. He intends to kill Casimir's troops when they arrive in Thalvar, and he's about to lose a large part of his army.

Bewilderment crosses his features. "How do you know about that?"

"Don't ask questions you won't like the answer to." I quote Casimir's words back to him; it is the same excuse he used in Avelisar.

"They haven't been moved."

"Don't send them."

"That's a particularly suspicious request, Princess." He raises a brow at me as we stop in front of my bedchamber door. "It appears you know something I don't."

"The warlord always says a divided kingdom falls, but a united one cannot be conquered," I say sweetly, stepping closer to him.

"Is that so?" Casimir tucks a stray hair behind my ear, his fingers not lingering on my skin for long. "It sounds like you had the most prolific teacher."

"Pfft, your ego is out of control," I tease, a grin on my lips.

He laughs, warm and low, like sunlight slipping through morning mist. I find myself smiling, too, excitement pulsing through my veins. Being near him softens the weight I've been carrying, allowing me to relax in his presence.

"I heard there's a banquet tomorrow night." I hope he will allow me to come. Nikolas will likely be in attendance, and I want to watch the Scorpion's Haze in action.

"Are you asking me to invite you?" Casimir's eyes light up with challenge.

I give him an aloof shrug. "I do like a good party."

"Come." Casimir studies me with a quiet intensity, almost

as if he's memorizing every detail of my face. "And slander another duke for me."

My brows lower. "You're not mad I ruined one of your great houses?"

"No, it was quite comical, actually."

"Really?" I blink in surprise.

"Horatio's reputation will never recover after being ousted by the human princess." He sounds amused. "I had no idea that we lost Crossgate due to his actions. You're quite the menace for that, Princess."

"I'm pretty sure you believed me to be a menace long before that."

"To me, yes. But to others?" Pride shines in his gaze. "Absolutely priceless to watch them squirm."

"I didn't start it." I point out.

"Start what?"

"The scene."

"I'm aware," Casimir replies. "Penelope is a pretentious person. It's not entirely her fault; her father has raised her to act that way."

I try to hide my smile. Casimir isn't mad about my spectacle. He actually seems proud of me. Where I expected reprimand, I found approval. And gods help me, that is far more dangerous.

"Goddess above, you are truly something." Casimir notices my thrill. "Delighted to wage war across the seven kingdoms, but distraught because I wrote your favorite book."

"It's not even *that* good of a book." I try to hide the burning in my cheeks.

"Says the woman who has read it hundreds of times." Casimir cups my cheek in his palm, thumb gently stroking my skin.

I want to kiss him again.

"Why did you tell me your namesake?" I ask, genuinely curious to know the answer.

Before Casimir can reply, someone clears their throat beside us. "Your Majesty."

Our heads turn in unison. Barnham stands a short distance away, his gaze fixated on the space between us. His jaw tightens, and his fist crumples the letter he's holding. It's as if our closeness offends him.

"What?" Casimir grinds out through a slightly clenched jaw as he lowers his hand.

"It's urgent." Barnham holds up the crinkled letter.

Casimir releases an angry breath before returning his attention to me. "Tomorrow night." His words carry a quiet promise that we will continue from where we left off, as if we have unfinished business to attend to.

"Goodnight," I reply softly, turning to walk in the opposite direction.

CHAPTER THIRTY-NINE

I DESCEND several winding staircases until I finally find the small room that houses the servants. They are busy washing and folding clothes, cleaning, and doing other small tasks. I scan the room for Serafina, but I'm unable to find her.

An older woman stops before me, bowing slightly. "How may I assist you, Highness?"

"Is Serafina here?" I ask. "I require her assistance."

The Elvarran turns. "Serafina! At once!" she calls loudly across the room, her voice booming with authority.

Serafina dashes from around the corner, a dirty rag in her grip as she approaches us. Her eyes slightly widen at the sight of me, but she quickly curtsies.

"Thank you," I reply softly. "I'll be needing her for a few hours."

"Of course," the woman coos.

Turning, I stride out of the servant's quarters and back into the main halls. Serafina trails behind me like a shadow, gaze locked on the floor. She stays deadly silent the entire walk to my room, entering shortly behind me.

I close the door to my room and open my wardrobe. "I need you to help me dress."

"Yes, Highness."

"Thank you," I say, sorting through Rowena's gowns and picking the best one.

It's not as grand as the one I wore to the ball, but it will do nicely. The dark navy fabric hugs my frame with quiet elegance, the high neck lending an air of poise while the long sleeves trail delicately to my wrists. Simple silver embroidery traces the cuffs and collar, catching the light.

Serafina helps me remove my day dress, leaving me in my chemise. She then bends down to guide the formal dress around my ankles as I pull it on. Sliding the thick fabric over my arms, she tightens the corset strings in the back.

"I asked for you specifically…" I break the silence, hoping she will speak to me. "Because of the other night."

Serafina doesn't reply.

"I wanted to make sure you were all right," I say softly. "As someone who has also experienced that… my heart is heavy with you."

What Olav nearly did to me in Avelisar left a permanent stain on my soul. I'd never felt such horror and dread as in that moment when he shoved me down into the bed. His hands are like a brand on my skin, and no matter how many times I scrub myself in the bath, I can't shake the sensation of his forced touch.

The edges of Serafina's eyes start to water as her composure wavers. "Thank you."

"Does he hurt you?" I ask, treading a fragile line.

A tear rolls down her cheek. I can see her struggling to keep her composure, her breath ragged as she keeps her gaze pinned on the floor. Turmoil rumbles beneath the surface, moments away from erupting. Serafina stands, wiping away her tears. She refuses to look at me, her hands coiled so tightly that her knuckles turn white.

I place a hand over hers, causing her to lift her eyes.

"Nikolas killed my parents. He torments me every time he visits." Serafina finally speaks, her voice filled with sorrow.

"You used to be a lady?" I ask in disbelief.

She nods. "My father used to be the duke of Thalvar."

Her words stun me. Serafina was born into a lavish life, attending parties and social events; her only worry was catching the eye of some handsome lord. Now, her days consist of scrubbing floors and folding laundry, her back aching from labor.

"Would you like to hurt him back?" I say gently.

Serafina watches me closely, searching my gaze for any sign of jest. I allow her to see the ferocity within me and the keen focus of my resolve. Nikolas is my target. He will rue the day he ever thought himself above me. I stitch every thread of vengeance with care, and I will stop at nothing until *his* rebellion ends by *my* hand.

Serafina gives me a curt nod. "Yes."

"Slip this in his drink tonight at the party." I move over to my satchel, pulling out the vial of Scorpion's Haze and handing it to her. The liquid is slightly green in hue and is thick and viscous. "You should also slip a little into a few other cups as well, particularly Leander Vaughn's, if you can. It will make it seem less like a targeted attack. Do not get it on your skin and toss the empty vial immediately out a window."

She nods again, her sadness slowly fading into a determined resolve.

"I will handle the King," I tell her. "You will stay in the shadows."

"I understand." She tucks the vial into her dress.

"Good," I reply firmly. "You are dismissed."

Serafina gives me a small curtsy. "Thank you... Princess Raelys," she says before exiting my room.

Moving quickly, I rummage through my belongings, pulling out the riding outfit Rowena made for me. I set it just beside my cloak and boots, and then toss all of my notes and letters into the fire, leaving no remains. I place my two copies of the Warlord Chronicles on the bedside table, my fingertips lingering over the cover.

Once Serafina poisons Nikolas, he will be incapacitated and won't be able to kill off Khalessor's troops when they arrive in Thalvar. The extra troops will stay here, and the rebellion won't be able to attack without their leader. With the rebellion squandered and the North destabilized, I can slip away in the chaos and finally be free. I have enough money from Kaia to pay someone to take me far, *far* away from here. I dream of a place where no one knows my face or name, and neither duties nor curses can bind me.

I want to be free, but if I am being truthful with myself, it's because I'm not ready to say goodbye. The bonds I've forged in the North are some of my fondest, and I didn't expect to build such a strong companionship with them. I can't stay here. I've done too many awful things. Casimir will never forgive me if he finds out I caused the famine that led his people to starve.

I came to the North because I had no choice if I wanted to survive, but I used this opportunity to play the games of war with Casimir as my opponent—to prove to myself that I am capable. I swore to him that letting me into Khalessor would be his greatest error, but it is mine. This mark on my skin was once my plight, but now it's my salvation, and I've crossed the person I'm falling for.

I scan every inch of my room, slowly taking in the space around me one last time. I may never see it again. It feels different than the time I left my room in Cathros. That version of me is practically a stranger; she was kind, sheltered, and naive.

I am not.

Every part of me breeds vengeance. Lies roll off my tongue like sermon. Manipulation serves as my only companion. I hate myself for it because I *love* it. As I approach the banquet hall, my resolve strengthens. The game of court is one I refuse to lose.

Lifting my chin, I glide into the room with a crafted air of grace and poise, looking for one person in particular. I take note of the gathered guests, filing the details of the guest list in the back of my mind. Breaking from the crowd is Casimir, his long steps crossing the room to greet me. I slip my hand into his, allowing him to guide me through the room.

"Horatio Horne seems to be missing," I say quietly.

"As well as Sebastian Black," Casimir replies in an equally subtle tone. His gloved hand wraps around my waist as his thumb makes maddeningly slow circles across my hip.

Sebastian isn't here? That is odd. I haven't seen him since the night at the ball. Perhaps he traveled back to Rykaris? But that can't be; now that winter has fully set in, the snow is thick and the land barren, making traveling long distances far too much of a challenge. Sebastian also wanted me to take his king's deal; he wouldn't give up and leave that easily, would he?

"Wine?" Casimir nods to a passing servant with a tray of wine.

I lock eyes with Serafina, who only stares at me with silent determination in her gaze. Casimir reaches to pick one up, and a sudden realization shoots through me. With Serafina holding trays with several goblets, not serving each glass individually, I have no idea which goblets contain poison and which ones don't.

"Don't drink," I whisper, and his hand freezes.

Casimir's arm lowers. "You know something I don't."

"Do you trust me?" I'm stunned by my question.

His grip slightly tightens around my waist. "I do."

I want to tell him of the attack and Nikolas' plans to betray him—that he's the leader of the rebellion—but I can't. Eyes follow my every movement like daggers waiting to strike. I take note of the long table of food, the display of wealth and prosperity, while the town is in shambles. Highborns never go hungry. I should have crafted a better plan, one that would have had a more direct impact on them.

"Your Majesty." Barnham approaches us. "A word, please."

"One moment." Casimir drops his hand from my waist and walks away.

I'm left adrift in a sea of staring royals. I don't blame them, not after what happened with Horatio. They are justified in being wary of me. I don't mind the ones who stare; after all, I'm the human among them.

"Princess." Someone approaches me.

A man stands to my right. He faces the room, keeping a watchful gaze on the people around him. The man is tall, his short black hair streaked with strands of gray, thin age lines etched into his face. There is a familiar force to his presence... unyielding and powerful, like a violent storm.

Casimir's father.

"Your Grace," I comment, returning my focus to the room. "Roderick, correct?"

"You would be correct." His voice is a low baritone with a stern edge. "A question, if I may?"

I don't reply right away. The longer I wait, the more Roderick's magic digs into me like thorns. Clenching my jaw tightly, I inhale a sharp breath as I try to bear the pain without letting it show. He is going to force something out of me, the same way Casimir does.

Roderick can't find out about the things I've done. It will ruin all of my plans. I bite the inside of my cheek and hold my breath, fighting the magic as it claws deeper into me. Roderick can't know. Casimir can't know. No one can know the awful things I've done.

A scream pierces the room.

The sound of glass shattering reaches my ears, and wine spills onto the floor as Nikolas falls to his knees, his head between his hands. I spot Serafina slipping out the doors as the entire room focuses on the scene. Nikolas spirals into a rampage, throwing punches and waving his arms wildly through the air, shoving people over in the crowd.

"Get them off me!" he screams in agony, fingers tearing his skin as he tries to fight off the invisible force that's swallowing him whole. Nikolas falls over the banquet table, the food crashing to the floor as he knocks it over.

I feel a piercing gaze on me.

Turning my head, I meet Roderick's stare.

CHAPTER FORTY

DUKE LEANDER VAUGHN of Valneth also exhibits signs of madness, bashing his head against the wall, blood running down his face and dripping onto the stone below. Guards rush across the room in an attempt to calm Leander, but he only takes a sword from his belt and stabs it into the gut of another, causing a mass panic as people flee the room.

Someone grabs a piece of shattered glass from the floor to examine it, sniffing the liquid before calling out. "Scorpion's Haze! Don't drink the wine!"

The room descends into chaos. Nobles scatter in a frenzy, pushing one another out of the way as they race for the doors. The thunder of hurried footsteps and the sharp edge of panicked cries fill the chamber as wine glasses fall. Glass shards scatter across the stone, coating the floor with red, causing people to slip as they flee.

"My, Princess, you seem rather relaxed given the circumstance," Roderick points out.

Shit. I stood there in silence, watching the manic scene unfold before me without reacting. I didn't gasp or flinch, my face an unreadable calm mask while others ran for their lives.

It is my error—not playing the part, letting Roderick observe me so closely.

I lift my gaze to meet his. "So are you," I counter.

"Was that truly necessary?" Roderick's voice turns harsh.

"Nikolas is the leader of the rebellion," I whisper.

"Then you should have told the King that."

"I was going to tell Casimir myself, but he seems a bit preoccupied now," I reply calmly.

The chaos around us grows. Leander dives into the crowd of nobles, punching one across the face. White foam spills from Nikolas' lips as he screams in agony, writhing on the floor. More highborns fall into psychosis, the poison taking hold of their bodies as they go insane. Casimir and Barnham enter the room, confusion crossing their features as they take in the scene around them.

"He told you his namesake?" Roderick's brows lower into a scowl.

"He did."

"He shouldn't have."

I scoff. "He can do what he pleases."

Roderick's aura is wildly threatening. "You are a little hellion who is a *stain* on this court and a direct threat to our people."

"You have no idea what I'm capable of," I threaten, clenching my jaw.

"Spoken like a true Valantis." He watches me with precise scrutiny.

I gather the fabric of my dress into my hands and move through the sea of royals. My body weaves in and out of the disorder, dodging blows from nearby fights as people try to defend themselves against the crazed ones. Running down the hall, I push open the door to my room and slam it shut behind me.

I quickly loosen the corset strings to undress myself. I pull on the pair of riding pants, tuck in the tunic, and cinch a belt around my hips. With my satchel and dagger in hand, I tie my cloak around my shoulders and dart from the room.

The halls are alive with chaos as I run toward the library. Kieran, Gilead, and Marek move past me as they head toward the banquet hall, alerted to the scene. As I turn the corner, the ornate doors of the library come into view. Once I escape through the secret tunnel I found, I will be free.

"Hey!" A voice booms across the space.

Glancing behind me, I see men running in my direction. They wear a strange set of armor, the plates made of bronze, with a wolf stamped in the center. Underneath, they wear blue and gold, their clothing oddly patchworked together.

Rebellion soldiers.

An arrow whizzes past my head, narrowly missing me. A yelp escapes my throat as I duck and turn to keep running toward the library. This is bad. They shouldn't be here. The rebellion must be mounting an attack on the castle the same night I decided to poison Nikolas. Casimir is in danger—a pit forms in my stomach at the thought.

"Get the princess!" I hear a man's voice call out.

A gust of wind hits me, causing me to stumble as I run. I grasp at the walls to hold me up as I continue running, desperate to get away. My fingers close around the library door handle, but a vine shoots out, wrapping around my ankle. I try to lift my foot, but it's too late. I hit the stone, and the impact forces the air from my lungs.

Vines drag me across stone, panic surging as I dig through my bag and pull out my dagger, swinging my arm to cut the tendril. It snaps, curling back down the hall as it retreats. Standing, I turn and keep running. Up ahead, a few stray Elvarrans are lingering in the narrow hall, blocking my path.

"Sorry!" I cry out, shoving past them as I run through.

"Stop her!" I hear someone call out, their voice echoing after me.

My boots slide across stone as I run around the corner, desperate to get away. I descend deeper into the chaos, the reverberation of blades clashing as I step over fallen bodies. A bolt of panic strikes through me—I *must* escape now, otherwise I may never be free. An arrow narrowly misses me once again, the tip scraping against my arm and tearing the fabric of my cloak. Glancing over my shoulder, I see a rebellion soldier lining up another shot in my direction.

"Rae!" I hear someone call out.

Turning, I see Hans and Lucio. Relief floods through me like a tidal wave as I run toward them. They will be able to fight off these soldiers and rescue me from certain death.

"A little help!" I call out, adrenaline pumping through my veins. My steps slow as I realize Hans and Lucio are wearing *bronze* armor, and I come to a sudden halt.

They are rebel soldiers.

An arrow hits my shoulder, causing me to stumble as I cry out in pain. Grunting, I twist and yank it out. The pain is excruciating as a river of hot blood runs down my back.

"Rae, I've got you." Hans stops in front of me, concern filling his features. "Are you hurt?"

I shake my head, backing away slowly. "No…" My voice trembles with fear as I glance over my shoulder at the men closing in on us. "I must go." I turn to my left and dash down a nearby corridor.

The smell of ash invades my senses, and when I look up, I can see banners aflame in the hall. Thick smoke makes it difficult to see and stings my eyes as I run. An arm bands around my waist as someone yanks me back.

I turn to swipe my dagger at the man, but he knocks my

attack away with ease. I thrash in his grip, kicking and punching to break free, but his grip only tightens around me. In a panic, I swing my arm and feel my dagger make contact with flesh. He lets out a roar of pain from the stab. The soldier's fist closes around a section of my scalp as he throws me against the wall. The stone is hard and unyielding when I hit it, and the breath knocks from my lungs once more.

Head spinning, I try to remain standing, but the man grabs me again.

"What do you want?" I cry out, swinging my dagger.

He lets out a hearty chuckle at my distress. "The commander requested we fetch you."

The commander of the rebellion? I don't understand what Nikolas wants with me. He should be incapacitated entirely by now, the poison taking control of his whole system. He is not of sound mind to give any orders—likely still in a frenzy in the banquet hall—which means this plan to capture me was in place long before.

I kick out my boot, his knee crunching from the force. The brute stumbles back. In the slight moment of opportunity, I pull the burning banner off the wall and wrap the fabric around the soldier. Ash rains down around us, and the man screams in horror. The smell of scorched flesh invades my senses, acrid and pungent.

He attempts to pull himself free from the fabric, but I keep wrapping it over his head, pulling it taut from behind to suffocate him. The soldier's fingers claw away at the banner. I reach out and yank more fabric back, the black smoke growing around us. I feel no pain, the fire blazing against my skin as I hold the burning banner in place.

Eventually, the soldier stops moving and falls to the floor.

CHAPTER FORTY-ONE

ALL AROUND ME, rebels and royal soldiers clash, steel ringing and bodies falling as battle erupts on every side. The sounds of swords clashing and battle cries echo off the walls so loudly that I feel as if my eardrums will burst. The floor is littered with corpses and discarded weapons, obstacles in my escape.

Each step sends a shockwave of pain through the wound in my shoulder. Blood soaks through my tunic, running down the length of my arm. I dodge chunks of stone and gusts of wind as Elvarrans sling their magic at one another. I run as quickly as I can to cut through the chaos. As I emerge on the other side, someone bumps into me in a clash of swords.

"Raelys." A deep voice calls out my name, a hand wrapping around my waist as they yank me against their chest. Their blade clashes against their opponents, shielding me from harm. The mark on my arm ignites from his touch, and I know who it is without having to look.

"Casimir," I gasp out as he pushes me behind him, continuing to fight.

"You must escape. Now," he demands, kicking the soldier back.

"What about you?" I ask, keeping my eye out for any more soldiers who may attack us. "What if they kill you?"

"Worried about me?" Casimir's lips quirk up as he strikes again. "If I fall, I fall protecting my crown." He whirls, sinking his blade directly through the man's gut.

The rebel soldier falls to the floor in a heap.

Casimir quickly closes the space between us, gloved hand cupping my cheek as he kisses me. It's brief, as the sounds of approaching footsteps echo across the hall. Casimir releases me, stepping in the direction of the adversaries.

"Run, Raelys," he commands.

"Are you sure?" I back away slowly, watching four soldiers approach.

"Yes. Get to safety." Casimir readies his blade.

I don't know why I'm hesitating. It's not like I'm any help when it comes to battle. I'll just get in his way. None of this was supposed to happen. These rebel soldiers shouldn't be here. I took care of Nikolas, shielding Casimir from his ploy.

"Raelys." Casimir barks, snapping me out of my trance.

"Please don't die," I urge.

"You are etched into my skin and bound to my soul, Raelys. No distance, nor time, nor magic could ever sever you from me, even in death," he calls over his shoulder before rushing into battle.

I turn and run.

Tripping over a few bodies, I stumble as I head toward the foyer. To my horror, the castle doors are broken off, shattered to pieces. Before I can reach the exit, something crashes into my side, slamming me into the wall. The taste of blood is sharp on my tongue as my head snaps back. My shoulder screams in pain as it's pressed into the stone, causing me to cry out.

A sword barrels toward me. I dodge as fast as I can, the

blade catching on my cloak, ripping the fabric. I try to run, but a hand closes around my throat, pinning me to the wall.

Nikolas.

His eyes dilate into large black voids as he bares his teeth at me. "You!" he seethes, restricting my airflow.

Kicking out my legs, I try to get Nikolas to release me. I claw away at his grip, gasping for air as spots form in my vision. Nikolas snaps his head back and forth, his eyes searching for something that isn't visible.

"Not again..." His voice wobbles as he slashes the air beside us. "Go away!"

Using his state of mania to my advantage, I sink my dagger into his arm. Nikolas lets out a cry of agony, throwing me with a heavy shove. The air knocks from my lungs as I hit the stone, my body rolling to a stop. I plant my hands on the ground, forcing myself to rise through the pain. I have to keep going. If I don't, I will certainly meet my end here.

I start patting the ground around me, searching for a weapon. When my fingertips brush against the hilt of something, I grab it. As I stand, Nikolas swings his sword at me. The blade hits above my left hip, slicing through the skin with ease as my blood paints the floor beneath us.

My hand instinctively goes to cover the wound, my blood hot and slick across my palm. I lash out, but he dodges with ease. Nikolas starts to laugh, but another hallucination grips him, causing him to turn.

"Fuck off!" he yells, swinging his blade at nothing.

I surge forward, swinging the dagger with all of my force. It sinks directly into Nikolas' amber eye. He screams, stumbling back as he reaches up to pull the blade free. Blood spurts from the wound as he dislodges the weapon from his eye socket, the gore making my stomach turn.

I run.

The wound on my side is deep, blood running down my leg and into my boot. I look down to see my tunic stained with red. My chest heaves as the world grows fuzzy, but I will my feet to continue running. Each step is agony, the edges of my vision darkening, but I push forward—one foot in front of the other—driven by sheer will and the desperate hope that I'm not too late.

"Raelys!" I hear someone call out for me.

Turning, I waver, tripping over myself as the world spins. I hit the wall, my knees buckling under the weight as my head hits the stone with a thump. My blood makes thick streaks against the stone as I fight to remain standing. A groan leaves my lips as I force air into my lungs. I can't faint—not now; there is too much at stake.

It's Sebastian who darts in front of me, his body shielding mine as his blade meets Nikolas', launching into intense combat. Blood rushes down Nikolas' face, a hollow socket the only remnant of his left eye. There are flashes of steel as the two clash in a battle of wills.

The mark on my arm burns with a sharp, searing pain. It's the same pain I felt when I tried to do something deceitful. Only this time, I am not betraying Casimir. I quickly yank my sleeve up to look. A diagonal slash cuts across the mark, the edges looking fractured. The silver lines slowly wither like broken vines.

Something is wrong.

I am compelled to rush back to Casimir, but someone steps in my path. I look up to meet a pair of brilliant green eyes. Sebastian's hands grasp my shoulders to stop me.

"What happened?" Sebastian takes in my state. "Are you all right?"

My fingers close around the edge of his armor as I try to steady myself, my body wavering. Glancing over his shoulder, I see Nikolas face down on the ground, lifeless. Sebastian saved my life. If he did not find me, it would have meant my end.

"I-I don't understand…" I struggle to speak. "The rebellion—"

"I lead the rebellion, Raelys." Sebastian cups my face gently in his hand. "Come, let's get you out of here."

I poisoned the wrong man.

How did I not see? There is no one rooting for Casimir's downfall more than Gottfried, and Sebastian is his most prominent loyalist. In my quest to gain my freedom, I've walked into a larger cage—trapped again.

"No!" I pull away. "Your soldiers tried to capture me."

My entire body wavers, and I struggle to stay standing, clinging to the last threads of strength in my limbs. Every movement feels heavier than the previous, haze forming in my vision. Sebastian's grip is the only thing keeping me upright, anchoring me to the ground.

"It's for your protection." A tick forms in Sebastian's jaw as he tightens his grip. "You'll be much happier in Rykaris, Raelys—"

"Why didn't you tell me?" I demand.

"We did not trust one another yet," Sebastian explains. "That's why I'm telling you now. We *must* go."

"Where's Wrath?" I ask between pained breaths as I fight the darkness that threatens to consume me.

"He's dead."

My heart breaks in two.

"You're lying!" I look down at the mark on my arm.

It's still there, but faint and lifeless—a pit forms in my gut. He can't be dead. I saw him moments ago. Felt his lips against mine moments ago. I refuse to believe it. Horror and dread lace my every muscle as I shove him away.

"Don't fight me." Sebastian reaches down, scooping me up

in his arms and tossing me over his shoulder. "You're losing too much blood. I must get you to a healer."

"Stop!" I scream.

"You'll thank me later." Sebastian moves. "Fall back!" he commands to his men.

"Let me go!" I thrash, but the world spins, weakening my resolve.

Sebastian descends the front steps of the castle and makes a sharp turn to the left, heading for the trees. Several rebel soldiers flank us on either side, and I see Hans, Lucio, and Gavriel as they guide us into the forest. We rush through the thick brush and into the snow-covered bushes, the sound of hurried footsteps and labored breaths filling my ears. The world around me fades quickly as we reach a nearby clearing, and I don't know how much longer I have left before I faint.

My feet suddenly hit the ground. I stumble, head spinning as I gasp for breath that won't come. The sensation of heavy weight presses down on my chest. Confusion floods me, my vision blurring with every frantic turn of my head as I try to run the other way.

"Raelys." Sebastian's voice reaches my ears as he rides towards me. He reaches down, yanking me onto the saddle and pulling me flush against him.

"Commander," Gavriel says, circling us on his horse. "You go. I'll gather what's left."

"Don't wait too long," Sebastian replies, kicking the horse and taking off into the night.

The rhythm of the horse's gallop sends sharp jolts of pain through my side. Each movement pounds like a hammer against the wound. I press my hand harder against it, warm blood still flowing like a river that won't stop.

The world closes in around me as darkness swallows me whole.

EPILOGUE

CASIMIR

WHEN MY BLADE fells the final soldier, I can finally breathe again. Glancing around me, I catch sight of Gilead and Stanik, each taking off in the opposite direction to sweep the halls for any lingering soldiers or spies.

Everything happened in the blink of an eye.

One moment, I was with Raelys at the banquet, my mind solely preoccupied with getting through the mind-numbing facade of socializing before spending the rest of my evening with her. She is all I can think about, all I've been able to focus on for days—no, weeks now. Her magic has taken root on my skin, claiming me as hers long before either of us ever realized it.

My brother pulled me away to tell me that a battering ram destroyed the front gates. A few moments later, Nikolas and Leander were plunged into a frenzy from Scorpion's Haze. Everything descended into chaos after the rebellion stormed the castle.

A sudden, sharp pain shot through the bond from Raelys, right above her left hip, signaling to me that she was in danger. Without warning, it suddenly ceased. She wouldn't vanish—

not without a trace, she is too intelligent, too precise for that. Something is wrong… very wrong, and my mind races with every possibility as I storm down the hall towards the foyer.

Stalking down the corridors, I look for her.

Each moment stretches into eternity, dread filling my veins with every echoing step down the empty halls. The silence around me screams that I am already too late, and everything around me feels lifeless without her presence.

Don't send your forces to Thalvar.

Her words echo in my mind, haunting me.

She knew.

With my forces sent west, the rebellion would have easily killed me. My death would have released her from our oath, yet she chose to warn me. I should have kept a closer eye on her, but I set her loose in my kingdom, knowing she deserved freedom.

"Your Majesty!" Kieran approaches me. "Are you all right?"

"The Princess," I snap. "Where. Is. *She.*" I grab the front of his armor, the last pieces of my restraint ready to snap.

"T-the rebellion c-captured her," he stutters, fear in his gaze.

I see red.

"Should she remain lost, Dratheria will cease to exist." My grip tightens. "I want every soldier in Khalessor at the front gates to go after them. Do you understand?"

Kieran nods. "Y-yes."

"Gather my forces." I release my hold.

Before I can reach the front gates, my father steps in my path, cutting me off. "You are not leaving after a siege to go after *one* princess." Roderick's voice is firm. "Your court needs you. Your people need you."

"Get out of my way," I growl, stepping around him.

Roderick's magic wraps around me like a million tiny thorns, halting my movements. "You are hurt," he counters, reaching out to grab my right arm. "I'll call a healer."

I pull it back before he can touch me. He can't see the mark, can't know it exists. I close my fingers around the gash on the inside of my arm, my blood coating my fingers. Someone caught me with a blade across the mark while fighting, and I did not get a chance to examine it.

"I'm going." I grind out, fighting against his magic's hold.

"You are not," Roderick replies calmly. "I will not allow you to throw away everything I have worked for. Your kingdom falls apart around you. I suggest you remedy it quickly, or you will *lose* your crown." He places a palm on my shoulder, turning me around and forcing me in the other direction. "I called for a healer."

I am helpless against Roderick's magic. My body is exhausted from fighting, my injuries settling in as the pain grows. My head is foggy from blood loss. I'm too weak to shield myself against his magic, leaving me like a puppet on his strings.

Although I am worried for Raelys' safety, I know she will be able to care for herself until I can free her. She is an architect of chaos, navigating court politics and rebellions with precision in the shadows. The person who lands in the crosshairs of her vengeance will quickly meet their demise.

She is by far the most destructive thing I have desired, yet she is the strategist to my ruthless blade. She is a fuel that burns hotter than the sun, and I would let that fire consume me if she allowed me to. It is a truth I have been blind to for so long, yet now it feels undeniable; she is irrefutably *mine*.

The stars dim with her absence… and soon, the world may follow.

ACKNOWLEDGMENTS

If you made it this far, Thank YOU for taking the time to read Oath of Ruin. I sincerely hope you enjoyed this story and were able to get lost in this world. I wrote to Raelys at a time in my life when I felt lost, stuck, trapped, and aimless. For all of those who also feel that way, may you always find the strength to keep fighting through the noise. Your light may dim, but it can never be fully extinguished.

Thank you to my alpha reader, Hope, who read through my jumbled first draft. To my dearest friend Sydney, who gave me the confidence to publish my writing. To my feedback partner, Marjorie, who helped this story take shape. And to my editor, Dana, for making this story shine.

ABOUT THE AUTHOR

Kaley Kae is a California girl born and raised, whose love for reading has developed into a passion for storytelling. She is obsessed with coffee, video games, and electronic music. When she's not writing, she is a full-time DJ at major clubs and festivals worldwide.